NECESSARY DOUBT
COLIN WILSON

the most unusual mystery story you have ever read

free

Necessary
Doubt?

- Professor Zweig reached for the brandy, poured himself a quarter of an inch, and warmed the glass in his hand.

- "And was it suicide?" Inspector Grey asked.

- "That is the question I asked myself. The suicide note could have been forged, of course. But in that case Gustav must have pushed the old man off the cliff. And that, as far as I can see, is impossible. The hotel was five miles away...."

- Grey stood up and paced across the room, tugging his moustache. "I agree, it's a nice little puzzle. No evidence.... I just don't know.... If I were still in the police, and you brought me this information, I don't know whether I'd bother to take any action."

- "Why not?" his wife asked. "Supposing this old man Zweig saw with him tonight is going to be murdered too!"

NECESSARY DOUBT
was originally published by Trident Press.

NECESSARY
DOUBT

Colin Wilson

A POCKET CARDINAL® EDITION published by
POCKET BOOKS, INC. • NEW YORK

156489

NECESSARY DOUBT

Trident Press edition published July, 1964

A Pocket *Cardinal* edition
1st printing.........January, 1966

This Pocket *Cardinal*® edition includes every word contained in the
original, higher-priced edition. It is printed from brand-new
plates made from completely reset, clear, easy-to-read type.
Pocket *Cardinal* editions are published by Pocket Books, Inc.,
and are printed and distributed in the U.S.A. by Affiliated Publishers,
a division of Pocket Books, Inc., 630 Fifth Avenue, New York, N.Y. 10020.
Trademarks registered in the United States and other countries.

L

To DAN *and* JEANETTE DANZIGER
with affection

Epigraph

Is it possible that nothing important or real has yet been seen or known or said? Is it possible that mankind has had thousands of years in which to observe, reflect, record, and allowed these millennia to slip by like the recess interval at school in which one eats a sandwich and an apple?

Yes, it is possible.

Is it possible that, despite our progress and discoveries, we still remain on the surface of life . . . ?

Yes, it is possible.

Is it possible that the whole history of the world has been misunderstood?

Yes, it is possible.

Is it possible that these people know with perfect accuracy a past that has never existed? Is it possible that all the realities are nothing to them, that their life runs on unconnected with anything, like a watch in an empty room?

Yes, it is possible . . . ?

But if all that is possible—if it has even no more than a semblance of possibility—then surely . . . something must be done? The first comer . . . must begin to do some of the neglected things . . . there is no one else at hand.

RILKE. (The Notebooks of Malte Laurids Brigge)

Note

The title of this book is borrowed from the theology of Paul Tillich. The central character, Karl Zweig, is, like Professor Tillich, an 'existentialist theologian' holding a university appoinment. No personal resemblance to Professor Tillich is here intended.

I am indebted to Professor P. J. Reiter's book *The Antisocial Act, Crime and Hypnosis* for the various facts quoted on the question of crime and hypnosis, and also for details of the Sala case and the Heidelberg case. Other titles are those of actual books on the subject of crime and hypnosis, but these were not consulted.   *C. W.*

'In what sense, can it be said that man possesses boundless freedom? He cannot fly through the air; he cannot dispel an illness by shrugging his shoulders; he cannot even dismiss tiresome obligations by turning his back on them. In what sense, then, does he possess more freedom than he realizes?

'The mistake here lies in supposing that this freedom is on the physical plane. It is not. It can only be explained by analogy. When a man is sick, every effort drains him of energy; if he wishes to do something, and finds obstacles in his way, he wants to sit down and cry. And yet when a man is healthy, all obstacles are treated casually, and easily overcome. The state in which human beings have lived for thousands of years has been analogous to sickness. It costs us a certain effort to live, and this effort is so consistent; is apparently so inescapable a part of the human condition, that we assume it is a feature of life itself. But in doing so, we are only reading our own state of sickness and exhaustion into our vision of the world. Man is capable of a state of freedom that would make his present condition appear in its true light: the exhaustion and distrust of a sick man.

'But what confines us to this condition? Original sin? Biology recognizes no such state. It is habit alone that confines man to his two-dimensional world of sickness and fear; the million years of habit that lie between us and our primate ancestors.

'. . . It is a truism to say that our civilization is in a state of intellectual bankruptcy, but there is much truth in it. It would be more illuminating to say that it is like a small business that finds itself sinking because its methods are old-fashioned. Possibly we require a few efficiency experts. . . .

'. . . To call life a dream is meaningless; it is merely to compare the whole of life to a mere part of it. The interesting thing about life is that we are constantly, and mostly unconsciously, engaged in the work of interpretation. (Phenomenology.) We read the "signs"; we read a hungry stomach or a pain in the back just as we read a newspaper. A dream is a series of shapes and symbols to be interpreted, like everyday life, so it is meaningless to call life a dream. . . .'

NECESSARY DOUBT

AS THE TAXI TURNED THE COR-
ner at Shepherd's Bush, the first flakes of snow drifted against
the window. Before they were halfway to Notting Hill, it was
snowing so heavily that visibility was limited to a few yards.
The driver said:

'I thought so. Been expectin' this all day. Either that or
rain.'

Professor Karl Zweig did not reply—not because he disliked the driver's familiarity, but because he could think of
nothing to say. The man seemed to understand that this
silence was not intended as a snub; he went on:

'I said to the missus this mornin'—if we have a snowy
Christmas it'll be the first one since 1948.'

Zweig managed to say: 'Really?'

'Not that I care. It's just a bloomin' nuisance for me.
Still, it's nice for the kids.'

Notting Hill Gate looked strange and bare with half its
buildings demolished; it brought back to Zweig a memory
of Hamburg as he had seen it in 1945, and a feeling of chill.
He thought of the snow falling into the black waters of the
Aussen Alster and the smell of rotting bodies that blew from

1

over the lake. The taxi driver's voice dissipated this feeling of nostalgia and disgust.

'Don't mind my askin', but 'aven't I seen you some time on TV?'

Since the taxi had picked Zweig up outside the Lime Grove television studios, the question was not unexpected. He said:

'That is possible. I occasionally appear on a programme called "Ask The Experts".'

'I thought so. I knew I'd seen you. I often pick up TV stars over there. 'Ad Arthur Askey in here the other day. . . .'

He continued to talk as the taxi crawled along the Bayswater Road in the Christmas Eve traffic, but Zweig no longer listened. The thought of Hamburg had brought back other memories, and the snow seemed to encourage them to rise. Oxford Street was still crowded with late shoppers and with children who were sheltered under awnings from the snow and stared into shop windows. Zweig was fond of children, and he was now reminded that he would spend Christmas Day with his sister and her children in Hampstead; his hand strayed out to touch the overfilled paper carriers that were wedged into the other corner of the seat; these contained toys that he had bought on the way to the studio.

The taxi now turned into North Audley Street. Zweig, who was inclined to abstract musing, now reflected: 'Adults love Christmas because it allows them to forget that life is a perpetual defeat. And children love it because it gives them the illusion that life is kind and culminates in rewards.' His mind played with the idea, developed it with a few bold strokes; he decided to turn it into a brief essay: 'A Defense of Christmas'; why the popularity of Christmas remains untouched—even increases—while belief in Christianity declines. . . . He lowered the window to throw away the butt of his cigar, and then leaned forward, staring. His taxi had halted at a traffic light in Curzon Street. On the other side of the lights, another taxi had stopped outside a hotel, and the commissionaire was now opening the door and helping an old man to climb in. A younger man, wearing evening clothes, stood waiting, sheltered under the commissionaire's umbrella and staring idly towards Zweig's taxi. It was this young man who had aroused Zweig's sudden interest. He leaned out of the window, prepared to call out as his own taxi drew behind the other, tempted to leap out and wave in case the other taxi drew away before the lights changed. But he was afraid the driver might misinterpret his action as an attempt to escape paying, and while he hesitated, the young man climbed into the other taxi and slammed the door. The traffic lights remained obstinately red. The taxi in front pulled away, and turned almost immediately into Shepherd's Market. Zweig rejected the idea of asking his own driver to follow it; instead, he leaned forward and said:

'Would you please stop outside that hotel.'

'Thought you wanted to go to Clarges Street.'

'Yes, but this will do.' The taxi pulled across the lights, and stopped. The commissionaire came forward to open the door. Zweig remembered the bags of toys and made a decision:

'Wait for me a moment. I shan't be a minute.' He addressed the commissionaire, fumbling in his pocket for money.

'The gentleman who just got into that taxi—can you tell me if he is staying here?'

'I don't believe so, sir.'

'Did you by any chance hear the address he gave the driver?' He added quickly: 'He's an old friend of mine.'

'Sorry, sir, I didn't. He didn't give the address until he got inside. But why don't you inquire inside, sir? They might be able to help you. Thank you, sir.'

Zweig went through the revolving doors into warm air and the smell of burning wax; this came from the enormous Christmas tree, covered with lighted candles, that stood in the corner. A smiling young man came towards him.

'Can we help you, sir?'

Zweig explained his problem again. The young man—probably an assistant manager—looked dubious.

'They're not staying here, I'm afraid. They'd just been in for a meal. I don't believe I'd seen them before. If you'd like to wait here a moment, I'll inquire for you.' He disappeared into the dining-room. Zweig now began to regret the impulse that made him stop the taxi; after all, he had seen the young man through a curtain of falling snow; he might easily have been mistaken. A moment later the assistant manager beckoned him over; he was standing in the entrance to the dining-room, talking to the head waiter. This man was very tall, and looked like a Spaniard; but when he spoke, it was with a cockney accent.

'Sorry, sir, I can't help you at all. The two gentlemen you're referrin' to came in for dinner.'

For want of something to say, Zweig asked:

'Do you usually get customers who are not residents?'

'Oh yes, sir.' The smile was ingratiating, the voice smooth with years of thanking customers for tips. 'Our catering is famous, if I might say so, sir.'

'Of course,' Zweig said hastily.

'All I can tell you, sir, is that the old gentleman was a Scot, and the young man was a foreigner. The old gentleman called him Gustav."

'Splendid!' Zweig said excitedly. 'That is my friend, Gustav Neumann. I haven't seen him for over thirty years.' His excitement made him want to say something pleasant, so he added: 'I must congratulate you on the sharpness of your observation. You would make a good detective.'

'All in the day's work, sir.' The waiter looked delighted.

'What a pity he's not staying here . . . ah well.' Zweig turned to the assistant manager. 'I must apologize for disturbing you like this.'

'Not at all, Professor. It's a pleasure.'

'You know me?'

'Saw you on TV half an hour ago.'

This made Zweig feel better, less of an intruder. He patted the head of a child who was staring at the Christmas tree, thanked the waiter and manager again, and went out. The commissionaire opened the door of his taxi.

'Find what you wanted, guv?' the driver asked.

'Unfortunately, no,' Zweig said.

•

His sitting-room was cold; he had told the caretaker not to bother to make up the fire, since he meant to spend the evening at his club. He had forgotten the unpleasant sensation of coming into a cold room in the early evening.

Zweig was proud of his rooms. He had had them now since 1933, although they had been sub-let to a colleague for twelve

years since then. They were old-fashioned, with fireplaces in
every room, dark green wallpaper, which he refused to have
changed, and heavy brown carpets, very worn, but still very
luxurious. He liked to say that they were the sort of rooms in
which Sherlock Holmes and Doctor Watson had lived. They
were slightly more expensive than he could afford—the new
landlord kept increasing the rent—but the mere thought of
giving them up brought a feeling of chill depression like
impending death.

Zweig plugged in the single bar electric fire—an innovation
which he disliked, and used as little as possible—and poured
himself a dry sherry. He went into his study, opened the
bottom drawer of the bureau, and took out a worn leather
photograph album. Then he went back into the other room,
settled himself in an armchair, and placed his reading spec-
tacles on his nose. As he looked through the album, he sipped
the sherry, and the fire diffused warmth along his shins. The
mood of nostalgia returned, and he reminded himself to take
two aspirins before he went to bed, for this state usually
presaged a cold. The pages of the album had inscriptions:
Hamburg, 1921, Zermatt, Christmas, 1926, Los Angeles, 1928
(this had been for an academic conference). There were
honeymoon photographs, dated 1927, and later in the volume,
he deliberately hurried past the page that contained a photograph of her grave in Heidelberg. Then came the photographs
he was looking for: 'Alfons and Gustav, dressed for "Land of
Smiles",' 'Albert and Gustav in Bonn.' 'Gustav as Herr Schind-
ler in "Pskov".' 'Pskov' had been Gustav Neumann's own
composition, owing heavy debts to Arthur Schnitzler.

Zweig finished his sherry and changed his slippers for
shoes. They were very small shoes of patent leather; Zweig's
feet were one of his few vanities; he liked to see people notice
their smallness, their eyes drawn by the elegance of his shoes.
Over these, he pulled on rubber overshoes. He unplugged the
fire. Finally, he carefully removed three photographs from
the album, found a clean envelope for them, and slipped them
into his wallet.

The snow had stopped; he walked carefully, afraid of slipping, jabbing the pavement with his closed umbrella. In
Piccadilly, the snow was well trodden, so that he could walk
with less caution. He crossed at the traffic lights by the Ritz
and turned into St James's Street. A figure that was turning

the corner into Pall Mall seemed to him familiar, and he hurried after it. The light of a streetlamp confirmed the identification. He called: 'Hi, Grey,' and the man halted and turned, waiting. Zweig said:

'Good evening, Charles. On your way to the club?'

'Yes. You?' Grey was at least a foot taller than Zweig. His smile, as he looked down at Zweig, showed real friendliness, and pleasure in this encounter. They walked on together. Zweig asked:

'Will you eat at the club?'

'No. I shall go home. My wife was expecting a couple of priests to supper, but they rang to say they couldn't come. So I'm going to keep her company. Why don't you join us?'

They turned into the club and handed their overcoats to the doorman. Zweig said:

'If you are sure it is no trouble, I shall be delighted.'

'I'm sure my wife will be delighted. She wants you to autograph one of your books.'

'Which one is that?'

'I believe it's called *Necessary Doubt*.'

The bar was crowded. Near the door, a famous African explorer, who had plainly been drinking heavily, argued in a loud voice with an actor whose knighthood was less than a year old. The Christmas decorations, made of silver paper in various colours, gave the room a carnival atmosphere. The explorer saw Grey and winked:

'Hello, old fellow. Caught any crooks lately . . . ?'

He laughed noisily with a curious gulping sound that the club wit had once compared to the noise of a dog being sick. Grey smiled thinly and said: 'You're looking well, Robert.' There was an empty table in the corner of the room, but Zweig knew that Grey would not sit there, for it was underneath a caricature that showed the two of them drinking at the bar. This sketch, one of several by a noted cartoonist, contained no element of humorous exaggeration; it simply showed Zweig and Grey standing side by side in typical postures: Zweig, short, thick set, his mass of white hair swept straight back without a parting, his head barely reaching the top of the bar, talking earnestly and forcefully; Grey, very tall, the shoulders slightly stooped, the thin, elegant hand caressing a brandy glass, listening with an expression of benign bewilderment. The two friends were flattered to be linked together in this way; but Grey obviously felt that to sit anywhere near the portrait would be tantamount to publicity-seeking. Zweig anticipated his response by saying:

'Let's go and sit in the lounge.'

'Good idea. Too crowded here.'

Deep in a worn leather armchair, Zweig sipped a dry sherry; Grey drank Irish whisky.

'My wife's been wanting to talk to you. She claims your books converted her to Catholicism.'

'I would be sorry to hear that,' Zweig said.

'It's true. She says she can't understand why you're not an R.C.'

'I shall try to explain to her,' Zweig said gravely, although he did not relish the prospect.

Grey said laughing: 'I'll try to keep her off the subject tonight. I can't promise, though.'

Zweig opened his wallet and took out the white envelope.

'Incidentally, I have a rather interesting story that I want to tell you. It comes within your professional field.'

'Soldiering or police?'

'Oh, police. I never think of you as a soldier.'

'I was in the Army a great deal longer than I was at Scotland Yard, you know.'

Zweig smiled and sipped his drink. To speak of himself as a soldier was one of Grey's vanities. His military career had been distinguished but unspectacular; it had certainly not brought a tenth of the notoriety of his years as Assistant Commissioner in charge of the CID. Grey affected to despise this notoriety, which was due partly to his best-selling volume of memoirs *My Years at the Yard*, partly to well-deserved newspaper publicity about his success in dealing with post-war crime.

Grey pretended not to notice the smile. He asked:

'What's the story, anyway?'

'It starts a long time back. . . .'

'Is it a long story?'

'Perhaps.'

'In that case, tell it when we get home. It'll keep Edna off the Catholic Church. Let's have another drink and then go.'

Zweig replaced the envelope in his pocket. Grey snapped his fingers at the waiter.

Lady Grey smiled when she saw her husband helping Zweig

off with his overcoat; like the cartoonist, she found the contrast between them amusing.

Zweig bowed slightly as he took her hand:

'I hope I do not intrude. . . .'

'Not at all. I'm delighted that Charles brought you back. We've got an enormous duck to get through. Is it still snowing?'

'It has just started again.'

'It's a pity Father Lawrence won't be coming. I so wanted you to meet him. We've both been reading your books.'

Grey interrupted quickly: 'That cooking smells good. We're both ravenous.'

'All right, go and sit down. I'll go and tell Mary there's a third.'

Zweig liked Grey's flat even more than his own. The dining-room always made him think of a lake in autumn. This may have been due to the brown, polished expanse of the table, in which reflections of the candle flames lay like yellow leaves.

'Another sherry?'

'Perhaps just one,' Zweig said. He felt a certain internal warmth, an expansiveness. It made him think of a colleague in Heidelberg who, when he had drunk a bottle of Niersteiner, used to say: My memory is leaking. . . . For a moment Zweig toyed with the idea of explaining his essay on the Spirit of Christmas to Edna Grey, and then changed his mind; it might lead them back to Catholicism. He seated himself at the table, and looked at the candle flame through his sherry glass, saying:

'Three sherries, and time stands still. Four, and I would fall asleep. Werd ich zum Augenblicke sagen: Verweile doch! du bist so schön!'

Grey said, smiling: 'You're in good form this evening. I always know you're happy when you start quoting German poetry. What does it mean anyway?'

'Faust's bargain with Mephistopheles: If I should say to the passing moment: Linger awhile, thou art so fair. . . . Yes, it's true I feel happy. But I'm not sure about feeling happy. Our whole concept of happiness needs revising. A man could be happy while suffering pain—provided the pain strengthened his vitality. . . .'

Zweig thought again about the melting ice of the Alster

and the odour of decaying flesh, and savoured the mixture of revulsion and nostalgia; it seemed to be a symbol of the Germany he loved, the Germany of brutality and decadence, the Germany that swayed like a snake to the music that spoke of suicide and death.

Edna Grey came in. She cried: 'Good, you've got a drink. It won't be a moment.' She spread the table cloth, saying to her husband: 'I've told Doris she can go home, so you'll have to carve.'

Zweig discovered he was hungry. He helped himself to a large plateful of anchovies and stuffed olives, and nodded eagerly when Grey suggested vodka to wash it down. Zweig's interest in food was spasmodic and rare; when it came upon him, he knew it to be a sign of relaxation, of acceptance of the physical world, which he usually regarded as a tiresome barrier to pure thought. Lady Grey knew him well enough to know this; she smiled as she saw him fill his mouth with anchovy and brown bread. She said:

'I've rung Father Lawrence, and he says he'll try to get over later. I think he rather wants to ask you if you'll contribute to an anthology he's editing.'

Zweig swallowed the vodka, and felt the heart rise from his throat to his forehead.

'How is that possible? He is a Catholic; I am a Lutheran.'

Grey saw his hope of avoiding theology vanishing, but it was too late to intervene. He respected his wife's religious convictions as he might have respected her membership of a sewing circle or a mother's union, but it struck him as a boring irrelevancy nevertheless.

'That's where you're quite wrong.' Edna Grey filled her glass with Perrier water. 'Surprising things are happening in the Church. There's a new spirit of tolerance. This anthology will include people like Bultmann and Tillich and . . . that American, what's his name . . . Niebuhr.'

Grey was sharpening the carving knife, and wondering where to start on the duck. He said grumblingly:

'I don't know how you remember all these names. . . .'

'Because they interest me, my dear,' his wife said sharply. 'Karl, would you mind opening that bottle of Chianti? Look, it's there, in the fireplace. . . .' The subject of theology was dropped for a moment while the meal was served. The maid came in to take her leave for the evening, then the cook came to ask their opinion of the duck. Zweig said with sincerity: 'It is one of the finest I have ever tasted in my life.' Grey said: 'It was my idea to use tangerines instead of oranges,' and for the next ten minutes the conversation remained on the subject of food and Christmas cooking. Lady Grey asked Zweig if the Austrian peasants had not any special Christmas recipes, and laughed when he admitted that he did not know. (Zweig's father had been a small farmer in a Tyrolese village, and Zweig had spent the first twenty years of his life in Austria.) In a lull in the conversation, Grey said:

'Karl's got a story he wants to tell us afterwards.'

'If you are not too bored,' Zweig said. The meal was making him sleepy, and he would have preferred to listen rather than talk.

'Of course,' Lady Grey said, 'I'll tell Mary to bring in the coffee. Will you take yours black?'

'I want you to try a brandy I've discovered,' Grey said. 'It's Portuguese, and my wine merchant assures me it was bottled before 1900.'

They moved into the next room, where a log fire burned; this was the point where Zweig wished he was not alone with his host and hostess. He wanted to stretch out his feet and close his eyes as he pretended to listen to the conversation. This was the disadvantage of these sudden bursts of interest in food; his stomach was taken unawares and complained of overwork. In these moments he thought of himself as a boa constrictor trying to digest a whole pig. His head throbbed, and he felt slightly deaf.

Grey noticed his somnolence. He said:

'Here, try this. It'll improve your digestion.'

They both lit cigars, and then sat in opposite armchairs, their eyes closed, feet stretched out to the fire. Grey was wearing a woollen smoking jacket and a new pair of embroidered slippers, obviously a Christmas present. Neither spoke. The only sound in the room was the hissing of the log that Grey had just thrown on the fire, and the distant murmur of traffic. Zweig reflected that this was why he was fond of Grey; his silence was restful, devoid of tension or question marks.

Edna Grey came in, pushing a trolley with coffee.

'Both asleep?' Her voice was casual and pleasant, but they both sensed in her a faint contempt, the disapproval of the ascetic for the gourmand, and opened their eyes guiltily. Since her conversion, nine months before, Edna Grey had drunk little but charged water, and she occasionally expressed irritation with the people whom she called "hearty Catholics" of the Chesterbelloc brigade. Her own confessor was a thin man with a face like wrinkled parchment, and a stomach that rejected all rich food. Although he was a Jesuit, he encouraged her to read Pascal, and the copy of *Provincial Letters* by her bedside was heavily marked from end to end. Grey knew nothing of Pascal—he had a vague idea that he was a scientist who discovered how to sterilize milk—but he was aware of his influence, as if it was a cold wind blowing from her bedside table, and he was stirred by a cautious but powerful revolt. He now said, with barely perceptible irony:

'No, my dear. Zweig and I are trying a little experiment in telepathy.'

'I don't know why. There *are* easier ways of communicating.' She poured the coffee, while Grey poured brandy for himself and Zweig. Zweig tasted it and nodded slow approval. The momentary drowsiness had gone; again, his senses were awake to the warmth of the room, the excellence of his cigar and the mellowness of the brandy; he still wished there were people in the room, but it was now because he felt he could do justice to his story, and wanted the inspiration of a bigger audience.

Lady Grey pulled the settee closer to the fire—it moved easily on silent castors—and took up her knitting. This was a scarf for Father Lawrence, at which she had worked patiently for months. It was made of a fine, blue-grey wool, and a week's work seemed to add very little to its length.

'Now,' Grey said, 'we're all ready for your story.'

'I am not sure that you can call it a story. It's a kind of problem, a detective problem. . . .'

He noticed the look of disappointment on Edna Grey's face, and added quickly:

'But it also has its . . . religious aspect, so to speak. I will tell you. When I came home today, only two hours ago, my taxi stopped outside the Chesham Hotel in Curzon Street. . . .'

He told them about his glimpse of Neumann through the snow, of how he had made inquiries in the hotel, and of how the waiter had overheard the old man calling his companion

'Gustav.' 'And then, you see, I was certain. It *was* Gustav Neumann, the son of my old friend Alois Neumann. Have you by any chance heard of Alois Neumann?'

Lady Grey shook her head. Grey said: 'Sounds familiar, but I can't think why. Scientist, was he?'

'A brain surgeon—one of the greatest brain surgeons in Europe. His book on the *Neurology of Hallucination* is still the major classic on the subject. We fought together in the first war, and after the war, we lived within a few hundred yards of one another at Heidelberg. So I knew his son, Gustav, from the age of seven.

'Now this Gustav was a curious boy. When I first knew him he looked like a girl. Long, dark hair, very large eyes, a full mouth. He was an intelligent boy—an excellent musician. Also good at languages. But he was quiet. It was very difficult to make him talk. I got the feeling that there was something morbid about the strength of his attachment to his mother. Well, when he was ten—in 1921—she died of a blood disease. Alois was worried about the boy; he wouldn't speak for days. So they went off traveling—Greece, Egypt, Japan. And when they came back I thought that Gustav had changed. Something had hardened inside him. His face had changed. He seemed to brood—as if he was wondering how to take revenge.'

Lady Grey said: 'I can understand. Poor boy. . . .'

'I don't know how far he'd changed, or what happened to him on that trip around the world. His father didn't know either. They were close . . . and yet there was a constraint between them. They didn't talk about feelings. But when Gustav was thirteen, I got rather a frightening insight into his character. This was in 1924, and there was, as you know, a strong anti-Semitic movement in Germany. Gustav went to a private school—a rather expensive one. Gustav, I should mention, did not look Jewish. His features were small and sharp-cut, and his lips were rather thin. But, of course, he was known to be Jewish—his father was a famous man. And there were a group of boys in the school who went in for Jew-baiting. They were led by a boy called Ernst Junger. I saw a lot of this boy—he was my pupil later—and I disliked him. He was a blond young thug with the skin of a girl and a definite sadistic streak. And he took a great deal of pleasure in tormenting Gustav. Well, one day this Junger had an accident. It was a rather curious accident. They had come back from a cross-country run, and Junger rushed into the shower and turned it on. The shower ran cold and he tried to adjust it. Then it turned into a blast of steam and boiling water. He screamed and tried to get out of the door, but it was jammed. It was Gustav Neumann who let him out. The scalds were bad, and for a few days there was some doubt whether Junger would live; then he began to recover slowly. He was in hospital for six months.

'Now the whole accident puzzled everybody. The man in charge of the boiler was dismissed, but he declared that he could not understand how it had happened.

'One day, a few months later, I was sitting with Alois Neumann and talking about Hitler and anti-Semitism in general. Gustav sat listening, but apparently not paying much attention. His father was called to the telephone. Suddenly, Gustav looked up at me and said: "The trouble with the Jews is that they don't try to defend themselves. They take everything lying down." He launched into an attack on Jewish religion—his father was an orthodox Jew—and said that it encouraged weakness and masochism. Then he said: "What the Jews need is more hatred—a healthy capacity for resentment and revenge. If we had that, people would be afraid to offend us." I was slightly irritated by his tone, and said mockingly: "Do you have it?" He looked at me in silence for a moment, then said: "You don't think that business of the boiling shower was an accident, do you?" At that moment he heard his father returning. He grimaced at me, and said: "Don't mention it in front of father." And for some reason, I didn't, although I sat there petrified. I think I was afraid of hurting his father . . . And the consequence was that Gustav became more friendly towards me. He seemed to feel—quite falsely—that I was on his side. He told me about the shower business later—much later. He knew that Junger was always one of the first into the shower—apparently he used to stand there for about half an hour, refusing to make room for anybody else. He examined the mechanism and found out how the temperature of the water was varied—by a kind of lever that mixed hot and cold water. And while the others were on their cross-country run, he hid in the changing room, and then took the thing to pieces with a screwdriver. He also discovered how to make the lock on the door stick. When the others came back, he started a conversation with the other boy who was usually one of the first into the shower, and made sure that Junger got there first. I asked him what he would have done if another boy had been first into the shower. He shrugged and said: "It would have been a pity. I would have thought of some other method of revenge on Junger. . . ." It obviously didn't strike him that I was asking whether he would have tried to prevent the wrong man being scalded!'

Zweig paused to drink his coffee, now half cold. Lady Grey said:

'He sounds a criminal type to me.'

'I don't know,' Grey said. 'The first characteristic of the criminal type is a kind of stupid vindictiveness. This lad doesn't sound stupid. I imagine his type could just as easily become a Napoleon or an industrial baron. . . .'

'In short, a criminal type,' Edna Grey said.

Grey grimaced. His wife's radicalism was theoretical, but it made him uneasy.

Zweig sipped his brandy, taking his time. He was aware of having gained their interest, and wanted to do justice to the story.

'What you have failed to take into account is that Gustav is Jewish, and that he was living in Germany in the mid-twenties. At his age—in his early teens—he was more sensitive to anti-Semitism than his father was. He only wanted to fight back.'

'Didn't you try to use your influence on him?' Grey asked.

Zweig finished the brandy, and waved his hand to decline more.

'Quite. . . . That, you see, was the trouble. To some extent, my influence was bad. I don't mean I corrupted him. But my ideas were, perhaps, unsuitable for a young man of his type.'

'In what sense?'

'There was a revolution in the air—in philosophy, I mean. Heidegger had published his *Being and Time* in 1927. My colleague Jaspers at Heidelberg was working on his *Philosophy*. Spengler's *Decline of the West* was all the rage in the universities. Students used to walk around with it under their arms. I was writing my *End of an Epoch*. . . .'

'Which I haven't read,' Lady Grey said softly.

'Which I have not read myself for twenty-five years,' Zweig

said. 'It started with a sentence that gained a certain notoriety: "Western culture is dying in debt." I went on to say that western culture is like a small business that is sinking because its methods are old-fashioned. I was thinking of a little sweet-shop in my native town. Each year it seemed to get smaller and dustier, and the man who kept it seemed to get more discouraged and bewildered. One night, he died, and when they went into the living quarters, they found that he had been living in the most complete poverty for years—no furniture, no fire, no blankets. Towards the end, he had been keeping alive by catching rats and cooking them. . . .'

'Oh, don't,' Lady Grey said, shaking her head with sudden violence.

'I am sorry. I mention it because the university at Heidel-berg always made me think of that sweetshop—teaching ex-hausted and useless ideas. I welcomed the new philosophy, even though it was destructive. Perhaps I welcomed it be-cause it was destructive. I felt that existentialism was a sign of the end of an epoch.'

'I don't understand existentialism,' Lady Grey said. Her husband said quickly: 'Never mind, Karl can explain it later.'

'When Gustav was eighteen, he became one of my pupils. At first, I thought he had changed. He was no longer sullen. He had a close friend called Georgi Braunschweig, who was a student of chemistry. This Georgi was a remarkable youth. Although his family were Jewish, his mother was a Roman Catholic, and Georgi was also a Catholic. He was a very tall, gentle boy, rather shy, slightly feminine. The odd thing was that although he was studying chemistry, his real interest was in religious mysticism, and he was fascinated by the lives of the saints. Gustav was very fond of him. I think his attitude was basically protective, because Georgi was frequently ill. Anyway, Georgi seemed to turn Gustav into a different per-son. I saw a great deal of them both, because Gustav used to bring his friend to argue with me, and sometimes they stayed until four in the morning.

'Now as I say, this youth Ernst Junger was also one of my pupils, and by this time he had joined the Brownshirts. I'm afraid I used to seize every opportunity to jeer about Hitler in my lectures. This was not difficult, because Junger could not resist dragging in Nietzsche and the polemical works of Wagner during the question periods. Well, one day, Gustav's

father and I both received typewritten letters, denouncing
Gustav as a sexual pervert. The writer claimed that he had
seen Gustav and Georgi actually engaged in these practices
in a field outside the town. Now I was certain that this was
nonsense. Even if Gustav had homosexual tendencies—which
I thought possible, in view of his mother's early influence
over him—I was certain that nothing of the sort could take
place between Gustav and Georgi. What is more, I was certain that the letter was written by Junger. That morning I
deliberately asked Gustav to stay behind after the lecture, and
as I did so, I noticed the look of triumph on Junger's face.
This convinced me. So later in the day, I sent for Junger, and
told him that I knew he wrote the letters. At first he denied
it; then I tried bluffing him, and said that I had had the letter
tested for fingerprints. That caught him off balance; he admitted that he had written the letters, but declared that
everything in them was true. I told him that, whether it was
true or not, I could have him expelled from the university for
such behaviour. Finally, I sent him away with his tail between
his legs. But I knew that he would begin to work out methods
of revenge, so I sent for Gustav, showed him my letter, and
warned him to be on his guard. He seemed indifferent. He
said: "I think I can take care of myself." I pointed out that
Georgi was also in danger, and he became worried. He swore
that he would kill anybody who touched Georgi. I think he
even went to Junger and made the same threat. But it made
no difference. A week later, Georgi and a Jewish rabbi were
ambushed in an alleyway as they were walking home; they
were both knocked down and kicked. The rabbi was knocked
unconscious; Georgi managed to drag himself to a telephone
and get his father to come and pick them up. But they had
broken one of his ribs. A week later he died of pneumonia.
Ernst Junger left Heidelberg two days after the ambush; I
was told that he had joined the Brownshirts in Berlin.

'A few days after Georgi's death, Gustav tried to commit
suicide by cutting his wrists. His father found him half an
hour later in a bath of warm water. He was rushed to hospital and given a blood transfusion, which saved his life. A
month later, he came back to the university. But he had
changed again. He was sullen, he hardly ever spoke. At the
same time, he became my most brilliant pupil. At first, I was
puzzled by his industry. He worked with a grim, quiet pur-

pose, as if his work was somehow a revenge on Ernst Junger.
He read the English philosophers, and Kant and Schopenhauer and Hegel. Then he read Kierkegaard and Heidegger.
In 1930, my *End of an Epoch* was published. I sent one of the
first copies to Alois Neumann—naturally. This was on a Saturday. Well, on Sunday morning, at about two o'clock, I
was just about to get ready for bed when someone rang my
doorbell. It was Gustav, in a state of tremendous excitement.
He had read my book—seven hundred pages of it—in about
sixteen hours' continual reading, and now he wanted to talk
about it. If it had been anyone else, I would have told him
to go home and come back in the morning. But I was glad
enough to see that Gustav had stopped hating the world and
wanted to talk. So we made coffee and made up the fire and
talked until dawn.'

Lady Grey said, sighing: 'That must have been very exciting.'

'It was more exciting than I can tell you. Because I realized
that Gustav was probably a man of genius. Never before had
he opened out his mind to me in this way. The way that he
talked about my book—and about Heidegger and Jaspers—
convinced me that his brain was probably a great deal finer
than my own. I am not being modest. My own brain is slow.
It lumbers like an elephant. But because it is slow and heavy,
it keeps on the same track. It is not easily put off. Sooner or
later, it achieves its results. But Gustav's brain was like a
swallow. He had all his mother's intuition and his father's
intellect. He seemed to be able to express, in a few quick
flashes, conclusions that it would take me days to perceive
and put into words. But all this came from the extraordinary
depth of his *feeling* about philosophy. He seemed to be tor-
tured by the problem of why men are alive. For the first time,
he talked to me openly of Georgi's death. I asked him if he
still wanted to take revenge on Ernst Junger. He shrugged
and said: "I suppose so, but not very deeply. What difference
would it make if I killed Junger? It would not solve the problem of why Georgi died. I want to know why the universe
is so constituted that a man like Georgi can die. My quarrel
is not with Ernst Junger but with God." It was this that
made me realize that Gustav had become a remarkable person. For example, we talked about anti-Semitism. I thought
that the subject would upset him. But he talked about it as

detachedly as if he was an Eskimo living on Mars. He said: "Both are to blame: the Nazis for being idiots, the Jews for being weaklings. Self-pity invites cruelty."

'I will tell you frankly that when Gustav left me at eight o'clock the next morning, I felt very proud of myself. I wrote in my journal: "Gustav Neumann may well be one of the great thinkers of our age." Naturally, I talked about him to my colleagues. Jaspers was particularly interested. Shortly after this, Gustav wrote a brilliant paper on Husserl that appeared in the phenomenological *Jahrbuch* and excited a great deal of discussion in the philosophical department. People began to point Gustav out; other students treated him with a new respect, almost as if he was a member of the faculty instead of a student. At least two girls showed their interest in him very openly. All this appeared to have no effect on him. If anything, it made him more moody than ever. It was also at about this time that he began to take an interest in his father's subject—the brain. This was at the time when all brain physiology was dominated by the reflex theories of Pavlov. But new men were doing exciting work—like Berger and Golla. Gustav took all the medical journals and read everything he could find about the brain, as if he expected to discover the answer to philosophy there. In fact, he wrote a remarkable paper on Leibnitz—an attack of course —entirely from the viewpoint of brain physiology.

'He talked to me very freely at this time. Often he came from some student party, just as I was getting ready for bed, and talked through the night. It was about this time that I published my *Necessary Doubt*. . . .'

'Which I *have* read,' Lady Grey interrupted.

'Good. That book made a surprisingly large impact, considering its size.' Zweig explained for Grey's benefit: 'It is a very short book, and its argument is that true religious faith must be built on doubt—not on blind acceptance. It argues that man's capacity to doubt is his greatest dignity, and that even a saint should never discard his ability to doubt.'

'I must read it,' Grey said, without conviction.

'It would probably bore you. However, I was saying that it was remarkably successful in 1931. Gustav was completely carried away by it. So much so that his father became worried about my influence over him. As an orthodox Jew, he disliked what he called my "nihilism." One day, the thing was brought to a head when Gustav got himself into trouble. He stole a car, drove it to the top of a cliff about twenty miles away, and crashed it into the valley. It was a Rolls-Royce belonging to an American visitor. Luckily his wife was a patient of Alois Neumann and they managed to avoid scandal. At the time this happened—in Easter, 1931—I had not seen Gustav for several weeks. I gathered later that he was involved in an unhappy love affair. Gustav refused to say why he had crashed the car; he refused even to speak to me about it. Later he told me that he wanted to test his courage. He leapt out of the car just before it went over. For the first and only time in our acquaintance, Alois and I had a quarrel. He said it was my insane ideas that had unsettled Gustav's mind. Finally, he admitted he had been unfair, and we made it up. Still, the matter was whispered around the university, and it got Gustav a bad name. And Alois actually came to me to ask me if I thought his son was insane! I managed to reassure him. Still, Gustav's behaviour was beginning to worry me. To begin with, he got drunk far too often. I realized that he was under some mental strain. For example, he came to see me one day and sat on my bed playing with a kitten. He was playing roughly, and the kitten suddenly got frightened and bit him. Gustav went white and grabbed it round the neck. I was shaving and saw it in the shaving mirror. Then he looked up and saw my eyes watching him. It obviously cost him a tremendous effort to recover himself and let go of the cat. If I had not been there he would have strangled it. But this was not sadism—it was the outcome of some nervous strain. Sometimes he talked to me seriously about suicide—not about his own suicide, but about writers like Kleist and Stifter, and whether they had a right to take such a way out; but I was certain that he was thinking seriously about it. The worst of it was that I could offer him no real reasons against it. I think perhaps it was Gustav who first made me aware of the inadequacy of my philosophy. . . .

'Well, in August, 1931 I made up my mind to leave Germany. I was certain that Hitler would come to power. I was known as an anti-Nazi, and I was certain that I would lose my appointment at the university. Then I was offered a post at the University of Los Angeles, and I accepted it. When I told Alois and Gustav they were both depressed; Alois had already started to transfer his money to Swiss banks; but his research centre was in Heidelberg, and he hated to leave it. Gustav said very little, but I could see that he was miserable. I tried to persuade them to come to America, but Alois said he preferred to wait.

'When I left Gustav that day, I lent him the manuscript of an article that I had written for an American philosophical magazine. This article did not strike me as particularly important. It was an attack on the academic method of philosophy. I said that the philosopher has to be like an eagle—to plunge down on truth from a great height, from sudden moments of vision, and try to seize it. I jeered at the philosophers who are like ants—who grub in the dirt and try to build systems according to a mathematical formula. As I say, this article did not strike me as in any way revolutionary; Nietzsche had said the same kind of thing many times.

'Two nights later—I remember the exact date—it was the 18th August—I was preparing to go to bed at about midnight when there was a knock on my door. It was Gustav, of course. I was feeling rather tired, so I was not particularly pleased to see him. When he first came in he seemed perfectly sober, and I offered him a glass of kümmel; it was only when he began to talk that I realized he had been drinking. He was in a strange mood, and his manner irritated me. You know that academic discipline in Germany is far stricter than over here. Well, I had never insisted that Gustav should treat me with the full respect due to his professor; I treated him as a son, and he always showed me the same kind of respect and affection that he showed his father. Now he was different; he treated me ironically, with a carefully concealed disrespect, and I was annoyed by it.

'I had been reading a small monograph on the sex murderer Kürten, written by a friend in Dusseldorf. Kürten had been executed two months earlier. Gustav picked up this monograph and started to talk about Kürten. In spite of my annoyance, I was interested by what he said. He said that Kürten was a pathetic attempt at a real criminal. He wanted to be an enemy of the human race, but he only succeeded in being a victim. Then he went on to talk about the relationship between the victim and the murderer, and said that Jews accept the role of victim too passively. He ended by saying: "So far, the human race has never produced a great criminal." I asked him whether he did not think that Hitler might qualify. He said: "Pooh, he's a fool, and how can a fool be a great criminal." I said that perhaps only a fool could be a great criminal. At that he grinned and said: "That is good academic logic." This annoyed me, and I told him that if he was too drunk to talk seriously, he had better go home. He poured himself more kümmel—without asking my permission —and said: "No, I won't go home. This may be the last chance we shall have of a serious talk, and I want to tell you something important." So I sat down and said: "All right, go on." He then launched into a violent attack on all academic philosophers like Jaspers and Heidegger. I shrugged and said: "Very well, I agree with you. Have you not read the essay I left with you the other day?" "That's not it," he said, "that's not what I mean. Did you have to *suffer* to write that essay—to suffer as Nietzsche suffered?" I said: "Perhaps. How do you know whether I suffer or not?" "I know because *I* suffer when I think. If it had not been for an accident, I would not be alive now." He then told me that he had read my essay the previous night, and that it had made him decide to commit suicide. . . .'

Lady Grey said mildly: 'Good heavens.'

Zweig shrugged. 'I told you he was very excitable. He thought my essay proved that all thought is useless—that nothing matters except vision. I had given an example from the life of Ramakrishna, the Hindu saint. Ramakrishna kept praying to God to reveal himself, but nothing happened. Finally, in despair, he seized a knife and was about to kill himself, and at that moment he received his vision of God. I argued that this vision is the aim of all philosophy, and that no amount of thinking can reveal it. Well, Gustav read this, and decided that he would commit suicide. He said: "I knew your story was true, because at the moment I leapt out of that car and it plunged over the cliff, I also had a sudden vision. But it vanished almost immediately." Anyway, Gustav determined that he would kill himself. Then he remembered that he had always wanted to meet Heidegger, who lived in Freiburg. Heidegger, as you know, also argues that man only knows reality in the face of death. Gustav then decided on a wild plan. He would go to see Heidegger and ask him why, in that case, he did not commit suicide—why he preferred to go on living and writing long-winded books. And in order to prove his sincerity, he would take a revolver out of his pocket and kill himself in front of Heidegger.

'The following day, Gustav took a train to Freiburg. He took my essay with him, because he wanted to read it again to decide if there were any flaws in my logic. He also took a loaded revolver.

'He told me that he ate a big lunch on the train—he felt that this was the equivalent of the condemned man's supper —and drank a whole bottle of champagne. But instead of cheering him up, it made him feel more depressed. He saw a newspaper headline about a speech made by Hitler in which Hitler said that Jews pollute the human race. And then, he said he had a kind of vision. All the people sitting around him seemed to be insects. He said: "I suddenly realized that the gods created the human race as a kind of joke. I realized that if I was a god, I would be tempted to exterminate all human beings, or at least torment them out of their stupid complacency. And then I thought: 'But I am also a human being, and the best thing I can do is to kill myself.' For a few moments I was tempted to kill myself there and then, until I remembered that I had left my revolver in my briefcase in the carriage. I went back to my seat. There were two other men in the carriage—fat bankers with faces like pigs—and they were talking about the Kürten case, and agreeing that something is wrong with the world today. For a moment, I was tempted to shoot them first. I sat there thinking about it, imagining their faces as I pulled out the revolver. Then I thought: 'Why should I shoot myself? Why not let them arrest me and execute me? It would be worth it for the fun of shooting these pigs.' And it was then that the idea came to me—my great idea." I asked him cautiously what he meant. He said: "Don't you see? I'd found the answer—to be a criminal, a master criminal. All human beings are insects, and the gods laugh at us. There's nothing we can do to become great. All the so-called great men are self-deceivers, like these two pigs. They pat themselves on the back for trying to help the human race, and they don't realize that they're insects trying to help other insects. What *can* a man do to try to be more than an insect? What could he do so that the gods would say: 'He is different from the others?' The answer is: take the side of the gods against human beings. Try to be a real criminal, the first criminal in the history of the human race who is not just an underprivileged victim. . . ."

'At first I thought he was joking. I thought that this was some brilliant idea that he'd thought up and that he was trying out on me—to shock me, to make me angry, perhaps. Then I realized that he was really serious. He went on talking—compared himself to St Paul on the road to Damascus. And suddenly I began to wonder if he was completely insane—if his mind had collapsed. I remembered that Nietzsche and Strindberg had both suffered from syphilis, and it struck me that perhaps Gustav had contracted it from a prostitute and that his mind was also collapsing. So I pretended to agree with what he said, and began asking him if his master criminal had to be in perfect health. Gradually, I turned the subject to his own health, and then asked him flatly if he was suffering from a venereal disease. At this, he became angry. He said: "I am completely healthy in every sense. Would you like to examine me?" He started to take off his clothes, but I stopped him. I decided that he was probably suffering from some form of alcohol poisoning, and advised him to go home and sleep. Anyway, he finally left. But his last words were: "One day I shall prove to you that I am right." I said: "Why do you want to prove it if you think I am an insect?" He said: "Because you have the capacity to be great—but you're afraid to use it."

'The next morning I rang his father and warned him that I thought Gustav was mentally ill. He seemed very frightened. However, a few hours later he came to see me, and said: "I've talked to Gustav about last night. It was all a joke. He wanted to upset you." I could see that this was what he wanted to believe, so I didn't contradict him. When he left, he said: "That Gustav's a clever lad. But he's as sane as you or I. I've talked to him for two hours, and there is not the faintest sign of a psychosis. I'll make him come and apologize to you later." But Gustav never came. And that was the last time I saw Gustav in Germany.'

Grey lit another cigar and stared at it reflectively. Lady Grey was looking into the fire, frowning slightly. Zweig said:

'I apologize for taking so long. I am just about to reach the point. . . .'

'Not at all,' Grey said, 'I find it fascinating. Go on.'

'Gustav did not come to see me. Occasionally, I saw him

around the town. He was always with an old man—a friend of his father's called Seyfert—Gerhardt Seyfert. When I mentioned this to Alois, he told me that Gustav was able to cure Seyfert's headaches by a kind of mild hypnotism—stroking his forehead—and that the two had become close friends. I had my own ideas. I knew that Seyfert was rich, and that he had no immediate family. So what was more likely than that he would leave some of his money to the son of his best friend? I also knew how much money Alois had spent on his research laboratory, and that if he was forced to leave Germany, he would lose it all. So perhaps Gustav was thinking about the future. Who could blame him?

'Well, a week before I left Germany, Gustav and Seyfert went to Switzerland together. Alois told me that Gustav was now acting as a kind of secretary to the old man. And a few days later, Gerhardt Seyfert was found dead at the foot of a cliff near the Matterhorn. He left a suicide note in his hotel room, saying that he was suffering from a cancer of the spine, and preferred to die this way. At the time of his death, Gustav was in the hotel, several miles away. When I was in America in 1932 I heard that Seyfert had left all his money to Gustav—two million marks.'

Zweig reached for the brandy, poured himself a quarter of an inch, and warmed the glass in his hand. He was aware that they were waiting for him to answer a question. Finally, Grey said:

'And was it suicide?'

'That is the question I asked myself. But how could it have been murder? The suicide note could have been forged, of course. But in that case Gustav must have pushed the old man off the cliff. And that, as far as I can see, is impossible. The hotel was five miles away. . . .'

'But you said he was using hypnotism on the old man?'

Zweig smiled, anticipating her question: 'You think Gustav might have hypnotized Seyfert into killing himself? No, that is quite impossible.'

Grey said: 'Even the writers of detective stories have dropped that one, my dear. You know you can't hypnotize a person to do something he wouldn't do when awake. Isn't that so, Karl?'

'Not quite. My friend Rowland carried out an experiment with a poisonous snake . . . however, yes, it is more-or-less true. I don't believe for a moment that Gustav hypnotized Gerhardt Seyfert.'

Edna Grey said reflectively: '*If* it was murder, I suppose it was what you'd call the perfect murder?'

'Perhaps,' Zweig said. 'But do you think it was murder?'

Grey shrugged and pulled at his moustache; it was a gesture that indicated mild impatience. He said: 'You know, all this is very theoretical. If I was asked to investigate a case like that, I'd want a lot more evidence than you've offered me so far. From what you've told me, I'd say there was no possibility of murder—or at least, no great probability. People who talk like your young friend don't suddenly turn into murderers. Surely you must feel that yourself?'

'I agree. But I still have a little more evidence to offer you.'

'All right. Let's hear it.'

'I heard very little from Alois Neumann after I came to America. Then, in 1936, I heard that he had committed suicide.'

'How?'

'He shot himself.'

'I mean how did you find out?'

'I read it in an American newspaper. It gave no details, except that he had shot himself at his home near Zurich. It said that he was thought to be depressed about the position of relatives still living in Germany.'

'That sounds likely enough.'

'I agree. The newspaper also mentioned Gustav. It said that for the past four years Neumann had been living alone with his son in retirement.'

Grey asked: 'Is that the lot?'

'Not quite. There is one more detail. In 1938 I spent a summer holiday in Mentone. As I was packing to leave, I noticed a sheet of newspaper that had been used to line a drawer in my hotel room. My attention was caught by the name "Gerhardt Seyfert." This, of course, could have been coincidence. The newspaper was dated two years earlier—September 1936. The news item was about a man—Gerhardt Seyfert—who had been arrested after a boating accident. This man Seyfert was the private secretary of a Belgian underwear manufacturer called Schmoll, and the two of them were in Mentone on holiday. They went out sailing, just the two of

them, and somehow the boat overturned. Seyfert managed to
swim to shore, but Schmoll was drowned. But on the day
after the accident, a man came forward who claimed that he
had been looking out to sea with a pair of binoculars when
he had noticed the boat. He thought he saw two men fighting
in it a moment before it overturned. Seyfert was arrested immediately, and this was the substance of the news item.'

'And did you find out any more?'

'Yes. Luckily, the owner of the hotel remembered the case
quite clearly. He told me that Seyfert had been released the
next day. He was able to prove that the witness had attempted to blackmail him before he went to the police. Apparently this witness was a man of bad character, already
known to the police. A few hours after the accident, he approached Seyfert and threatened to go the police with his
story about the fight—unless Seyfert paid him a large sum of
money. Seyfert refused, and was later able to prove that the
man had come to his hotel on the day before he went to the
police. So the case against him was dropped.'

Edna Grey was frowning at her knitting. She said: 'I don't
quite understand. Why do you connect this Seyfert with the
old man who died in Switzerland?'

'Because there was a photograph of this private secretary
in the newspaper. It was a bad picture, of course—rather
blurred. But it looked remarkably like Gustav Neumann.'

Zweig reached for the brandy bottle and poured himself
a small measure. He was obviously enjoying the impression
produced by his words. Grey said:

'Are you quite sure it was Neumann?'

'No, of course not.'

Edna Grey asked: 'Did you go to the police?'

'Yes, I called on the police before I left Mentone. They
were not very helpful. They had no photograph of the man
called Seyfert, and they said that the case was closed. I went
to the office of the newspaper that printed the story and
asked them if they had the original of the photograph, or any
other pictures of Seyfert. But they had destroyed the original,
or lost it.'

'Did you think of contacting the family of this man
Schmoll?'

'I thought of it, but I did nothing about it.'

'Why not?'

'Mainly because I was not convinced that there was anything suspicious.'

'You think it was coincidence about the name and the photograph?'

'That seems probable. Consider: we know that Gustav Neumann was living with his father in 1936. Alois Neumann died in July 1936. Six weeks later this boating accident takes place in Mentone. Is it likely that Gustav would change his name— and get himself a false passport—and find himself a job as someone's private secretary? Why should he do it? And why should he commit murder?'

'Perhaps this rich Belgian left him money in his will.'

'After a six-week acquaintance?'

'That's true. Still, we don't know about that, do we?'

Edna Grey lay down her knitting with a startled expression:

'You don't think . . . this old man tonight . . .'

Zweig said: 'That is why I told you the story. What do you think?'

Grey stood up, and paced across the room, tugging his moustache. He said:

'I agree, it's a nice little puzzle. No evidence . . . no evidence.' He laughed, a brief, snorting guffaw. 'It's the kind of case where a policeman needs to use his nose rather than his head.' They watched him as he walked up and down the room. He said: 'I just don't know.'

'What don't you know, dear?'

'I don't know. . . . If I was still in the police, and you brought me this information, I don't know whether I'd bother to take any action . . . I think probably not.'

His wife said: 'Why not? Supposing this old man that Karl saw tonight is going to be murdered. . . .'

'Ah, that's a different matter. *If* this old man's murdered, or if he appears to commit suicide, I'd agree there's something to go on. The balance of probability would definitely make the thing smell fishy.'

'*I* think it smells fishy already.' She looked with misgiving at Zweig, who was smiling as he sipped his brandy; his amusement puzzled her.

'I quite agree, my dear. But there's nothing in what Karl has said to give the police a definite lead. Now if I'd been

Karl back in 1938, I'd have made it my business to contact the family of this man . . . what's his name?'

'Schmoll.'

'. . . and find out what happened to the old boy's money. Incidentally, you did say he was an old man, didn't you?'

'No, I didn't. But you are right. He was sixty-eight.'

'But then, I daresay the family had some inquiries made anyway.'

'Is it too late to find out?' Edna Grey asked.

'No. I don't suppose so. But it's a bit late for following up clues.' He asked Zweig: 'Didn't you ever report your suspicions to the police?'

'Not exactly. I repeated the story once or twice to policemen of my acquaintance. They said what you have said.'

'I don't see that at all,' Edna Grey said patiently.

'No? Then I'll try to explain, my dear. It's a matter of the weight of evidence. Now take, for example, the Smith case—the Brides in the Bath murders. Smith married these women for their money, then arranged for them to drown in their bathtubs. Now there was never any real evidence against Smith. Three women were drowned in their baths. All of them suffered from fits, so it could have been accident. In each case, Smith had an alibi, and no one suspected murder. Then a relative of one of his victims read an account of another woman who drowned in her bathtub, and thought it couldn't be coincidence. So Smith was arrested and tried. There were no marks on the bodies—no signs of violence. But the prosecution alleged that Smith lifted the knees of the women and drowned them without a struggle. Now if only one woman had died in that way—or even two—Smith could never have been convicted. But the jury thought that three was too many to be coincidental, so he was executed. It was a matter of weight of evidence. Now on the evidence that Karl has just given us, I'd say that no jury would ever convict Neumann of being a murderer. On the other hand, if it happened again, then I doubt whether he could get away with it.'

'You mean he has to murder this poor old man before the police could do anything?'

'I know it sounds absurd, but I'm afraid that's about the truth of it. What do you think, Karl?'

'I agree. I think it remotely possible that Gustav had something to do with Gerhardt Seyfert's death. But I think that it would be impossible to prove it.'

Edna Grey asked: 'And do you think it possible he might be planning to murder this old man you saw this evening?'

Zweig stared at the fire before answering. He said finally:

'I think the chances are against it. I would be interested to know where Gustav is at this moment.'

'Then why did you tell us the story?'

'To begin with, because I think it is an interesting story. And secondly, because I wanted to ask Charles's advice. How would I set about tracing Gustav Neumann—assuming, that is, that it *was* Gustav Neumann whom I saw this evening?'

Grey sat down again and knocked the ash off his cigar.

'That could be difficult. I'd ask questions at the hotel. Somebody might know more than that head waiter. Did you notice the number of the taxi?'

'I'm afraid not.'

'That shouldn't be too difficult to check. The commission-aire might know the driver. Did you say they'd been to the hotel before this evening?'

'No. The manager said he hadn't seen them before.'

'Hmm. Well, the question is: why should they go to a Mayfair hotel for dinner on Christmas Eve? If they were staying in one of the big London hotels, presumably they wouldn't go out to eat.'

'Perhaps they're staying at a boarding house,' Edna Grey said.

'Or a cheap hotel. But why dine at a hotel when there are plenty of good restaurants around? That suggests some previous experience of the hotel.'

Zweig said: 'It's the kind of place where people go for a business lunch.'

'Still, there's something odd here. Why should they stay in a boarding house, or a cheap hotel, and then take a taxi to an expensive hotel for dinner?'

Zweig blew out his breath vigorously, making a noise like a walrus as he shook his head.

'I can think of no explanation. Or there might be a very simple explanation. . . .'

Edna Grey said: 'What does he look like, this friend of yours?'

'Ah.' Zweig took the envelope out of his wallet and handed it to her. Grey leaned over her shoulder. Zweig said:

'That is a studio portrait of Gustav. It was taken for his nineteenth birthday.'

'He's rather good looking,' Edna Grey said. But her voice was dubious. All three of them stared at the photograph; Neumann's face was thin; the eyes and the compression of the lips showed alertness. The chin was prominent and pointed. It was the face of a brilliant young scientist or doctor. But it was also a nervous face, a face that could only lose flesh and become more tense and angular.

Zweig showed them the other pictures. 'This was his father —a great man. If he had been able to continue his researches in Heidelberg, he might now be one of the most famous names of our time.'

The egg-shaped head was almost hairless, except for bushy grey eyebrows; the face had the same expression of tension and alertness as that of his son. It was a revealing snapshot. The two stood on a snowy hillside. Alois Neumann stared at the camera with a kind of hostility, his hands deep in the overcoat pockets, his shoulders hunched as if prepared to be attacked; Gustav Neumann, nearly a foot taller than his father, wore no overcoat, although a scarf was thrown over his right shoulder; he stood with his legs slightly braced apart, his left hand on his father's shoulder, the head thrown back and looking over the camera.

The third photograph showed Gustav Neumann standing beside an even taller youth. 'That is Georgi,' Zweig said. He noticed the disappointment on Edna Grey's face. 'He is not handsome, and he carries himself rather badly. That is because he was shy. But he had great sincerity and insight.'

'That's strange,' Grey said.

'What?'

'This picture'—Grey pointed to the photograph of father and son—'seems to indicate that he's left handed. You notice he's thrown the scarf over his right shoulder. A right-handed person naturally throws it over his left. And yet in this other picture, he's smoking a cigarette with his right hand.'

Zweig chuckled with delight. 'That is astonishing. In fact, you are right. Gustav was left handed, but he had an idea that he might want to disguise his identity one day . . . that was one of his odd notions. I suppose he thought the Nazis

NECESSARY DOUBT 31

might put a price on his head. So he trained himself to use his right hand as well as his left, so that he couldn't be described as left-handed.'

Edna Grey said with admiration: 'You should still be in the police force, dear. You're very perceptive.'

Grey grunted. 'Believe me, the Sherlock Holmes stuff is the least important part of police work. The main thing we need is more men on the beat.'

Edna Grey stared at the portrait photograph. She said: 'He doesn't look in the least like a criminal to me.'

'I see what you mean. Still, I'm not sure that I haven't seen a criminal with a face like that. Steinie Morrison was one. I wonder. . . .'

'What?'

'I don't suppose I *have* seen him before. It's unlikely that he'd have a police record in this country. Yet that picture with his father looks familiar.'

'You should ask Colbright, dear.'

'That's an idea. I wonder if he's doing anything now.'

'I didn't mean tonight!'

'Well, why not? It's not ten o'clock yet. He only lives in Fulham. Are you anxious to go, Karl?'

'Of course not.'

'Then let's try it. It can't do any harm. I'll give him a ring and see if he's at home.'

'Not on Christmas Eve!'

'Oh, he won't mind.' Grey went out of the room. Zweig observed her look of dismay, and said: 'I must apologize for this. I wasn't serious, you know.'

'Not serious? About what?'

'About Gustav. I would like to see him if he's in London. But as Charles said, he's simply not the type to be a murderer. I simply think that it makes a good story. In the hands of a writer of detective stories, it could be fascinating. In reality, I'm sure there's nothing to it.'

'Then why don't you try to stop Charles from phoning?'

Before Zweig could answer, Grey came back into the room. He looked cheerful and brisk.

'That's all right. He says he'll be delighted to see us. So we'll go right away.'

Edna Grey said: 'Karl has just been saying that he's quite

sure there's nothing in it, Charles. I don't think it's right to burst in on someone on Christmas Eve. . . .'

'That's all right. I'd like to see old Tubby again. It'll make his Christmas.'

Zweig said cautiously: 'I see your wife's point. Even if Gustav has a criminal record—and I am sure he hasn't—it wouldn't be in England.'

'Never mind. Colbright's looking forward to seeing us now. You'll come, won't you, my dear?'

'Certainly not, Charles. I think you ought to phone him and tell him you'll go tomorrow or Boxing Day instead.'

'No, no. Can't do that. Anyway, we shan't be gone more than an hour.' He pulled the curtains aside and peered out. 'Ugh, snowing like mad. Hope we can get a taxi. I'll ring for one.'

●

The snow in the Old Brompton Road had been flattened and churned by traffic, but in Redcliffe Square it was thick and undisturbed. Zweig had forgotten to bring his overshoes, and regretted it as he stepped out of the taxi and into a drift that covered his ankles. The driver said:

'It's goin' to freeze over in an hour, you see.'

Zweig looked at the luminous dial of his watch, and wished he was back in his rooms with a glass of good port. He watched with regret as the lights of the taxi turned into Redcliffe Gardens as if it was his last link with the West End. The wind was strong and icy, and it was uncomfortable to keep the face turned to the east.

The front door opened before they reached it. A cheerful London voice said: 'C'mon out of the cold.' A short, fat man stood there, trying to hold open the door and leave enough room for them to get past him; the size of his stomach made this difficult. He was wearing a paper hat and a bright orange dressing gown.

'Le' me take your coats. . . . Well, it's nice to see you again,

Sir Charles. ''Aven't you brought the missus? Pity. Blimey, what a night. . . .'

The house smelt pleasantly of burning holly and mince pies. He led them into a small room whose walls and ceiling seemed to be invisible under bunches of holly and paper chains. A fire that was big enough to heat a barn made its atmosphere stifling. Zweig felt the snow in his trouser turn-ups melting and soaking through his socks. Two children, a boy and a girl, were playing snakes and ladders at the table.

''Ave a seat. The missus's in the kitchen. She won't be a minute.'

Zweig was introduced to ex-chief inspector Colbright. Grey was staring at the dressing gown with startled fascination. He said:

'You . . . er . . . cold, are you?'

The boy said: 'Naoh, he just won't take it off. He likes the colour.'

'Daughter gave it me for Christmas,' Colbright said proudly. 'The married one. I think it's rather striking, don't you?'

Zweig took a seat on the far side of the table, and tried to avoid direct radiation from the fire by sheltering behind a tall girl with pigtails. Colbright said:

'Now, let's have a drink. Would you like to try a spot of this cocktail? It's called Two Over the Eight. The wife gets it special for Christmas. It's ninety proof.'

''Ave to keep it away from the fire,' the boy said, and guffawed. His father said:

'You talk when you're spoken to, or you'll get a flea in your ear.'

The girl was staring intently at Grey. She asked suddenly: 'Where's your garter?' When Grey looked at her uncomprehendingly, she explained: 'They said at school that knights don't wear armour any more, just garters. You *are* a knight, aren't you?'

They were interrupted by Mrs Colbright, who brought in a dish of mince pies. She was as fat as her husband, but a foot taller. When Zweig had been introduced, and had declined a mince pie, she asked:

'What'd you want Albert for? Want him to go out on a job?'

'Oh, can I come?' the boy said.

'Not quite, Mrs Colbright. We just want to call on his encyclopedic knowledge of crime and criminals.'

''Old on a minute,' Colbright said, 'let's get the drinks settled, eh?'

Grey and Zweig accepted whisky. The children were induced to go to bed, and warned not to listen outside the door. Grey produced the photographs and handed the portrait to Colbright.

'Cheers,' Colbright said. ''Appy Christmas and many of 'em.' He continued to stare at the portrait as he savoured and swallowed the mouthful of whisky. He said: 'Mm. That's the Maidstone bloke, isn't it?'

Grey and Zweig leaned forward at exactly the same moment, and wearing exactly the same expressions.

'Who?'

Colbright held the picture at arm's length and frowned. 'Yes, it couldn't be anybody else, surely? The private nurse in the Maidstone shooting case. Of course, sir, you wouldn't remember it, 'cause it was 1938.' He looked at them inquiringly.

'Tell us about the case,' Grey said. 'Were you on it?'

'No. But is it the bloke?'

'We don't know. Who was shot in this Maidstone case?'

'Old boy called . . . er . . . I can't recollect his name now. Something like skin . . . Erskine, Buskin, Boleskin.'

Zweig and Grey stared at one another over the table-top. In spite of the heat, Zweig felt the cold flowing across his scalp and shoulders.

"Think it must have been Erskine. Anyway, you could easily check up.'

'What happened?' Grey said; the edge of impatience was barely perceptible in his voice.

'It was supposed to be a suicide case, I believe, but it had one or two odd features. The window was open, and they suspected a burglar. The weapon was a shotgun.'

''E's got a wonderful memory, our Albert," Mrs Colbright said. 'I've often said he ought to be on TV.'

'Anything else you can recall?'

Zweig leaned forward; he asked:

'What was the secretary's name?'

'Oh, there you've got me.'

'Can you recall any more details?' Grey persisted.

Colbright stared at the wall, frowning. He muttered: 'Le'me see . . . open window . . . somebody came in. . . .' But after a few minutes of this, he said: 'Sorry, Sir Charles, but it's so long ago, and we wasn't really involved. I 'appened to 'ear a bit about it because my brother-in-law—that was my first wife's step-brother—was a sergeant in the Maidstone police. It might come back to me if I could think about it . . . or it might 'ave come to me if I wasn't trying so 'ard to remember. . . .'

Grey said: 'I suppose we could try the Maidstone police. Who was Chief Constable then?'

'Oh . . . what was his name . . . got it on the tip of me tongue . . . Scottish, he was—Macpherson, that's it. But I bet he retired years ago. He's probably dead.'

'Would you mind very much if I used your phone?'

'Of course. But don't mind me saying so, you'd probably do better to leave it till after Christmas. Is it all that urgent?'

'We don't know. My friend Zweig'll tell you about it while I try and ring Maidstone. Could you show me the phone?'

Zweig tried to explain briefly, but his excitement and uncertainty made the narrative unconnected. In spite of this, Mrs Colbright listened with strained attention, and nodded periodically to encourage him. Zweig kept wishing he was in the next room, standing beside Grey; he found this tension unbearable. He wanted to ask if they had an extension telephone in the house, but felt that this would be rude.

Colbright listened without displaying any reactions and without commenting, even when Zweig's account lost itself in ambiguities. But when Zweig said: 'So you see, if you are right, and Gustav Neumann *was* the secretary in this Maidstone case . . .' he whistled and said, 'Blimey.' He reached over and took up the photograph again. But staring at it did nothing to settle his opinion.

Mrs Colbright had failed to grasp the implication of Zweig's most recent glimpse of Gustav Neumann. She said:

'But isn't there a law that you can't try a man for a murder that's more than twenty years old?'

Colbright said: 'If we can find 'im, we might 'ave something a bit more recent to go on.'

For some reason, Zweig was comforted by Colbright's use of 'we'; it seemed to make everything more definite. At the same time, he found himself, for the first time, realizing that this might prove to be a murder hunt.

They heard the telephone bell tinkle as the receiver was replaced. When Grey came back in, he looked pleased.

'That was a piece of luck. The sergeant on duty had served under Macpherson.'

Zweig was so delighted that he seized his friend's hand. He found it icy cold; evidently the next room was unheated.

'And what news, then?' he asked.

Grey stooped down, holding his hands out to the fire. He accepted a second whisky from Colbright.

'Not as much as I'd like. Macpherson died earlier this year. The sergeant hadn't actually been on the case—he was on the beat at the time—but he knew some details. The old man, Benskin . . .'

"That's it!' Colbright said.

'. . . came from abroad with his private secretary. Apparently he was either an entomologist or a lepidopterist—the sergeant wasn't sure which. He was ill when he arrived and spent most of his time in bed. The secretary told people he was suffering from the aftereffects of malaria. One night the secretary went out to get some special medicine from the doctor— it contained a drug—and when he got back, the old man was dead on the dining-room floor. They assumed he'd heard noises and come downstairs to investigate, carrying the shotgun. The burglar must have grappled with him and shot him in the face. . . .'

'That's it,' Colbright said. 'You bring it all back now. And they couldn't find any marks of breaking and entry. I remember! It was something about the gardener. At first the police thought the burglar must have got in by a side gate that led into the back garden, but the gardener said he'd rigged up some sort of a burglar alarm inside it because there'd been a lot of burglaries in the neighbourhood. And for some reason— I can't remember what it was—they knew he hadn't got in through the front gate, so they assumed that the secretary had done it and tried to fix himself an alibi. Then what 'appened . . . let me see. . . .'

'A local burglar was arrested,' Sir Charles said, 'and was able to prove he hadn't been near the house. But he confessed to the other burglaries.'

'That's it. But didn't they arrest the secretary then?'

'Apparently not. The post-mortem proved that the death had taken place when the secretary was out of the house.'

Zweig was unable to repress his excitement any longer: 'This secretary . . . does anyone have a description of him?'

'He looked like your photograph,' Colbright said.

'Yes, but was he a foreigner? What was his name?'

Grey shook his head. 'That I couldn't find out. The sergeant will ring me back if he can find out anything about it. He couldn't remember the name.'

Zweig subsided into his chair, expelling his breath.

'Ah, so we still know nothing, nothing at all.'

They were all sitting; now they stared at one another. Mrs Colbright asked:

'Couldn't you go down to Maidstone? There must be somebody who'd have all the details.'

Grey said, shrugging: 'We can get the details from police files. I'd have no difficulty at all if I still had an official position. As it is, I'm caught off balance. This whole thing may turn out to be a bubble. We've got nothing solid to go on—just a series of guesses. If I was still in the police, I'd send a couple of men down to Maidstone to find out what they could, then I'd check with Interpol about the Mentone case —see if we couldn't connect the two, see if the Zurich police know anything about Neumann's whereabouts during the war. But we've only the two of us. . . .'

'Three,' said Mrs Colbright, beaming at her husband.

'Well, that's very kind . . . but even with three the big question remains. . . . Do we spoil our Christmas by chasing a murderer who may not exist?'

Mrs Colbright saw the force of this argument; she looked gloomy.

'Couldn't it wait . . . I mean until after Christmas? Surely there's not much you can do on Christmas Day?'

After a silence, Zweig said: 'I am inclined to agree.'

Grey said slowly: 'On the other hand, if I approached the Yard immediately, we might get a few men to work on locating your friend Neumann over Christmas.'

The clock on the shelf struck eleven with noisy echoing chimes. Zweig wanted to go home to bed, but was ashamed to say so. The heat of the room was making his eyelids heavy. He felt useless and helpless; it was an irritating situation, a mystery that might not be a mystery; and he could do nothing to resolve the incertitude. He stared from Colbright to Grey, then to Mrs Colbright, and decided to suggest going home. But as he opened his mouth to speak, another idea crossed his mind, and he heard himself asking Colbright:

'Where did you see that photograph of the private nurse?'

'Er . . . let me see.' He bent his head, digging his chin into his chest and clutching the back of his scalp. 'It could have been a newspaper. . . .'

Grey looked interested.

'Was the story in the national Press?'

'Not exactly. If I remember rightly, it didn't make much of a sensation after the first day.'

'But which papers carried it?'

'Let me think. . . . I used to take the *Mail* and the *Chronicle*. But then the bloke I worked with took the *News*. So it could have been any of them. On the other hand, perhaps I didn't see it in a newspaper at all. Per'aps my brother-in-law showed me a photo.'

'Worth trying, anyway,' Grey said. He looked at his watch. 'Look here, we don't want to keep you up, so let me ring for a taxi, and we'll do it from my flat. . . .'

'Or mine,' Zweig said hopefully.

Grey stood up. 'I'll ring for a taxi, and while we're waiting, I'll try and ring a friend of mine on the *News*—he's a night sub.'

When Grey came back into the room, ten minutes later, Zweig was dozing in an armchair. Mrs Colbright had gone to attend to her cooking, and Colbright had been called upstairs to subdue a disturbance between the children. There was a ring at the doorbell, and Grey said: 'Good, that'll be the taxi.' He went to answer the door, and Zweig shook himself into reluctant wakefulness. A cold wind blew into the room through the open front door. Colbright came in, and Zweig shook hands with him but was unable to remember his name. Grey said: 'That's our taxi. Say goodnight to your wife for us, Albert. Don't disturb her. . . .'

'Any luck with the *News*?'

'Not yet. My friend wasn't there, but I've managed to persuade somebody to have a look in the files. Unfortunately, I don't know the exact date of the murder. Early October sometime, wasn't it?'

'Ah, I can tell you that one. It must have been the day before Michaelmas Day, because Ted—my brother-in-law—always brought the wife some Michaelmas daisies.' He opened a bureau drawer, and took out a diary. 'Must have been twenty-eighth of September, or thereabouts.'

'Splendid. What a memory you've got! I wish I'd known that five minutes ago. Never mind. I'll phone again from my place.'

They went out into the icy night air. Zweig dropped, shivering, on to the seat of the taxi, closed his eyes, and realized how much he had drunk since seven o'clock. The driver asked the address, and without thinking he gave his own. Grey climbed in and slammed the door. Zweig envied his liveliness. The taxi wheels spun in the snow, skidded, then gripped. The driver turned and asked: 'Which end of Clarges Street?'

'Not Clarges Street!' Grey said. He stopped and looked at Zweig. 'At least, unless. . . .'

Zweig felt uncomfortable. 'I feel very tired, but if you think I can be of use. . . .'

'Knightsbridge,' Grey said to the driver. 'Just beyond Wilton Place.' He turned to Zweig. 'Come in for a moment, and let's find out if there's any information waiting for us. I doubt whether there will be. They've got a skeleton staff on the *News*.'

Zweig pushed aside his tiredness, rubbing his hand over his cold cheeks.

'Of course. Under the circumstances it is the least I can do.'

'You see, Karl, it's remotely possible that Sid Hopkins—my friend—might turn up a picture of the secretary. *If* he did, I'd want you to look at it immediately. You understand why, don't you? If it *is* your friend Neumann, I'd feel justified in phoning the assistant commissioner tonight and starting a murder hunt.'

'Of course. I understand.' But Zweig's heart was compressed by fatigue at the thought of travelling down to Fleet Street by taxi. He no longer believed in what they were doing; he was slightly puzzled by Grey's enthusiasm.

Grey's dining-room was empty; in the lounge, the fire was almost dead. 'Edna must have gone to bed,' Grey said. He threw a log on the fire, and applied the bellows.

Zweig watched with fascination as the underside of a half-burnt log glowed red, then took fire, realizing at the same time that this interest was the result of exhausted attention. He closed his eyes and leaned back into the cushions that caressed the back of his head and neck. Grey went out of the room, then returned; Zweig kept his eyes closed, preferring that Grey should think him asleep. He could see the glow of the flames through his closed eyelids. Grey piled more logs on the fire, arranging them quietly in case he disturbed his friend. Then Zweig's pretence of sleep drifted into unconsciousness, and he slept more deeply because a part of his mind still anticipated being awakened.

He dreamed that he was playing chess with Gustav Neumann. Neumann was a boy of seventeen. Then, somehow the chessboard was a floor with big squares, and he and Neumann were chessmen standing at opposite ends, facing one another. As well as being a chessman, Zweig was also above the board, looking down on it. The board was not the floor of a room, it was part of a long, oval-shaped patch. But there were no walls; the oval was defined by banks of clear grey mist, a mist like grey crystal. When Zweig looked closer at this mist, he observed that there was nothing to stop it from flowing forward and covering the floor and the chessboard; it swirled in small eddies, and sometimes seemed to recede slightly; otherwise it might have been held back by a glass wall.

Zweig woke up, and thought for a moment that Grey, sitting in the opposite armchair, was Gustav Neumann. Grey noticed his movement and looked up, smiling.

'There's no word yet. I can't understand what's happened. Would you like me to order you a taxi?'

Zweig shook his head, and stared at the fire, then at the clock. He had been sleeping for half an hour; it was after midnight. He was inclined to tell Grey about his dream, but was too lazy to speak. Instead, he thought about it, and of the strange feeling of significance that had been with him in the dream. Grey would say: 'But you simply thought of yourself as an adversary of Neumann, playing chess against him,' and that was the least important part of the dream. What had impressed him had been an insight that came as he looked at the walls of mist. *Out there* was nothing, no meaning, no values; in here there were rules, rules of the game; and the game was played in a small area of apparent normality and reality, surrounded by the mist.

The telephone rang. Grey jumped up, saying: 'Ah, at last.'

He picked up the phone and announced his number. Zweig, suddenly awake, listened carefully.

'Ah, Sidney . . . oh, it's not Sidney. Robin Davis, of course I remember you. What's happening? . . . I see. I'm sorry to put you to so much trouble, but it's important. If there's a story in it, I'll see you get it first. . . . Yes. What would you like us to do? Come over there? . . . You can? Of course. When? . . . Are you sure it's no trouble? No. That's very kind of you. . . .'

He replaced the telephone.

'He's coming here right away. He's bringing the picture.'

Zweig, delighted not to be asked to go to Fleet Street, said: 'Amazing! How did you persuade him?'

'I didn't have to. He's on his way home, he says. It's strictly against the rules to bring library clippings out of the office, but I think he's hoping for a story.'

'But he had a photograph?'

'Yes. He says he's got a fairly good picture of the private nurse—whose name, incidentally, was Bernstein.'

Zweig's excitement mounted suddenly. The photograph would be in his hands in a few minutes, and he would have definite knowledge. It now seemed that the photograph would decide everything. If it was not Gustav Neumann, then Neumann was not a murderer, and the other evidence was coincidence, an accident. Then, with sudden clarity, Zweig saw himself holding a newspaper photograph of Gustav Neumann, and it was like a shock of cold water. He said:

'Charles . . . supposing it *is* Gustav? What will you do?'

Grey shrugged. 'There's only one thing for me to do. Lay all the information before the police immediately and start the murder hunt.'

'Tonight?'

'I'm afraid so. There'd be no room for doubt that Neumann is a murderer. At least, not in my mind. How about you?'

'Of course,' Zweig said; his voice was without expression. He was imagining Christmas morning spent at Scotland Yard, repeating his story.

'How about a final drink?' Grey said.

Zweig stood up. 'Thank you. I'll have a large brandy.'

'Excellent idea. So will I. Meanwhile, we'd better decide what to tell our friend from the Press.'

'Does it matter?'

'Not at this stage. He won't print anything until we tell him. But if they start investigating the story themselves it could be awkward. Neumann might decide to vanish.'

'Then let us tell him. . . .'

The ring of the doorbell interrupted him. Grey said:

'He's damn quick.'

A moment later, Grey came back into the room, preceded by a young man whose raincoat was powdered with snow.

'Robin Davis, this is Professor Karl Zweig.'

'How do you do, sir. I know your face, of course.'

'Let me have your coat, Robin. You'll have a drink, won't you? Try this brandy—it's a special Portuguese brandy.'

The young man had a plump, good-natured face, and a shy manner of speaking, with a slight stammer.

'That's very k-kind of you, Sir Charles. I'd love some.'

'On the contrary, my dear Robin, it's kind of you to take all this trouble on Christmas Eve . . . Christmas Day. Have you eaten? Could I make you a sandwich?'

'No, no, r-really, thanks. I'm on my way home. I told my wife I'd try to be home early.'

'Where have you been until now?'

'In St Albans. This body in the river case. The husband confessed a few hours ago.'

'Did he indeed? So it was the husband. . . .'

Davis took a gulp of the brandy, swallowed with his eyes closed, then said, more cheerfully:

'Ah, that's a brandy.' He held out his hands to the fire. Zweig cleared his throat and said:

'Pardon me, but the photograph . . .'

'Oh, I'm so sorry. It's in my overcoat.'

Zweig shivered. He was afraid that his hands would tremble as he took the photograph. Grey, aware of the tension, poured more brandy and said casually:

'Did Sid give you any idea of what it was all about?'

'Not much. To tell the truth, I was feeling so cold and damp when I got in that I didn't listen carefully.' He held out a long envelope, on which was written: 'Benskin case, September 28, 1938.' To Zweig's relief, Grey took it, and sat down on the settee. He shook out its contents, and smoothed them out. Zweig stood looking over his shoulder. Grey said:

'There you are. Is that him?'

Zweig looked unbelievingly at the bearded face, photo-
graphed in half-profile.

'I . . . I don't understand. Gustav had no beard.'

He stared at it helplessly, blankly, as he had stared at
the burning logs earlier, his brain flatly rejecting it; he felt
intense relief when Grey said:

'Obviously, he may have grown a beard for the occasion.
But does it look like Neumann? Can you tell?'

It was a good photograph, although the paper had turned
yellow at the edges. But to Zweig, it could have been a picture
of a man wearing a hood like a member of the Ku Klux
Klan. The eyes were not looking at the camera; the man wore
a trilby hat. Zweig suspected himself of not wanting to recognize it, to avoid the inevitable complications that would follow, so he felt embarrassed about admitting that the picture
meant nothing to him.

'Let's have a look at your photograph of Neumann,' Grey
said. They placed them side by side. Grey murmured: 'Could
be.' He looked at Zweig. 'What do you think, Karl?'

'I don't know. I just don't know. I don't think it is . . . but
I don't think it's not. I just can't tell.'

Robin Davis came over timidly. He said:

'Do you mind . . . or is it strictly private?'

'Not at all. After all, you brought the picture.'

Davis stared down at the two photographs. He said:

'I would have said that they're the same man . . . but
with the reservation that I might be wrong.'

He picked up the envelope, looked inside it, and shook it.
A thin, folded clipping fell out. Grey opened it eagerly; but
the photograph showed only an oldish man with a totally
bald head; the caption said: 'Walter Benskin, taken a few
days before he was killed.' The date of the cutting was a
few days after the murder; it mentioned that Benskin's collection of rare moths had been valued at several thousands
of pounds, and speculated whether the burglar had been hoping to steal it. There was little else of value in the house.

Davis said: 'He already looks dead, doesn't he?' It was
true; possibly it was the newsprint reproduction that gave the
old man's face the appearance of lifelessness. Zweig found
himself unable to look away from the face, and wondering
if it was his imagination that made it seem the face of a
destined victim.

'What's the story?' Davis asked. 'Or is it a secret?'

'Not really. If this man and this one are the same, then is probably a murderer.'

'And if not?'

'Then the probability is greatly reduced.'

'What sort of a murderer?'

'One who kills old men for their money.'

'Sounds a terrific story.'

'Don't worry. If anything seems to be definite you'll the first to get it.'

Zweig read through the article that described the death Walter Benskin. The headline said: 'Man killed in dea struggle with burglar.' It contained few details that he did n already know. Benskin had returned from South America month before his death; the Maidstone house had been le to him by his brother, who had died while he was in Americ

Grey was looking over his shoulder. He said:

'From the wording of that account, it looks as if Bernste was more of a secretary than a nurse.'

Grey said: 'It looks as if I'll have to go down to Maidsto after Christmas and see what I can find out. I'd like to kno about the nationality of the secretary.'

'There is one thing about Gustav,' Zweig said. 'He was fine linguist. He spoke French and Italian perfectly. It m: not have been obvious that he was not English.'

'That's worth bearing in mind. But the police must ha asked to see his credentials, his passport and so on.'

Davis said: "Well, if you gentlemen have seen all yc wanted to see, I think I'd better be going. I'm afraid I'll ha to take those cuttings away with me.'

'Not at all. I don't think we shall need them again. Inc dentally, I'm surprised there's no follow-up to the story.'

'I don't know. It could have been mislaid, of course. The again . . .' he stifled a yawn. 'I'm sorry . . . then again, pe haps there wasn't any follow-up.'

He pulled on his coat.

'Professor, can I give you a lift anywhere?'

'No thank you. I live only a hundred yards away.'

When Davis had gone, Zweig reached for his coat.

'So there is no evidence. And I'm afraid I have wasted you evening.'

Grey said: 'I'm not sure. You see, I got an idea that I'

een that photograph of Neumann before. And Colbright immediately thought it was the secretary in the Maidstone case.'

'That is true. I wonder why?'

'I wonder. . . . You see, Colbright's got an extraordinary memory for faces. He was one of the best men in criminal records; he could often identify a wanted man just from a bad photograph or a description. So either he saw a photograph of the secretary without his beard, or he saw another photograph, with the beard, that was far more like your picture of Neumann.'

'Do you think that possible?'

'Yes. If you noticed, that newspaper photograph was taken from the worst possible angle. Evidently the photographer was crouching slightly, so the beard is seen from underneath, and looks fairly prominent. Even if it was a fairly small beard —perhaps only a fortnight's growth—it'd look prominent from that angle. If a photograph were taken from above—or with the man looking down—it might be almost unnoticeable.'

Zweig was tired; Grey's words flowed past his ears as a stream of sounds. He was thinking: 'I am getting old. I have been awake for a few hours past my normal bedtime, and I feel exhausted.' He said: 'I must go, Charles. I can hardly keep awake.'

'I'll walk across with you. Or would you like a taxi?'

'No. The walk will wake me up.'

It had stopped snowing, and the air was icy. In spite of Zweig's protests, Grey walked with him. But the wind was so cold that talk was impossible. Their feet crunched through the icy crust that had formed on the snow with every step. Ahead of them, the open expanse of Hyde Park corner looked strangely beautiful in its desertion, and made Zweig think nostalgically of the Brandenburg Gate in Berlin. The cold penetrated Zweig's indifference, but only to the extent of making him think with pleasure of the prospect of a warm bed and a hot water bottle. It was tiresome that he had to be up fairly early in the morning to go to Hampstead; perhaps he could sleep until eleven o'clock, and get there for lunch.

At the bottom of Clarges Street, he said:

'My dear Charles, I really insist that you walk back now. I am not going to fall down and break my neck in the last twenty yards. Thank you for a delightful evening, and please thank your wife. If you need me tomorrow, you have my

sister's telephone number in Hampstead. I shall probably be
back late tomorrow night.'

'Have a merry Christmas. I'll try and contact the Maid
stone police in the meantime.'

As he let himself into the flat, the clock struck one. He
reflected that he had left the flat less than six hours before
to go to the club; it seemed a long time ago.

Before removing his coat, he filled the electric kettle and
plugged it in; the hot water bottle came first. Then he placed
his coat and jacket on coat hangers and hung them in the
wardrobe of his bedroom. He removed the photographs from
his inside pocket and took them into his study, where the
album still lay on the desk, and carefully re-inserted them. He
stared for a long time at the photograph of Gustav Neumann,
then turned back to the previous page, and looked at a photo
graph of Neumann at the age of six, sitting on his mother's
knee. The mother and child were amazingly alike; two dark
eyed, sensitive faces staring at the camera. Zweig had met
her several times in the last year of her life; he remembered
her as a gentle woman with a passion for the songs of Hugo
Wolf and Robert Franz. How could it be possible that her son
should be a murderer? He thought again of the photograph
of the bearded secretary, then looked at the serious-faced
child, and suddenly wondered what could have possessed him
to suspect Gustav Neumann of multiple murder.

He took the album under his arm, and went into the bed
room. The condensed moisture on the inside of the window
had turned into frost; he scratched it with his fingernail. This
bedroom was the warmest room in the flat, since the hot
water pipes from the bathroom ran through it. He undressed
slowly, and savoured the pleasure of being back in his own
room, independent again.

It was his usual practise to read for a few minutes before
turning off the light; this evening, he opened the photograph
album again and turned over the pages. Looking at a picture
of himself in battledress, it suddenly seemed incredible that
he was now an old man, with perhaps only another ten year
to live. Forty years had passed like a dream, leaving as little
behind; a few memories, a little achievement—and the wall
of mist ahead, as inscrutable as his beginnings. He thought
Strange how my sense of reality changes. In youth, every
thing is too real; towards the end, nothing is real.

He turned the pages idly, no longer caring, and no longer interested in the photographs. The album fell open at its end flyleaf. There, a pocket made of reinforced paper contained photographs that had been creased or damaged, and also a few photographs that seemed interesting enough to preserve but not interesting enough to label and insert. One of these now caught his attention. It showed about a dozen men sitting round a dinner table, all formally dressed. Alois Neumann was far from the camera and hardly recognizable. It was a photograph that Neumann had presented to him; he was not even sure what it was supposed to be, although he had a vague memory that it was either a civic banquet or the society of surgeons. His own face was not present, and he recognized none of the others.

And yet there was one face that seemed familiar, and it was this that kept him staring at the photograph. It was the man sitting next to Alois Neumann. When he peered at it the familiarity vanished, and he became aware of the badness of the photograph; but held at a distance, it again troubled his memory. The man seemed to be middle aged and almost bald; the eyelids, as far as one could judge, were large and drooping. Zweig had a theory that the memory worked on a certain electricity generated by the brain cells, and that if memories were deeply submerged, it would take a considerable charge to get them to the surface. He said aloud: 'The battery is flat', and switched off the bedside lamp. It was unimportant and he was tired.

He was almost asleep when another face seemed to superimpose itself on the image of the photograph. He opened his eyes and lay, wide awake, staring into the darkness. Then he sat up in bed, switched on the light, and opened the album again. The identity of the face had come back. He had seen it only an hour ago in a newspaper photograph: the face of the old man who had been killed at Maidstone, Walter Benskin.

And yet with the light on it, he was again uncertain. If this man who sat beside Alois Neumann was Walter Benskin, then Grey should be informed immediately. But how could he be certain? He was tired; it was a cold night, and his bedroom was the warmest room in the flat. He reasoned with himself as he stared at the picture. Newspaper photographs are unreliable; and a blurred, twenty-five-year-old snapshot was certainly unreliable. Moreover, the reporter had by now reached home with the press cuttings and was probably in bed. This was not evidence; Grey might well be irritated to be awakened at this hour. . . .

He lay down and switched off the light. He thought: It is absurd; I feel sleepy, and then realized that he was not sleepy. Instead, he was staring into the darkness and thinking: So Gustav is a murderer. He was surprised that the thought produced an excitement that was close to pleasure. He wondered: Why should I be pleased if Gustav is a murderer? Am I senile enough to welcome the excitement? No, Zweig thought of the few murder cases of which he had had personal experience. There was a man in California who had murdered his wife and set the house on fire; but he was a hysteric. And Zweig had accompanied Alois Neumann to examine Haarmann, the Hanover butcher; he had been repelled by the man's degeneracy, a certain peasant cunning. As to Kürten . . . all murderers are. . . . His mind groped for a phrase and found it. Victims of their own crime. Who had said that? Alois? No, it had been Gustav, speaking on that last evening they spent together. When Zweig had described this evening to the Greys, Gustav Neumann had been a blurred face, evoked by effort of memory. Now he became a presence, as clear as if Zweig had opened his eyes and found him standing in the room. Even his voice was reproduced, with the accuracy of a gramophone record, saying: 'A murderer like Kürten is the victim of his own crime. The horror of the act lies in the confusion of killer and victim. But can you imagine a murderer who remains outside his own act? Wouldn't this be the final expression of free will—to kill without involvement?'

And yet it was precisely because Neumann could express himself with such clarity that Zweig could not believe him capable of murder. A man who could devote his life to killing old men for their money must be himself a fool and a victim. Was this the source of Zweig's pleasure—the thought that Neumann was also one of the defeated? Or was it, perhaps, a kind of hope?

He was no longer thinking seriously of telephoning Grey. And the memories of Alois Neumann now carried him away from the present until the sense of comfort merged into sleep. In his sleep, he was on leave in Berlin in 1917; it was a grey, cold day in February, and he and Alois Neumann had found a café where they could buy schnapps. It was expensive, and almost certainly diluted; but they were talking of the future, of the Germany that would emerge after the victory, and of their part in it, and feeling nothing but optimism and a sense of impending victory. He was going to be the greatest German thinker since Kant; Neumann was developing theories on the relation of will power to the brain that would revolutionize psychology. And Neumann, emptying the last of the schnapps into their glasses, said: 'It's strange that we should be here together. But the great ones of every age come together. . . .'

He half-awoke, and remembered that this was forty years ago. The feeling of loss choked him, became too intense to bear, then it vanished as he found himself lying in bed. He thought: 'It's strange how grief in life is easier to bear than grief in dreams.' Then the thought of Gustav Neumann returned, and for the first time, he saw everything in perspective. How could he reconcile himself to sending him to the gallows? How had it happened that everything was now in Grey's hands? Obviously because five hours ago he had not believed Gustav Neumann a murderer. He now understood why it was that he had not contacted Grey as soon as he discovered the photograph of the man who looked like Walter Benskin. It was not fatigue or laziness, but an instinctive loyalty to Alois and Gustav Neumann.

He now felt regrets; regret for not leaping out of his taxi and accosting Neumann outside the Chesham Hotel; regret for telling the story to Grey. But then, if he had not talked to Grey, he would not now be certain that Gustav Neumann was a. . . . His mind rejected the word before the sentence was completed. He was certain of nothing—not even that the man outside the Chesham had been Gustav Neumann. His whole chain of evidence might yet prove to be a paper chain. Only one thing was certain: he must find some way of contacting Gustav Neumann. And then? And then. . . . This time the sleep came so suddenly that he was unaware of it until he woke up and found grey daylight filtering through the frosty panes.

Someone knocked; before he could rouse himself enough to shout 'Come in', Grey entered, pushing the dumb-waiter with coffee.

'Morning, Karl. Sleep well?'

'Very well,' Zweig said. His first thought was for the photograph album on the bedside table, but it was too late to conceal it. 'What time is it?'

'After eleven. I've just come from the Chesham.'

Zweig sat upright, and rubbed his palm over the stubble on his chin.

'What news?'

'None, I'm afraid. I talked to the same doorman who hailed the cab. He said he didn't know the cabbie and couldn't recollect the number.'

He was pouring coffee into two cups. Zweig, feeling somehow ashamed to be in bed, pulled on his dressing gown, and lit the gas fire.

'Why don't you come into the other room? It's warmer there.'

'I'm not awake yet,' Zweig said, rubbing his eyes. Then, recollecting the album, he said: 'Still, we may as well.' But before he could stand up, Grey said:

'This is the album, isn't it? Any more pictures of Neumann in there?'

'A few.' There was no point in lying.

'May I see?' Grey was already holding the album. Zweig put sugar and cream into his coffee, saying: 'There's nothing that could help.' He sat in the armchair by the fire, and stared at the hot elements, willing himself not to watch Grey. After a moment, he heard Grey replace the album.

'I've got another piece of news,' Grey said. 'I don't think Neumann could have been the secretary in the Maidstone case.'

'What? How is that?'

'I've been on the telephone to Edwin Stephens, who was in charge of the case. He tells me that he thinks Bernstein was Scottish—in spite of his name.'

'Was he sure?'

'More or less. Surely Neumann couldn't have spoken with a Scotch accent? He wasn't all that good at languages, was he?'

Zweig said slowly: 'Yes, he was good at languages . . . but. . . .'

'Quite. Not that good. I've often heard about foreigners who speak English "like a native", but never met one. Your own

English, for example, is perfect from the grammatical point of view, but you've a slightly explosive way of accenting short words. . . .'

Zweig was interested. He prided himself on his English.

'In what way? I've taken great trouble not to pronounce my w's as v's and my v's as f's.'

'I can't quite explain. An Englishman speaks somehow . . . smoothly. All the words sound connected together. A foreigner speaks English as if there's a little barrier at the end of every word that has to be surmounted . . . sorry, I don't make myself clear.'

'Not quite. But never mind. I see your point about Gustav. I have only one objection. Surely a Scottish accent is also slightly like a German or Italian accent?'

'Is it?'

'I have heard a record of Caruso singing in English, and anyone would take him for a Scotsman.'

Grey stared at his coffee, and Zweig found himself wondering why he was saying all this. Grey said:

'But was Neumann all that good as a linguist?' Zweig smiled and shrugged.

'No.'

'Good. Because frankly, I don't believe that the secretary was Gustav Neumann. That was a false trail that Colbright started.'

'But did not your friend in the police ask to see the man's papers?'

'No. At least, he didn't ask him to prove his identity. You see, this Bernstein was released almost as soon as he was arrested. In fact, technically speaking, he was never under arrest—just at the police station helping the police. And incidentally, Edwin Stephens tells me that he's quite sure the secretary had nothing to do with the murder. He thinks it was accidental death. The old boy was nervous. He heard a noise and went charging downstairs with a gun—and somehow it went off.'

'What about the open window?'

'Stephens says it was opened from inside. The old man probably opened it himself.'

All the time Grey was speaking, Zweig was thinking about the photograph in the pocket at the back of the album—a photograph showing the victim sitting beside Alois Neumann. Zweig and Grey had been friends for many years; there was a habit of frankness between them, and Zweig now found it hard to break. When Grey stopped talking, they both sat in silence, drinking coffee, and he decided to mention the photograph. Instead, he heard himself saying:

'In short, the case against Gustav Neumann collapses?'

'Not quite. I still think there's a possibility he may be a murderer. At the first opportunity, I'm going to get Scotland Yard to check with Interpol to see if he's known to the police.'

He replaced the cup on the tray, and stood up.

'Time I got home. I expect you want to get dressed. Anyway, thought I'd come and rest your mind about the Maidstone business.'

The telephone rang. Zweig said:

'That will be my sister. . . .'

'I'll go then. I'll phone you if there's any news.'

Zweig walked with him to the bedroom door.

'Thank you for calling in, Charles. You are very kind.'

Grey took his leave quickly, aware that he was keeping Zweig from the telephone.

Zweig said: 'Hello. Who is that?'

A strange voice said:

'Professor Zweig?'

'Speaking.'

'You don't know me. I'm the manager at the Chesham. I believe you were in here last night asking after two diners. . . .'

'Yes.'

'And I gather a friend of yours was here again this morning. Well, I think we can tell you a little about them, although I don't know if it will be of any help.'

Zweig was aware that he should now be asking the manager to hold on, while he called Grey back up the stairs. Grey would not yet be out of the building. It was at this point that he faced the decision that had been implied in his earlier reticence with Grey. He said:

'Just one moment. I will be over there in twenty minutes. Will you still be there?'

'Yes, sir. And you can also speak to the secretary. She took the order for dinner. . . .'

'Excellent. This is really very kind of you. I will come over right away.'

'Thank you, sir.'

He poured himself more coffee and sat on the bed. The album was lying on the pillow, and he threw it open without changing his position. There was a photograph of himself and Alois Neumann as soldiers; it had been taken in Baden in 1916. This helped to soothe his disquiet; it seemed almost an omen. He talked softly to himself as he dressed: 'No, it would not be kind to Charles to tell him. . . . He is a policeman. It is his duty. . . . But Alois and Gustav were my friends. . . .' He rang for a taxi, then went into the kitchen and buttered some matzos. He was too excited to be hungry, but was old enough to know that leaving the house without breakfast would be disastrous. He now asked himself why he had offered to go to the hotel, and realized that it was because Grey was still in the building while the manager was talking. This attempt at evasion made him smile. He crunched the biscuits without appetite, and washed them down with cold water. He was honest enough to discern that his motives were less creditable than he would care to admit to Grey. In self-justification, he would claim that he was divided between his old friendship for Gustav and his duty as a citizen; in fact, he was divided between excitement at the prospect of a murder hunt, and irritation at the amount of his time that it threatened to take up. The feeling of friendship for Gustav was almost nonexistent. He had always been slightly offended by Neumann's lack of respect; now, after twenty-five years, it was mainly the irritation that remained. Yet the excitement was not the morbid absorption of a man who is secretly fascinated by the idea of crime; Zweig was not. If Gustav Neumann proved to be a second Landru, Zweig would be disappointed and saddened. What excited him was a prospect that he was unwilling to define, because it seemed too unlikely; but it was connected with his final conversation with Gustav Neumann in Heidelberg.

The manager recognized him as soon as he entered the foyer, and came towards him smiling. He was a small, elderly man with an effusive manner that probably covered shyness.

'Good morning, Professor, and a happy Christmas. Can I offer you a small drink?'

A group of women who were entering the dining-room stared at Zweig; he heard one of them mention television. This kind of recognition usually flattered him; this morning, it brought a sense of discomfort, as if his shoes were full of water. He turned away from them and said:

'I'm afraid I've only just had breakfast . . . but thank you all the same.'

'No? Not even a small sherry for Christmas? Would you like to come into my office for a moment?'

A plump woman in a maroon dress followed them into the office. The manager said:

'This is Mrs West, our secretary. She's been with us for thirty years. *You*'ll have a sherry, won't you, Mrs West?'

'Thank you, Mr Gascoigne. I don't mind if I do, seeing it's Christmas.'

Zweig felt awkward standing there, and unwilling to hint that his taxi was waiting. The manager glanced at him as he filled two glasses, and Zweig said:

'Perhaps a very small one, then.'

'Good. . . . Yes, Mr Chambers, my assistant, told me that you'd been in to inquire about your friend. But of course, he didn't know about it because he didn't come on duty until five. It was Mrs West who took the phone call and booked them for dinner.'

'Do you know their names?' Zweig asked her.

'Not both of them. But I knew the old man. He was Sir Timothy Ferguson, the Scottish baronet. He used to come in here regular before the war—often with his father.'

'Splendid!' Zweig took out his diary, and scribbled the name. 'You don't happen to know anything more about him?'

'Only what's in *Who's Who*,' the manager said. He brought the book from the table; it was already open. 'There you are.'

Zweig bent over it, and read it through quickly. 'Third baronet . . . son of Major-General Sir Kelvin Ferguson . . . chairman Hospital board of management . . . Scottish Ship-building Research Association . . . Perth. Perth? Isn't that in Australia?' Geography had always been Zweig's weakest subject. The manager smiled at the secretary; in imagination, he was already telling his wife: 'He's on "Ask the Experts," and he doesn't even know where Perth is!' 'There *is* another Perth in Scotland, Professor,' he said.

'Of course, of course, I see it now. I'm not wearing my reading glasses. . . .' Zweig copied the address and telephone number into his diary. 'This is very helpful indeed. I'll telephone this number and see if they know where he's staying.' He looked at the secretary. 'I suppose you've no idea where he telephoned from?'

'No, sir. It was his secretary who phoned. Isn't that the man you want to find?'

'Yes. Why do you say his secretary?'

'That's how he announced himself on the phone.'

'Ah. But he didn't tell you where he was staying?'

'There was no need, sir. He just asked if they could book for dinner, and I said yes. . . . I suppose they must be staying with friends somewhere. . . .'

Zweig finished his sherry. He now felt expansive; he even found the manager likeable.

'I cannot tell you how grateful I am for the trouble you've taken.'

'It's a pleasure, Professor. I never miss your programme. Incidentally, I wonder if you'd be so kind as to sign my nephew's autograph book? He's only eight. . . .'

Zweig signed his name with a flourish, then signed a piece of paper that Mrs West said she wanted for her son's collection. Then, shaking hands with both of them, he took his leave. As he climbed back into the taxi, he reflected that celebrity also has its advantages. . . .

●

Seated on his sister's bed, an hour later, Zweig put through
a trunk call to Scotland. There was a long silence, with no
ringing tone, until the operator's voice said: 'I'm sorry, sir,
there seems to be no reply . . . oh, excuse me one moment.'
After another silence, she said: 'You're through.'

Zweig said: 'Hello, is that the residence of Sir Timothy
Ferguson?'

A muffled voice said that it was.

'This is Professor Karl Zweig. I am a friend of Sir Timothy.'

The voice said: 'I'm afraid he's not here.'

'Who is speaking?'

'This is his housekeeper.'

'I believe he's in London at present. Do you happen to . . .'

'He's not in England, sir,' the voice interrupted sharply.

'Are you sure? How long has he been away?'

'For two months. He's in Cologne.'

'Then you must be mistaken. I saw him here in London
last night.'

There was a silence, then:

'Why are you ringing up here?'

'To find out if you can tell me his London address. He
went off before I could get it from him. . . .'

'But I'm certain you must be mistaken. Sir Timothy always
sends a telegram before he returns to England. And he
wouldn't spend Christmas in London. He'd come straight
home.'

Zweig took a deep breath, and restrained himself from
bellowing: 'I tell you . . .' He said: 'I can assure you that
Sir Timothy is in London at the moment. Now have you any
idea where he might be staying?'

She asked him to hang on; he waited what seemed an
interminable time, and the pips sounded twice. The operator
came on the line once to ask: 'Are you still speaking?' He
shouted: 'Yes, don't cut me off,' and the operator said ir-

ritably: 'I can hear you quite well, sir.' There was another long silence. The woman's voice said:

'I'm sorry I've been so long. I couldn't find his address book. Sir Timothy will probably be at his flat at 74 Pelham Place, South Kensington. If he's not there, then he may be staying with Joseph Atholl Gardner at 200 Cromwell Road.'

She repeated the addresses, and Zweig copied them into the diary. He asked: 'Is the Pelham Place flat on the telephone?'

She gave him the number, and added:

'If you speak to him, would you ask him to ring me and let me know what he's doing? It's Mrs Kirkup.'

Zweig promised and hung up. He leaned back against the wall, closing his eyes. From outside came sounds of children screaming with laughter. Zweig grimaced. He was fond of Ottolie's children, but today they were an irrelevancy.

The door opened and his sister came in. She was fifteen years younger than Zweig; until she married, ten years previously, she had acted as his housekeeper. Ottolie had the same strong features and firm mouth as her brother; her flat, red cheeks looked as if they had been painted on with enamel. They spoke in German; she still used the dialect of their village.

'Are you tired?'

'A little.' He had been close to her for too long to keep secrets. 'I have a lot on my mind today.'

'Can't you forget it for Christmas?'

'No, my dear. It's serious. You remember Gustav Neumann?'

'The murderer?' She was acquainted with the Neumann story as far as 1936; she had heard Zweig tell it several times in America; like her brother, she had never taken it wholly seriously.

'Yes, the master criminal. He may be in London.'

'Good. But what is there in that to upset you?'

'With an old man.'

'So?'

'Don't you see?' He stared at her.

She laughed. 'You don't think he's going to kill this one?'

'You think it impossible?'

She stared at him incredulously.

'Are you serious?'

He said defensively: 'Why not?'

'Because . . .' She shrugged, and began picking up clothes, putting them into a drawer. 'I didn't think you ever really believed that story. I mean, I know it's *possible*. But . . .'

'Why do you think I've repeated it to friends in the police?'

'Because it's a good story. And because you wanted to marry me off to that detective.'

This happened to be true, so Zweig changed the subject.

'I've got his London telephone number. I think I'd better ring him now.'

'You might interrupt him while he's disposing of the body.'

She went out as he picked up the telephone. Before she came in, he had not meant to ring the Pelham Place flat; but her scepticism deflated him, made him feel that he was playing at detectives and losing sight of common sense. Besides, it could do no harm. If Neumann really meant to kill Sir Timothy Ferguson, then Zweig's intervention would stop it. And if it was all a mistake, they could meet and talk about old times.

The telephone made a number of strange sounds; then the operator's voice said: 'What number are you calling, sir?'

He told her.

'I'm afraid that number has been disconnected, sir.'

'For how long?'

'I can't tell you that, sir. Would you like me to put you on to inquiries?'

With a sense of futility, he agreed. It took another ten minutes for inquiries to tell him that the phone had been taken out a year ago, and that no other telephone had been installed. He asked:

'Can you tell me if there are any other telephones in the house?'

'I could look up the street directory. Is there any particular subscriber you wish to speak to?'

'No. I'd just like to see if I can contact my friend. . . .'

'I'm sorry, sir, but we can't do that. I can't tell you a number unless you can give me a definite idea of the person you wish to speak to.'

'Can't you tell me which flat Sir Timothy Ferguson lived in?'

'Yes, sir. The basement.'

'Then tell me if there is a telephone on the ground floor.'

'I'm sorry, sir. I can't do that unless you know the name of the subscriber. You see, we have to protect subscribers. . . .'

He hung up in exasperation. Ottolie came in while he was still swearing. She said unhelpfully: 'All English telephone operators are like that.' Zweig chewed at the nail of his index finger. She said: 'Come and have some lunch.'

'I wonder . . . perhaps I should ring this man . . . Gardner.'

'After lunch.'

'I would prefer to do it now. You see, they may be staying there. Besides, Cromwell Road is only around the corner from Pelham Place. He might go and see if Ferguson is at home. . . .'

'On Christmas Day! Why should he?'

Zweig was already dialling. She stood, watching. A female voice replied. When Zweig asked for Joseph Atholl Gardner, she said:

'I'm afraid Mr Gardner and his wife are out for the day. Can I take a message?'

'No. But could you tell me something. Do you happen to know if Mr Gardner has seen anything of Sir Timothy Ferguson this Christmas?'

'No, sir, not as far as I know. I don't believe Sir Timothy's in London. But I'd know about it if he was, because he always spends a lot of time here.'

'Ah. Thank you very much. I'll phone back tomorrow.'

'Well?' Ottolie said.

'I wonder if I should take a taxi down there myself? The maid there says she doesn't think Sir Timothy's in London. That means that he may be keeping his presence a secret.'

Ottolie hunched her shoulders, clasping her hands as if praying; this was meant to indicate that she found her brother hopeless. Because Zweig had always been the 'thinker' of the family, and she had been the practical one, she was inclined to treat him sometimes as a stupid child. This attitude of hers annoyed him; besides, she was wrong as often as he was. And yet he allowed himself to feel convinced by her. He stood up, saying:

'All right, I'll leave it until after lunch.'

'Leave it until tomorrow. There is nothing you can do on Christmas Day. Forget it and enjoy yourself.'

Hence it came about that Karl Zweig spent the afternoon

of Christmas Day in helping Ottolie's eldest boy to construct a meccano crane, and the evening in discussing West German politics with a Düsseldorfer who kept a Soho restaurant, and a Swiss civil engineer, a colleague of his brother-in-law. He also drank at least two bottles of an excellent Rhenish wine, supplied by Herr Schneider of Soho, so that when the subject of Gustav Neumann occurred to him, it came through a haze of well-being and a tipsiness that was due to the food as much as the wine. At two o'clock in the morning, his brother-in-law drove him home, driving in second gear over the icy snow. A few minutes before he fell asleep, the thought of Gustav Neumann came back with a certain freshness, brought about by thinking of other things for twelve hours. Seen with this new detachment, it was suddenly obvious that Gustav Neumann could not be a criminal. The criminal is the man without a destiny; Neumann was a romantic, obsessed by the idea of his destiny. This thought comforted and soothed Zweig, and carried him into sleep.

He was awakened at nine-thirty by the charlady, who also cooked his breakfast. He sat up and rubbed the sleep out of his eyes.

'Shall I make a fire, Professor? Will you be in all day?'

Zweig disliked having to make decisions when he was only half awake. He said: 'Let me think about it.'

'Would you like a kipper for your breakfast?'

'That would be excellent.'

He was dozing off again when the phone rang.

'It's Sir Charles Grey.'

Muttering under his breath, Zweig pulled on his dressing gown, and padded out to the phone. Grey's voice said:

'Sorry if I woke you. This is important. Can I come around in twenty minutes?'

'You know you can come around at any time.'

'I know. But I want to bring somebody with me—John Stafford-Morton, the psychiatrist.'

'All right. Come when you are ready.' He called to the charlady: 'Perhaps you could light the fire after all? Sir Charles will be over in a few moments. Would you make the coffee in the large pot?'

It was too cold to get dressed immediately. He lit the bedroom fire, fetched the 1951 edition of *Who's Who* from the study, and climbed back into bed. He had never heard of John Stafford-Morton, but from his entry, it was evident that he was a man of importance. His name was followed by two lines of letters: M.A., B.Ch. (Cantab.), F.R.C.S. (Eng.), F.I.C.S., etc., various hospital appointments connected with psychological medicine, and a long list of publications including *The Mind of the Recidivist* and *Nervous Disorder and Crime*.

The charlady came in, saying: 'You'd better eat this before they arrive. The coffee's nearly ready.'

He ate absently, continuing to stare at the entry in *Who's Who*. Why should Grey want him to meet this man? It seemed pointless. But this was not what really disturbed him. He had been hoping to have a chance to call at the address in Pelham Place before he saw Grey, and to speak to Gustav Neumann. Now he had once again to face the decision of whether to tell Grey what he had learned. This one was more difficult than the decision not to show Grey the photograph, for Grey might at any moment learn that Zweig had spoken to the manager of the Chesham Hotel. Zweig cursed himself for not having the presence of mind to ask Grey to call in two hours' time. For a moment, he contemplated rushing out of the house, and taking a taxi to Pelham Place, leaving a message asking Grey and Stafford-Morton to wait. He imagined their faces as he walked into the room, saying: 'Let me introduce you to Gustav Neumann, the young man we suspected of being a murderer. . . .' The thought was interrupted by a ring at the doorbell. Zweig went into the bathroom, looked at his unshaven face in the mirror, and decided that there would be no point in getting dressed. Instead, he knotted a silk scarf round his throat, and changed his moth-eaten jaegar dressing gown for a less comfortable but newer-looking one.

Grey said: 'Sorry to disturb you at this hour, Karl. Doctor Stafford-Morton has a busy day ahead.'

Zweig shook hands with the psychiatrist, and decided immediately that he disliked him. Stafford-Morton looked younger than his fifty years, but his face had the pale, nervous look of a man who is afraid that the world will not take him as seriously as he takes himself. His voice was high and abrupt.

'I know a lot about you. Always wanted to meet you. It's a pity we've got to talk shop today. . . .'

'Coffee for you both?' Zweig said.

'I'll tell you the reason we came so early, Karl. I've talked to Mitford at Scotland Yard, and he agrees that it would be a big job to trace Neumann. It'd mean sending out descriptions to all police stations and doing a terrific amount of routine inquiry. It might occupy dozens of men for weeks. And he doesn't seem to feel we've got any real evidence that Neumann might be a murderer. Now I've talked to Doctor Stafford-Morton here, and he seems to agree that it's probably all a mistake. . . .'

Stafford-Morton said: 'I wouldn't put it as strongly as that. But I can see Mitford's point. Allow me to say frankly, Professor, that on what Grey has told me, I don't think your Gustav Neumann sounds like a murderer.'

Zweig stared into the smoking fire, that was so far giving out almost no heat. He asked: 'Why do you say that?'

'From what Sir Charles has told me, this Neumann is a sort of rebellious intellectual, fascinated by the idea of being a great criminal. In my own experience, such people never take to crime.' His voice, shrill and crisp, had a lecturer's tone, and Zweig kept looking away from him, to conceal his distaste. 'You will, of course, have observed that the literary men who preach criminality never actually practise what they preach. De Sade and Lautréamont are obvious examples. When De Sade actually had a chance to get revenge on some of his enemies during the reign of terror, he magnanimously forgave them.' He paused, then, as if aware that his tone sounded patronising, added quickly: 'But of course, you are as aware of all this as I am.'

What he was saying suited Zweig's purpose, yet he had a perverse desire to contradict. He said gravely:

'But surely it is not true to say that the literary man is never a criminal. There have been many criminals who wrote poetry, for example. . . .'

'Oh, quite. But never very good poetry. You couldn't really call Wainwright or Lacenaire "literary men," except as a polite compliment. You see, the poet's attitude is the opposite of the criminal's. He's too much an egotist to stoop to deceiving society. He automatically feels that he is in the right and society in the wrong. The criminal. . . .'

'Is also an egotist,' Zweig interrupted.

'Of course. But of a different kind. He's a petty egotist, a selfish animal. For him, society is always in the right. Society has a right to condemn him. The poet feels he has a right to condemn society.'

Zweig found himself feeling a certain admiration for this reasoning; it was only an expansion of the idea that had come to him on the point of sleep. And yet it was impossible for him to express agreement with Stafford-Morton.

'But has not Sir Charles explained to you that Gustav Neumann believed that he had a right to condemn human beings? He felt that crime is a natural expression of this condemnation.'

Stafford-Morton said explosively, his voice becoming higher still:

'But my dear Professor, that is precisely what I am saying. All crime is an expression of fear. It's the natural expression of an inferiority neurosis. Would you say your friend Neumann was a bad case of inferiority?'

Grey intervened: 'I don't understand you, Karl. Yesterday you agreed that Neumann wasn't really the criminal type. This morning you sound as if you want to believe he is.'

'It is not a question of what I want to believe. I hope that Doctor Stafford-Morton is right. But if he is wrong, it may cost a life.'

Stafford-Morton now sounded definitely irritated. 'There *are* other lives to consider. The police are using every available man in the hunt for the Ealing child murderer. There is also this case of the watchman at Dollis Hill. While they're trying to trace your friend Neumann, another child may be murdered.'

This was the moment when Zweig was tempted to say: 'There is no need to look for Neumann. I think I know where he is.' But Grey was already talking:

'The point is this: if you can convince Doctor Stafford-Morton that he's wrong about Neumann not being a criminal type, he will advise Mitford to start the search. I must say that he seems to me to be making good sense. . . .'

Zweig said: 'Very well, Charles, let us assume that you are right. For the moment, I will carry on with my private search for Gustav. . . .'

Grey persisted: 'But *do* you think the doctor's right? That's all I want to know. You know this Neumann, and we don't. Could the doctor be mistaken? Could he be ignoring some important factor about Neumann's personality?'

Zweig suddenly wanted to get this interview over; his impatience was like something swelling in his chest, threatening to explode. He stood up abruptly.

'Very well. I agree. I will get dressed and. . . .'

'You agree with what?' Grey asked. His voice betrayed suppressed annoyance.

'I agree that there is no point in asking the police to take any action. I think I can find Gustav myself.'

This was more than he meant to say, and he noticed Grey's look of surprise.

'How? If the police can't do it. . . .'

Zweig smiled. 'I have a few ideas. I promise to tell you about them later.'

'Wouldn't it be better to tell me now? We might be able to do something together.'

Zweig said: 'Let me ring you up about it in two hours' time.'

Stafford-Morton stood up. 'I'm afraid I have to go in any case.' It was evident, from his tone, that he was now aware of Zweig's hostility; he reacted by becoming more impersonal and precise. Grey tried to soothe him by being particularly affable as they said good-bye, and promising to ring him. Zweig bowed stiffly as Stafford-Morton went out. When the door had closed, Grey said:

'Well, you certainly made him feel unwelcome.'

'I am sorry. He irritated me.'

'Why? I agree his manner isn't very friendly, but that's probably shyness. . . .'

Zweig said: 'He reminded me of a modern history professor at Santa Barbara, another Englishman. . . .' He was surprised by his own remark; while he had been listening to Stafford-Morton, he was not consciously aware that he was comparing him with the professor in California, and transferring to him all the dislike he had felt for his former colleague. The realization now made him feel embarrassed. Aware that

Grey was staring at him curiously, he said: 'I agree, it is strange how we allow these stupid factors to influence us.' Now that Stafford-Morton had left, he had already forgotten the unique flavour of the interaction of their personalities, and was prepared to be tolerant—in theory.

Grey, unaware of what was passing in his friend's mind, said: 'It's a pity you don't like him. He was very anxious to meet you. He's apparently read all your books and thinks you're the most important living philosopher.'

This made Zweig feel ashamed of himself. He said:

'I felt he was talking on a subject about which he knew very little. Perhaps if you see him, you will apologize on my behalf? Say that I am naturally upset at the idea that my old friend might be a murderer. . . .'

'Quite, quite,' Grey said. He appeared to become abstracted for a moment, fumbling in his pocket for his pipe; this was a device for affecting the transition to the subject that interested him. He said: 'Now about this phone call . . .'

'Phone call?' Zweig said, although he understood perfectly.

'You said you'd ring me in two hours. What've you got up your sleeve?'

Zweig laughed, and poured the last of the coffee. Grey filled his pipe, and pretended that the silence contained no interrogation, although, in fact, he had no desire to smoke. Zweig was reviewing the alternatives; but they all pointed in the same direction: to being frank with Grey. He said, sighing:

'Very well, I might as well tell you. I think I know where to find Gustav.'

Grey was startled. 'Good God, how?' His astonishment was flattering, and Zweig was sorry to deflate it with explanations. He said:

'You remember when you left me yesterday, the telephone rang? It was the manager of the Chesham. . . .'

He told of his visit to the Chesham, his telephone conversation with the Scottish housekeeper, and then with the housemaid at the flat of Joseph Atholl Gardner. Grey said:

'My God, you *have* been holding out on me!'

Zweig noticed the tone of reproach, and became more vehement.

'But don't you see why? Look, Charles, *I* do not believe that Gustav Neumann is a murderer. And when I finally meet him, what am I to say? That I have been helping the police

to hunt him? At least I want to be able to say: "Circumstances made it seem that you might be a criminal, but I
never seriously believed it." '

Grey said: 'That's all very well, Karl, but supposing he is?
You'd send him scurrying off to the other end of England.'

'I do not see that,' Zweig said. 'If he *is* a murderer, then the
sooner he knows we suspect him, the better. It will perhaps
save the life of this man Ferguson. And if he's not. . . .'

Grey started to light his pipe, changed his mind and pushed
it into the tobacco pouch.

'But what did you intend to do when you saw him?'

'Find out all I could. . . .'

Grey walked across to the mantelpiece, frowning at the
carpet.

'Well, I don't know. I suppose it wouldn't have done any
harm. . . .'

Zweig knew what he was thinking. He said quickly: 'How
could it? My story would seem plausible enough to Gustav—
that I saw him coming out of the Chesham, managed to find
the identity of his companion, and traced them to the flat.
I could ask him casual questions about his plans. . . .'

He was beginning to convince himself when he remembered the photograph. For a moment he considered showing
it to Grey, then knew it was impossible. It would only confirm
Grey's suspicion that he believed Neumann a murderer. He
looked at his watch, and said: 'I must dress. . . . That is, if
you think I should call on Gustav. . . .'

'I don't see it will make any difference.'

Zweig left his bedroom door open as he dressed, so that
they could continue talking. He said:

'Do you want to come with me?'

'No. Not if you want to see him alone. It might be an idea
for me to go and wait outside.'

'You might have a long wait.'

'And on the other hand, there may be no one there.'

'And what do we do in that case?'

There was a silence; then Grey said:

'In that case, I think we call in Interpol, and find out what
Ferguson was doing in Cologne, and whether he knew Neumann.'

'But of course he did.'

'Not of course. The only evidence we have is your glimpse of a man at twenty yards on a snowy night. You could have been mistaken.'

'And the waiter. He said the man's name was Gustav. . . .'

'Ah, yes. I'd forgotten that. Anyway, we'd better go and look at this Pelham Place address. I'll ring for a taxi.'

•

In Pelham Place snow on the pavements was thick and unmelted. Grey said:

'Good weather for detective work. Notice whether there are footprints leading down to the basement.'

Zweig felt guilty about leaving him outside. Although a wintry sun made the snow dazzling, the air seemed colder than ever. He said:

'Perhaps you should come in with me.'

'No. If it gets too cold, I'll wait in that restaurant across the road. Off you go.'

The path to the front door was well trampled. Steps ran off to the left and down to a side door; but, like the steps that led up to the front door, these had been swept of snow. Three dustbins at the bottom of the steps indicated the reason for this. Zweig looked out at Grey—who was standing on the other side of the street—and shook his head. The space in front of the basement door had also been swept. Zweig observed the curtains of the front window twitching as he went down the steps; he caught a glimpse of the white face of an old lady.

He knocked on the door and waited. There was no reply. He noticed a bell push, and held his thumb against it, but could hear no ringing sound from inside. He glanced at his watch; it was almost midday. They could be out for lunch. The curtains behind the barred windows were drawn.

Grey called: 'No luck?' Zweig shook his head. Grey came in at the front gate and the two of them stood at the bottom of the steps leading to the front door. Grey said:

'There's no point in pretending I'm not with you. An old

woman looked out of that window and spotted me. Let's go and find out what we can.'

The front door opened almost immediately. A young girl said: 'Can I help you?'

'We were looking for Sir Timothy Ferguson? Is this where he lives?'

A door opened and the old lady came out.

'It's a great pity. You've missed them by half an hour. They went off in a taxi.'

'Do you happen to know when they might return?'

'I'm afraid it won't be for some time. They took their baggage with them.'

Grey muttered: 'Damn and blast.'

Zweig said: 'Thank you very much. Sorry to have troubled you. . . .'

Before he could turn away, Grey said:

'Excuse me, but would you mind if we had a word with you? Are you the owner of this house?'

'I am. What is it about?' She came to the door, leaning on a stick. The girl excused herself and went in.

'It's about Sir Timothy. It's very important that we find out where he's gone to. Did you see the man who was with him?'

'Mr Neumann? Yes.'

They refrained from looking at one another. Grey asked softly: 'Have you any idea where we might find them?'

'I'm afraid not. Unless they've gone to Sir Timothy's place in Scotland.'

Zweig had noticed the look of half-recognition of her face when she came to the door. He said:

'This is Sir Charles Grey, and my name is Zweig—Professor Karl Zweig.'

It had the effect he had hoped for. She smiled and said: 'Of course! Now I recognize you. I knew I'd seen you before. . . .'

Grey said: 'Do you think we might come in for a moment?'

'Of course. Come this way . . . I didn't know you were a friend of Sir Timothy's, Professor. He never mentioned you. . . .'

Grey and Zweig exchanged glances. Evidently she was fairly well acquainted with Ferguson. Zweig said:

'Not a close friend.'

She led them into the front room. Grey said:

'We tried to ring Sir Timothy, but the exchange said it was disconnected.'

'That's right. He had it taken out a year ago. He said it wasn't worth paying rent for it when he only used it every six months. He makes use of my telephone if he wants to make a call.'

Zweig was already wondering how much they should tell her. He decided to leave it to Grey. Grey asked:

'Do you see much of Sir Timothy?'

'Not a lot. I let him have the downstairs flat very cheaply, but he doesn't use it more than twice a year.' She sat down in a high-backed armchair, wedged her stick firmly between her knees, and looked up at them. 'I'm afraid I can't really help you at all. He may have gone to Scotland and he may have gone elsewhere. Is it important?'

Grey said: 'It *is* rather important. Had you met Mr Neumann before?'

'No. Sir Timothy met him in Germany a few weeks ago.'

'I see. Did he speak to you about him at all?'

'Yes . . . but why? Why do you want to know?'

'Do you mind if I sit down?' Grey pulled a chair from the table, and sat facing her. 'You see, madam, we're a little worried about Sir Timothy.'

'Are you from the police?' The question came so abruptly that Zweig was startled; but Grey seemed undisturbed.

'Yes. I am. But this is not yet a police matter. It's more or less private.'

'Who is it you're after? This Neumann?' Her eyes gleamed with voracious and unabashed interest. Grey said cautiously:

'Have you any reason for suspecting him?'

'Oh no. But if it's not Sir Timothy, I suppose it must be his secretary.'

'Yes, it is Neumann we're interested in. . . .'

She interrupted: 'What has he done?'

'He has done nothing, as far as we know. His description corresponds to that of a German confidence swindler who has no right to be in this country. If Neumann turns out to be the same person, we shall simply have him deported. . . .'

Zweig listened with admiration, impressed by the glibness and plausibility of Grey's invention. Grey went on:

'But we may be completely on the wrong track, you see, so we have to be extremely careful. We can't go around openly making accusations. That's why we'd be grateful for any help you can give us.'

The old woman glanced at Zweig. She asked:

'And would Professor Zweig recognize him—the confidence swindler?'

Zweig, anxious not to entangle himself in subterfuges, said: 'Er . . . no. I happened to hear that Sir Timothy was in London with a secretary who answered the description. . . .' He was floundering, and Grey interrupted quickly:

'What can you tell us about this secretary? Did Sir Timothy tell you anything about him?'

'Not a lot. He didn't have much chance to talk to me on this visit. Usually we spend a lot of time talking.'

'When did they arrive?'

'The day before Christmas Eve.'

'Is Sir Timothy a rich man?'

She shrugged. "That's something I'm afraid I can't tell you. Sir Timothy is a good and kind man in many ways, but he doesn't like to talk about money.'

Zweig seized on the *non sequitur*.

'You mean he doesn't like to spend money?'

'Well . . . yes. Although that's something I can't really tell you about. He always pays his rent.'

'Why does he need a secretary?'

She smiled. 'He doesn't, of course. He just calls this man his secretary. In fact, he's something more like a doctor.'

'Is Sir Timothy ill?'

This time, she laughed. Zweig could see that she was enjoying every moment of the conversation.

'He thinks he is. Perhaps he really is, for all I know. He's a worrier, you see. There's always something wrong with him. His stomach's his weakest part—he's always being sick after meals. And I believe there's something wrong with his bowels . . . although, of course, he doesn't tell me about that.'

Zweig asked the question that had been in his mind since he entered the room.

'Was he ill over Christmas?'

'No. On the contrary, I've never seen him looking so well. If this man Neumann's a confidence swindler, he must know something about medicine.'

'You think he seemed a lot better than the last time you saw him?'

'Certainly he did. The last time I saw him was in August
. . . I think . . . or perhaps September. I can't remember.
At all events, he looked awful. He thought he had some rare
disease of the bowels. That's why he went to Cologne—to see
a specialist.'

Zweig asked: 'Do you happen to know the name of the
specialist?'

'I did. . . . He mentioned it several times . . . but I've
forgotten.'

'Was it Wertheimer?'

'That's right!'

'Do you know him?' Grey asked.

'A little. He is the greatest European specialist on diseases
of the stomach and bowels. He was a friend of Gustav's
father.'

'Ah! Then that's almost certainly where Neumann met Sir
Timothy. That may be a useful lead. Now, madam, could you
repeat to us exactly what Sir Timothy told you about his new
secretary?'

'He didn't have time to tell me much. He only came up
here once, and that was on the day he arrived. He said he'd
discovered an amazing doctor who was doing wonders for
his health. I said he looked as though he had. He had colour
in his cheeks, his eyes were brighter—he looked twenty years
younger.'

'Did he tell you anything about the treatment?'

'No. Except that he wouldn't be seeing much of me on this
trip because he had to spend a lot of the time lying down.
I thought this seemed a bit strange, as he looked so healthy.'

'And how about Neumann—did you see him?'

'Once or twice. He seemed to me very pleasant. I could
see why he's such a good doctor.'

'Why?'

'Why? Because . . . oh, because he's very . . . persuasive.
He has great charm . . . and warmth. Still, I suppose you
can't really judge by appearances. Do you really think he *is*
a crook?'

Grey stood up and replaced the chair, saying slowly:

'The description fits, but the description could very well be
wrong. My dear lady, you've been very helpful indeed. *If*
they return, I wonder if you would be good enough to telephone me at this number?'

She looked disappointed as she took the card. She was obviously reluctant to let them go. She asked:

'Will you be coming back?'

'That is impossible to say. The next problem is to try and find Sir Timothy. You say you have no idea where he is?'

'I'd guess they've gone to Sir Timothy's place in Perth. I could give you the address.'

'We have it, thank you. But do you know whether Sir Timothy has any other place in England. Does he keep another flat—or a cottage—anywhere?'

'I doubt it—knowing Sir Timothy.'

'Why?'

'He doesn't like expense. That's why he had the telephone taken out.'

'Ah, of course. Well, many thanks indeed for your help.'

Outside in the snow, Grey said: 'Well, Karl, I owe you an apology.'

'Why?'

'If I'd let you handle this your way, we wouldn't have arrived half an hour after they left.'

'It was simply bad luck. What now?'

'I suggest we try this other chap . . . what's his name?'

'Gardner? Joseph Atholl Gardner.'

'I know his name. I wonder where I've heard it?' He interrupted himself to shout: 'Taxi!' The taxi stopped suddenly, skidding in the half-melted snow and throwing spots of mud on their trousers. Zweig scrambled in, saying:

'I may be mistaken, but I think he wrote to me about something. . . .' He gave the driver the address, and the cab turned past South Kensington underground. He added: 'I want to congratulate you on the way you handled the old woman. Your story about the confidence trickster was convincing. I think we might try the same thing on this Gardner man.'

'That depends. It's always best to get the person summed up first. If I'd told that old lady the truth, it'd be all over London by this evening. I'd be willing to bet that she's on the phone at this very minute.'

'But do you think it would be advisable to tell anyone that we suspect Gustav of murder?'

'I don't know. It could be.'

The taxi was stopping outside a block of flats close to Earl's

Court Road. Here the snow had thawed completely, and the road was strewn with gravel chippings.

Grey glanced down the name-plates outside the door. Looking over his shoulder, Zweig observed that most of the names were suggestive of money, rank or celebrity. 'Third floor,' Grey said.

The girl who opened the door said: 'Who did you want to speak to, sir?'

'I believe I spoke to you yesterday on the telephone,' Zweig said. 'I wanted to talk to Mr Gardner.'

She looked dubious.

'Would you mind waiting a moment, sir? Mr Gardner is usually working at this hour. What was the name again?'

They stood there, looking at the closed door. Grey said: 'Exclusive sort of bloke.' As soon as he had spoken, the door opened, and a tall, soldierly man in tweeds stood there. He said:

'My dear sir, this is a great honour. . . .' He looked surprised to see Grey. Zweig wondered if he had made a mistake, since he had no recollection of seeing him before. He said:

'I am Professor Karl Zweig, and this is Sir Charles Grey of Scotland Yard.'

'Ex of Scotland Yard,' Grey said.

'Splendid! Splendid! Do come in.' He moved fussily, rubbing his hands. 'My wife is out at the moment. She'll be so sorry she missed you.' Zweig was bewildered by this effusiveness; the only explanation that occurred to him was that he was one of his television 'fans', and this seemed somehow unlikely. And, in fact, no television set was visible in the room into which he now led them. This room was large and well furnished—basically identical with all the thousand-a-year flats that Zweig had ever entered, including Grey's; the chief difference lay in the number of curious and barbaric ornaments on tables, shelves and in wall cabinets. At a first glance, these seemed to be mainly African trophies—there was an enormous coloured shield and two crossed spears over the fireplace—but on closer inspection, Zweig observed relics of Egypt, India and Japan. A corner cabinet contained a large stone figure—about two feet high—with an inscription that might have been Celtic. Gardner was saying:

'I was wondering if you'd ever follow up your letter as you promised. After eighteen months I'd given up hope.'

This baffled Zweig, so he smiled, shrugged, and said:

'It has been a long time, but . . .'

Grey, glancing oddly at Zweig, said: 'I didn't realize you two had corresponded.' He was perfectly aware of Zweig's embarrassment, and amused by it. His own memory for faces and names was almost infallible.

'Oh, certainly,' Gardner said. 'We exchanged several letters after the second volume of *Protestant Theology* came out. I was intrigued by Professor Zweig's footnote on the saviour figure in Celtic mythology. You see, I have definite proof that the Welsh are one of the lost tribes of Israel.'

Now the memory returned, Zweig was not sure whether to be relieved or dismayed. He smiled at Grey, but tried to indicate, by a movement of his forehead, that he wanted to be rescued. Grey said smoothly:

'I'm delighted by this. But I should tell you that our reason for coming here was not primarily to discuss Celtic mythology —no matter what private motives my friend Zweig kept undisclosed to me.' He coughed, lowering his eyes, and Zweig knew this was to prevent himself from seeing Zweig's face and smiling. 'We came to see you about your friend Sir Timothy Ferguson.'

'I see. I see. Won't you sit down? What'll you drink, whisky or sherry?'

Both asked for whisky. Gardner handed them both tumblers that were half-full, and went out to fill the water-jug. Zweig said quickly, in a low voice:

'I didn't realize, but he's a complete madman. He has some theory about the Great Pyramid being a burial-place of Druids.'

'But you must have replied amiably.'

'No doubt. Probably I said that his theories struck me as fascinating, but that I couldn't see any. . . .' He broke off as Gardner came back into the room, and said: 'I was just telling my friend that I thought your ideas fascinating, but couldn't see that there is sound evidence to support them.'

Gardner said, wagging his finger: 'Aha, so you said in your letter. And I told you that if you'd care to come and see me, I'd be delighted to give you all the evidence you needed.' Zweig tasted his drink, and reflected that Gardner's whisky was of a less dubious quality than his ideas. Gardner said:

'Now, you wanted to talk about Tim Ferguson. So let's get

that over, then we can discuss the important questions.' They sat down, and Zweig observed that the soles of Gardner's shoes were made of crepe more than an inch thick. Gardner said: 'He's in Cologne at the moment, I believe.'

'I think you're mistaken, sir,' Grey said. 'Up till an hour ago, he was here in London. I believe he's now on a train, or about to get on a train.'

'That's impossible. He never fails to see me when he comes through London. We were out in Ceylon together for years.'

'That,' Grey said, 'is one of the things that worries us. We have definite evidence that Sir Timothy spent Christmas in his flat in Pelham Place with a man whom he calls his secretary.'

'I don't quite understand. Can't you be more explicit?'

'All right. We have reason to suspect that the man who calls himself Sir Timothy's secretary may be a criminal. Has he written to you from Cologne?'

'No. We seldom correspond. What sort of criminal?'

'He may be a confidence trickster. Is Sir Timothy rich?'

'Good lord, yes. Probably a millionaire. What reason have you got for thinking this secretary's a crook?'

'We aren't certain. But his description corresponds to that of a man who is wanted by the German police.'

'How do you know this? You said you were ex-Scotland Yard.' Zweig observed that, even if Gardner's religious ideas were insane, he seemed to have his wits about him in other respects. The way he was listening and staring at Grey from under lowered eyebrows, convinced Zweig that he was no fool.

'Yes. And that's partly the problem. At the moment, this is a private affair. We're not sure that any crime has been committed or is contemplated.'

Gardner said: 'Don't you think you'd better tell me the story from the beginning?'

Grey looked at Zweig; he knew that Zweig objected to spreading the idea that Neumann might be a murderer. Zweig said, shrugging:

'I don't suppose it can do any harm.' He said to Gardner: 'But we must ask you to treat it with the strictest discretion.'

Gardner said nothing, but nodded slightly, without taking his eyes from them.

Grey said: 'All right. We think it just possible that this man Neumann may be a murderer.'

'That is the secretary?'

'Yes. He is also apparently acting as Sir Timothy's doctor.'

'Is he wanted by the German police?'

'Not as far as we know. The possibility that he might be a murderer has come to light only over the past two days—and by an odd coincidence. Karl. . . .' Grey gestured at Zweig, and left Zweig to tell the rest of the story. Having now repeated it three times, Zweig found himself able to compress it into about ten minutes. When he had finished, Gardner said:

'But it's perfectly obvious—the man's a murderer.'

'Is it?' Grey asked.

'You don't happen to have anything that belongs to this chap, do you? Neumann?'

'No. Why?'

'Pity. I could probably find out. . . .'

'Find out what?'

'I know,' Gardner said. 'I've got a pair of gloves that Tim left here.' He rang a bell, and when the maid appeared, said: 'Bring me those gloves Sir Timothy left here, would you?'

Zweig and Grey eyed one another, and Grey raised his eyebrows.

'I want to try an ancient Celtic method of divination,' Gardner said. 'That'll give us something to go on.'

Grey suppressed an urge to say that they had an appointment; curiosity outweighed his exasperation. They watched Gardner take a number of notched sticks out of a cupboard, and then remove his shoes. Zweig said: 'Pardon me, but why do you wear such thick soles?'

'Ah, thought I saw you looking at 'em. It's to do with the currents in the room.'

'Currents?' Grey said, glancing at the electric power plug.

'Etheric currents from these various things. You see, as Professor Zweig'll tell you, all objects that have been associated with powerful feelings—especially religious feelings—pick up bits of the hidden powers of the people they come into contact with. When I handle them, some of this current passes into me unless I'm earthed. Then if I touch some other objects, I get two conflicting currents. You see, the beliefs these things represent often conflict violently. So I'd be in danger of a kind of psychic electrocution if I didn't wear thick soles.'

Zweig asked: 'And how about us?'

'Oh, it depends on whether you're sensitive to it. You may not be a conductor. But I am. And since my wife's a medium, I could do her a great deal of damage.'

He was now sitting in front of the Celtic statue in the corner of the room. The glass in front of its case lowered on two chains to form a kind of table top. On this, Gardner placed his sticks, then sorted them into heaps. He said over his shoulder:

'You recognize the procedure, of course, Professor?'

'It seems similar to the method the Chinese use to consult the I Ching.'

'Quite. Very similar. Now, the gloves. . . .' He placed the gloves at the foot of the statue, then proceeded to move the sticks, placing some on the floor behind him, and moving others from one heap to another. After five minutes of this, he had only one heap of sticks left. He then took these one by one, and scrutinized them carefully. He said finally:

'That's odd. They seem to say that Tim's in great danger, but not physical danger.' He stood up, glowered at the stick in his hand, then said with annoyance: 'That's *insane.*' Grey turned away quickly, and Zweig could see the broad smile on his face. To stop himself from laughing, he asked:

'What is insane?'

'Just that. He could hardly be in spiritual danger . . . an old roughneck like that.'

Grey had recovered himself. He said:

'Mr Gardner, I hope you'll realize that I'm just an ordinary policeman, and although I have seen something of divinatory magic in the East, I didn't expect to find it invoked in the middle of London. You'll forgive me if I say that I can't really attach too much importance to your joss sticks.'

'Not joss sticks, old boy. You burn those.' Gardner hardly seemed to have heard Grey's speech; he was still frowning at the stick. He said: 'I couldn't have done anything wrong. . . .' He finally shrugged, and threw the stick on to the rest of the pile. 'Can't be helped. Anyway, apparently he's in no physical danger.'

Grey asked with irony:

'Can those sticks tell us where to find him?'

Gardner said seriously: 'Oh, no, that's quite impossible. They only have a limited number of symbols. My wife might be able to help if we could get her in a trance, but she's best in the evenings.'

This time, Zweig had to take a gulp of his whisky to hide his smile.

'Have you any idea where he might be?'

'I don't know. . . .' Gardner was preoccupied. He shook his head, and switched his attention back to Grey. 'I beg your pardon. Let's see . . . where could he be? He's a funny old boy. He's got three or four hideaways in different parts of England.'

'Are you certain of that? His landlady seemed to think it unlikely.'

'Why?'

'She thought he wouldn't enjoy paying rent for a place he wasn't using.'

'Oh, that's true enough. He doesn't like spending. But he doesn't pay rent for his various cottages—they belong to him. He likes to buy places very cheap—I was once with him in Cornwall when he got two cottages for ten quid each—and put a caretaker in one of them. Then he gets his own cottage looked after free, you see? He's a curious old boy, Sir Tim, as you'll discover. His father was once sold up by bailiffs, and I think having all these places gives Tim a sense of security.'

Grey said, sighing: 'It complicates our problem, though.'

' 'Fraid it does. Let me think. He's got this place in Cornwall, another in Wales, near Abergavenny, another in the Lake District near Coniston, another somewhere near Birmingham. . . .'

Grey said suddenly: 'Why didn't I think of it? We should have asked at the cab rank near South Kensington station.'

Zweig asked blankly: 'Why?'

'He couldn't have rung for a taxi or the old lady would have heard him. The telephone was in her front room, remember? If you ring for a taxi, they always ask you where you want to go. So the chances are that Neumann walked the fifty yards round the corner and got a taxi from the rank.'

'Simple enough,' Gardner said. 'My car's outside. Let's go and find out.'

'Don't bother,' Grey said hastily. 'We can get a taxi or a bus.'

'Nonsense, I may as well help all I can, since I can't help in any other way.' He led them out into the hall, striding vigorously, shouting: 'Margaret, if my wife comes home, say we shan't be gone more than ten minutes.' He clamped a deerstalker hat on to his head. 'Come on, off we go.' Zweig caught Grey's expression as they went out of the door; his eyes were raised to the sky in supplication.

Gardner's car, a grey Rover 90, was parked outside the flats, under a no-parking sign. Somehow, Zweig had expected him to drive a red convertible sports car. It seemed to add a dimension of respectability to his personality that was lacking in the flat. Although the windscreen was covered with melting snow, revealing that the car had not yet been used that day, the engine started at the first twist of the key. Gardner tugged both sides of his moustache in turn, as if to adjust it for driving, and said: 'Well, I had a feeling I'd have an interesting Christmas. I'm never wrong.' The car slid into the traffic, the wipers working silently.

It was now one o'clock. Grey said:

'If the taxi driver took them to the station at half past eleven, he'd be back by half past twelve, presuming it was Paddington, St Pancras or Victoria. So we might have to wait if he's gone off again. . . .'

Gardner parked his car opposite the taxi rank. There were three taxis waiting. As they stopped the car, the front one started to pull away. Grey leapt out of the car and ran over to it. They watched him talking to the driver. After a moment, he took out his wallet and gave the man a note. He turned and came back. 'Hello,' Gardner said, 'he's found something.' This was evident from the smile on Grey's face. He opened the back door and climbed in.

'My God, there was a piece of luck for you! That was the man! He picked them up at 74 Pelham Place at half past eleven, and drove them to King's Cross station. He didn't know what train they wanted to catch, but said they didn't seem to be in a hurry. He said the young man came over here at about 11.25—dark eyes and dark hair.'

Gardner said: 'King's Cross. That could mean they're on their way back to Perth. Or it could mean Bury St Edmunds.'

'What about Bury St Edmunds?'

'I've just remembered—Ferguson's got a place there. I

should have thought of that first. Of course! If he's on his way back to Scotland, he might stop there anyway.'

'The next thing,' Grey said, 'is to ring King's Cross and find out what trains left there between twelve and one.'

'No need to do that. Come back to my place, and we'll look it up in Bradshaw.' He started the engine before they could argue. As they got out of the car, a few minutes later, Grey was able to mutter in Zweig's ear: 'This is the craziest murder case I've ever been on.'

Gardner said: 'Ah, good. I see my wife's home.' A cream sports car was now parked where the Rover had been. Grey said: 'Don't you ever get tickets for parking?'

'Got to park somewhere,' Gardner said mildly. 'Anyway, we've got an understanding with the local police.' He turned to Zweig: 'My wife'll be so pleased to see you. She's a great admirer of yours—tremendous.'

'I'd be delighted,' Zweig muttered, and avoided Grey's eyes.

'Not half as delighted as she will be,' Gardner said heartily. 'By the way, I hope you're both staying to lunch?'

They began to protest at once, but as they were now in the enclosed space of the lift, both felt that they were somehow predestined to eat lunch with the Gardners. It came to Zweig that Gardner had something oddly compelling about his personality, in spite of the appearance of crankiness.

As they entered, Gardner yelled: 'Coo-ee, Natasha!' From an open bedroom door, a soft but clear voice said distinctly: 'Don't shout, Joseph. It's vulgar.'

'Sorry, dear.' For the first time since they had met him, Gardner looked sheepish. Zweig found himself already approving of the unseen woman.

'Guess who I've got with me?' Gardner said.

'I know whom you've got with you,' the voice said. Zweig observed a slight foreign accent. 'Margaret told me.' The woman now came out of the bedroom. She was a great deal younger than they expected—her age might have been anything between twenty-five and forty. Her face was of Russian type, with high cheekbones and slanting eyes, and her hair was long and black. The tight woollen dress she wore was also black. She wore no make-up except a touch of lipstick, and the paleness of her face, contrasted against the darkness of hair and dress, gave the impression that she was startlingly beautiful. In fact she was not, as Zweig was able to see as he talked to her; the nose was slightly irregular, the chin a little too pointed, to maintain the first impression.

'It is kind of you to come, Professor.' She shook hands with him in a way that somehow managed to imply that he had come especially to see her. Gardner introduced her to Grey. Then she said: 'Let us go and have a drink. Lunch will be ready in ten minutes. You must be frozen.' She turned to Zweig and said: 'I can't tell you what a pleasure this is to me.' Her manner was warm and inviting, even intimate, without being coquettish. And yet Zweig was not entirely charmed. Although he was, at sixty-five, as susceptible as he had been at twenty, his ideal woman had light hair, blue eyes and an expression of innocence. There had been three women of this type in Zweig's life—the last had been one of his students, a Swedish girl—but the appetite remained. The innocence—or its appearance—was important. Since his chief interest was in ideas, he was generally bored by a woman with a strong personality, feeling that it was an unfair substitute for an interesting mind.

Gardner was looking through a Bradshaw, muttering as he did so. Zweig and Grey allowed Mrs Gardner to pour them more whisky. Gardner suddenly shouted: 'Here it is. This must be it. The Norwich train goes from King's Cross at twelve twenty-five. It could be that. Or there's a train to Edinburgh at two-thirty, if they don't get the other.'

'Are you going to Norwich, dear?' Mrs Gardner asked. Her voice was silky, but there was no obvious irony.

'I might.' Gardner poured himself half a tumbler of whisky, then dropped on to the settee, beaming at them.

'My wife's a medium, y'know. It's a pity we haven't got anything belonging to this Neumann chap. She'd be able to tell you right away if he's a murderer.'

'Neumann? What is his first name?'

'Gustav. . . .'

Mrs Gardner leaned forward and stared into the fire. Gardner said: 'She often gets impressions from names. They're not always accurate, but she gets an astonishing number of direct hits.'

Mrs Gardner, ignoring him, said slowly:

'Neumann. I do not get an impression of a murderer. This may be mere association of ideas . . . but I see someone connected with the nerves, the brain perhaps.' She looked at Zweig. 'A psychiatrist, or a brain surgeon, perhaps?'

Zweig felt the thrill of astonishment stir his scalp.

'That is astonishingly accurate. His father was a brain surgeon. But perhaps you have heard his father's name? Alois Neumann. He is a celebrated authority on the brain.'

'That is very probable. I spent my childhood travelling on the Continent.'

The girl came in to say that the meal was ready. Gardner said: 'Perhaps you'd like to wash-up first? The bathroom's through there. There are two wash-basins there so you can go in at the same time.'

They were glad of this excuse to talk together for a moment. Zweig carefully closed the door, then said in a low voice:

'I think we shall have to dissuade our friend from following this any further.'

Grey, peeling off his coat, and disdaining to lower his voice, said:

'I must say, I can't make up my mind whether he's a fraud, or just slightly eccentric. Did you say he wrote you a cranky letter?'

'Completely insane. He seemed to think that a theologian should be an expert in magic rituals and ancient mythology. I didn't even try to explain that my theology begins with a preoccupation with language.'

They were now standing side by side, and bars of lilac-coloured soap were diffusing a curious fragrance that neither of them recognized.

'What do you make of his wife?' Grey asked.

'Strange. I expected her to be dumpy, with untidy hair. But I wonder if she is really a medium?'

'What do you mean?'

'I wonder if she wants to encourage her husband's ideas. . . .'

'You mean whether she's deliberately taken him in for the sake of his money? It's possible. What nationality do you think she is?'

'Russian or Hungarian. But she also gives me the impression that she has been trained as an actress—or perhaps as a model.'

'Actress,' Grey said. 'That voice'd make her fortune on the screen.'

Zweig dried his hands; he said: 'Frankly, what worries me is that Gardner might want to come with us to Bury St Edmunds. . . .'

'Might,' Grey said. 'Let's see what happens.'

They helped one another on with their jackets, and went in to the dining-room. Gardner looked up with a cheerful and welcoming grin, and both felt guilty about their conversation. Mrs Gardner glided across to Zweig, took his hand in both hers, and said in her caressing voice:

'Dear Professor, I want you to come with me for a moment.' Zweig felt himself responding to this intimacy with alarming promptness. Gardner, he noticed, did not even appear to notice; he was talking to Grey with that expression of absorbed enthusiasm that seldom seemed to leave his face. Zweig allowed himself to be drawn towards the door, noticing the coolness of Mrs Gardner's hand. They crossed the thickly carpeted passageway, and she pushed open a door; with an alarm that was half pleasure, he discovered that they were in her bedroom. She still held his hand as she led him across the room. The bed was folded back to air; a black nylon nightdress was thrown across the pillow. She pointed to the bookshelf.

'There. I wanted you to see that I am not joking when I say that I admire you above every other writer. I have all your books that have been translated. You are my bedside reading.'

It was true. At a casual glance, all his books seemed to be there. Her hand rested lightly on his sleeve for a moment.

'There is one exception . . . which I keep by my bedside. Your *Creative Nature of the Sexual Act*.'

To his own irritation, Zweig felt himself blushing. He coughed, and said:

'That is one of my earliest books.' He realized that this sounded as if he was making an excuse, and felt more irritated than ever.

'I think it the most profound and beautiful of all your books. I wonder if you would be so kind . . .' She took his hand, and drew him towards the bed, and for an incredulous moment he mistook her intention, and felt as though a bomb had exploded in his head. Then he saw that she had taken up his book, and was unscrewing the cap of a fountain-pen. He reached out, hoping that his hands would not tremble and betray him. As he did so, she looked up, and he noticed the smile of childish mischief, and was staggered. He scrawled in the book, aware that his words were illegible, then handed it back to her. She accepted the book, without taking her eyes from his face. She said:

'My husband laughs at me. He says I have a schoolgirl crush on you.'

'I'm most flattered.' Zweig was pleased because his voice had just the right note of dry gallantry.

'We must go.' She made it sound as if they had just been making love. She took his hand again and led him out of the room. 'Some day, when you have time, you must sign all your books for me.'

'We shall need more time,' he said.

She turned and smiled.

'A lot more time.'

Gardner was still talking enthusiastically to Grey; he was explaining something about Indonesian mythology. Mrs Gardner said:

'You must sit next to me.' She led him to the chair, still holding his hand. It amazed Zweig that she seemed to be unconcerned about her husband's reactions; she openly treated Zweig as her property. He found himself thinking: 'Her latest toy . . .' and this helped to restore a little detachment. As he started to eat his soup, he noticed the time on his wristwatch; it was twenty-three minutes past one. The last occasion when he had looked at the watch had been in the bathroom, as he slipped it back on to his wrist after washing; it had then indicated nineteen minutes past one. Mrs Gardner had completed her conquest of him in just under four minutes.

They ate in silence for a few moments, then Gardner said:

'I've explained the situation briefly to my wife. And she feels that we ought to go to Bury St Edmunds this afternoon.'

Grey said drily: 'That will hardly be necessary.'

Gardner glanced at him sharply. 'Why not?'

Grey cleared his throat. He said:

'Er . . . I don't wish you to feel that we're ungrateful for your help, and for your kind hospitality. But you do see, don't you, that this may be a murder hunt? And the more of us there are, the less chance of being successful. . . .'

'I don't really see that, Sir Charles. After all, if you were just a tiny bit more certain of your facts, you'd have half London's police helping you.'

'No. You don't quite see my point. This isn't a matter of finding and arresting a criminal. It's rather . . . how shall I say—a matter of tracking, of vigilance, you see . . . I think Professor Zweig will agree with me.'

Zweig pretended that his soup needed his full attention, and made a non-committal noise. The truth was that he liked the idea of travelling to Bury St Edmunds in company with Natasha Gardner. Mrs Gardner now said:

'Come, Sir Charles. You haven't really much idea of how to go about this, have you? I mean, you don't even know where to find Timothy's cottage. And when you find it, what do you intend to do? You don't know either of them, and if Professor Zweig goes, it will give the game away.'

Zweig felt it was time to make a tentative commitment.

'That is probably true, Charles.'

Grey said good-humouredly: 'It probably is. I never know what I intend to do in advance. We'll find some excuse for finding out what's going on. It may not be necessary to go and knock on the door of the cottage. We can have a look round after dark. The main thing is to make him realize he's under observation while we check up with Interpol to see if we can get enough evidence to arrest him.'

'But our method is so much simpler,' Natasha Gardner persisted. 'Listen. On the other side of the field from the cottage there's an empty cottage that we once thought of renting. Now what would be more natural than for Joseph and myself to pretend that's our reason for being in the district? We're on our way back from somewhere in the North, and we've decided to call and see about the other cottage. We notice smoke coming from Timothy's cottage and we naturally go over to call on him. If necessary, we could take the other cottage for a few weeks. While we're there, this man Neumann wouldn't dare to try anything. And yet he still doesn't have any suspicion that the police are after him. And you can check up on his criminal record at your leisure.'

Zweig looked at her with admiration. What she said destroyed Grey's arguments and made it clear that she and her husband were invaluable allies. Grey was nodding slowly as he frowned at his plate, and to Zweig, his thoughts were as apparent as if he had spoken them. He was divided between the orderly instinct of a soldier—which told him to get rid of these charming but dubious allies—and his perception that her plan was the simplest and most convenient. Zweig said gently:

'She may be right about the importance of not letting Gustav know he is under observation.'

Grey became aware that the girl was waiting to take his soup plate, and that he was the only one who had not finished. He said, laughing:

'Very well. If you don't mind the boredom and inconvenience, we'd be glad of your help.'

'Good-oh,' Gardner said. 'Let's open a bottle of wine to that.'

'Not for me, thank you,' Grey said. 'If I'm travelling to Bury this afternoon, I'd rather stay awake.'

Mrs Gardner said: 'Joseph, if you're driving, you hadn't better have any more to drink either.'

'Driving?' Grey said. 'Do you think that is wise in this weather?'

'It'd be best if we can get through,' Gardner said. 'Otherwise, the whole story collapses. We wouldn't be likely to be travelling through Bury St Edmunds by train, would we? I'll ring the AA and find out what the roads are like.'

●

Three hours later Zweig woke from a doze and peered out of the window of the car. It was already dusk. He asked: 'Where are we?'

Gardner said: 'This place is called Sudbury. We'll be there in less than half an hour if the road stays O.K.'

'I think we'd better check in at a hotel before we do anything else,' Grey said.

Zweig asked: 'Is that a good idea? Supposing we are mistaken about Gustav coming here? Supposing they are actually on their way to Scotland at this moment? Would it not be better to return to London tonight?' The prospect of a night in a strange hotel did not appeal to him.

'Afraid not, Professor,' Gardner said. 'The roads'll be frozen in a few hours. I'd rather drive during the day.'

Zweig stared gloomily at the snow-covered landscape, and suppressed a yawn. Natasha Gardner turned in her seat and smiled at him. She said:

'Never mind. You and I can spend the evening in a corner talking about your ideas.'

Her husband said mildly: 'Don't keep him entirely to yourself. I'd like to talk to him as well.'

'I would be delighted to talk to both of you,' Zweig said diplomatically. He closed his eyes again, and pulled the sheepskin car rug closer round his knees. This exchange had improved his humour; he now allowed himself to daydream of a warm face close to his own, a feminine perfume, and came close to falling asleep again. Gardner woke him up by saying:

'The cottage is down there, off to the right. But I suppose we'd better find the hotel first?'

A few minutes later, he said:

'Damn, it's snowing again. Thank heavens we're nearly there.'

'I'm rather glad,' Grey said. 'I hope it goes on.'

'Why?'

'The problem of footprints. We can't get anywhere near the cottage without giving ourselves away with footprints. If it's snowing, this doesn't matter.'

The car was going slowly, taking a steep gradient. Suddenly the wheels began to spin on the icy road, and they came to a stop. Gardner said: 'Looks as if we'll have to get out and put chains on. That's bad luck.'

'Why don't you try backing to the bottom and trying it on the other side of the road? There's less snow there.'

'I need a cup of tea,' Natasha Gardner protested.

'We'll try it.' Gardner allowed the car to drop back down the hill. In the hollow at the bottom, sheltered by trees, the road was relatively free of snow. Zweig was already experiencing boredom and dismay at the prospect of helping to get the chains on the car, particularly since it was now dark. He wiped the back window free of mist, so that Gardner could see through it. They stopped under the trees, then the car pulled over to the right-hand side of the road, and went forward in second gear with full acceleration. To Zweig's relief, the wheels gripped and they swept up the hill. Gardner said: 'Hurray, we've done it!' when his wife shouted: 'Look out.' Another car came over the top of the hill, its headlights glaring at them through the falling snow. For a moment it looked as if there would be a collision; then both cars swerved and stopped almost abreast. Gardner lowered his window and shouted: 'Sorry, old boy. Can't get up on the other side. Snow's too thick.'

'Look out,' Grey said, 'we're slipping backwards.'

Their headlights swung on to the other car as Gardner tried to straighten out, and Zweig could see it was a taxi. At the same moment, Natasha Gardner called: 'My God, it's Tim.' Zweig could see a white face peering out of the rear window.

'Quick,' Grey said, 'drop back and get past them. Don't let them stop near us.' He turned to Zweig. 'Karl, get down below the level of the window in case his headlights shine in the car.'

Zweig crouched down, his head against Grey's overcoat. Gardner said:

'It's all right, they're going on.'

'Would Sir Timothy recognize the car?' Grey asked.

'Luckily, no. We only had it a few months ago.'

Gardner was forced to drop to the bottom of the hill again; this time they got over the hill without mishap. Ten minutes later the car stopped outside the George Hotel, Bury St Edmunds. Grey was saying:

'That was a piece of luck. They must have caught that later train. I'd assumed they'd be staying in a hotel overnight.'

'I'm surprised they're not,' Natasha Gardner said. 'Tim's a terrible hypochondriac about cold and damp. Perhaps they telegraphed the caretaker to get the place ready.'

'Where does the caretaker live?'

'Twenty yards away, in another cottage. They both belong to Tim.'

The desk clerk asked them: 'Staying long?'

'Just for the night,' Gardner said, 'although we may stay a couple of days if the snow's too heavy.'

Zweig and Grey booked separate rooms that were next to one another; the Gardners' were further along the same corridor.

'Shall I have the car put in the garage, sir?'

'No, don't do that,' Gardner said. 'We may want to use it later. Have you got anybody who could put the chains on the back wheel?'

'Certainly, sir.'

They drank tea in the lounge. They appeared to be the only guests in the hotel. In front of a large coal fire, with a plate of beef sandwiches, Zweig began to feel happy again. When the waiter had gone, Gardner asked:

'Now, what's the next move?'

Natasha Gardner said: 'My next move is to soak in a hot bath, then get changed.'

'There's only one thing that worries me,' Grey said, 'whether Neumann saw your face or heard your voice when you called out to that taxi driver.'

'Why? Does it matter?'

'Only if Neumann saw that there were more than the two of you in the car. The other thing, of course, is that you won't be able to claim that you're *en route* from the North.'

Gardner was standing by a map on the wall. He said:

'I don't know. I could claim we took the wrong road from Cambridge and went too far south. Anyway, I doubt whether he'd be certain of the identification. It was pretty dark and snowy.'

Natasha Gardner asked: 'What time do you intend to go to look at the cottage?'

'We may as well go fairly soon,' Grey said. 'But there's no need for you to come. We only want to take a look at the outside of the cottage. Why don't you stay and have your bath?'

She said, sighing: 'No, I had better come with you. I haven't come all this way to stay behind in the hotel!'

Gardner said: 'Why don't you and Professor Zweig both stay behind? There's no point in either of you coming.'

Zweig smiled; the idea struck him as excellent. Grey noticed his smile, and said drily:

'I'm afraid we might need Zweig. If Neumann's there, I'd like a definite identification.'

'Then we all go,' Natasha Gardner said. 'But first I must comb my hair and change these stockings. They have a ladder.'

'Nobody'll notice it in the dark,' Gardner said.

'*I* would notice it,' she said.

When she had gone upstairs, the three men moved close to the fire. Zweig lit a cigar; Grey and Gardner smoked pipes. Zweig was feeling schoolboyishly delighted with himself. Now he was warm and well-fed, the excitement of the chase was on him again. He looked at the oak-panelled walls of the lounge, relieved of their severity by the Christmas decorations, and reflected that there is an intimacy about masculine society—particularly when its members share a common aim —that women would find difficult to understand. Looking at the faces of his companions, both staring at the fire and occupied with their own thoughts, he came close to wishing that Natasha Gardner had stayed in London. But when his thoughts turned to Natasha Gardner, he had an image of her seated on the edge of a bed and pulling on a stocking, and his sense of well-being was intensified. For a moment, the two pleasures existed side by side; then they merged, fusing into a vitality that reminded him of youth.

Grey said: 'Sounds as if the wind's getting up.'

Although the windows were closed, the wind was disturbing the curtains. Gardner said:

'If it goes on like this, they'll be snowed in in that cottage by morning.'

'I think we'd better make a move as soon as your wife comes down. I don't want to get stuck in the snow.'

'She'll be half an hour yet. She never gets ready in less than three-quarters of an hour.'

'In that case, I think I'll go and freshen up myself.'

When they were alone, Gardner said:

'Seems a nice bloke, your friend. Known him long?'

'Several years. He is a very good man.'

They smoked in silence for another five minutes. Zweig asked:

'Pardon my curiosity, but is your wife a Russian?'

'Half Russian and half Hungarian. Her family had an estate at a place called Mateszalka.'

'She reads a great deal?'

Gardner said drily: 'Oh, she's highly educated. A real intellectual. And like most intellectual women, she's easily swept off her feet.'

His eyes rested on Zweig with what seemed an ironic expression. Zweig threw his cigar butt into the fire and stood up.

'I think I shall go and unpack my bag.'

'I'll find out if they've got the chains on the car.'

When Zweig was washing his face in his room, Grey came in.

'You know, Karl, I've been thinking about this. I wonder if it's a good idea to keep your presence a secret from Neumann?'

'He might be suspicious. What am I supposed to be doing here?'

Grey sat on the bed.

'That's what I've been thinking about. Presumably Sir Timothy Ferguson has heard Gardner's wife mention your name. Perhaps they've even discussed your work. Well, we've all spent Christmas in the North—we'll have to decide exactly where—and we're on our way back to London. I am interested in buying this other cottage, and the Gardners have brought me along to show it to me. That sounds plausible enough, doesn't it? It's a perfectly ordinary coincidence that you happen to know Neumann.'

'You could be right. Let's ask the other two what they think about it.'

The clerk said: 'You're not going out right now, are you, sir?'

'Oh, I think so,' Gardner said, 'after all, we don't want this snow to get any deeper.'

'I wouldn't go far, sir. With the wind like this, you'll get drifts all over the place.'

Gardner came back to the three of them in the bar. Drops of snow melted on the shoulders of his overcoat.

'I don't know whether there's much point in going out now. I've just been out to the car, and the weather's terrifying. But I suppose we can try.'

'Oh, yes, we must try,' Natasha Gardner said. She was drinking her second whisky, and looked flushed.

Grey looked at his watch.

'Dinner's in an hour, so we'd better get started. If the roads are as bad as all that, we'll have to turn back. How far is this place?'

'About five miles.'

Natasha Gardner pulled on a red woollen hat that covered her ears. Noticing that Zweig was smiling, she said:

'I have decided to abandon glamour for warmth.'

'You look enchanting.'

She said: 'Come, gentlemen. Into the night.' Zweig caught the look of mild disapproval on Grey's face. He obviously felt that she was treating this like a picnic. She said: 'Come, Professor, you can lead me to the car.' She took his hand. As they went out, Grey noticed that Gardner was shaking his head. He said: 'She's in high spirits.'

'It's not that,' Gardner said. 'She admires Zweig tremendously—thinks he's the greatest living thinker. Yet she can't resist flirting with him and behaving like a naughty schoolgirl.'

'You don't mind?' Grey asked. Something told him that Gardner was not the sort of person to resent the question.

'Good heavens, no. I've seen it too often. I only hope *he* doesn't.'

Grey said, smiling: 'No, I'm pretty sure he doesn't.'

The front door of the hotel had been closed. As Zweig and Natasha Gardner stepped out into the night, the wind tried to force them back into the hotel. Whirling snow blinded them. They stood there helplessly, pressed together, until Gardner came out. He said:

'The car's just down there by the pavement. Come on.'

Although the car was less than twenty feet away, they could not see it until they stood against it. As Natasha Gardner tumbled into the back seat, the wind drove the snow in after her. Her teeth were chattering as she called: 'C-close the door, quickly.' Gardner turned on the windscreen wipers, but the snow had packed them down and then frozen. Natasha Gardner said plaintively: 'You should have got in the car earlier and got it warmed up.'

Her husband stumbled out into the snow and rubbed the windscreen with his gloved hand. But even when the wipers began to move, the windscreen remained opaque; it was covered with a sheet of ice. Gardner switched on the engine and the demister. After ten minutes, the interior of the car was warmer, and visibility through the windscreen had been increased to four yards. Gardner said: 'Lovely night for a murder.' No one replied.

They drove through the town at five miles an hour. To Zweig, nothing was visible through the snow, even though the orange fog lamps were turned on. The sound of the wind drowned the noise of the engine, even in second gear. But Gardner appeared to know the road, and after a quarter of an hour, slipped the car into top gear and said: 'We're out on the main road now. It doesn't seem as bad as I thought.'

'It seems *terrible*,' Natasha Gardner said, pronouncing it 'terreeble.'

'No. This wind's driving the snow into banks against the hedges, and leaving the road comparatively clear.'

Now the car was warmer, Natasha Gardner had taken Zweig's hand again, and held it pressed between them, her arm and body tense, as if still resisting the cold. Zweig allowed himself to sink into pleasant daydreams about her. He had no illusions about his sexual attractiveness. If his face was still handsome—in fact, age had brought it a new kind of impressiveness, as if it was carved out of stone—he was aware that his voice was unimpressive; it had an almost feminine intonation; besides, he was too short. For Natasha Gardner, he was obviously a kind of father figure. It was apparent that a father was, to some extent, what she wanted; Gardner was probably fifteen years her senior, perhaps more. Zweig was even more satisfactory in this capacity, since he was not only ten years older than Gardner, but also a thinker whom she already regarded as a mentor. That there was no sexual element in this admiration was proved by Gardner's lack of jealousy. And yet the role of spiritual father was not unsatisfying; on the contrary, it promised concealed intimacies, unacknowledged pressures and contacts. Compared to this indefiniteness, an openly sexual relation would have seemed coarse. Zweig's romanticism had always been revolted by the French tradition of unconcealed adultery.

The car turned to the left, crunching through piled-up snow. Grey said: 'Good thing we've got the chains on. We'd be skidding all over the place otherwise.'

Natasha said fretfully: 'It seems a long way.'

'About two more miles.'

Grey said: 'I think the best thing is to try to get a look through the windows of the cottage. There's no point in calling on them tonight. It'd look too suspicious in weather like this.'

'And supposing we can't see in the windows?'

'I don't know. We'll think of something.'

'And supposing we can't get back?' Natasha Gardner asked. 'What do we do—ask Tim to find us a spare room?'

'No reason why not. We've got to find the place first. I can't see a damn thing.'

Gardner stopped the car, and wound his window down. He said:

'I believe it's over there. It's about twenty yards off the road. We'd better get out and walk from here.'

They clambered out into the deep snow, and tried to take shelter from the wind behind the car. Gardner shouted:

'You'd better all follow me. Stick close together, and avoid the side of the road. There's a ditch.'

Zweig found it impossible to tell where the road ended and the ditch began. The countryside around them was flat, with few trees or hedges, and the road might have stretched away in almost any direction. Holding Natasha Gardner's gloved hand, he stumbled in the direction of Gardner's voice. It was impossible to see; the wind drove the snow into his eyes if he raised his face. A moment later, he heard Grey shouting: 'Where are you? I've lost you.' Gardner said: 'Look, I think we'd all better hold hands in a chain, otherwise we'll get lost.' For another five minutes, they moved on, linked together. Grey shouted: 'Are you sure we're going in the right direction?' and Gardner called back: 'No.' Gardner stopped, and they huddled around him. He said:

'Can you see a light over there?'

'I can,' Grey said. He pointed off to the right. Natasha Gardner said: 'That's it. I'm sure it's the place. I recognize these trees.'

'What shall we do?' Gardner asked. His wife shouted:

'Take a look at it, then get back to the hotel. I'm hungry.'

Gardner said: 'Natasha, you'd better stick with me. We'll go first.'

The snow had almost stopped, but the wind was still so violent that this made no difference. In spite of a thick overcoat, Zweig felt naked. Grey said: 'Come on, Karl. We'll take a look round the back.'

The Gardners were no longer visible, but they had left a

path in the deep snow. They climbed over a stile, and crossed the corner of a field. Now the light was immediately ahead, and they could see the outline of the cottage. Grey leaned close to Zweig's ear, and said:

'Let's approach it from further down. I don't want to leave too many obvious footprints.'

They climbed over what appeared to be a chicken wire fence, then pushed through some apple-trees. The branches cut Zweig's face, but the flesh was so cold that he was unable to guess whether he was hurt. He stumbled, and blundered into an object that clanged metallically. Grey said: 'Look out, mind the dustbin.' As he spoke, a door opened, and a shaft of light fell across the snow. A voice called: 'Is anyone there?' Grey hissed: 'Get down.' They crouched under the trees, and Zweig whispered: 'That is Gustav.' As he spoke, Gardner's voice, coming from the left, called: 'Hello.' They watched Gardner and Natasha Gardner advancing along the garden path.

The man shouted: 'Who is it?'

'Is Sir Timothy Ferguson there?' Gardner called.

'Yes. Who is it?'

'My name's Gardner.'

From inside the cottage, another voice shouted: 'Hello there! Come on in.' A moment later, the cottage door had closed behind the Gardners.

Grey stood up. 'Come on.'

'Where?'

'Back to the car. There's no sense in waiting here.'

Five minutes later, they sat in the front of the car, the engine running, and the heater melting the snow on Zweig's shoes. It felt luxurious to be out of the wind, even though the heater seemed ineffectual. Zweig apologized about falling over the dustbin. He said: 'It was completely buried.'

'Never mind. It may be all for the best. The Gardners can take a good look around.'

'Do you think we should drive nearer?'

'No. Neumann might hear the engine. He must have pretty good hearing to come and investigate the noise of a dustbin lid.'

Slowly, the warmth returned to their hands and feet. Grey said:

'The old man sounded healthy enough.'

They sat in silence, but both were occupied with the same thought: that their murder hunt had been a mistake. This thought had been in Zweig's mind ever since Gardner announced that Sir Timothy Ferguson was in no physical danger. Although he would have refused to admit that he was impressed by Gardner's Celtic statue and his method of divination, Gardner's words had confirmed a certainty of his own: that Neumann was no criminal.

Grey said: 'It's snowing heavily again. I hope they don't stay too long, or the roads will be impassable.'

'Perhaps we should have gone inside with them.'

'No, not yet. If necessary, we can go and bang on the door —claim that Gardner left us waiting in the car. Let's give them another ten minutes first.'

He started the windscreen wipers again. Their steady clicking made Zweig drowsy. He was shocked into wakefulness when the door of the car opened, and Gardner's voice said: 'Sorry we've been so long.'

Zweig climbed into the back seat.

'Find out anything?' Grey asked.

'A bit. I'll tell you in a moment.' He turned the car with some difficulty; the road was narrow, and the ditches were concealed under snow. Natasha Gardner said:

'Give me a cigarette. That man made me feel strange.'

In spite of the snow, Gardner drove at twenty-five miles an hour, hunched forward and staring through the windscreen. Zweig lit Natasha Gardner's cigarette, and noticed the colour in her cheeks. No one spoke until the car turned on to the main Sudbury road. Then Grey asked:

'Did you tell him that Zweig was here?'

It was Natasha Gardner who answered.

'No. We just said we had two friends with us. We said you were back at the hotel. I'm glad you didn't come and knock on the door.'

'How did you explain your presence there at this time of night?'

'Natasha claimed she had a sudden "sixth sense" that Tim was at his cottage. I don't think Neumann believed her.'

'Did everything strike you as normal?'

'Not quite. But I'll tell you about it when we get to the hotel.'

The drive back took less than a quarter of an hour. Natasha

Gardner smoked all the time, and stared in front of her; Zweig was aware of her tension. They were half an hour late for dinner. The desk clerk looked relieved when they came in. 'I was afraid you'd been caught in the snow. Would you like to go straight into the dining-room?'

There were only two other guests in the dining-room. The three men sat down, and soup was placed in front of them immediately. Gardner said:

'We'd better go ahead and eat. You can never tell how long Natasha might be.'

Between spoonfuls of the soup, Gardner told them about the cottage.

'When you stumbled against the dustbin, I thought we'd better show ourselves. After all, he only had to look outside to find footprints. So we told him the story we'd arranged—about spending Christmas in Cambridge. Everything seemed all very normal. Tim was obviously delighted to see us—wanted us to stay for supper, but we said you were waiting at the hotel. They gave us some whisky, and Neumann seemed very friendly.'

'I didn't like him,' Natasha Gardner said. She had just joined them, wearing a different dress.

Grey asked: 'Did he seem at all worried by your appearance? Did he seem guilty, or shifty?'

'Oh no. Not at all. Very self-possessed.' She said this mockingly.

Gardner said: 'I know what she means. I didn't really dislike him, but there was a kind of . . . arrogance there.'

'How about Sir Timothy? Did he seem happy?'

Natasha said thoughtfully: 'He seemed very cheerful . . . but . . .'

Gardner interrupted her: 'He looked better than I've ever seen him. But there was one odd business. I told you that Natasha said she'd suddenly had a feeling that Tim was at his cottage. Well, I claimed that we'd phoned his London address—his landlady—from the hotel just to check. When I said this, I thought Tim looked nervous. Then Natasha said to Neumann: "You must be a wonderful doctor. I've never seen Tim looking so healthy." And Neumann immediately said: "I beg your pardon, but I am not a doctor. I am merely Sir Timothy's secretary." So I said: "But the landlady mentioned on the phone that you were a doctor." Then Tim interrupted: "That's my fault. We were talking about doctors, and she got mixed up. She's got doctors on the brain." So we dropped the subject.'

The main course had now arrived, together with a bottle of claret. Zweig was now feeling sleepy, the effect of warmth and food after exertion. He said:

'That does not seem strange to me. After all, if Gustav is not a doctor, why should he say he is?'

Grey said: 'The landlady seemed pretty definite about it this morning. I think he might have reasons for not wanting anyone to know that he's giving Ferguson medical treatment of some kind.'

Zweig asked: 'Did they say why they had come to the cottage?'

'Yes. Tim claimed that he wanted to write his memoirs, and wanted to be somewhere lonely.'

'Had he ever spoken to you about writing his memoirs before?'

'Never. In fact, I don't believe him. He's about the least literary person I've ever known.'

'But you didn't get the impression that Neumann has somehow forced him to come to the cottage?'

'No. Not at all. I don't believe he has. There's one thing of which I'm absolutely certain. Tim trusts Neumann completely.'

Grey turned to Natasha Gardner:

'What was your impression of Neumann, Mrs Gardner?'

'I . . . don't know. When we first went into the house I thought that we had been mistaken about him. He looked too young to have been in Heidelberg in 1930. Then, when I looked at him in a better light, I saw that this was false. He has the kind of youthfulness that I have seen before in men with a single purpose. He is a man with a one-track mind.'

'A crank?' Grey asked.

'No. Some sort of an idealist.'

Zweig laughed triumphantly, and turned to Grey.

'You see, that is exactly what I told you. He is not the criminal type.'

Natasha said slowly: 'I don't know.'

'Why?'

'He's not a criminal type, I agree. But he's a man who cares more about the end than the means. I think he could commit a crime to achieve some objective.'

'For money?' Grey prompted.

'Yes, if money was necessary for his main purpose.'

Gardner was looking at his wife with admiration.

'She's nearly always right about people, you know. She sees a lot deeper than I ever do.'

'Do you agree with her about Neumann?'

'I think so. He struck me as all right. A nice bloke. Terrifically intelligent, I'd say. But a bit inhuman.'

Grey asked Natasha Gardner:

'Would you say that Sir Timothy is in any danger from Neumann?'

'I . . . don't think so. I . . .' She was frowning at her plate, groping for words. 'Not really from Neumann. I don't think he is what we thought. . . .'

'And what did we think?'

'I know what *I* thought. That he was a completely cynical crook with no conscience and no morals, a man who would kill because he had no human feelings. You know what I mean, Sir Charles. The criminal type. A man who is an adolescent on the social level. . . .'

'Yes. I know what you mean. And are you sure he's not?'

'Quite sure. If he is a killer, then he is of the same type as Hitler—a man for whom killing is only the means to an end.'

Zweig almost choked on a mouthful of wine. He swallowed, coughed, then said:

'That is impossible. You forget that Gustav is a Jew, and that he suffered under Hitler. Hitler was a fanatic who was stupid enough to swallow the nonsense of Gobineau and Günther. Gustav is too intelligent for that.'

Gardner said: 'I don't think that's quite what she means. I think that what she means is that idealists have been responsible for more deaths than all the criminals in history.'

'Quite. But what is Gustav's ideal? When I knew him in Heidelberg, he had the crazy idea of becoming a master criminal. That is not an ideal—it is adolescent nonsense.'

Grey drained his glass. He said:

'In short, we're just as much in the dark as before . . . except for this one curious clue—that Neumann wants to be regarded as a secretary and nothing more.'

'That is understandable,' Zweig said. 'I believe that his

treatment is probably psychological. But probably he has no diploma to practise as a psychologist.'

'It's not illegal, provided he doesn't use false pretences. Why should he worry?'

Zweig said, shrugging: 'He could have many reasons.'

'I can only think of one,' Gardner said. Zweig did not reply. He knew what Gardner meant, but was not willing to think about it. Instead, he signalled to the waiter, and asked for another bottle of wine.

Grey said: 'I wish I could get inside that cottage and take a look round.'

'What do you think you might find?' Natasha Gardner asked.

'To begin with, whether Karl's right about the treatment being psychological.'

'You think Neumann is making Sir Timothy take drugs?'

'Not likely,' Gardner said, before Grey could reply. 'I don't know all that much about drugs, but I've seen a little of their effect. Tim looked completely normal and healthy.'

Zweig said: 'In that case, we may as well return to London tomorrow.'

'I'm inclined to agree,' Gardner said. They all looked at Grey. Grey shook his head.

'I don't agree. Why don't you and Mrs Gardner go back and leave Zweig and myself here? There's nothing much for you to do.'

'What do you intend to do?'

'I'd like to watch that cottage. Didn't you say there was another cottage nearby that you'd once thought of renting? How near is it?'

'Fifty yards away.'

'Is Sir Timothy's cottage visible from its windows?'

'Yes, I suppose so. But what's the point?'

'They're bound to go out sometime. I'd like to take a look inside when they do.'

'That won't be easy. The gardener's cottage is only ten yards away. You'd almost certainly be seen.'

Grey dropped a lump of sugar into his coffee.

'Then there's only one alternative. To warn Ferguson that Neumann might be a murderer.'

'How?' Gardner asked.

Grey looked at Zweig. 'Would you be willing to do it?'

Zweig said cautiously: 'Naturally, if you think it necessary. But are you sure that it's necessary? It would not be easy. It would depend on getting Sir Timothy alone, or getting a message to him. . . .'

'Or simply going to the cottage with Gardner and talking frankly to Ferguson—in front of Neumann, if necessary.'

Zweig grimaced. 'It seems unnecessarily . . . crude.'

'If we intend to go back to London and leave the two of them alone, I see no alternative.'

Zweig stared into his empty wine glass. He said finally:

'I would like to speak to Gustav alone.'

'You might give everything away.'

'I know. But you are asking me to act on the assumption that he is a man who murders for money, and I find this difficult.'

Grey said, sighing:

'All right. We may as well forget about it. The only alternative is for me to stay and watch them.' He turned to Gardner. 'If you can arrange it, I'll move into that cottage tomorrow.'

'There shouldn't be any difficulty, but it won't be very comfortable. It belongs to a local farmer. I'll see if I can get him on the phone tonight.'

Natasha Gardner said: 'You know the place is unfurnished and unheated?'

'We can build fires.'

'In that case,' Gardner said, 'I'll come with you and share the watch.'

'We had all better go,' Natasha Gardner said.

'We can decide about that later. The first thing is to find out if we can use the cottage. Can you phone the farmer now?'

'If you want me to.'

While Gardner was at the telephone, the three of them sat in silence. Zweig offered them both wine; when they declined, he poured the remainder into his own glass. He was drinking to try to relieve the feeling of oppression that had been on him since they returned from the cottage, but it made no difference. There was something elusive about the whole affair; it was at once too complicated and too simple.

Natasha Gardner said: 'I have an idea. Why do you not get the local police to call at the cottage and ask to see Neumann's papers? If he thinks the police are interested in him, he might give something away. . . .'

Grey looked pleased.

'That's not a bad idea. The village constable would probably do it. He could say that he was checking up to make sure that everything was all right—protecting Ferguson's property and all that. Then he could ask to see Neumann's passport.'

'What is the point?' Zweig asked.

'To make Neumann nervous.'

Natasha said: 'I think our visit this evening probably did that.'

'I hope so. I want him to be suspicious—suspicious and cautious.'

Gardner came back in; he was rubbing his hands and looking cheerful. He said:

'Well, my dear, we've now got ourselves a summer cottage.'

'You didn't offer to buy it?'

'Yes. It doesn't matter. I've been thinking about it for a long time. And I couldn't think of any other excuse for wanting to move in tomorrow morning. Anyway, it's all fixed. He'll go there at eight tomorrow morning with a load of logs for the fire. He tells me there's a certain amount of furniture in it. Don't look so worried. It wasn't expensive.'

Grey said, laughing: 'You certainly do things thoroughly.'

'In this case, there was no alternative. Shall we go into the lounge and have a brandy to celebrate?'

Natasha Gardner yawned, then apologized. She said: 'I'm afraid I shall have to go to bed soon. I can hardly keep awake.'

'Good idea,' Gardner said. 'I want to be up by seven. I'll get the desk to give me an early call.'

'I shall sleep until nine,' Natasha Gardner said, frowning.

'That's all right, Grey and I can go and get the place ready. I'll come and collect you two later.' He slapped Grey on the shoulder. 'We'll take a bottle of brandy with us too. You coming to have one now?'

'In a moment,' Grey said. 'First, I want to phone the local chief constable.'

'What on earth for?'

Natasha Gardner said, smiling: 'He wants to arrange for someone to give Neumann an early call in the morning.'

At nine thirty the next morning, Zweig and Natasha Gardner breakfasted together, then went out to look at the town. After the storm, the sky was cloudless. The snow was melting, and the damp air tasted already of spring. Both had recovered from the fatigue of the drive, and Zweig's feeling of oppression and foreboding had disappeared completely. Now they were alone, she no longer behaved in a manner that might have stirred her husband's jealousy; the gestures and looks that seemed to invite intimacy had vanished. In spite of this, the feeling of intimacy was somehow deepened. Zweig found it difficult to realize that they had known each other for less than twenty-four hours; she made him feel as if they had been close friends for years.

At ten o'clock, Gardner had rung to say that they were settled in the cottage, and would probably stay there for the rest of the day. He seemed to feel that the occupants of the other cottage would find it hard to resist the temptation of sunlight and the unexpectedly warm breeze, and would give him an opportunity to search their cottage. He advised his wife that there was a ruined abbey and two fifteenth-century churches that were worth seeing, and suggested that she take Zweig for a walk. They decided to take his advice, found a guide-book in the hotel, and spent the morning tramping through the melting snow, and learning the history of King Sigebert and King Edmund. An old churchwarden described the destruction of the monastery so graphically and at such length that they both felt a slight surprise on finding themselves back in the twentieth century. At this point, the striking of the church clock warned them that they had only ten minutes to walk two miles and prepare for lunch.

She asked the desk clerk: 'Any message for me?'

'No, madam, but there's a gentleman waiting to see you.'

'A gentleman?' She looked blank. 'Where is he?'

'Waiting in the lounge, I believe.'

She told Zweig: 'Perhaps you'd better go in to lunch while I see who it is. I suppose it's someone with a message from Joseph.'

'I will wait.' In saying this, he had no other motive than the thought of the pleasant intimacy of travelling up with her in the lift, and of knocking on her door in five minutes' time to find out if she was ready.

'All right.' She asked the clerk: 'Could you point him out to me?'

The lounge seemed to be empty. The clerk said:

'That's strange. Perhaps he's gone away again.'

As he spoke a man rose from a high-backed armchair that

was turned away from the door. He said: 'Good morning, Mrs Gardner,' then, looking at Zweig, who stood behind her, 'Good morning, Professor.'

Natasha Gardner showed no sign of surprise. She said: 'Ah, it's you.' She turned to Zweig. 'You don't know Mr Neumann, do you? He's Sir Timothy's secretary.'

Neumann said: 'On the contrary, we are old friends. He was my Professor.' To Zweig, he said: 'You don't seem surprised to see me.'

Zweig envied Natasha her self-command; he was aware that he was flushing, and for a moment found it impossible to speak. Then, stammering slightly, he said:

'Surprised! I am astounded. What are you doing here?' He advanced on Neumann, his hand outstretched. Neumann glanced down at it and smiled slightly, as if amused by an irrelevancy. Then he reached out and took it, quickly and casually, and dropped it almost immediately. He said to Natasha:

'I'm sorry to come at such an inconvenient moment. I was hoping to have a word with you and your husband.'

'I'm afraid he's not here. He's at the cottage. . . .' She stopped, and Zweig's mind completed her sentence: 'spying on you.' She caught herself immediately. 'Didn't you see him as you came past?'

'No. How unfortunate! I might have saved myself a journey here if I'd known. I came the other way, through Beyton. But now I'm here, and it's so late, I wonder if you'd be so kind as to let me offer you lunch?'

Although he was speaking to her gravely and with courtesy, he was at the same time managing to suggest that Zweig was not in the room. Zweig was too startled to resent the snub; he stood there, staring at Neumann's profile, momentarily out of his depth. After days of thinking about Neumann, this confrontation was too sudden; moreover, the man who was now talking to Natasha Gardner was completely unlike the Gustav Neumann of his thoughts. The physical resemblance was there; in this respect, Neumann had changed very little. But this self-possession, like a heavy rock balanced on a pivot, was something that he could not have anticipated.

Natasha Gardner was staring at Neumann with unconcealed irritation; more self-possessed than Zweig, she resented the snub that he was too bewildered to notice. Her voice was cold and polite as she said:

'I'm sorry, but I've already arranged to have lunch with Professor Zweig.'

'What a pity.' Neumann's manner was so casually formal, balanced between courtesy and unconcern, that an uninvolved observer would have been surprised by her reactions. Zweig noticed also that Neumann's accent had no trace of German; he might have been an English solicitor talking to his twentieth client of the day, covering his boredom with a polite façade of interest.

Natasha Gardner looked at her watch. 'I'm afraid we're already rather late for lunch.'

'In that case, would it be very pushing of me to ask if I might have the pleasure of joining you?'

She looked at Zweig, mollified at having reduced Neumann to asking a favour, but determined to press her advantage.

'If Professor Zweig has no objection . . .' Her tone implied that, if Zweig had any objection, then Neumann would have to dine alone. It was her way of forcing Neumann to acknowledge Zweig's presence. Zweig failed to use his advantage. He said hastily:

'Of course, of course. Certainly,' and then realized, from the set of her lips, that he had somehow directed some of her annoyance to himself.

She said, shrugging:

'I must go to my room. Perhaps you two would go to our table?' She added, to Zweig: 'I would like a dry sherry.'

Left alone, Neumann smiled at Zweig with the same controlled, social politeness.

'It's an unexpected pleasure to find you here. Shall we go into the dining-room?' He held the door open for Zweig. 'I'm afraid I'm rather hungry. Have you been looking at the town?'

'Er, no . . . that is to say, yes, at the abbey. . . .'

'I must see it before we leave.' They went into the diningroom, and their voices were those of two casual acquaintances who have nothing to say to one another.

The waiter came forward; Neumann said: 'I think I would like a dry martini—very dry. Will you join me? Yes? Two martinis and a dry sherry.'

As the waiter left them, Zweig said: 'You speak English like an Englishman.'

The compliment was intended to penetrate Neumann's reserve. But Neumann only said, in his driest voice:

'Your own English is excellent.' He stared across the room, ignoring the menu that lay open in front of him. There was no doubt that he meant Zweig to realize that he considered him a stranger. If his reserve had been due to shyness, he might have tried to conceal it by pretending to be occupied with the menu.

Zweig asked: 'Are you still a German citizen?'

Neumann looked at him coldly.

'Yes.' He looked away sharply, as if he considered the question an impertinence. After a moment, he added: 'In fact, a police officer came to see me today to inspect my papers. He appeared to be rather interested in my address.'

'Indeed?' Zweig said. He opened the menu. While he pretended to read, his mind was occupied with questions. Where were Grey and Gardner? Had Neumann deliberately avoided them, and if so, how much did he suspect?

Neumann said: 'I think I might try the oysters.'

'Yes,' Zweig said. 'Perhaps I shall join you.'

There was a pause, and he felt as if he had made a mistake; he looked at the head of the menu; oysters were not mentioned. He said: 'My menu makes no mention of oysters.'

There was no mistaking the sarcasm in Neumann's smile. He said: 'Ah, no, I made a mistake.'

The incident was trivial, yet it impressed Zweig. He felt that Neumann had known that he was not really reading the menu, that he was only staring at it in order to gain time to think. At the same moment, he felt a twinge of a superstitious fear that Neumann was able to read his mind. He was relieved when Natasha Gardner joined them a moment later. She glanced from one to the other, noticed that Zweig was looking as uneasy as when she had left them five minutes earlier, and said in a deliberately naïve and animated voice:

'I expect you two have been talking about old times?'

Neumann smiled. 'Not yet. I am not certain that we have a lot to discuss.'

'Indeed?' She widened her eyes. 'Why?'

'My own career has been very unexciting. I cannot boast of any progress or development to compare with that of Professor Zweig.'

Zweig wondered if this was a belated attempt to offer him

a compliment. He asked: 'Have you read any of my later books, then?'

'A few. I have even seen you on television.' The smile was not openly sarcastic, but there was no mistaking the meaning. But Natasha Gardner only smiled more charmingly than ever.

'Won't you tell us what you've been doing since you were Professor Zweig's student?'

Neumann raised his martini carefully; the glass was too full.

'I wouldn't dream of boring you, Mrs Gardner.'

They ordered the meal, and Zweig had another chance to stare at Neumann's face. It was astonishing how little it had changed. The mouth was still too sensitive, the forehead unlined. The eyes had the same alertness as in the photograph in Zweig's album; the lines around the mouth showed no trace of weakness or defeat. It was the face of an arrogant youth, not of a middle-aged man. And yet it was a face that Zweig was prepared to like; this was why he felt puzzled and hurt by Neumann's deliberate coolness.

Natasha Gardner was asking him about his work for Sir Timothy. He explained that he was helping Sir Timothy to work on an autobiography, and that he would also be examining and cataloguing various family papers when they arrived at Perth. The story sounded plausible. When Natasha Gardner asked for more details about the family papers, he explained that one of Sir Timothy's Elizabethan ancestors had been an indefatigable diarist and correspondent, and that a later ancestor had corresponded with Creevey and Dr Burney. The details seemed too circumstantial to be invention. In the silence that fell as they began to eat, she asked suddenly:

'Why were you so unsurprised to see Professor Zweig just now? Did you know he was here?'

Neumann carefully chewed a slice of beef before replying. 'I make a point of never being surprised. Besides, Sir Timothy happened to mention that Zweig was your favourite writer, and I gathered that you knew him.'

There was something insidious in the way that Neumann managed to imply disrespect without being obviously rude; referring to Zweig without his academic title could have been a kind of deference—after all, no one speaks of Professor Schopenhauer or Professor Nietzsche—but Zweig knew better; speaking of him as her 'favourite writer' also seemed to convey that Natasha Gardner was an intellectual dilettante. And yet Neumann was smiling at them as if his one desire was to make himself agreeable to his dining companions.

Natasha Gardner asked abruptly:

'What did you want to see me about?'

Neumann laid down his soup spoon for a moment.

'About Sir Timothy. But it's rather a delicate matter, and I'd prefer to talk about it when your husband is here too.'

'I don't think either of us would feel it correct to talk about Sir Timothy behind his back, and with a comparative stranger.'

'I was sure you'd feel like that. But I think you might feel differently when I explain the circumstances.'

She shrugged. 'Then the best time to see us both is after dinner tonight.'

'Your husband won't be back for lunch?'

'No. He's looking over a cottage we've bought.'

'I see.'

They finished the soup and sat in silence. It seemed impossible to continue the conversation without a change of subject. Neumann seemed unembarrassed; the waiter had brought a carafe of wine, and he sipped absently, staring at the diners at the next table. Natasha Gardner asked:

'Where did you two know one another?' It was a deliberate attempt to bring the conversation back to Neumann's past. It was Zweig who answered:

'Gustav's father was my closest friend in Heidelberg. I was also Gustav's professor of philosophy.' This was the first time he had used Neumann's Christian name, and it gave Natasha Gardner the lead she wanted.

'You knew one another well, then?'

'Moderately well,' Neumann said, in the same non-committal voice.

'But wasn't that many years ago—in the late 1920s?'

'It was,' Neumann said.

'In that case,' she said, smiling at Zweig, 'you seem to have very little to say to one another.'

There was a silence, during which Zweig looked at Neumann; the glance said that he would also like to know the answer to her question. Neumann sighed.

'My dear Mrs Gardner, you were kind enough to allow me to join you for lunch. There were certain subjects that I hoped would be avoided. You admire Doctor Zweig's work; I cannot entirely share your feeling. Under the circumstances, it would be rude and ungrateful of me not to keep my opinions to myself.'

'Nonsense,' Natasha Gardner said. 'You're perfectly at liberty to say what you like. I'm sure Professor Zweig doesn't mind.'

'Not at all,' Zweig added.

'Have you read many of his books?' Natasha Gardner asked. It was clearly meant as a challenge.

Neumann was still smiling. 'Enough to grasp the basic ideas.'

'And do you object to the basic ideas?'

The food had arrived, but Neumann ignored his knife and fork, staring at her across the table top, as if he had to settle more important issues first. He said quietly:

'You urge me to be frank. Very well, and I hope you will not be offended. There were certain German philosophers and artists who were criticized for remaining in Germany and supporting the Nazis—Heidegger, for example. Others preferred to leave the country and gain a reputation as martyrs. . . .'

Zweig tried to interrupt: 'But my dear Gustav . . .'

'Allow me to finish. You were one of those who went to America and became a symbol of humanitarianism. So not many people were surprised when you declared yourself a Christian. But I could remember your telling my father that only a fool, a knave or a weakling could be a Christian in our century.' Neumann now made no attempt to hide the cold hostility in his glance. 'But I agreed with what you said at the time, and I still agree with it. There is only one thing I would like to know. Which of the three do you think you have become?'

Neumann turned his eyes from Zweig, and carefully sliced his steak. Zweig stared at him for a moment, unable to find words. The insult seemed so gratuitous that at first he was simply astonished; then, as his feelings adjusted themselves, he felt the blood rise in his face; Neumann's air of indifference as he cut the steak increased the anger. The man had stated plainly that he was either a fool, a knave or a weakling. Zweig was not a conceited man, but he was used to respect; and Neumann, after all, had been his student. The response that leapt into his mind was the obvious one: 'Is it better to become a Christian or to become a murderer?' But before he could say it aloud, Natasha Gardner's voice asked with astonishment:

'Do you think it necessary to be so rude?'

Neumann looked up, and there was an element of brutality in his smile. He said:

'Professor Zweig understands me.'

'On the contrary,' Zweig said, and realized that his voice was choked, 'I fail to understand you in every way.' He spoke deliberately, because he was thinking of all he knew and guessed about Gustav Neumann.

Neumann smiled and said: 'Then perhaps I'd better say no more.' He began to eat as if this now demanded all his attention.

'It's a little late for that,' Natasha said.

What angered Zweig was not that Neumann questioned his sincerity, but that he questioned it in this way. His manner left no room for a reasonable reply; it seemed designed to irritate, and his natural response was rage. At the same time, he realized that it might lead him to say something he would regret. Could this be Neumann's purpose in provoking him? With an effort he took a drink from his lager glass, stared at the surface of the beer as he drank, and allowed his mind simply to contemplate the pattern of foam on its surface. This steadied him. Then he made himself face the alternative explanation: that Neumann might be genuinely indignant about his work since 1930. It seemed implausible, but had the effect of soothing his feelings. He began to eat again, and for a moment it looked as if conversation had dropped. When Zweig spoke again, his voice was reasonable, interested, almost friendly.

'You seem to feel very strongly about all this, Gustav. But is it really such a terrible thing to become a Christian?'

Neumann looked at him, and it was obvious that the hostility was still there.

'In your case, yes, although I agree it is no worse than Heidegger becoming a Nazi.'

Zweig felt again master of himself.

'But Heidegger has denied that he was ever a Nazi. In any case, would you equate a creed of racial violence with a creed of love?'

Neumann said slowly: 'In both cases, a man has sold his

intellectual integrity for security. You told us once never to deal with fools or cowards—and above all, never to deal with men who had surrendered their reason to a myth, or to an emotion, or to a Saviour. You told us to ignore such men and go our own way.'

Zweig asked: 'And have you gone your own way?'

'I think so. But that is hardly the point at the moment.'

'It could be the point,' Zweig said. He caught Natasha Gardner's warning look, but went on: 'I do not consider that compromise is always weakness, so I admit that, in certain respects, I may have compromised. But not in important matters. Can you say the same?'

Neumann said, coldly and deliberately: 'I repeat, I hardly think that relevant to the present conversation.'

Natasha Gardner, who had been eating, said: 'You mean you make the rules?'

'I mean,' Neumann said, 'that we are not talking about compromise, but about dishonesty and cowardice.'

She said, without looking up from her plate: 'Would you tell us why you want to be offensive?'

He smiled, and took up his knife and fork again. 'I am sorry. I had no wish to start this conversation. You asked me to be frank. . . .'

'But not rude.'

Neumann seemed apologetic, but Zweig suspected this was only another mask.

'I would like to make it clear that I am not unaware of the charm of Professor Zweig's ideas, the persuasive quality of his writing . . . and the appeal of his television personality. I understand why you should admire him. I am told that many women's clubs regard him as a great philosopher, and I can see why. But not being a woman, I feel I should be allowed the right to criticise the quality of his ideas. . . .'

Natasha Gardner was flushing; it was the first time that Zweig had seen her angry, and he found it made her look younger. Her voice sounded slightly breathless as she said:

'Mr Neumann, either you will leave this room, or I shall.'

Neumann smiled, as if listening to a child.

'I would be very sorry indeed if you found that necessary. Professor Zweig will tell you that I do not mean to be offensive.' He returned to his meal as if the matter was settled. She continued to stare at him, realising that she had been made to look foolish; she had expected him to leave or to apologise profusely. Instead, he was treating her as a child. If she accepted his almost contemptuous apology, it would be like accepting a rebuke. If she pressed the matter, she would sound hysterical. Zweig said:

'I hardly think it is necessary to be rude to Mrs Gardner.'

'If you insist that I am trying to be rude, there is hardly anything I can do about it.'

They ate in silence. Natasha Gardner finished her steak and stood up.

'I am going up to my room.' She turned and walked away before either of them had time to react. Neumann returned to his eating immediately. He said:

'I am sorry to offend one of your female admirers.'

Zweig suddenly felt there was no longer any point in controlling himself and playing this game of concealment. He said:

'I fail to understand why you insisted on having lunch with us, unless you wanted an opportunity to be insulting. You have behaved very badly. . . .'

The waiter's cough made him turn.

'Will the lady be coming back, sir?'

'No. She's finished, thank you.'

'What sweet would you like, sir?'

The thought of spending another ten minutes with Neumann was distasteful to him. He was tempted to stand up and walk out. Only curiosity held him back.

'I will take coffee, please. And a little brandy.'

Neumann said: 'And the same for me.'

He finished eating and pushed away his plate. The waiter took it away. Neither of them spoke. It was Zweig who said finally:

'Why did you come here?'

'Out of curiosity.'

'About what?'

Neumann said smoothly: 'First, allow me to ask you a question. What are you doing here?'

Zweig drew a deep breath and stared at his finger-nails; they were blunt and square, and needed manicuring. This evasiveness revolted him, but he was aware of the possible consequences of being frank. He said, smiling:

'I feel that we are talking at cross-purposes.'

'Indeed?' Neumann's look of innocence was obviously insincere. 'Could you explain what you mean?'

'All right. I suspect you are here because you want some information. Very well. Tell me what you want to know.'

Neumann stared across the room with an expression of abstraction. Then he smiled.

'Beautifully put. But I don't quite know how to answer. Let us say—to begin with—that I would like to know why you call yourself a Christian?'

For a moment, Zweig was surprised; it was not the question he had expected. He shrugged.

'Very well. If you are serious.' It was difficult to begin; the insincere tone of the conversation was a hindrance. He drew a deep breath and tried to forget Neumann's presence. 'Like most young men who had read Nietzsche, I began by rejecting Christianity as a myth propagated by weaklings. In my first books, I concentrated on the problem of man's position in the world—his lack of freedom, his helplessness. I tried to create a philosophy of freedom based on man's ability to take a detached view of his own sufferings. I believe these books exercised some influence on your own ideas? Then came the Nazis. I saw my friends persecuted. I saw what happened to your friend Georgi Braunschweig.' He was watching Neumann closely as he said this, expecting some response. Neumann was staring away across the room; his face showed no emotion. Zweig stopped speaking while the waiter brought coffee. He went on, his voice level and quiet:

'All these things made me feel that the human race had gone mad. And one day—on the boat travelling to New York—the answer suddenly came to me.' Neumann's eyes were now turned on him, but their expression was hard to read. 'I realized that no philosopher has ever said anything that has really changed the human race—not even Socrates with his "Know yourself." The only men who have altered history—man's spiritual history—have been the religious teachers. And it became obvious to me that no one has ever said anything as important as Christ's "Love your neighbour as yourself." You will tell me that this was an emotional reaction to Nazi brutality. I do not deny this, but I think it remains true.' Neumann's momentary look of interest had vanished and he was now looking away. 'After that, many things fell into place. I had been obsessed by man's lack of freedom, his limitedness.

Now I saw that this was another name for original sin. The same was true of human suffering, man's subjection to pain and death.'

Without looking at him, Neumann said: 'And redemption?'

'That was not difficult. I had never been able to accept the idea of atonement because it seemed obvious that no man can atone for another. We are all slaves in our own prison, and we all have to escape individually. And yet now it suddenly seemed to me that Christ *had* produced an incalculable effect on human history with his gospel of love. Do you understand me? Since Christ died, love has been an active component in human history.'

'In spite of the Nazis?'

'In spite of the Nazis. Imagine human history without Christ. There would be *nothing but* the Nazis. Man's natural law is self-interest, and self-interest leads to sadism, and destruction unless it is transformed by intellect. For every self-interested Socrates there are a million self-interested Goerings and Himmlers. I had believed that the human race must be redeemed by intellect, and I felt despair when I saw how easily intellect can be destroyed by a fanatic. Now I realized that only love is strong enough to oppose the evil of stupidity and brutality. And Christ had given a form and expression to that idea of love—made it a force in history. Can you deny him the title of redeemer?'

Neumann said softly: 'Redeemer, perhaps. But the son of God?'

'Are we not all sons of God?'

'You are being evasive. A Christian believes that Christ was the son of God in a unique sense.'

Zweig said, shrugging: 'Very well. Then perhaps I am not a Christian after all.'

'I see.' Neumann was smiling as he sipped his coffee. Zweig now felt sure of himself; he tried to compel Neumann to look at him as he spoke.

'There was one other thing that caused me to revise my position. A few weeks after I arrived in America I received a letter from your father. He told me that his friend Gerhardt Seyfert had committed suicide in Switzerland while he was on holiday with you.'

Neumann was looking at him now; at the mention of Seyfert's name, he smiled slightly. Zweig said:

Of all the books ever written
why have the Editors of TIME
chosen these four to
send you for only $1?

To introduce you to the
reader service that ranges the entire
towering works for about $1.25 each

THE DOCTOR AND THE DEVILS
by Dylan Thomas

Dylan Thomas wrote a dramatic dialogue with death in this portrait of an early 19th Century doctor who held human life cheap enough to buy it on the hoof. Sacrificing his soul to his science, the Faustian Dr. Rock became an unforgettable Frankenstein of modern medicine, a potentially great man who fell from grace with a terrible grandeur.

BEND SINISTER
by Vladimir Nabokov

The author of **Lolita** brings the stiletto edge of his superb satirical gift to the story of a philosopher whose faith defied a dictator. With Nabokov's crackling style showing to even greater advantage, **Bend Sinister** dissects the machinery of tyranny much as **Lolita** did the masquerades of morality.

JOHN PAUL JONES
by Samuel Eliot Morison

John Paul Jones won the Pulitzer Prize for its salty portrait of America's first naval hero — a paradoxical genius with an unruly passion for glory and women. Capturing all the color and action of Jones' sea conquests, the book is also a deeply moving examination of a disgraced idol who was buried in an obscure French grave until Teddy Roosevelt sent an armada to bring him back in state 158 years later.

THE SEA AND THE JUNGLE
by H. M. Tomlinson

A cool, highly civilized Englishman doffed his bowler, abandoned his umbrella and deserted his desk to ship for the hottest, wildest place in the world — the unexplored upper Amazon. Here's an immensely absorbing and amusing classic in the great tradition of odd-ball English adventurers.

Time Reading Program...the only literary world to bring you the

We're offering you these four titles at a fifth of the usual price—only twenty-five cents each—to prove our basic premise: that the most important books can also be the most enjoyable books to read.

Arthur Koestler, Aldous Huxley, Graham Greene, J. P. Marquand, James Joyce, George Orwell, James Thurber, Joyce Cary—the Program brings you the best of authors like these too. Each book is a literary landmark, a compelling chapter in the complex of ideas, events and emotions that makes our world a fascinating place in which to live and learn. Demonstrating that higher learning needn't resemble hard labor, they allow you to live up to your intellectual income and like it. Though there's something to set you thinking on every page, each book offers you just as many opportunities to luxuriate in the sheer delight of good writing.

Making the Most of your Reading Time

Publishing houses pour forth an avalanche of books every day. How do you go about separating the good from the bad, the best from the good? How do you achieve balance or perspective in your reading? How do you distinguish books of permanent value from those of only passing interest? With 700,000 volumes currently in print, you could hardly be expected to know the answers. But the Editors of Time have to know, because it's their daily occupation. In satisfying 13,000,000 literate, demanding and discriminating readers every week, they're obliged to keep up with almost every area of human endeavor—including the books on every subject. And now, in the Time Reading Program, they'd like to pass on to you the best that they encounter, to share their unending intellectual adventure with you.

TRP offers more, demands less

The Time Reading Program is not a book club—it is a reader service. You join it entirely on your own terms. There are no minimums, no obligations, no strings of any kind—you pay only for the books you want to keep and you may cancel the entire Program at any time. The most you ever have to do is send back any book—1, 2, 3 or the whole package—you may not want, and you can use the container they came in. Nor does the Program offer you a random collection of best sellers, chosen on the debatable grounds of hoped-for or passing popularity. Instead, its carefully planned diversity gives you a massive, many-sided insight into the most provocative pursuits of man. Taken together, the selections form a rich mosaic that shows our civilization at its most inspired—as well as its most revealing moments. Ranging through the whole spectrum of literature—from fiction to philosophy, science to satire—the Time Reading Program brings you the kind of books you'd like to read but can't always find for yourself.

For each book, a dual perspective

Since great books can be enjoyed on two levels—the immediate experience, as well as the ultimate impact—most of the Program's selections contain not only an introduction, but a preface as well. The preface, by the Editors of Time, places the book in the broad perspective of literature and shows what part it plays in the over-all picture, the contribution that makes it a classic. The introduction, by an outstanding authority in the book's own field or by the author himself, is more in the nature of an intimate appreciation, in terms of the "feel" or heartbeat of the book. Between them, they interpret each volume in a way that will prove invaluable not only to the general reader, but to the college student or candidate as well.

Each book is a visual work of art too

Designed by leading artists, TRP books are beautifully decorative. Some are illustrated inside too with old prints, maps, drawings and photographs. They are not paperback books: they are covered in a tough, flexible plastic, especially developed to withstand wear and tear. The surface of these covers lends itself to color processing much as a painter's canvas does, so that each book is a delight to the eye as well as to the mind. Much larger than most comparably priced books, more expensively bound, printed on finer paper in handsome, generously spaced type faces, these volumes are possible at about $1.25 apiece only because there is no middleman between you and the publisher, and because the Program's wide membership permits large printings.

Read the books first—decide later

The way the TRP works is simplicity itself. The four-book set shown here is yours for only $1, without further obligation. If you want to inspect the other books in the Program, just sign the order card and send it to us. This merely means that every other month you'll receive another four-volume set. Browse through them for ten days, and then decide whether you want to keep them. You pay only for what you keep, at $4.95 per set, plus postage and handling, and any time you please, you may cancel the entire Program with a stroke of your pen.

The order card commits you to nothing more than the fun of browsing through four stimulating books with no cost or obligation—so why not sign it and send it now? You'll be glad you did.

'I remembered what you had told me about becoming a master criminal. And I wondered . . . if his death was really suicide.'

Neumann said: 'I see.' He spoke indifferently, as if listening to some unimportant explanation.

Zweig drank his coffee; it was cold. He wanted to force Neumann to reply. Watching Neumann's face, which showed no sign of inner conflict, or even of interest, he found himself admiring Neumann's self-possession. Once again he felt the need to break through these defences, the desire to be allowed to like the man who was now glancing at his watch and signalling to the waiter.

Neumann said: 'Could I have my bill, please?'

'You are my guest,' Zweig said.

'That is kind of you but I couldn't dream of accepting.' Neumann nodded at the waiter, who left. 'I'm afraid I'm a somewhat unsatisfactory guest.'

Zweig said, with controlled exasperation: 'Gustav, why don't you answer me? Why do you join us for lunch and then refuse to speak? What are you trying to hide?'

Neumann stared at him; Zweig caught a flicker of cold irritation in his eyes.

'I have nothing to hide.' He added, more deliberately: 'You may search as hard as you like. You will find nothing.'

Zweig said: 'Why do you treat me as an enemy?'

Neumann's voice contained a note of contempt as he replied:

'I think you know the answer to that.'

'But good heavens . . .' Zweig stopped speaking as the waiter returned. Neumann dropped two pound notes on to the tray. He returned the wallet to his pocket, and said:

'Thank you for allowing me to join you. I am sorry Mrs Gardner felt it necessary to leave.' He started to push his chair back. Zweig said:

'Listen, Gustav, please.' Neumann stopped politely. 'I'd like to speak to you completely frankly, but you realize that that is impossible.' He was saying more than he intended to, but he went on: 'I wish I could convince you that I have tried to be your friend in this matter.'

'And Mrs Gardner—is she also my friend?'

'I have known Mrs Gardner for exactly twenty-four hours. She is no more than an acquaintance.'

'I'm sure she'd be upset to hear you say so.'

'Why do you feel so hostile towards her? What has she done to you?'

Neumann said quietly: 'Since you ask me, nothing. And if I betray a certain . . . irritation, then it is because I am concerned about what she has done to you.'

Zweig was astonished. 'Why?'

Neumann placed his elbows on the table, and leaned forward.

'You have explained why you became a Christian. But you have not explained the other compromise. I think you know what compromise I am talking about. Mrs Gardner is a symbol of that compromise. A delightful woman, I can see. She admires your work. She admires you. She is anxious to give you all she can. . . .'

'Are you trying to suggest. . . .'

'I am suggesting nothing. No doubt you will develop a sincere platonic friendship. She will adore you. She will make sure that you are the guest of honour at all her dinner parties. She will read all your books and recommend them to her friends. But do you suppose she will understand a word you write?'

Zweig knew he should be angry, but it was impossible; he wanted to believe everything Neumann said. He shrugged.

'Very well. Supposing that is true. What has that to do with my ideas? I am an old man . . . and sometimes I feel as if I have not even started to work. Everything I have written seems a mere preparation for the real work. If Mrs Gardner is willing to offer me friendship, why should I reject it?'

'And her husband?'

'What are you talking about?' This time he allowed his irritation to appear.

'Her husband is Joseph Atholl Gardner, is he not? The author of *The True Story of Atlantis* and various other curious works.'

'I have no idea. I have not read them.'

'He is very popular in Germany. As you know, the Germans love strange ideas . . . Perhaps the two of you could write a book in collaboration. It would be a great success.'

Zweig said: 'If I wanted to, I would not ask your opinion.'

'I am sure.' Neumann began to stand up. Zweig said:

'Have you nothing else to say to me?'

'Nothing that would not increase your annoyance, Professor. But I will tell you one thing.' He paused, looking down at Zweig. 'Gerhardt Seyfert was suffering from a cancer of the stomach when he committed suicide.' He picked up his bill and slipped it into his pocket. 'I will now wish you good afternoon.' He bowed slightly, and walked away. Zweig stared after him, tempted to catch him up and ask another question. He was deterred by the curious stare of the waiter. When he saw Neumann walk into the revolving door of the hotel, he stood up and went out.

He knocked on Natasha Gardner's door. When there was no reply, he walked in. She was sitting by the window, looking into the street. When she turned, he saw that she no longer wore any make-up. The corners of her eyes looked red.

'Have you been crying?'

'It was nothing. For some reason, rude people always upset me. I get a lot of feelings I can't control, and then I want to kill them.' She smiled. 'What happened?'

'After you left? I was tempted to leave too. I'm not sure whether I did right to stay. . . .'

'Why?'

'I tried to get him to talk. He only fenced. Finally I told him that I had suspected him of killing Gerhardt Seyfert—the first old man.'

'What did he say?'

'Nothing. But before he left he said: "Seyfert was dying of a cancer when he committed suicide." '

'Do you believe him?'

'I don't know. It is obvious that he knows we are following him. He knows all about your husband's books too. I suppose Ferguson could have told him about that. But I can't understand his attitude. He said that I could search as much as I liked, but I wouldn't find anything.'

'How much did you tell him?'

'Nothing more. Nothing except my suspicion about Seyfert. For most of the time I was trying to explain my attitude to Christianity. I wanted him to talk. But he seemed to want information without giving any.'

She crossed to the mirror and looked at her face.

'I look awful. I haven't felt so furious and impotent for years. He's one of the most provoking men I've ever met.'

'I think he intended to be. I think he wanted to annoy us into giving him information.'

She applied a touch of lipstick to her mouth.

'There's one consolation anyway. He wouldn't dare to try anything with Tim now. At least it's out in the open.'

'I hope you are right.'

'I wonder if that policeman called on him this morning?'

'Yes. He mentioned it to me.'

'Then that explains why he came to the hotel. He probably saw Joseph and Sir Charles arrive at the cottage this morning, and came here to investigate.'

'But how could he leave without being seen?'

'That's easy enough. He said he came through Beyton. That means he turned to the right outside his cottage. They wouldn't be able to see him. . . .'

The ringing of the telephone startled them both. She said: 'I suppose that's Joseph.' Zweig noted with pleasure that she sounded almost resentful.

She listened for a moment, then said: 'It's for you. From London.'

'For me?' He took the phone. 'Zweig speaking.'

'Professor Zweig? This is Bert Colbright.'

'Who?'

'Colbright. Remember me? We met the other night.'

'Of course.'

'I was trying to get Sir Charles, but they say he's out. Lady Grey told me where you were staying.'

'Have you found anything?'

'Not really, but I've got a lead. I've found a bloke who met the secretary at the time of the Benskin case. Chap called Sams. He says he'd recognize him anywhere. The thing is, can you send me a photograph of Neumann?'

'I'm afraid that's impossible. They are in my flat in London. Who is this man?'

'He was the photographer on the *Maidstone Courier*—the bloke who took that photograph of the secretary.'

'Have you explained that Neumann has no beard?'

'Yes, but he thinks he could recognize a photograph all the same. Anyway, it's worth trying. Anything happening there?'

Zweig explained briefly about the lunch with Neumann. Colbright said: 'You'd better watch him. He sounds a slippery customer.'

Zweig promised to ring him back when Grey returned to the hotel. He hung up. Natasha Gardner was lying on the bed, her eyes closed. Zweig asked her:

'Tell me, what is meant by a slippery customer?'

She looked at him.

'Someone who is difficult to hold. Why?'

'He said Gustav was slippery.' He sat down beside her. 'I think he is mistaken. There is something strangely unslippery about Gustav.'

'How do you mean?'

Zweig said slowly: 'It is hard to explain. But he is like a man who knows his own mind. Today, for example, when I spoke to him . . . I felt he was concealing something from me . . . and yet not in the way that a criminal conceals something. In a way, he was laughing at me all the time.'

She said: 'I think I know what you mean.'

'Do you? Even though he made you so angry?'

'What made me angry was that I felt he wanted to be insulting. It was just as if he was poking me with a stick.'

Zweig was tempted to tell her what Neumann had said about her, then he changed his mind. Instead he said:

'I did not know that your husband's books were famous in Germany.'

'Oh yes. He gets translated into all kinds of languages.'

'Do they interest you?'

'I suppose so, but . . . I can never really tell whether he's serious. I don't mean that he's insincere. But he's so enthusiastic. He lets himself get carried away by things. I try to make him read your books.'

'Why?'

'Oh, to . . . to try to get him down to earth. No, I don't really mean that. To try to make him more serious.' She was staring past him, frowning slightly. She said: 'I don't suppose it matters so much now.' Zweig stared at her, and she smiled. 'I mean . . . you can talk to him.'

Outside, it was already becoming dark. He said: 'I should leave you now.'

'Why? What do you intend to do?'

'Work on my new book. I am writing a commentary on Heidegger's *Sein und Zeit*.'

'Then do it in here. I'm going to rest.'

When he returned from his room, carrying his brief-case, she had switched on the standard lamp; her dress was hanging over the back of a chair, and she lay under the eiderdown on her bed, one silk-stockinged foot protruding. She was already breathing quietly and regularly. Zweig took out his heavily marked copy of *Sein und Zeit* and his own manuscript, held together by a bulldog clip. The pages, scrawled with a ball-point pen, were covered with crossings-out, interjections, new sentences written sideways in the margin. He read through the final sheets, until he came to the last paragraph: 'In what sense can it be said that man possesses boundless freedom? He cannot fly through the air; he cannot dispel an illness by shrugging his shoulders; he cannot even dismiss tiresome obligations by simply turning his back on them. In what sense, then, does he possess more freedom than he realizes?' A calm yet intense joy took possession of him. His brain leapt forward like a horse that is released into a meadow after a long winter. He realized with pleasure that the five days since he had last looked at the manuscript had sharpened his perception of the problems, made his grasp on them firmer. The memory of Neumann became unimportant. A moment ago, the thought of Natasha lying there in her underclothes, covered only by an eiderdown, had disturbed him; now she might have been in another city; if the eiderdown had slipped off while she was asleep, Zweig would have replaced it without interest, and returned immediately to his work.

He began to write quickly, without pausing, leaning the manuscript on the arm of the chair. An hour later, when Gardner looked into the room, he was still writing, and Natasha was still asleep.

Zweig lifted his finger to his lip and tiptoed out of the room. He closed the door carefully behind him. Grey was on the other side of the corridor, knocking on Zweig's door.

Zweig asked: 'Have you seen him?'

Gardner grimaced: 'Yes.'

Zweig pushed open the door of his bedroom, and beckoned them in. He felt under no necessity to explain his presence in Natasha Gardner's bedroom; somehow, he felt that Gardner took it for granted.

'Where did you see him?'

Gardner sat on the bed.

'He called on us an hour ago. His taxi just pulled up in front of the cottage. Then he said he'd been talking to you. How much did you tell him?'

'Nothing.'

Grey said: 'He's a cunning devil. First he took us by surprise by walking straight into the cottage. I only just had time to get away from the window and hide the binoculars. Then, just as we thought it was a reconnaissance visit, he mentioned that he'd had lunch with you and Natasha. Did you tell him about me?'

'What about you?'

'Well, who I am?'

'No. Why?'

'He knew. Now where the devil did he learn that?'

Gardner said thoughtfully: 'That's not so difficult. *I* knew you were a friend of Zweig's long before I met you. Can't think how I knew. . . . It's been mentioned in a newspaper or something. . . .'

'I know,' Grey said. 'The cartoons! The cartoons in the club bar! They've been published in some glossy magazine.'

'I think you're right,' Gardner said. 'I seem to remember something of the sort.'

There was a tap at the door. Natasha looked in. She yawned as she came into the room, but Zweig observed that she showed no other sign of having slept for the past hour.

'May I have a cigarette? What are you talking about?'

'We're just starting to pool information.'

While Natasha stretched out on the bed, her back propped against the wall, smoking greedily as if it was her first of the day, Zweig gave a brief account of the meeting with Neumann. He ended by mentioning the call from Colbright.

Grey said: 'It looks as if it's time to take some kind of action. If Colbright can identify Neumann as the secretary in the Benskin case, I'm going to tell the whole story at Scotland Yard.'

Gardner looked worried.

'I'm not sure we've handled this too well. He may have beaten us.'

'I know,' Grey said.

'There's one consolation,' Natasha Gardner said. 'He won't dare to try anything on Tim.'

'No,' Grey said. He spoke without thinking, staring out of the window. Zweig felt himself compelled to walk across the room to relieve the tension of conflicting ideas, the need to speak of several things at once. But all he could say was:

'That's not certain.'

'But what did *you* make of him?' Grey asked. 'Did he strike you as normal?'

'In what way?'

'Do you think he might do something against Ferguson . . . out of a kind of bravado? I got the feeling that he *wanted* to annoy us, to snap his fingers in our faces. I've seen criminals like that. . . . They get caught. They're easy to catch because they're too confident. But they get caught after the crime, not before. . . .'

Natasha said: 'I don't think you're right. If he *is* a criminal, he's not that type. His insolence was a deliberate attempt to annoy us into giving something away.'

They sat in silence for a moment. The room was already full of smoke, and seemed stuffy. Grey asked:

'Do you want to try and contact Ferguson?'

'Why?'

'Because we've done all we can for the moment. Neumann knows we know, although I doubt whether he knows how much we know. There's nothing for us to do now but wait. Unless you want to see Ferguson and give him a hint of what we suspect.'

'But what are we supposed to be waiting *for*?'

'For Colbright to get here with this witness—the man who can identify Neumann. I'm going to phone Colbright now and ask him if he can take the next train here.'

'And suppose Neumann decides to get away tonight?'

Gardner looked at his watch.

'There's only one way to keep a check on that. He'll have to ring the station for a taxi, or get a car from the local car-hire firm. I'll go and make sure that we find out as soon as he tries to get either a taxi or a car. I'll go now.'

Natasha Gardner said: 'But I doubt whether he'd try to leave tonight. After all, it'd be almost an admission of guilt, wouldn't it?'

Gardner asked her: 'Do you think he's guilty?'

She closed her eyes, but the look on her face was one of concentration. After a moment, Grey said:

'I'm afraid your wife's guess is probably as good as ours.'

'No.' Gardner kept his eyes on her. 'Sometimes she has sudden insights into people. She's a medium.'

She opened her eyes, and seemed almost surprised to find them there. Gardner said: 'Well?'

'I don't know. I have never met anyone who baffled me so completely.'

Gardner said, laughing: 'If he baffles you, he must be complicated.'

Grey stood up.

'I'm going to phone Colbright.'

Zweig asked: 'And supposing he can't bring this photographer with him? What then?'

'Then . . . I don't know. You could return to London. I might have to come with you. But someone would have to stay and watch Neumann.'

'Joseph could stay,' Natasha said, 'and I could drive you back to London.'

They looked at Gardner. He shrugged and said: 'I'll do whatever you like.'

'First of all,' Grey said, 'I'll talk to Colbright.'

Zweig said: 'There is one more alternative.'

'What's that?'

'Let me go and see Gustav this evening.'

'What for? What good would that do?'

Zweig threw his cigar butt into the ashtray with a gesture that revealed all his impatience.

'It might give us something definite to go on. Look, let us be frank. Gustav knows that we suspect him of something. But he also knows that we have no evidence.'

'How can you be sure?'

'Because if we had evidence, the police would be asking him questions. You agree? Very well. And we have no evidence. What if this witness identifies him as the secretary in the Maidstone case? What does that prove?'

Grey said: 'That's true, Karl. But how do you know we can't find some evidence? If we got Interpol to work on the case, there's no telling what we might not discover. What do you suppose Neumann's been doing since the Maidstone case, nearly twenty years ago? He might have killed a dozen old men in that time. We've got to find out.'

'You may be right. But in the meantime, we have nothing to work on. Supposing I went to see him later this evening—alone.'

'He'd only pump you for information without telling you anything.'

'Yes. And supposing I gave him the information he wants? Supposing I told him everything. . . .'

'He'd be out of the country by this time tomorrow.'

'Would that matter? He cannot disappear, once the police start looking for him. Don't you see—*if* he ran away, *that* would be proof of his guilt. Where could he go? The police could easily check how he left the country and where he went.'

Grey walked towards the door; there was impatience in the movement. He said:

'Look, let me phone Colbright first. Then we'll discuss it afterwards.'

●

For Zweig, the evening passed with incredible slowness. Colbright had promised to ring them back when he could contact the photographer; it was after nine when he finally called, promising to arrive the following afternoon, bringing the witness. They spent the hour before dinner drinking in the lounge, but Zweig felt no desire to drink. He felt bored and tired. He had tried to write in his room, but found he had lost the thread of ideas. At supper, he drank a bottle of hock to himself; but for some reason, he remained sober and bored. His companions were beginning to exhaust him. They had all talked too much about Neumann, then found it difficult to speak with interest of anything else. In the presence of her husband, Natasha Gardner had little to say. After supper, Gardner suggested that he should drive to the cottage again to make sure that Neumann was still there. Zweig offered to go with him. Natasha and Grey stayed behind.

They drove slowly on the icy road. The snow had started to thaw, then froze. The wind blew steadily; its whining depressed Zweig, who sat hunched in the passenger seat, wishing himself back in his London flat.

Gardner said: 'You know, Karl—you don't mind if I call you Karl, do you?—I've got a theory about Neumann. He is what I would call a Wahima type.'

'A what?'

'Wahima. You remember my letter—the one I wrote you last year? I explained about it there. . . .'

'My memory is bad,' Zweig said. He had read only the first and last pages of Gardner's twenty-page letter.

'When I first went out to Africa in '28, I was out in Ruanda, near Lake Victoria. People are mostly Bantus, but the rulers are a race of giants called the Wahima—all about nine feet tall. Odd lot. Anyway, these Wahima were a murderous lot of bastards, and the Bantus revolted against their king—chap called Musinga, which is how I got mixed up in it. But these Wahima are a strange crowd. My own opinion is that they're part of the tertiary race.'

'I beg your pardon?'

'You know—the race of giants that preceded the human race. I wrote you all about it. Anyway, my point is that these people base their whole social system on cruelty. Not just ritual cruelty, like the Incas and Aztecs, but the real thing—absolute bloody sadism. Yet they're an intelligent lot, and I imagine their ancestors were probably absolute geniuses compared to us. Anyway, it struck me as soon as I met your friend Neumann—he's a Wahima type. Same shaped head, same cast of feature, same tallness. I've got an instinct about these things.'

'You think Gustav Neumann is a sadist?'

'Not exactly. But these people of the old races have got different standards from ours. They look on us as a lot of Yahoos . . . aha, they're still there.' They had passed through Kirkfield and were now at the top of the incline leading down to the cottages; the lights of Ferguson's cottage were clearly visible. 'I suppose we'd better go down and make sure though.'

As they passed the cottage, Zweig saw Neumann's silhouette cross the blind towards the kitchen. Gardner said:

'I'll turn the car further on—don't want to make 'em suspicious . . . As I was saying, everything you've told me about him convinces me that we're not dealing with the ordinary crook. Natasha, for example—she could smell an ordinary crook a mile off. This chap puzzles her.'

Zweig cleared his throat.

'Presuming you are right about Neumann—how do you imagine that a pair of respectable Jewish parents managed to produce a—er—Wahimi?'

'Wahima? That's simple. Nothing odd about that. The Jews also had an intermixture of the tertiary race. You'll find the Bible full of references to giants of an older race. Goliath must have been one of them. Samson too. Miscegenation, you see. . . .'

When they arrived back at the hotel, twenty minutes later, Gardner was talking in the full tide of enthusiasm, explaining to Zweig how his own theories of cosmic catastrophe differed from those of Hoerbiger and Bellamy, and how he had discovered the clue to his own version in the similarity between the Welsh and Hebrew languages.

Grey and Natasha were still drinking coffee. As Grey was about to stand up, Gardner said:

'You'll be interested in all this, Sir Charles. This is also detective work, but on a vast scale—and some of the evidence has been buried for millions of years.'

Zweig listened with bewilderment. There seemed to be so many flaws in Gardner's reasoning that it was not worth pointing them out. After half an hour of this, Grey said:

'I'm afraid all this is well over my head. I think I'm going to turn in.'

Zweig expected Natasha to go too; she had showed no interest in her husband's ideas; but she lit another cigarette, and stared at her fingernails.

Ten minutes later, when Gardner had gone out of the room, she asked:

'Tell me the truth. Is it all as stupid as it sounds to me?'

'Let me be frank with you,' Zweig said. He was relieved to have an opportunity to state his feelings. 'Your husband has a completely untrained mind.' He glanced at the door to see if Gardner was coming back, then said: 'We cannot even begin to talk constructively. As you know, I have no great respect for the academic tradition—but at least it guarantees a common language, a common approach. Now it seems to me that your husband is not an ungifted man. He reminds me of

the archaeologist Edward Thompson. Do you know of
Thompson? He was a brave man, a kind of visionary, and
his researches into Mayan culture were of enormous value.
But he was not a serious interpreter of all the things he
discovered—he had too much imagination. I am sure your
husband would be a great archaeologist . . .' He stopped,
feeling embarrassed, and also thinking that he heard Gardner
re-entering the room. When he realized they were still alone,
he asked: 'Do you understand?'

'Perfectly,' she said. She was smiling ironically. 'You mean
that Joseph is a crank?'

'I . . .'

'Come, you don't have to mince your words with me. I can
bear it.'

'Very well.' He drew a deep breath. 'Let me put it this way:
most of my colleagues would have no hesitation in calling
him a crank.'

'But you're not quite the same thing as your academic colleagues. Do *you* see anything in his ideas?'

Zweig squirmed; he wished that Gardner would interrupt
them. But when the silence made further delay impossible,
he said, almost angrily:

'I must be frank. I cannot . . . feel any sympathy for the
things he has explained.'

Having said it, he felt relieved. She asked:

'You're quite sure that he hasn't got hold of some important
idea? He's always telling me that his theories will shake the
academic world. Is that just a delusion?'

This time, Zweig could answer without embarrassment.

'Yes. I'm afraid it is.'

'Are you quite sure?'

For the first time since he had known her, he had to repress
a feeling of impatience. It seemed incredible that she should
be unaware that her husband's ideas were absurd. He said:

'Let me assure you that no reputable anthropologist would
consider your husband's ideas for a moment. I am not saying
that he is wrong. For all I know, some of his ideas may be
right. But if he stood in front of an audience of professors
and explained his ideas as he has explained them to me, they
would all demand that he should be certified insane.'

'I see. Thank you.'

They sat in silence, both smoking, waiting for Gardner's return. Finally, she said:

'May I ask you just one more thing? Will you have to avoid us when we get back to London?'

He knew what she meant. He said:

'I would hate to avoid you. But if I am to remain on friendly terms with your husband, I would have to tell him the truth. Otherwise it would be impossible.'

'Then why don't you do it now . . . when he comes back?'

He faced his inner-coldness for a moment, and his face twitched with involuntary revulsion.

'Not tonight. It would . . . take too long.'

He was almost relieved when Gardner came back into the room, even though his first words were:

'I wrote a long letter to Margaret Mead about my theory of the phallic trinity and got rather an interesting reply. . . .'

Natasha said:

'Could you tell Karl about it later, dear? I think he's rather tired?'

'Are you? I'm sorry. All right, I'll cut it short, but I'm sure this'll fascinate you. . . .'

Zweig listened gloomily, feeling as if he was frozen inside a block of ice. He started to light another cigar, then changed his mind; his throat felt sore. He nodded and grunted periodically to show he was listening, but this was as far as he could force his desire to be sympathetic. The question that kept presenting itself was: What on earth has all this to do with *my* ideas?

A point came where Gardner said: 'I wrote an essay on my interpretation of the stone men of Malacula. I wonder if you'd care to look at it? It's in my room now. . . .'

Natashà said: 'Why not give it to Karl now and let him read it overnight, dear? I can see he's tired.'

Her tone of concern, and the proprietary way she referred to him, gave him pleasure, particularly when Gardner said:

'That's an idea. I expect you must be tired. . . .'

Zweig stood up.

'I don't know why I should be. I seem to tire very easily when I'm away from home.'

'Quite. We'll have more of a chance to discuss these things in London. We're having a little party on the tenth if you'd care to come. . . .'

'Ask him later,' Natasha said firmly.

'If I am in London, I would be delighted to come,' Zweig said. 'Now I hope you'll excuse me if I follow the example of my friend Grey. . . .'

As he went upstairs he congratulated himself on the evasion. It would be easy enough to be in Oxford on the tenth. When he thought about Natasha Gardner, he felt disappointment; it was beginning to look as if her concern for him was partly the concern of a hostess who realizes that the big fishes have to be wound in carefully.

His room was stuffy with the smell of stale cigarette smoke. He opened the window and leaned out; the cold night wind was comforting. The light in the next window—Grey's room —was already out. The wind had dropped, and the ice of the street reflected the moonlight. Something about the moonlit rooftops brought a feeling of impersonality, freedom, a free- dom from the mental nausea that hovered on the edge of his consciousness. He heard Gardner's voice in the passageway, then heard their door close. On an impulse, he picked up his overcoat and went out of his room. He turned right, so as not to pass their door and risk having to explain why he was not yet in bed, and went down the staff stairway.

As he walked, the problem clarified itself in his mind, but this brought no comfort. He could not think of Neumann as fundamentally an enemy, any more than he could think of Gardner as fundamentally a friend. He walked slowly, staring at the ground, and realized that it had been many years since he had experienced this kind of conflict. Although it was still half an hour to midnight, the streets were empty. The wind seemed to come from empty spaces and moorland, a wind like a huge animal, an animal that would feel only contempt for human beings if it could ever become aware of them, the contempt of the unenclosed for the imprisoned, for men suffo- cating in the shell of the personality. This thought brought him no pleasure, only an increased awareness of his dis- satisfaction. He found himself thinking angrily: 'Why did I have to tell Grey?' Then realizing the futility of the self-re- proach.

He found himself standing opposite the station; there was a single taxi-cab drawn up there. Without thinking, without considering his motives, he walked towards it. The driver was smoking. He asked:

'Could you take me out to Kirkfield?'

'Sorry, guv. I'm here to meet a train. You could get a taxi if you ring up for one.'

'Thank you.' He turned away and walked back towards the hotel. Already the impulse to talk to Gustav was disappearing, melting away. When he thought about it, it was senseless; he had promised Grey not to talk to Neumann until Colbright's photographer had seen him. And yet he realized that if he had now been sitting in a taxi-cab, driving out towards the cottage, this thought would have been dismissed. Even Grey belonged to 'them'. Zweig realized, with mild surprise, that he was already making little distinction between Grey and Gardner.

As he walked upstairs, a clock struck midnight. He was no longer tired; moreover, he felt a sudden appetite for a glass of wine—a cold hock served in a big, round glass with a green stem, as it had been served in his favourite café in Heidelberg, or at a small village at the junction of the Rhine and the Moselle where a half-pint of excellent wine could be had for about sixpence. He wondered whether it would be permissible to phone the desk and ask for a bottle to be sent up.

As he walked along the corridor towards his door, Natasha Gardner came out of the bathroom; she was wearing a green quilted nightrobe and slippers. Zweig said apologetically:

'I have been for a little air.'

He paused at his door, fumbling for the key. She said:

'Good. I'll come in and talk to you.'

'Now? What about your husband?'

'He's asleep.'

'In that case,' Zweig said, 'I'm delighted.'

Her hair was slightly damp, and hung over her shoulders, giving her the look of a schoolgirl. She was carrying a bath towel, and swinging a blue plastic toilet case by its handle.

The room was icy; Zweig had left the window open. But the cigarette smell had been dissipated. He slammed down the window and drew the curtains. She asked:

'Have you got anything to drink?'

'I'm afraid not.'

'I've got some whisky. Shall I fetch it?'

'Wouldn't it wake up your husband?'

'That doesn't matter.' She went out. Zweig stood in front of the mirror over his washbowl, and rubbed the grey stubble on his chin with the flat of his hand. He looked at the old face that stared back at him and thought: No wonder she thinks of you as a father.

'He's still awake,' she said, 'but he doesn't want the whisky.' She ripped the leadfoil off the top of a bottle of Jamesons. Zweig washed out two tooth glasses and placed them on the table. He asked her:

'Where would you like to sit?'

'In the bed. My feet are cold.'

She kicked her slippers on to the floor and pulled back the coverlet of his bed. She said: 'Ooh, good! There's a hot-water bottle.' She propped the pillows behind her, and leaned back, pulling the bedclothes around her throat. Zweig poured whisky into both glasses.

'Water?'

'A lot, please.'

As he handed it to her, he asked:

'And supposing Joseph comes looking for you?'

'He won't mind. Why should he? But he won't come, anyway.'

'Does he trust you?'

'I think he trusts you.'

'Are you wearing anything under that robe?'

'Of course not. I've just got out of the bath.'

'And he doesn't mind you being in another man's room?'

'He'd mind most men. But not you. The only thing that worries him at the moment is why you wouldn't comment on his theory about the lost tribes of Israel.'

Zweig said: 'Hmmm!' He tied the cord of his own dressing gown, pushed his feet into his slippers, and relaxed in the armchair. The whisky tasted pleasant; he drank half of it in two swallows.

She said: 'Why are you so worried tonight?'

'You noticed?'

'It was obvious.'

He stood up, leaving his glass on the arm of the chair. There was a feeling of internal release. This was not the whisky, or even the sight of her face looming at him from behind the bedclothes. It was the return of his affection for her, the possessiveness, the certainty that he could talk to her. He felt no more physical desire for her than if she had been his daughter.

He said: 'To be frank, I am worried about Gustav. . . .'

'Why?'

'I feel as if we were. . . .'

She smiled, and said: 'Cats hunting a mouse?'

'In a way, yes. I feel as if . . . when I started all this, I started something that I did not foresee.'

'And you still feel that, even after meeting him today?'

'Yes. Even after today.'

'But why? He struck me as an unpleasant, cynical little man. And I don't think I'm prejudiced because he was rude. I felt the same about him last night, when he was perfectly polite.'

'You do not understand, Natasha. You are too young. . . .'

'Why? I'm thirty-two.'

'I mean you cannot understand the forces that can turn a man like Gustav into . . .' he shrugged, as if throwing off a weight on his shoulders, 'a nihilist.'

'Can't I?'

'You see, you would have to understand something about Germany after the first war. It seemed to many of us that the world had entered a new era. We were all pacifists. We saw the wreckage of Europe around us, but this seemed a guarantee that no one would ever dare to start another war. We all believed that Geneva would be the symbol of a new world of reason and co-operation. New universities were opening— like Hamburg and Frankfurt. My friend Ernst Cassirer went to Hamburg; I was at Frankfurt for a time before I moved to Heidelberg. Cassirer was like me; he also believed in the future age of reason and enlightenment. . . .'

He was sitting on the radiator, his back to the window; now he collected his whisky from the chair and held it beside him on the radiator. The need to make her understand was like a dynamo inside him.

'You must try to grasp that this was not the usual optimism of philosophers . . . everything will work out for the best. It was far deeper than that. Cassirer was a Jew. When he was younger, he was denied a university appointment because of his race. We felt that human kind is divided into two races, as distinct as cows and horses—on the one hand, the mindless brutes with their passions and prejudices, on the other hand, the men of learning, the men of the mind. Before 1914, we sometimes wondered if the men of learning would one day be murdered in an uprising of the brutes. Sometimes we despaired of human beings. They seemed too incredibly cruel and stupid to be worth saving. I knew that if I was God, I would destroy the race. And then came the war, and suddenly it was as if all the destruction had left men clean, purged of their evil. I remember an evening spent with Cassirer in Berlin, just before he went to Hamburg, when he told me of his idea of symbolic forms, and of how he thought that this would be a new key to philosophy, a bridge between art and science, the beginning of a new age. We talked all night, and we both saw a Europe like ancient Athens, but without the cowards and the assassins, without the corruption and petty nationalism. That was our faith, our belief. We all held it— Husserl and Jaspers and myself and Alois Neumann. There were some of us who thought that the war had been a kind of Armageddon for the human spirit, and that now there would be a new age of enlightenment. And then came Hitler. It was sudden and unbelievable, like the Vandals on Rome. And there was Spengler, with his message that the West is dying because civilization is like any flower that has to die. We could hardly believe it. The night was back again. It was as if all our faith had been the most childish kind of illusion, like a young girl's faith in a seducer. But you see, it was not so bad for us—for men like Cassirer and myself and Jaspers and Barth . . . at least we held a kind of spark of belief. The ones who were most badly hit were the very young, men like Gustav. They were told that the world was ready for reason and peace, that they could dare to be optimistic. It was worse for them, because they felt they had been betrayed twice— by the militarists, and by their teachers. Can you see now why some of them became nihilists, why they tried to tear out their deepest convictions by the roots?'

She nodded slowly. 'Yes. I *do* see. But how could it turn a man into a professional murderer?'

'I don't know. Who am I to judge? My own struggle was hard enough. It suddenly seemed to me that pity and love were the only values that could save the world, yet I mistrusted pity and love. Perhaps men like Gustav distrusted them too and tried to strangle them. I know that some of my students joined the Nazi party. One of them became a camp commandant who was sentenced to death at Nuremberg for the murder of forty thousand Jews. Another wrote a book in which he claimed that I am a Jew—which, as it happens, is untrue.'

She said: 'And tell me, did you want to go to Nuremberg to defend your pupil who murdered Jews?'

'Of course not.'

'Then why do you feel pity for Gustav Neumann?'

'Ah!' He smiled, and went to help himself to more whisky. 'That is not easy to answer, but I will try. Tonight, as I listened to your husband telling me his ideas about the lost tribes of Israel and Hindu phallic worship, I suddenly felt as I used to feel when I heard a Nazi quoting Alfred Rosenberg's arguments to prove that Jews and Negroes belong to a lower racial type, like monkeys.'

She looked startled. 'As bad as that?'

'Please forgive my frankness. I do not speak to you as Mrs Gardner. . . .'

'And I don't listen to you as Mrs Gardner.'

'Good. Then understand that I am not accusing your husband of the same degree of insanity as Streicher and Rosenberg. His ideas could hardly lead to extermination camps. And yet it suddenly came to me: By what values am I hunting Gustav Neumann? If the world were really divided into two races, the brutes and the philosophers, then a philosopher would have a right to condemn a brute who commits murder. Yet we have no evidence that Gustav has committed murder. And whether or not Gustav has ceased to be an idealist, he is certainly not a brute.' He paused, and took a slow sip from his glass. When he looked at her again, he was smiling apologetically. 'And your husband and Sir Charles Grey are certainly not philosophers.'

She asked: 'What do you want to do?'

Zweig said: 'I wanted to go and speak to Gustav tonight, before Colbright arrives. I want to give him a chance to answer me frankly. Do not forget: many years ago, when he had this mad idea of becoming a master criminal, he came to tell me about it. He did not see me as an enemy. But today, when he had lunch with us, I was an enemy. And perhaps that was my own fault. . . .'

'Even though he may be a murderer . . . ?'

'Yes. If Gustav is arrested and tried and executed, I would know that this was necessary, just as I knew it was necessary when Hermann Denke was executed at Nuremberg. And yet

I would always feel, in some way, that the guilt was partly my own, that I failed him as a human being. . . .'

'Then why don't you go . . . tomorrow morning?'

He said ruefully: 'I tried to go tonight. By the station, half an hour ago, I had a sudden impulse to take a taxi. Luckily, it was already engaged.'

'Would you like me to drive you there now?'

He knew she was serious, but he knew the idea was impractical.

'No, my dear. Not now.'

She threw back the bedclothes and stepped out of bed. The air of the room was now warmer. She came across to him in her bare feet.

'I don't quite understand you . . . but I'm beginning to.'

'Does it matter?'

'Oh yes. It matters.'

She stood beside him, her hands on the radiator, leaning forward. Although the gown had fallen open so that he could see the outline of her small breasts, he knew there was no coquettishness in her movement; for a moment, she was unaware of her nakedness. She said:

'You suddenly make me feel . . . stupid.'

'Stupid?'

'No, I don't mean that. I mean cheap, as if I've been throwing myself at you for the past twenty-four hours.'

He said with pleasure: 'Have you?'

'In a way, yes. I suppose all women have it in them—the predatory instinct, the desire to lay claim. But now you suddenly make me feel . . . I can't explain it. As if I was trying to claim a gold mine. I don't really understand your philosophy. I try to. I'd like to. But a lot of it's above my head. And now you suddenly make me feel . . . like a cheap little flirt.'

'Good heavens, no!' He was genuinely shocked.

She glanced down, noticed the outline of her breasts, and quickly buttoned up the robe. He said:

'My dear Natasha, please believe me when I say . . . that I have enjoyed the past twenty-four hours very much indeed. Far more than I could tell you. I wouldn't in the least mind being appropriated by you. Although I can hardly believe that your husband wouldn't mind. . . .'

'He wouldn't.'

'Then please go ahead and appropriate me.'

'Do you mean that?'

'Of course.'

He let her take his hand, but was startled when she raised it to her mouth and kissed it. He said: 'No.' She said, smiling: 'All right,' and kissed him at the side of the mouth. She said: 'Ooh, you're prickly.'

Zweig found himself looking into the mirror over the top of her head, looking at his own lined face and thinking: 'Perhaps I shall have ten years more. Perhaps even longer.'

She said: 'I'd better go and let you sleep.'

He wanted to restrain her, but knew it was pointless. So he said instead:

'Yes, I feel tired now. Thank you for the whisky.'

'I'll leave the bottle here. Good night, Karl.'

'Good night, Natasha.'

When the door had closed, he drew back the curtains and looked again into the street. His face was burning and his eyes felt tired. Before climbing into bed, he looked again at his face in the mirror and said slowly: 'You stupid old man.' Then he felt the warmth that her body had left behind, and let it blend with him until the warmth and his own consciousness were both transformed into sleep.

At breakfast the next morning, Grey said:

'I think we'd better get back to the cottage today.'

Natasha asked: 'Is there any point?'

Gardner said: 'I think so. To begin with it's our cottage anyway. Don't you want to see it?'

She smiled. 'Not in this weather. And not without furniture.'

'All the same, I'd think we better stay there. If we don't bother to go, it'll confirm his suspicion that we were spying on him yesterday.'

The day was grey and cold; the weather forecast spoke of more snow. As they drove towards the cottage she said: 'I'm beginning to hate this place. I shall be glad when we can get back to London.'

'That should be later today, if it doesn't snow too heavily.'

The dampness of the living-room seemed even colder than the east wind outside. The cottage had thick, whitewashed walls, and all its doors were too low. It had obviously been two labourers' cottages converted into one. The floor of the living-room was covered with a coarse coconut matting. Natasha sat in the only armchair, hugging herself and looking miserable. Grey looked at the bottom of the garden and found a rotten tree trunk; when Gardner broke it in two with a blow of a hatchet, a colony of black beetles moved out sluggishly. The men dragged big sections of log into the living-room and hurled them into the fireplace, which was nearly six feet wide, and soaked them in paraffin. The resulting fire was so hot that they had to stand halfway across the room.

From the window, Grey said:

'There's no sign of smoke from their chimney. Of course, that doesn't mean much. They've got electric fires there.'

In the firelight, Natasha had suddenly regained her energy, and was looking into the next room. She called:

'Did you two leave this door unlocked?'

'There's no lock,' Gardner said. 'But it latches inside so you can't open it.'

'Well someone's left it open.'

Gardner and Grey went in to look. The wooden latch of the door was in its raised position, so that the door could be opened from the outside by pushing.

'Somebody's been in,' Grey said. 'I checked that door before we left yesterday. See any footprints outside?'

Gardner was looking at the path outside the door.

'There's nothing here. But if he walked close to the house he could avoid the snow. Look.'

The overhang of the roof, and the wall of a toolshed, had prevented the snow from covering the path round the side of the house.

Grey tried the latch.

'It's pretty stiff. He probably banged the door when he left and thought it had fallen back into position. Look, here's the mark of a knife where he forced it open.'

Gardner said: 'He didn't find anything anyway. I wonder what he was looking for?'

Natasha called plaintively: 'I wish you'd come in and close the door. You're letting all the heat out.'

Grey said: 'That man certainly doesn't let the grass grow under his feet, does he?'

Gardner said thoughtfully: 'I'd like to get a look inside their cottage. . . .'

Zweig had taken a seat at the table, and was reading through his manuscript. The visit to the cottage struck him as a waste of time, but he had been unwilling to suggest staying behind at the hotel with Natasha again. He had decided to make the best of it, and spend the morning revising his book. He said, smiling:

'Gustav is probably in your room at the hotel at the moment, going through your papers.'

'That's O.K. by me. I've nothing to hide.' Gardner was again standing by the window, looking through the binoculars. He said suddenly: 'Hello.'

'What is it?'

'Damn! There's a taxi stopping outside their cottage. I wonder if they're leaving.'

All four of them hurried to the window and stared across the field. Grey said:

'It'll be a nuisance if they are. Colbright will curse.'

Gardner said: 'If they leave with the luggage, I'll follow them in to the station. I'll find out where they're going, anyway.'

Grey had taken the binoculars from him. He said:

'I don't think they intend to take the luggage. The driver's waiting in the cab. If they meant to take their cases, he'd be helping them out with them.'

'Then what the devil are they up to?'

'Here they come,' Grey said. 'And they haven't got luggage.'

'Both of them. Good. As soon as the cab gets out of sight, I'm going to have a look in their cottage.'

Grey went back to the fire and threw the twisted root of the tree into the flames. He said:

'I don't understand. He *knows* we're here, because he can see the smoke, and the car's parked outside. So he must know that we'll try to take a look in the cottage.'

Gardner said: 'Come on, Natasha, let's go out to our car and get them to stop.'

'But why?'

'I want to make sure that Tim's still all right.'

They went out of the cottage, leaving the front door open. Zweig and Grey stood watching them from a window. As the taxi drew level with the parked car Gardner waved it to a stop. The back window was lowered and an old man looked out. They heard him calling: 'Hello there, Joe, you old rascal. What are you doing?'

Zweig said: 'He sounds healthy enough to me.'

Gardner was standing at the window of the taxi talking. After a moment he stepped back and waved; the taxi drew away. Natasha came back into the room, and held out her hands to the fire.

'He looks perfectly well. They are going to do some shopping in Bury St Edmunds.'

Gardner followed her in.

'It all seems innocent enough. They're going in for shopping and some lunch. Shall we go and take a look at the cottage?'

Grey shrugged.

'I think you'd better go alone. I don't think it'd do for an ex-commissioner of police to get arrested for unlawful entry.'

'I will go too,' Zweig said.

They looked at him in surprise.

'Why?'

'For no particular reason. I would like to take a look at Gustav's belongings.'

'If we can get in,' Gardner said. 'If I remember rightly, both doors have got pretty formidable locks. Come on, then.'

Grey said: 'If I see any sign of the taxi returning suddenly, I'll give a blast on the car horn. But you won't have much chance of getting away without being seen, I'm afraid. So you'd better have a good excuse ready.'

They tramped along the centre of the road, so as to leave no footprints. Gardner said:

'I wouldn't be surprised if he returned suddenly, pretending he'd left something behind, just to catch us in the cottage.' He chuckled. 'I can see the headlines: "Well-known professor jailed for burglary." '

Fifty yards beyond Ferguson's cottage stood another cottage; smoke came from its chimney. Gardner said:

'That's the caretaker's cottage. We'll just have to risk being seen from there. Luckily I know the man pretty well, so I could probably keep him quiet if necessary.'

The pathway to the front door of the cottage had been newly cleared; the snow had been piled on either side. Gardner pushed open the gate. He said:

'Looks as though he didn't want us to leave footprints, doesn't it? That's useful.'

They stopped outside the window.

'We might as well try the doors first. I don't suppose they've left them open, but . . . I'll be damned.'

The front door opened as Gardner pushed it. They both looked apprehensively into the room. Gardner knocked on the door and called: 'Anybody home?' When there was no reply, he beckoned Zweig in. They kicked the snow off their shoes against the wall, and carefully wiped their feet on the doormat. Gardner said: 'This begins to bother me. It looks too easy.'

Zweig found himself in a warm and comfortable living-room. An electric fire burned in the empty fireplace. The heavy grey carpet felt pleasant under his feet. It was obvious that a great deal of money had been spent on the cottage; the furniture was new and modern.

'Let's take a look upstairs first. We'd better hurry in case the caretaker spotted us.'

There were two rooms upstairs, their doors facing one another on either side of the staircase.

'You look in there,' Gardner said, 'I'll look in this one.'

Zweig realized he was in Sir Timothy Ferguson's bedroom. There was a cigar butt in the ashtray, and decanter of whisky on the bedside table. The leather suitcase on the table bore the initials 'T.F.'

Zweig unzipped the suitcase and glanced inside. It contained a soiled shirt and two crime paperbacks. He went systematically through the drawers, repressing his distaste. Gardner called: 'Any luck?' and he called: 'None so far.' As he spoke his hand encountered a box at the back of a drawer. He opened it and found a hypodermic syringe. He called Gardner, then unscrewed it and sniffed it. It had no smell. Gardner said:

'That's interesting, but it doesn't tell us much. Can you find any capsules or pills?'

'No. I've been through all the drawers.'

Gardner opened the wardrobe and rummaged inside. He said:

'There's nothing, as far as I can see . . . nothing at all.'

Zweig went into the other bedroom. It was similar to Ferguson's, but less comfortable. There was a suitcase on the floor, and a pair of pyjamas on the bed; otherwise, the room was completely anonymous.

He opened the wardrobe. It contained a suit and two pairs of shoes. When he closed the door, the suit caught in it, and he had to wrench it open again. As he did so, something slipped from the top of the wardrobe and fell behind. Zweig peered into the gap, and saw that it was a book. He eased the wardrobe forward, and reached in for it. The title was in German: *Das Hypnotische Verbrechen und Seine Entdeckung.* Zweig dropped it on to the bed, found a chair, and looked on top of the wardrobe. There was another book and several magazines. The magazines were issues of the *Monatschrift für Kriminalpsychologie und Strafrechtsreform,* with dates between 1936 and 1938. The book was Hollander's *Psychology of Misconduct, Vice and Crime.*

Gardner came in. He said: 'Hello, what've you got there?' Zweig held out the book.

'Hypnosis? Where did you find that?'

'On top of the wardrobe.'

'Well, I'll be damned.' He opened the flyleaf, the signature read: 'G. Neumann, Copenhagen, 1958.' Gardner indicated the magazines. 'What's all this stuff?'

'I believe it's the bulletin of an institute for criminal psychology. I found these books, too.'

'What's it mean? I don't speak German.'

'The Hypnotic Crime and its Detection.'

'I don't understand.' Gardner sat down on the bed and glanced into the volume. 'This is pretty old—1889.'

Zweig could follow the thought process. He said: 'Quite. We now know that hypnotic crime is impossible.'

'In that case . . . what's Neumann doing with such cranky stuff?'

'What is more to the point—why did he leave it on top of the wardrobe?'

'You think he wanted to hide it? Why should he?'

Zweig was looking through the magazines. He said: 'Ah, look! These contain articles by Gustav.'

'On what?'

'This one is called "An Examination of the Evidence in the Sala Case".'

'What's that?'

'I am trying to find out.'

They heard the sound of a car engine outside. Both of them ran to the window. It was a red post office van, and it had stopped at the next cottage.

Gardner said: 'If they returned now, we'd be caught here. There's no way to get away without being seen.'

'Do you think we should go?'

'It might be an idea. . . .'

'Give me a few minutes more. I want to look at this.'

'All right. I'll take a look downstairs.'

When Gardner returned, ten minutes later, Zweig was still reading.

'Anything interesting?'

'Very interesting. Very strange indeed.'

'It is important? We ought to leave.'

'No. I can probably find it in the British Museum or the Psychological Institute. I am ready to go.'

Zweig stood on a chair and replaced the books on the wardrobe, while Gardner smoothed the bed.

'Did you find anything downstairs?'

'Only this.' He held up a small glass ampoule. 'It was in the waste bin. It probably contained the stuff used in the hypodermic. It looks empty, but a chemist might be able to tell us what it contained.'

He looked out of the window.

'Nobody about. We'd better go.'

'It's a pity. I would like to spend a few hours in here. I would like a chance to read these things thoroughly.'

Gardner did not speak again until they were walking back along the road.

'Why did you say it was interesting?'

'Because Gustav's article was about the case of a man who used hypnosis to control a gang of criminals. It took place in Sala, in Sweden, in 1936. In another issue of the magazine, he had written another article about a case of criminal hypnosis that took place in Heidelberg in the same year—a case in which a woman was hypnotized without her knowledge, and then turned into a thief and a prostitute by the hypnotist.'

'Are you sure it's possible? It sounds like a fairy-story to me.'

'I must admit that I find it incredible. On the other hand, the *Monatschrift* is a perfectly reputable publication.'

They walked on in silence for a moment, then Gardner asked:

'It is possible?'

'It seems to be.'

'That's not what I mean. You know what I'm getting at.'

'I know. That is what I have been asking myself ever since I looked at the article.'

They had arrived at the door of the cottage. Grey opened it for them.

'Any luck?'

'We don't know.' Gardner placed the ampoule on the table. 'I found that in the waste bin. It may be nothing.'

Natasha said: 'He used to have injections of some sort for hormone deficiency.'

'I know. There's one other thing. . . .'

Zweig said: 'I found some books and magazines on top of the wardrobe. They all dealt with crime and hypnosis. Gustav had written several articles on the subject.'

Gardner asked Grey: 'Have you ever come across any cases of hypnosis in your police work?'

'Only once. A case in which a doctor seduced one of his patients under hypnosis. His defence claimed that she wanted to be seduced, because you can't make a hypnotized person do something she wouldn't do when awake.'

'That's what *I* said.'

Zweig said: 'According to Gustav's article, a hypnotist in Sweden made a man commit suicide under hypnosis.'

There was a silence. Then Natasha said: 'My God!' Her voice was almost inaudible.

'Is there any proof that this took place?'

'According to Gustav's article, it was a man who controlled a whole gang of criminals by hypnosis. You could easily get the records from the Sala police. The hypnotist was having a homosexual relationship with one of the gang, and at this time, homosexuality was punishable by law in Sweden. He was afraid the man might talk about it, so he hypnotized the man into shooting himself.'

Gardner sat down in the window seat. He said:

'I don't know about you, but I need something to drink. Natasha, pass me the whisky.'

Grey said: 'I think we could all do with some.' Natasha opened a hamper that had been packed by the hotel, and took out a bottle of whisky and four glasses. She poured some into a tumbler and handed it to her husband, who drank it in one gulp.

Grey said: 'Look here, we've got to be calm about this. Frankly, it all sounds improbable to me. To begin with, I've always been taught that nobody can be hypnotized against his will. All that stuff was exploded a long time ago.'

'Svengali and all that,' Gardner said.

'I don't know much about psychology, but I *can* remember what was said in court in this Marchmont case—the man who raped the woman under hypnosis. The man only got six months. And that was because the court believed that it wasn't really a case of rape at all. In other words, the woman would have allowed herself to be seduced whether she was hypnotized or not. She allowed herself to be hypnotized because it gave her an excuse for infidelity to her husband. Now you're not going to tell me that a man could be hypnotized into blowing out his brains. . . .'

'Unless he already wanted to commit suicide,' Gardner said. 'Quite.'

Zweig said: 'I quite agree with you. It is true that Freud disproved the whole notion that a hypnotist can gain power over an unwilling subject. But in these cases that Gustav quotes, I am not sure how far the subjects were unwilling. The man who committed suicide received "a long course of suggestion." Those are the words Gustav uses. I have no doubt that a stage hypnotist, for example, could not persuade someone to attempt suicide in front of an audience. But if the hypnotist lived in close proximity to the victim, he would be in a position to begin a "long course of suggestion," particularly if the subject trusted him completely.'

Gardner was walking up and down the room. He said excitedly:

'My God, it *is* possible. Why didn't Neumann want to be know as Tim's doctor?'

Grey said patiently: 'I think we're letting speculation run away with us. All we've found is a number of books about crime and hypnosis. We know Neumann to be interested in psychology, and also in crime. This doesn't prove that he's been committing murders by hypnosis.' He asked Zweig: 'Is there anything in these articles to suggest that Neumann himself was experimenting with hypnosis?'

'No. Nothing at all.'

'Do *you* know whether he ever tried to practise hypnotism?'

'Not as far as I know.'

'Well, I'm inclined to disbelieve it. I think he deliberately left those books there as a red herring.'

'In that case, why should he hide them?'

'Where were they hidden? On the wardrobe? Isn't that a pretty obvious place to hide anything? If he really wanted to hide them, why didn't he put them under the mattress of his bed? Or outside in the woodshed?'

Natasha Gardner said: '*I* don't think Tim looked as if he'd been hypnotized. I thought hypnotized people had dead eyes, like a fish.'

'Not necessarily.' It was Zweig who spoke. 'He need not be under hypnosis all the time. But all the same, I am inclined to agree. It sounds incredible to me. On the other hand, it would certainly explain some very curious features.'

Natasha said: 'Come and eat.' She had unpacked the hamper on the table; it contained two cold pheasants, a bottle of burgundy, and some fruit. They pulled up stools round the table. Gardner was looking flushed from the whisky. He said:

'The trouble is that *if* he made the old men commit suicide by hypnosis, there's no chance of ever convicting him.'

'That's not quite true,' Grey said. 'On the contrary, if the circumstantial evidence was strong enough, then the hypnosis theory might be the last link in the chain. As Karl says, it would explain everything. Take this case of the old man in Switzerland, what's his name . . .'

'Gerhardt Seyfert.'

'Well, according to the evidence you explained, Neumann couldn't have murdered him because he had the perfect alibi. But he might have persuaded him to commit suicide.'

'How could you prove it in court?' Gardner asked, his mouth full of pheasant.

'That wouldn't be absolutely necessary. In the Brides in the Bath case, no one proved that Smith drowned his wives. It was circumstantial evidence. But as I say, I don't really believe that Neumann's a hypnotist. I can't explain why. It just doesn't smell right to me.' He filled his glass with wine, and sipped it appreciatively. 'Tell me, did you have any difficulty getting into the place?'

'None at all.' Gardner stopped eating, frowning at his plate. 'I see what you mean. I was a bit surprised to find everything so easy. On the other hand, why should they bother to lock the door? There's no one around here who might break in, and their caretaker lives next door.'

Grey said: 'This hypnosis theory is a good idea to work on.

It strengthens the case. We could probably check through Interpol to find out if Neumann ever practised as a hypnotist. But I don't think this case is going to depend on the answer.'

Natasha asked: 'What do you think it depends on?'

'To begin with, whether this photographer can identify Neumann as Bernstein. If he does, I shall be convinced we're on to something.'

'What time is Colbright arriving?'

'At two fifteen—an hour from now.'

'How do you propose to let him see Neumann?'

'Quite simple. By calling on Sir Timothy and taking the photographer with me. Or by getting you to take him.'

Zweig said: 'I would like to go to the British Museum as soon as possible, and check on these books of Gustav's. I would like a chance to read them carefully before I make up my mind on this question of hypnotism.'

'Will they have the books there?' Natasha asked.

'They should have. If not, I can probably locate them at the Psychological Institute.'

'I'll tell you where you could locate them,' Grey said. 'At the house of John Stafford-Morton. He has an enormous library on the psychology of crime.'

Zweig grimaced. 'I would prefer not to trouble him.'

'All right. But I think you're making a mistake. He's an excellent man. *I* shall go to see him about this hypnotism theory.'

Zweig smiled, but said nothing.

●

Two hours later, Zweig and Grey stood together on the station platform watching the London train steam in. It had started to snow again, and Zweig felt depressed; the train was an hour late and he was cold. Gardner had said that if the snow continued it would be impossible to return to London later that day.

'Here he comes,' Grey said.

Colbright waved to them from the other end of the platform. He was accompanied by a small man with a toothbrush moustache and the appearance of a provincial bank manager. Colbright called cheerfully:

'Gor, what a journey! Hello, Professor, how are you?' He shook hands briskly. 'We couldn't even get a bottle of beer on the flippin' train.'

'Come and have one at the hotel.'

'Good idea. This is Terry Sams, who's a photographer.'

'It's very kind of you to come all this way,' Grey said, shaking hands with the little man. Mr Sams grinned..

'It's a pleasure. Bert's done me a few favours in his time.'

As they walked back to the hotel, Grey explained briefly about their plans, with a minimum of detail. Colbright asked:

'You mean you intend to knock on the door, just like that, and bring the two of 'em face to face? Isn't it a bit risky? I mean, if he recognizes Terry, he'll know the 'ounds are getting a bit close.'

'There's not much he can do. If he tries to leave the country, I could have him pulled in for questioning.'

Zweig asked Mr Sams: 'Do you think he will recognize you?'

'I dunno. Might not. That's why I'm wearing my Sunday get-up. That was Bert's idea. I used to dress . . . a bit carelessly in the old days.'

It was Zweig who saw Natasha crossing the street to intercept them. She looked excited, and was waving to attract their attention. Zweig followed her glance, and recognized Neumann and Sir Timothy Ferguson standing outside the hotel. Neuman was waving his umbrella at a taxi. She said:

'Thank God you've come. They've been having lunch in the hotel.'

Grey gripped Colbright's arm.

'Quick. Get over there with Mr Sams and see if you can get a look at him before he gets into the taxi.'

They could no longer see Neumann; the taxi had stopped in front of him. Sams and Colbright ran across the street towards it. Zweig said:

'Too late. They're getting inside.'

'It's not,' Grey said. Sams had grabbed the outside door of the taxi and pulled it open. He was talking to someone inside. A moment later, he withdrew his head and slammed the door again. The taxi started forward immediately. They hurried across the road to rejoin the two men in front of the hotel. Sams was chortling with pleasure.

'That's him all right. I couldn't mistake him.'

'Are you sure?'

'Absolutely certain. I pretended I thought the cab had stopped for me and started to get in. Then I saw him, and said: "Oh, sorry, is this your taxi?" and he said: "Yes, I'm afraid I rang up for it from the hotel." As soon as he spoke, I knew him. So I dodged out quick.'

'Do you think he recognized you?'

'I don't know. I doubt it though. After all, I'm not exactly the sort of bloke you'd recognize after twenty years, am I? 'Specially in this get-up.'

'Good man!' Grey said. 'That was a splendid piece of quick thinking. Luck's really on our side. You're *quite* sure it's Bernstein?'

'Absolutely one hundred per cent. He looks a bit different without the beard, but I can tell his voice anywhere. Reminds me of my dad's favourite actor a bit.'

'Come and have a drink. You deserve it.'

Zweig asked: 'What happened?'

'It was absurd. We didn't want lunch, of course—after the meal at the cottage—so we didn't go into the dining-room. Otherwise we'd have seen them having lunch. Luckily, Joseph came down to see if there was any mail, and heard the desk clerk ringing for a taxi in Tim's name. So he went to try and hold them in conversation while I came rushing out to look for you.'

Gardner was standing in the hall; he called: 'Any luck?'

Grey nodded. 'It's him all right. Come on, let's go and get a drink. I need one.'

'There's plenty in our room. I've ordered sandwiches too. That Neumann's a rude beggar, isn't he? I did my best to keep them in conversation but he practically walked through me.'

They were all feeling elated. Gardner poured whiskies, then said: 'Here's to success.' Only Zweig, standing by the window, did not raise his glass. He realized that Natasha was watching him. She came over, holding out the plate of chicken sandwiches; as he took one, she said quietly:

'Are you sorry about it?'

Zweig smiled. The talk in the room made their voices inaudible. He said:

'I am not sorry. I already knew that Gustav was the secretary at Maidstone.'

'You did? How?'

As Gardner approached them, he said:

'I will tell you later.'

Gardner said: 'Well, my love, you'll spend tonight in London after all.'

'Why?'

'Grey wants to get back to see Scotland Yard. And I'm going back to Maidstone with Colbright to see what I can dig up.'

'But what about Tim and Neumann?'

'Neumann can't get away now. Grey's going to get the local police to report to Scotland Yard if he tries to leave. Anyway, he couldn't get far. And I don't think Tim's in any danger now, Neumann wouldn't dare.'

When Gardner had moved away again, she asked:

'Aren't you pleased to be returning to London?'

'Yes, I am pleased. But . . . I cannot share this emotion.' He indicated the others; Colbright was helping himself to more whisky and beaming cheerfully at Sams; Grey and Gardner were talking animatedly. 'Your husband finds all this exhilarating. He would have made an excellent detective. As to me, I cannot stop thinking. . . .'

'About Gustav?'

'About everything.'

Sams approached them.

'Professor, I wonder if you'd do me a little favour? My wife wants your autograph.'

'With pleasure.' Zweig groped for his fountain pen.

As he wrote his name across a pink, scented page, Sams leaned his head closer.

'There's just one more thing. If we've got time before we leave, I'd like to get a photograph of you and Sir Charles.'

'Of course. But why?'

'Well . . . you know . . . it might come in useful. I wouldn't use it until I got the O.K. from you, of course. But when this story breaks, it'll be nice to have the scoop. Big 'eadline: Professor Zweig turns Detective. It'll be quite a piece of publicity, won't it?'

Zweig was startled. 'But you mustn't misunderstand . . . I had very little to do with it.'

'Really?' Sams stared back with raised eyebrows. 'That's not what Bert Colbright told me. He said you put 'em on to it.'

'Yes, but . . . that was all.'

'That's all right, Professor.' Sams winked. 'A bit of the right kind of publicity never did anybody any harm. Look, the sun's comin' out. Let's get that picture while the light's good.'

●

Zweig sat in the back seat between Natasha and Grey. Sams and Colbright were next to the driver. Both were in a cheerful mood, and talked noisily while they passed the bottle of whisky between them. Zweig was glad of Natasha's warmth against him—they shared a travelling rug—but felt in no mood to talk. He also kept his hands on top of the rug, knowing that if he put them underneath, Natasha would take his hand; his unwillingness was not a feeling of guilt about Gardner or Grey, but a more complicated emotion.

She said: 'You're very quiet.'

'I am thinking about my book.' He made the excuse because he was aware Grey was listening.

Grey asked: 'What will you do this evening?'

'Very little. Probably have a meal at the club, then go to bed. And you?'

'I'm going to see Blaydon at the Yard as soon as we get in. He's the Interpol man.'

When they passed through Chelmsford, Colbright was asleep. Gardner switched on the radio; a blast of Wagner came out. She felt Zweig stiffen against her, and she looked up.

'Don't you like Wagner?'

'On the contrary . . . he used to be my favourite composer.'

'Mine too. It's the "Rheingold," isn't it?'

The full orchestra gave out the Thunderstorm motif, rising

to a noisy climax that made the radio crackle. Gardner said over his shoulder:

'He's not really my cup of tea. Too bloody noisy and German . . . if you'll excuse my saying so, Professor.'

'Not at all. I am an Austrian.'

They listened in silence until the announcer said: 'That extract from the last act of Wagner's "Rheingold" was recorded at Bayreuth last year. . . .' Gardner said:

'I think everybody has a Wagner phase. I used to like him when I was eighteen.'

Natasha said: 'I still like him.' She looked at Zweig, as if hoping for him to defend her taste. He was looking past her, into the darkness. When he spoke, it was as if he had not heard them.

'We had a society in Göttingen—a Nietzsche society—in 1910. Half a dozen of us used to meet and talk about the superman. We had piano scores of all Wagner's operas, and Alois and I used to start the meetings by playing bits of Wagner as a piano duet. . . .'

'I didn't realize you could play the piano.'

'I have not played for many years.' Colbright snorted suddenly, stared at them with surprise, then closed his eyes again and leaned his head against Zweig's shoulder. 'Our favourite piece was that storm music from "Rheingold".'

'Nothing like a bit of old Gilbert and Sullivan,' Sams said. He began to sing: 'Oh my name is John Wellington Wells. . . .' He beat time with the empty whisky bottle. Zweig felt Natasha's hand move across the blanket and take his. Colbright snored gently.

●

Zweig had telephoned the caretaker before they left the hotel; when he arrived back home, fires had been lighted in the study and sitting-room. Gardner had dropped him at the end of Clarges Street at seven thirty.

He threw his coat over the settee, poured himself a sherry, and sat in front of the fire. The flat seemed somehow different, more silent and empty than he remembered it. He thought with regret of Natasha Gardner. He knew that Gardner intended to drive Sams back to Maidstone, and that she expected him to ring her and spend the evening with her. He had already decided not to do so. This was not because he was any longer concerned that Gardner might feel jealous; the past two days had convinced him that nothing was less likely. It was the fear of being caught up in something that might lead nowhere. His increasing dependence on her worried him, and his attempts to be completely honest with himself were not reassuring. It was true that he felt no physical desire for her; but it would be equally absurd to pretend that the basis of his feeling for her was not sexual. Neumann had talked about 'platonic friendship' and implied that she wanted to capture Zweig to show off at her dinner parties. He no longer believed this; for some reason—he could only guess at it—she was as infatuated with him as he was with her. But it could lead to nothing; he was too old to become her lover, and too afraid of getting hurt; and there was no question of Natasha leaving her husband. Every aspect of their relationship baffled him. And yet he still felt the warmth of her body against him, and the touch of her hand in his, and was tempted to lift the phone and dial her number.

He drank the last of the sherry, pulled on his overcoat, and went out. Halfway down the stairs the telephone started to ring; he hesitated, half turned, then hurried on down the stairs. At the door, he told the porter: 'If anyone calls, I shall be at the club.'

Once inside, he felt better. Members waved and nodded to him. He went straight to the dining-room and ordered another sherry. The head waiter said: 'Nice to see you back again, Professor.'

'It's pleasant to be back.'

Suddenly he felt happier. He had decided to drink Perrier water with his meal, but he now changed his mind and ordered a half bottle of hock.

'I can recommend the salmon today, sir.'

'Good. Then I'll have salmon. With anchovy butter.'

He stared around the dining-room as he sipped his sherry, and reflected that a man's life is less complicated without a woman. The past three days now seemed shadowy, as if they had taken place many weeks ago. His manuscript was waiting at home, still in his suitcase; he would go back and do a few hours' work before going to bed—removing the phone from its rest in case Natasha should ring. A chapter on the full significance of the natural standpoint . . . He snapped his fingers at a passing waiter. 'Another sherry, please.'

He had reckoned without the hock. At half past nine he took his coffee and the latest philosophical quarterly into the smoke room, and found his favourite armchair unoccupied. He read halfway through an article on Teilhard de Chardin, but found his attention gliding over the sentences, declining to grapple with their abstract complexity. He closed his eyes to consider a particularly difficult statement, and fell asleep.

The voice that woke him was saying: 'Excuse me, Professor. You've dropped your magazine.' He tried to remember where he had seen the man before. Something about the narrow face made him think of unpleasantness. He took the magazine, saying: 'That is kind of you. . . .'

'Stafford-Morton. Remember me?'

'Of course.'

'Do you mind if I have a word with you?'

Zweig sat up and polished his glasses in an attempt to throw off the sleep. He asked:

'Are you a member of this place?'

'No. I've been having dinner with a colleague. But I guessed I'd find you here. Sir Charles Grey rang me a few hours ago.'

Zweig said stiffly: 'I see.' Now he was fully awake, he felt less vulnerable.

'Grey told me that I might be able to help you—that you want to consult some psychological journal?'

'That is unnecessary. I can probably find it at the British Museum.'

'That's possible, but not certain. What was the journal?'

'The *Monatschrift fur Kriminalpsychologie* for 1937 and 1938.'

'In that case, I can help you. I've got them all.'

It was at this moment that Zweig recalled something Grey had said: that Stafford-Morton regarded him as the most important living philosopher. The thought made him remember that he felt guilty about their last meeting. He said, smiling:

'It is extremely kind of you to make the offer. I hardly like to put you to any inconvenience.'

'It would be a great pleasure, Professor.'

Zweig said: 'Can I offer you something? Coffee? Brandy?'

'No, thank you. I've got some over there. I just came over to speak to you.' He looked at his watch. 'I don't know whether you'd like to see them tonight, but I shall be going home at about eleven. You could take the volumes home with you.'

'Do you live far away?'

'In Harley Street.'

'Of course.' Harley Street was conveniently close, and the idea was appealing. 'In that case, I would very much like to come back with you.'

'Splendid.' Stafford-Morton stood up. 'Then we leave in a quarter of an hour.'

•

Neither of them spoke until the car turned into Regent Street. Then Stafford-Morton said:

'Grey tells me there have been some surprising developments?'

'Did he explain what they were?'

'He said you'd found Neumann.'

'Yes.'

'Did you actually speak with him?'

'Yes. We had lunch.'

'And do you still think he might be a murderer?'

Zweig had to make an effort not to resent these questions. There was something about Stafford-Morton's dry manner that annoyed him. It was true that he reminded him of the history professor at Santa Barbara, who had been responsible for some inconvenience in Zweig's academic life, but this was not enough to explain it. He said:

'He seems to have changed a great deal since I knew him— for the worse. But there is one thing you should understand. I have never wanted to believe him a murderer.'

'No, of course. And perhaps I owe you some explanation myself. I can quite understand why you should have felt some . . . er . . . irritation with me the other morning. But I wasn't really being as arbitrary as perhaps I sounded. What I really wanted to know was *why* you thought Neumann should be capable of—er—making a career of murder. From what Sir Charles told me, you seemed to feel he'd become a murderer out of a theory. Now my own experience is that no one ever murders for a theory.'

'I agree. And I'm afraid that all I have to offer now is another theory.'

'Would it be rude to ask what it is?'

'Let me ask you a question first. Have you ever heard of anyone using hypnosis to make someone commit a crime?'

'Er . . . yes. I suppose so.'

'Do you believe that a man could be forced to do something under hypnosis that he would not do in his fully conscious state?'

'No. I don't.'

Somehow, Zweig had known that this would be his answer.

'Have you read any of the articles by Gustav Neumann in the *Monatschrift für Kriminalpsychologie* that appeared in 1937?'

'No. I didn't know he'd ever written any. As a matter of fact, I bought a bound set of the *Monatschrift* when a colleague died, and I haven't studied it very carefully. What are they about?'

'Crime and hypnosis. He claims that hypnosis can be used to gain complete power over people—even an unwilling subject.'

'Ah, I've heard a great deal about that theory. A colleague of mine published articles about it in the *Journal of Abnormal Psychology* in 1939, and I joined in the controversy. He had a box containing a poisonous snake and a glass partition. The partition was supposed to be quite invisible and hypnotized subjects were told to thrust their hands into the box. Several of them did as they were told—and were, of course, stopped by the glass wall. So my colleague argued that a hypnotized person could be made to perform an act that might endanger his life.'

'Did you not agree?'

'No. I'm certain the hypnotized person somehow *knew*

there was a glass wall in the box. Perhaps the senses of a person under hypnosis are sharper than when awake. It might be something even subtler than that, a kind of childish faith in the hypnotist, a willingness to load him up with your moral responsibility. For example, they tried an experiment in which a hypnotized person was ordered to fling a flask of vitriol in somebody's face. Again, there was an invisible glass wall to prevent any damage being done. . . .'

'And did the subject throw the acid?'

'Oh, yes.'

'But doesn't that seem to prove that a man can be made to commit a criminal act under hypnosis?'

'No. Because again, I believe that the subject somehow knew that it could do no harm. Now if the hypnotist had said: "Go out into the street and kill the first person you meet," the subject would probably have wakened up immediately. Laboratory conditions somehow falsify the whole thing.'

'I see.'

The car had drawn up in Harley Street. Before they got out, Stafford-Morton said:

"One more question. Where does the question of hypnosis arise? You don't think someone hypnotized Neumann into murdering people?'

'No. But I wondered if he could hypnotize a man into committing suicide.'

Stafford-Morton gave a hoot of laughter.

'Completely impossible, my dear . . . Professor. Quite impossible.'

He spoke again as they removed their overcoats in the hall.

'Because *that* would really be the ultimate test of power over a man, wouldn't it? Nobody wants to die really. Most suicides are so confused they don't know what they want. Is this your theory of how Neumann killed old men?'

Zweig tried hard not to sound irritable.

'It is not my theory. Please understand that. . . .'

'I'm awfully sorry. Don't imagine I'm trying to be sarcastic. . . .'

'We happened to discover several books on the subject of crime and hypnosis in Gustav Neumann's room. I also saw his articles in the *Monatschrift*. And he claims in one of them that a Swedish gang leader hypnotized a man into shooting himself.'

Stafford-Morton said diplomatically:

'Well, let's take a look at the article.'

His room struck Zweig as typical bachelor quarters. It was tidy enough, but completely cheerless. The walls were lined with books from floor to ceiling. The dark blue rug went badly with the brown carpet and reddish armchairs.

'The *Monatschrift*'s up there. Brandy?'

'A very small one, please.'

He took down one of the grey cloth-bound volumes, and quickly found the article. He said:

'Here is the passage in question.'

'I see. Thank you.'

While Stafford-Morton read the article, Zweig took down the cumulative index, and looked under 'Neumann'. Four articles were listed, the first in 1935. It was on the use of truth drugs by the American police.

Stafford-Morton looked up, smiling, from the book.

'If Neumann does turn out to be a murderer, he'll be quite unique in the annals of crime. I can't think of any other murderer who wrote articles for an official journal of criminal psychology.'

Zweig said ambiguously: 'I hope you are right.' He took down the 1935 volume, and found the article. Before he started to read, he turned to the last page of the magazine and looked at the notes on contributors. The entry on Neumann read: 'Son of a famous brain surgeon who has often contributed to these pages, Gustav Neumann was born in 1911, and educated at Heidelberg. Since 1932, he has lived in Switzerland. He is at present collaborating with his father, Alois Neumann, on the third volume of *Brain Physiology*.'

Stafford-Morton said: 'Really, I can't bear his style. Sentences like this have no place in a scientific article: "The question of the human will and the nature of its dependence on the brain has been ignored by Freudian psychologists. Why this strange silence?" ' He read slowly, translating as he went along. 'I ask, is that a sentence you'd expect to find in a reliable article?'

'Not in England,' Zweig said.

'Or anywhere else. And listen to this. "The problem is to

isolate the will from reflexes of habit." What on earth does he mean by that?'

He read on in silence, his occasional grunts indicating disagreement. At one point, he said: 'You see, he's writing as a philosopher, not as a scientist. But in that case, why doesn't he publish in a philosophical journal?'

Zweig was still reading when Stafford-Morton had finished. 'What are you reading?'

'An article on the use of truth drugs. I think I see what he means about isolating the will from the reflexes.'

'In that case, I'd be glad if you'd explain it to me.' But Stafford-Morton's manner made it plain that this request was not intended to be taken seriously.

Zweig said: 'You will find two more articles by him listed in the index.'

He continued reading. A moment later, Stafford-Morton said irritably: 'I told you so. There's an article here on Nietszche's philosophy applied to psychology. Really! These German publications!'

Zweig made no reply. Ten minutes later, when he finished the article on truth drugs, Stafford-Morton was reading with absorption. Zweig asked, smiling:

'You find it interesting?'

'I beg your . . . oh, er, yes. Quite impossible, of course. But he has an interesting mind, this protégé of yours. That's the trouble. He lets it run away with him.' Stafford-Morton allowed the volume to rest on his knee. 'I once had some ideas like this in my teens. . . .'

'About Nietzsche?'

'Not exactly. About a new basis for psychology—to explain neurosis in social and historical terms. This chap suggests that neurosis is the outcome of Christian morality.' He chuckled drily. 'Not a bad idea.'

'No?' Zweig was surprised.

'There's nothing more irritating than some of these self-sacrificing patients who don't seem to think they have a right to get well. I had one only yesterday. I had to tell her: "Damn your family, damn your responsibilities. Be totally selfish until you've got yourself better." '

'You agree with Gustav Neumann then?'

'No! By no means! He takes it to a point of absurdity. But he's got something. He quotes Nietzsche here about the

Christian being the most puerile and backward man of his age. He says: "Since the Christian is by nature a sufferer, states of happiness and peace make him feel uncomfortable." There's a lot in that. I've known patients who would have felt guilty about being really happy. So they're almost impossible to cure. But your friend here goes beyond that. He seems to think that religion is the cause of all modern ills. He says that the religious man daren't face his own capacity for greatness, so he cuts himself off from it and develops a split personality. I mean, listen to this sentence: "They prefer to believe that the bearing of exalted men—the prophet, the poet, the great criminal—proves that they have been possessed by a power higher than themselves. They do not dare to face the idea that they *are* the higher power." Now have you ever heard anything so nonsensical? To begin with, this stuff about the poet and the great criminal—adolescent romanticism. . . .'

'May I see it?' Zweig could not keep the excitement out of his eyes as he reached for the book. Stafford-Morton glanced at him curiously. Zweig read in silence for a few minutes, then said:

'This goes further than anything he said to me.'

'In what way?'

'This is a justification for crime.'

'Oh, I wouldn't say that.'

Zweig said: 'Yes, there's no mistake about it.'

'A little more brandy?'

'No, thank you. If you will forgive me, I would prefer to go home. I feel very tired.'

'Certainly. I'll ring for a taxi.'

After Stafford-Morton had replaced the telephone, Zweig asked:

'Would it be possible for me to borrow these volumes?'

'But, of course. Keep them as long as you like.'

'Thank you.' Zweig found it difficult to ask a favour of Stafford-Morton; he found it difficult to reconcile himself to the dry manner that seemed always to be on the edge of sarcasm. 'I shall not need them for long.'

Stafford-Morton poured himself more brandy.

'You may be right, of course—they may have some connexion with the case. But I doubt it. To my mind, it looks a bit too good to be true. . . .'

Zweig asked suddenly: 'Have you had any experience with the use of scopolamine?'

'Scopolamine? Poison, isn't it?'

'An alkaloid poison. In small doses it can be used as a truth drug. It causes depression of the central nervous system.'

'Where did you learn so much about it?'

Zweig indicated a volume of the *Monatschrift*.

'From an article by Neumann. He claims that it can be used with morphine to cause a twilight state of consciousness when the subject becomes incapable of telling lies. He points out that in this state, the subject is also abnormally sensitive to suggestion—just as under hypnosis.'

Morton was frowning. 'I . . . see. Does it occur in nature—in any plant, I mean?'

'Yes. In *Datura stramonium,* the thorn apple or jimson weed.'

Morton said nothing: he pulled back the curtains and looked out of the window. After a moment, he said:

'Here comes your taxi.'

'Thank you.'

Morton stacked the three volumes of the *Monatschrift* on the table. Then he said:

'I may as well confess that . . . I'm not sure what to think. What you're suggesting is as fantastic as the old stories about Svengali and Mesmer—murder by hypnotism, drugs, and the rest. . . .'

Zweig interrupted: 'I am not suggesting anything of the sort. I only wish to consider the evidence.'

Morton smiled unexpectedly. He picked up the three volumes of the *Monatschrift* as his phone started to ring.

'All right. Well, you take these home and have a good look at the evidence. Let me think it over.' He picked up the phone, said: 'All right, thank you,' and replaced it. 'All I'm trying to say is this: if you ever get Neumann into a courtroom, these theories are going to be more of a nuisance than they're worth. The judge would laugh it out of court.' Zweig followed him downstairs. He could see that Morton was worried, and this pleased him. He said casually:

'I remember Gustav used to be an excellent chemist. He used to distil atropine from deadly nightshade and use it in experiments on rats. . . .'

'My God!' Zweig was glad Morton was in front of him, and was unable to see his smile.

Zweig climbed into the taxi; Morton placed the books on the seat beside him.

'Thank you for the loan of the books. And for your hospitality.'

'It's a pleasure. . . .' Morton shook his head. 'It's all very interesting, but . . . not enough evidence for a conviction.'

'Perhaps I don't want to see him convicted,' Zweig said. He turned away and gave the driver the address, to avoid seeing Morton's startled face. He waved as the taxi drew away. Morton was staring after it.

●

The tiredness had disappeared when he arrived home. It was half past midnight. He was tempted to ring Grey, then decided against it; Grey would probably be in bed. He plugged in the electric blanket, then poured himself a brandy. The fire was out, so he lit the gas fire in the bedroom and sat in front of it, reading Neumann's article on truth drugs. After ten minutes, the need to speak to someone made him pick up the telephone again. He decided to try Natasha's number; if there was no reply after two rings, then she was probably asleep, and he would hang up. But after the ringing tone had continued for a few seconds, he was overwhelmed by the weight of his disappointment, and had to force himself to replace the receiver. He went back to the bedroom and swallowed the rest of the brandy in one gulp, then poured himself another. His mind felt like a microscope that is slightly out of focus; the problem that was raised by the *Monatschrift* articles was blurry, and no mental effort could make its outlines more clear. A musical theme ran in his head, and he whistled it suddenly: the six notes of the Thunderstorm motif from 'Rheingold.' For a moment, the mental picture cleared, then blurred again. He opened the 1936 volume of the *Monatschrift* and turned to Neumann's article on the psychology of suicide. Its opening sentence read: 'The act of suicide is a protest against limitation; the suicide regards life as a prison.' He went back into the sitting-room and opened his suitcase; he took the manuscript of his Heidegger commentary back into the bedroom, and leafed through its pages. The third chapter opened with the words: 'Man's experience of the world is basically an experience of limitation. . . .' He said aloud: 'Astonishing.' The doorbell rang and he started guiltily. He stood, staring at the bedroom door, taking pleasure in the hesitation, and in the complete silence that followed the ringing. Then he went out. Natasha said:

'Good. I'm glad you're still awake.'

'My dear Natasha. What are you doing here?'

'I'm on my way home. Your porter didn't want to let me in. Seemed to think I was one of the ladies of the town.'

'Where is your husband?'

'At Maidstone. I've been having dinner with his aunt—a terrible old woman. I tried to telephone you half an hour ago and got no reply.'

'I tried to telephone you.'

'Good.' She flung her leopardskin coat across the armchair; she was wearing a black dress that fitted tight around the throat. He thought her face looked pale and tired. 'I came past the end of your street and couldn't resist seeing if you'd come home yet. Where have you been?'

As he told her, he was aware that neither of them was listening to what the other said. The talk was a kind of alibi, as if there was another person listening outside the door; he had wanted her to come and she wanted to be here, and they both knew this.

'It's cold in here. Can I have some of that brandy?'

As he poured her a drink she peeped into the bedroom.

'Oh, you've got a gas fire. Let's come in here.' He smiled, and she said: 'We seem to spend most of our time in one another's bedroom.' She pulled out his pillow and propped it against the back of the bed, then curled up on the bed, her legs under her. Zweig returned to his armchair. She indicated the books: 'What are you reading?'

'They contain Gustav's articles. I have just discovered a coincidence.' He showed the sentence about suicide, then his own sentence: 'Man's experience of the world is basically an experience of limitation.' She lit a cigarette.

'I don't quite see what's so remarkable in that. Just a similarity of wording.'

'No, no. It is deeper than that. It is the thing we are both trying to say. I have been talking with this man Morton . . . he doesn't understand.' He stood up and walked up and down the room. 'You see, it is nothing definite, but a feeling, an intuition. I feel as if I am about to see something important . . . but I cannot explain what. It is to do with the idea of limitation. The natural standpoint . . .'

'The what?'

He did not reply, staring at his feet as he walked slowly. She watched him, waiting. He whistled as he moved, and she said: ' "Rheingold." ' He looked at her in surprise. 'You're whistling that "Rheingold" theme again.'

'Yes. It stuck in my mind.' He ran his fingers through his hair. 'I started to tell you this afternoon . . . about our circle. We used to talk for hours about the superman, about human freedom. . . . And now, these articles of Gustav make me think. . . .' She waited, making no attempt to hurry him, although he was aware that she failed to understand him. He said explosively: 'You see, we really *felt* the need for freedom. It was a *real* problem, not just words. Now these articles of Gustav make me feel . . . almost ashamed. Because he feels it too. It is there.' He tapped the volume with his knuckle. He said, shrugging: 'I have become an old man. I had forgotten what it feels like to feel the need for freedom like a toothache.'

She said softly: 'Nonsense.'

'No. But . . . there is something that escapes me about Gustav. There is . . . a key.' He snapped his fingers. 'It is in these articles. Suicide. That is one problem. He asks: Why do people commit suicide? He quotes one of my essays: suicide is the ultimate absurdity of human existence, like a millionaire killing himself because he is afraid of starving to death. You see? I used to tell my students a story about our village preacher. He was fond of beginning his sermons by telling us that there are millions of souls in heaven who want to be born on earth—millions of souls waiting in a line for the opportunity to assume a human body. Unfortunately, there is only one body for every million souls, so most of them have to go on waiting, and waiting, and waiting. Sometimes they have to wait for a million years. And this is why children are always so glad to be alive—they can still remember how long they had to wait to be born. Then they grow up, and they grow bored and dissatisfied. . . . You see? Our preacher —Doktor Eichbaum—used to tell us that we should be more grateful for being alive. You see? So I used to say to my students that suicide is the ultimate absurdity—a soul that has queued up for a million years gets so confused that it imagines it wants to escape. The suicide weighs up life and decides it is not worth living. But think of the absurdity! Most of these men cannot even add up a column of figures, and yet they imagine they can summarize the whole of life. And this, I would explain, is the essence of philosophy. That is philosophy —an attempt to create a giant adding machine that will summarize all human existence. You ask the machine: Is life worth living? And then you feed in your data—all human joy and suffering—and that million years of waiting for a body. . . .' There was a bumping noise under Zweig's feet. He looked down in surprise. Natasha asked: 'What's that?' Zweig said: 'Ah, I am keeping my neighbours awake by walking up and down. I must walk more quietly. They are banging their ceiling.' He kicked off his shoes, and sat down in the chair.

She said: 'You must write all this down.'

'Yes, of course.' His tone was dry, almost impatient. 'I shall write it in my Heidegger book. But that is not what troubles me. I am trying to think . . . about the key in Gustav's work.' He was silent, staring into the gas fire.

'I don't quite understand. Surely these articles seem to prove what you suspected? He writes about suicide and about hypnosis. . . .'

He grunted, shaking his head.

'No, you do not understand.'

'No?'

He stood up and began to prowl up and down again. Absentmindedly, he whistled the six notes of the Thunderstorm motif. Then he said: 'Why did Alois Neumann commit suicide?'

She stared at him. 'Why?'

'The others, yes. He might murder the others. But why his own father?'

'Suppose his father found out? He might commit suicide out of despair?'

'No. Alois was not that kind of man.'

'Then supposing Gustav murdered him . . . because he knew too much?'

'No. That is also impossible. Alois would never betray his son to the police. . . .'

'Then what . . . ?' She watched him as he walked back towards the window, his hands clasped behind him, his face set into a scowl. He turned, and pointed to the volumes of the *Monatschrift* beside the bed.

'The answer is in there. I am certain of that.'

'Are you sure? I mean, are you sure they're not just a red herring? Joseph thinks so.'

'No. He left the books there, deliberately, for me to find. But perhaps he hoped I would read them carefully—and understand.'

There was a thumping on the floor again. Zweig said: 'Ah, I forgot. These old floors creak, and I am keeping them awake. Let us go into the other room.' She stood up without speaking, and went out in her stockinged feet. The sitting-room felt cold. He plugged in the fire, and carefully closed the bedroom door behind him. Natasha crossed to his study, and switched on the light.

'So this is where you work.' She looked through the bookcase, and took down a volume. She said: 'It's terribly dusty. Don't you have a cleaning woman?'

'Yes.'

'Then she's not very good. I'll come and dust for you tomorrow.' The photograph album was lying on the desk. She sat down and opened it.

'Who is this?'

'That was my wife.'

'Oh. . . . I'm sorry. She's very attractive.'

Zweig came and stood behind her, leaning over her. He opened the back of the album, and took out the photograph that showed Alois Neumann with Walter Benskin. He placed it in front of her.

'I told you this afternoon that I already knew Gustav was the secretary in the Maidstone case. Here is the reason.' He placed his finger on the photograph. 'That old man sitting next to Alois Neumann is Walter Benskin, the man who was killed.'

She stared at it. 'How long have you known?'

'Since Christmas Day.'

'But why didn't you tell Grey?'

He shrugged. 'Why? I am not sure. Perhaps because I suddenly felt that I was betraying Alois as well as Gustav. . . .'

'But . . . I don't understand. If you don't want him to be caught, then why did you come to Bury St Edmunds?'

'It is not true that I don't want him to be caught. I felt then as I feel now. This is not a simple murder case. I hoped for an opportunity to speak to Gustav alone, to find out the truth.'

'And you had your opportunity.'

'Yes. And he treated me as his betrayer. Perhaps I deserved it.'

'But do you mean you want him to escape—even if he *is* a murderer?'

'No. I only want to understand.'

She stood up suddenly, and looked into his face. She said quietly: 'Of course.'

'It's cold in here. Come back into the other room.' The single-bar fire made almost no difference to the temperature of the sitting-room. She shivered as she sat in the armchair. Zweig went to the bathroom, and returned with a green jaeger dressing gown.

'Put this on.'

'Thank you.'

He sat on the arm of her chair.

'I think I have decided what I must do. Tomorrow I shall take a train to Bury St Edmunds and go and see Gustav.'

'Is that a good idea?'

'I don't know. But I must talk to him.'

'What about?'

He smiled at her. 'About suicide.'

'You don't mean . . .' She stared at him. '. . . You don't want him to commit suicide?'

'Good heavens, no! You think I should offer him a revolver, like an officer who has been caught cheating at cards?'

She said: 'Well, it might come to that.'

'No! Listen.' He went into the bedroom, and returned with the *Monatschrift*. He sat on the arm of her chair to find the place. 'Listen, does this sound like the writing of a man who would kill himself?' He read aloud: 'In spite of its unpleasantness, there is something humorous about suicide. As an evaluation of life, it has some of the quality of a schoolboy howler.' He closed the book. 'That is the last sentence of his article. He wrote it after his father had killed himself.'

She stared back at him. 'That's extraordinary. That's . . .'

'Yes?'

'I was going to say: That's either insanity or genius. But I'm not sure it couldn't be something else—ordinary heartlessness.'

Zweig said slowly: 'I am not sure that Gustav was heartless . . . no.'

When he looked back at her, from the door of the study, he saw that she was looking at him oddly.

'What is it?'

She laughed. 'I'm not sure. I don't think I understand you at all.'

He said: 'That is unimportant.' He tapped the volume of the *Monatschrift*. 'That is more important.' He sat down on the arm, allowing his hand to rest on her shoulder.

'My German isn't very good. Why are you so impressed by it?'

'Ah!' He gestured, nervously and helplessly, then shook his head. 'If only I could explain. You see . . . here is this man, Gustav Neumann. He is obsessed by suicide, by the idea of violent death. I remember, his favourite writer was the Russian Andreyev, who attempted suicide several times. . . .'

'Ah, yes. I have read him.'

'And then there was a book on Legal Medicine that belonged to Alois Neumann. This book has many photographs of strange suicides, like a man who killed himself by banging a six-inch nail into his skull, and a woman who made all the furniture into a pile, lay down on it and set fire to it. . . . Gustav was fascinated by this book. He once said jokingly that he would write a treatise on philosophy illustrated with these photographs. And you know he often talked of suicide. He stole a car and drove it over a cliff. . . . All this. Also, he had this idea of becoming a great criminal. Now what happens? Five years later, he writes this article, and all the morbidity has vanished. Why? I tell you, the Gustav I knew would have been *incapable* of writing that suicide has its humorous aspect.'

'I still don't see. . . .'

'No.' He interrupted, standing up suddenly. 'Then what of his idea of becoming a great criminal, what of that?' He smiled at her triumphantly and walked across the room, as if he had now made his point. She stared at him with incomprehension. He said: 'You see. It does not fit?'

'You must think me very stupid, but . . . what does not fit?'

'A man who outgrows the idea of suicide also outgrows the idea of murder.'

'Yes. . . .' She sounded doubtful.

'Ah, never mind. We must wait and see what happens. But I would like to see Gustav tomorrow.'

'Very well. I'll drive you.'

'I could go by train.'

'No. I'll take you.'

'Good. In that case, we set out early.'

'I'd better get some sleep then.' She stood up. He started to pick up her coat, when she said: 'Do you want me to go home?' He looked at her in astonishment. 'If we're setting out early, I'd better stay here. That settee will do.'

'But . . . what about your husband? Supposing he is waiting at home?'

'He's not. He won't be back until tomorrow anyway. Are you worried about your reputation with the other tenants? In that case, I'll go.'

'No, no. We all lead separate lives, but . . .' He hastily changed what he was about to say into: 'But I could not let you sleep on the settee. You must have the bed.'

'I don't mind. It looks very comfortable.'

He covered his excitement and embarrassment by collecting an armful of blankets from the bathroom cupboard and making up a bed on the settee. Then he filled a hot-water bottle at the kitchen tap, allowing the water to run until it was too hot for the naked hand. When he came back in, she had forestalled his arguments by climbing into the makeshift bed. She took the hot-water bottle, smiling.

'Good night, dear.'

He lay in his own bed, staring into the darkness. The thought of her in the next room made it difficult to sleep. He raised his wrist and stared at the luminous dial of his watch; it was two o'clock. As he did so, the telephone started to ring. He listened incredulously for a moment, then sat up in bed and turned on the light. As he reached the bedroom door, the ringing stopped. The light from the bedroom showed Natasha standing at the table; she was saying:

'Hello, dear. What on earth do you want?' She looked across at Zweig, covering the mouthpiece with her hand. 'It's Joseph. He sounds drunk.' She was wearing a black slip, and her hair flowed loosely over her shoulders; with her bare feet, she seemed no more than ten years old. She said: 'No, he's not asleep yet. We were just about to go to sleep . . . What? Yes, I'm staying here overnight. Karl wants to drive back to Bury St Edmunds in the . . . Yes, wait a moment. He can tell you himself.' She handed the receiver to Zweig, and climbed back into bed. Gardner's voice sounded slurred, but not thick:

'Hello, Karl. Thought I'd find Natasha there when there was no reply from our place. Sorry to disturb you at this hour, but I've just found something important.'

'Yes?'

'I've been out with Terry Sams all evening, talking to various people. And we've just got rid of an old friend of his . . . chap called Ted Houghton. He was the son of the gardener out at Highfields—that's the house where Benskin was killed. He's been drinking here since eleven. Can you hear me?'

'Yes.'

'He's told me something that came as a shock. I'd got the impression old Benskin was pretty feeble and sick before he died. But Ted Houghton claims he was as lively as a cricket. Says he looked a picture of health for about two weeks before he died. Apparently he was ill when he moved into the house, but he made a quick recovery. They were all amazed. Houghton says the old man suddenly looked thirty years younger.'

Zweig said: 'Mein Gott.'

'Quite. You see what I'm getting at. Tim's exactly the same. Now this Houghton thinks that the secretary was giving the old man some kind of drug, because he saw him injecting something with a hypodermic one day. What do you think? It doesn't sound like hypnosis to me.'

'But why didn't this gardener report it to the police?'

'Report what? That the old man looked healthy? Everybody knew it.'

'About the hypodermic syringe.'

'There was nothing in that. After all, the old man had been

ill—it could have been some ordinary injection. Now look, what's all this about going to Bury St Edmunds?'

Zweig said carefully: 'I cannot explain over the telephone. But I would like to have a frank talk with Gustav before we go any further.'

'Listen, old boy. *Please* take my advice and do nothing of the sort. You do see why, don't you? This case is tying up very nicely. Do you know what I think? I think it's all a matter of drugs. I think Neumann's got some drug that has a terrific uplift, and a terrific after-effect of suicidal depression. But it's going to be hard as hell to prove it in court. I'm hoping the Scotland Yard analysts will find something in that ampoule we discovered. And if Tim's already suffering from its effects, we've got to be pretty quick . . .'

'Of course. But I also have my reasons for wanting to see Gustav.'

'Then listen—please promise me you won't do anything until I get back tomorrow? I'll leave here early and come straight to your place.'

'Very well.'

'Good, splendid. Can I talk to Natasha again?'

Zweig said: 'He wants to speak to you.'

She threw back the bedclothes and came across the room, taking the phone. He could see the outline of her legs against the light from the bedroom, and experienced a lurch of desire that embarrassed him; it was the first time he had thought of Natasha simply as a woman. He looked away quickly. As if sensing his feeling, she reached out and took his hand as she talked.

'All right, I'll make sure he doesn't leave early. But I still don't think Tim's been taking drugs. He hates drugs, and I didn't notice any of the signs. . . . Well, like bright eyes. We'll see. I must get back into bed. I'm standing here in nothing but my slip. No, I won't be a nuisance. Bye-bye, dear.' She hung up and said: 'You see, I have my husband's permission to stay here. He trusts you.'

Zweig was unable to keep his eyes from her bare shoulders. 'I wish I trusted myself.'

She came closer to him; her eyes were completely candid, without a trace of coquetry or seductiveness.

'Why do you let these things worry you? I know what you

are feeling. I know why you went to your club tonight instead of phoning me. You don't trust me, do you?'

He said, surprised: 'What do you mean?'

'You're worried. You've only known me for three days and I've been running after you shamelessly. I know the way your mind works. You want to know where it can all end.'

He reached up and put his hand on her shoulders, it was a protective gesture, and the coldness of her flesh made him want to draw her to him. His own feet, without bedroom slippers, were uncomfortably cold. He said quietly:

'Yes, you are right. And I still feel it. Why are we standing here now? Why are you here instead of at home? Would anyone believe that you were not my mistress?'

'What does that matter? Life isn't as obvious as plays and novels. Its ways are more devious than any playwright ever dreamed. You'll get used to me . . . given time. When you've known me for six months.' She laughed, and he felt her body shiver under his hands. She said teasingly: 'You shouldn't try to think things to a conclusion. It doesn't work. Let things go. Let them drift.' She leaned forward suddenly and kissed him at the side of the mouth, then said: 'It's cold,' and went back to the bed. She pulled the sheets around her throat, and looked up at him. She said: 'Don't worry about me. I shan't disappoint you.' He bent over and kissed her. Her lips were soft, and lay so passively that he was tempted to rest there, drawn into her warmth. He straightened up quickly, and went back into the bedroom without saying good night. But in his own bed, he realized that the feeling of frustration had vanished. It was now no longer strange that she was in the next room. In a sense he could not define, it would have made no difference if she had been lying at the side of him in his bed. As he closed his eyes, her warmth enveloped him and drew him into sleep.

The sound of the telephone woke him; but before he was fully awake, he heard her voice answering it. A few minutes later he opened his eyes and found her standing by his bedside with a cup of coffee. He sat up, blinking, and peered at his wristwatch. It was half past ten. She grimaced and gestured towards the other room, saying in a whisper:

'Your cleaning woman's scandalized. I was still walking round in my slip when she came in.'

Zweig rubbed his chin; he felt ashamed to let her see him unshaven, his eyes still full of sleep.

'Who made the coffee?'

'I did.'

He took it from her, and tried to massage away the heaviness of his face with his right hand. She said:

'Sir Charles Grey just phoned from Scotland Yard. He's coming round in half an hour.'

'What did he want?'

'Something about Interpol. He sounded rather pleased with himself.' She closed the bedroom door, then sat in the armchair. 'Do you mind if I stay in here? Your cleaning woman's been looking at me as if I were a prostitute.'

Zweig said with embarrassment: 'Then I'm afraid it won't improve things if you stay in here. Still, perhaps you could light the gas fire?'

She sat with her face turned away from him. His mouth had the powdery, livery taste that warned him that he had drunk too much on the previous evening. The coffee was good, and he began to feel better as he drank thirstily.

'Any news from your husband?'

'Not yet. He'll be here soon, I expect.'

In the cold light, Zweig no longer felt so happy about her presence, and he felt uncomfortable at the thought of facing Grey and Gardner. There was probably not a single person of his acquaintance who would believe that he and Natasha had spent the night in separate beds—except, perhaps, Grey and her husband. And even they might wonder. . . .

There was a perfunctory knock on the bedroom door. The cleaning woman said:

'If there's nothing more to be done, I'll be going.'

He found himself looking at Natasha, as if for advice. She said: 'There's the dusting in your study.'

Zweig said quickly: 'No, no, that's all right. Thank you, Mrs. Macrae.' The door slammed. She said, laughing:

'I'm compromising you so much, you'll have to marry me soon.'

He asked: 'What about your husband?'

She stood up. 'More coffee?' She took the cup from him and went out. When she came back, a moment later, she said:

'You don't need a wife.'

'What do I need?'

'A half-wife. Someone to pay you a lot of attention when you need it, and leave you to your bachelor existence when you don't.'

He wanted to ask her seriously how many of a husband's privileges could be expected from a half-wife, but could think of no way of saying it that would not sound offensive. The ringing of the doorbell broke into his attempts to formulate the question. He heard Gardner's voice saying:

'Are they up yet?'

There was a murmur of voices for a moment, then Gardner knocked on the door.

'Hello, may I come in? Good morning. How are you?' The slamming of the outer door made him wince. 'Ooh, my head's thick this morning. Who's the gorgon?'

Natasha said, laughing: 'His housekeeper. What did she say?'

'I asked her if you were up yet, and she said: "Who?" and I said: "Profesor Zweig and my wife," and she snorted and flounced away. Odd sort of woman.' He sat down in the other chair. 'The old head's a bit tender. I'll be glad to get home and mix one of my hangover specials. What's happening?'

Natasha said: 'We don't know. Sir Charles will be here in a few minutes. I'm going to wash.' She went into the bathroom. Gardner said:

'Oof, I feel terrible. How are you?'

'I am also terrible.'

'Who was it who said: "There is no cure for a hangover but death?" Any coffee?'

'In the kitchen. Let me get it for you.'

'Don't worry. I'll get it.' He went out. Zweig climbed out of bed and pulled on his dressing gown. Gardner came in carrying two cups:

'I brought you some more. Who made it, Natasha? She makes splendid coffee. That's why I married her. Hope she hasn't been a nuisance?'

'No, no certainly not.'

'Did you go out yesterday evening?'

'Not with your wife. She arrived . . . later.'

'What time?'

'About one o'clock.'

'Ugh!' Zweig could not tell whether the exclamation was a reaction to his answer, or a twinge of pain in the forehead.

'She's really pretty disgraceful, that girl. Ah, that's better.' He gulped the coffee, then looked across at Zweig with sudden frankness. 'She's rather enthusiastic about you, as you gather.'

Zweig asked: 'Why?'

'I don't know. She's always admired your work. But my theory is that it's a father thing. She was in love with her father. . . .' He broke off as the key turned in the bathroom door. Without changing his voice, Gardner said: 'I discovered some interesting things. The first was that old Benskin was apparently pretty thick with Neumann. People thought they were father and son because they seemed so close.'

Natasha asked: 'Who told you this?'

'A friend of Sams. I talked to a couple of people who knew something about it. One was a French polisher who did quite a bit of work in the house—he was there for several days . . . ah, excuse me.' He went out to answer the ring at the door-bell; a moment later, he returned with Grey.

'Morning, Karl. Only just up? You look tired.' Grey's face looked as healthy as if he had just returned from a brisk walk in the wind; his moustache seemed to bristle with energy. He flung his bowler on the bed. Gardner said:

'We're both under the weather. Don't talk too loud.'

'Are you? Sorry to hear that. Thank you, my dear.' This was to Natasha, as she handed him coffee. 'Well, I've had another session with Blaydon, and things are moving.'

'Any news about that ampoule we found?' Gardner asked.

'Ah yes, but nothing cheering. It was quite empty, so they hadn't much to go on. But they managed to make a very weak solution of whatever it had contained, and their lab man is completely baffled. He says the only constituent he can swear to is a small quantity of one of the atropine group. . . .'

'What?' Zweig jumped up in his excitement.

'Atropine. You know it?'

'Not scopolamine?'

'He didn't know. . . .'

Gardner interrupted: 'Why do you mention scopolamine?'

'Because I have found an article on truth drugs in the *Monatschrift*. . . .'

'. . . Because that's one of the things that came into my mind last night. I had something to do with scopolamine during the war—intelligence used it on spies. And its effect isn't unlike the one described by this French polisher . . .'

'What French polisher?' Grey asked.

'Look, let's take it in turn. You tell us what you've found out, then I'll tell, then Karl can tell us what he's found in the *Monatschrift*. All right?'

Grey said: 'Very well. My news isn't all that exciting. I've spent several hours with Blaydon of Interpol and Chesson of the CID—been there all morning. They both agree that we need more evidence, but that it looks very much like a murder case. So we're doing a systematic check with the police in Mentone, Heidelberg and Geneva—the address on Neumann's passport is at a place called Gex, twenty miles from Geneva. The next thing is to find out if he has a criminal record in any of these countries. What have you found?'

Gardner said: 'I spent last night with Sams, who's an awfully nice little bloke. We went around to several pubs, and talked to several people who remembered the Benskin case. It seemed to be the general opinion that he'd committed suicide. I began to get a bit discouraged—until I met a chap called Houghton, who was the son of Benskin's gardener.' He paused, then said: 'He told me that Benskin was exceptionally cheerful and healthy just before his death. The way he described his appearance made me think of Tim Ferguson. It all sounded very strange. The old man came back from South America in a pretty feeble state—then he made a sudden terrific recovery.'

'So it could hardly have been hypnosis?' Grey said.

'I shouldn't think it likely. You see my point, don't you? I'd stopped believing that Tim's in any real danger, but now I've changed my mind. I think we've got to act fast. I think I've got to see Tim, put all facts in front of him, and ask him what "treatment" Neumann's been giving him.'

Grey had lit his pipe.

'Perhaps you're right. It couldn't do any harm. Still, I never know quite where I am with this case. I've got Blaydon and Chesson convinced that Neumann could be making use of hypnotism. . . .' He asked Zweig: 'Incidentally, could you prepare a short report on these articles of Neumann's? The ones on hypnosis? Blaydon needs it.'

'Of course. But we shall need other sources besides his articles. I suggest you tell Blaydon to contact the Stockholm police about the Sala case, and get details of the other case from Heidelberg.'

'What were the cases, briefly?'

'The Sala case took place in 1929. A young man who was interested in hypnosis used it to dominate a whole gang.'

'How do you mean, dominate?'

'They regarded themselves as a secret magical society as well as a criminal group, and all submitted to being hypnotized. They committed various crimes—car thefts, robbery with violence, sex murders, even white slavery. According to Neumann, he hypnotized a number of under-age girls into having sexual relations with him, then made them go into the white slave traffic. He also killed a member of his gang by giving him an injection of poison while he was in a trance. And, as I told you, he made another member commit suicide by means of hypnotic suggestion. It should be easy enough to get all the details from the Swedish police. The Heidelberg case concerns a young woman who was hypnotized on a train, without her knowledge. The man who hypnotized her posed as a doctor, and later made her steal money and prostitute herself. Neumann also writes about a case that occurred in Thuringia in 1921, in which a gamekeeper hypnotized a school teacher and made him commit various crimes. Incidentally, he also made him shoot himself through the hand with a revolver —which proves that the subject *can* be made to act against his own interests.'

Grey sucked at his pipe. He said slowly:

'Well, if Neumann *has* been using hypnotism to make them commit suicide, he's justified his boast about becoming a master criminal.'

Gardner said: 'I stick to the drugs theory. Although I suppose that drugs would make a man much more susceptible to hypnosis, wouldn't they?'

The telephone rang. Grey said: 'That might be for me. I told Chesson to ring me if anything turned up.' He went into the other room. They heard his voice say: 'Grey here. Hello, John. . . . What? At what time? . . . The twelve-thirty? Good. Will you have someone there to meet the train and follow them? Splendid. I'll be at home in a quarter of an hour if you want me again.' He came back into the bedroom. 'Neumann and Ferguson caught the ten-thirty train back to London. They're arriving at King's Cross at twelve-thirty.'

'Splendid!' Gardner said. 'It looks as if we've got him worried. But I wonder if he's thinking of leaving the country?'

'It's possible. Whatever happens, we'll keep on his tail. The first question I want to ask him is why he was using a false passport in England in 1938.'

Gardner stood up. 'Well, if you gents don't mind, I'm going home to get an hour's sleep and a pick-me-up. Coming, Natasha?'

'Yes. Unless there is anything I can do here?' She looked at Zweig; he could see that she wanted him to provide her with an excuse for remaining. But with Grey's eyes on him, he had to reject the appeal.

'No. I shall work for the next few hours. I shall also be here if anyone needs me.'

'I'm off, then,' Gardner said. 'Do you want a lift, m'dear?'

'No. I have my own car round the corner.'

Grey said: 'I'd be grateful if you'd drop me off in Knightsbridge.'

'With pleasure.'

As they went out, Grey said: 'I'd be glad if you'd prepare that report, Karl. Blaydon wants to keep it for future reference, no matter what happens.'

'I will do it later today.'

When they had gone, Natasha asked:

'What do you propose to do?'

'I don't know.' He sat down in the armchair, sniffing with slight distaste at the tobacco smell that filled the bedroom. 'It begins to look as if it is out of my hands.'

'Do you still want to talk to Neumann?'

'I would like to, but it will obviously be impossible if he is under police observation all the time.'

They walked back into the other room. The fire was now burning brightly. She picked up her coat.

'How about going out now and getting a meal?'

He said, smiling:

'I would like to, but there is something I must do. I must read carefully those four articles of Gustav's in the *Monatschrift*. I want to re-read them now my mind is fresh.'

'But why?'

'Because I have an irritating feeling that there is something I keep missing, something I ought to see but cannot see. . . .'

'Then let me get you something to eat while you read. I shan't disturb you.'

'Thank you. I'm not hungry at the moment. Won't your husband expect you back?'

'No. He'll go straight to bed. Let me make you some coffee, anyway. I'll be as quiet as a mouse.'

He brought the volumes of the *Monatschrift* from the bedroom, and placed them on the coffee trolley beside the sitting-room fire. He had not wanted Natasha to stay, because he was afraid she might prevent him from concentrating; but as soon as he started to read, he forgot about her. She slipped off her shoes, and moved about in her stockinged feet; ten minutes later, when she brought him his coffee, he took it absently, murmuring, 'Thank you,' and went on reading without looking up. She went into the study and closed the door. Zweig did not even notice the noises she made as she lifted books and moved furniture, although he had forbidden the cleaning woman to dust in his study because he resented anyone touching his papers.

At first, the remains of the hangover made his perceptions sluggish; but after reading two pages, the fatigue ceased to be important. The reading produced a feeling like pain, and yet it was a pain that he found strangely moving, and that made him aware of his age, and of his body's inability to bear a certain kind of pleasure. This feeling was so strong when he came to the end of the first article that he found it impossible to go on reading. He drank the coffee, which was now cold, then began to walk up and down the room. Natasha came in; he looked at her as if he had never seen her before; then, when he saw her stockinged feet, suddenly smiled. She said:

'I'm going out to buy some food. What would you like to eat?'

'No, not yet. I don't feel like eating.' He sat down again and stared into the fire.

'Would you like me to go now?' She was standing behind his chair, and he took her hand.

'No. But this'—he gestured at the book—'is more important than eating.'

'Have you found what you're looking for?'

He laughed. 'Do you know what I'm looking for?'

'A clue . . . to Neumann's motives . . .?'

'In a way. But that is not so important.' She sat in the opposite armchair, sensing his need to express it. He closed the book, and pushed away the trolley as if rejecting a temptation. 'Ever since we drove back yesterday, I have been thinking about our Nietzsche society in Göttingen. Alois Neumann was the founder and president. . . . And now, when I read this, I keep thinking about Alois, and I understand something about Gustav. But I also understand something about myself.' He was not looking at her as he spoke; he was afraid that her expression might distract him from what he was trying to face. 'We believed . . . we believed . . . in everything, in the future, as only young men can.'

She said: 'But you still do.'

'Yes, but not with the same . . . confidence that everything will change. In those days, we all *felt* so much more. But you see, the things we agreed about were not necessarily intellectual issues. For example, a man called Fritz Haller was studying to become a minister, and he was converted to Roman Catholicism. He thought that we were talking nonsense about Christianity. But we all had a common feeling—that man *is not big enough,* that no man who has ever lived has achieved a fraction of the greatness of which man is capable. Do you understand that belief? It is difficult for a woman, I know. It seems to involve too much contempt. And yet that is not true. It was not a matter of contempt. We used to read articles and stories to one another—not our own, but articles out of literary magazines—and then we would say: "It is all too small. It is all written in a little room with a stuffy atmosphere." We believed that man is on the edge of a new development.'

'But you say this in several of your books.'

'Yes, I *say* it. But I sometimes feel that I have forgotten what we originally meant by it. One evening, Fritz Haller read us a paper on Nietzsche's idea of the superman. And what he said was this: "We need not accept all Nietzsche's ideas, because a lot of them are the screams of a sick man. The man who calls himself a Nietzschean is a fool, because Nietzsche was far too small. And yet Nietzsche expresses something that is happening to man's spirit in this century." ' By now, Zweig was walking up and down the room; his old habit of lecturing made it impossible to sit down when he wanted to talk. 'He said: "Let us forget Nietzsche and all his books, and concentrate on this new phenomenon, that Nietzsche was one of the first to observe. It is this; for the first time in history, men are beginning to feel stifled by their own humanity. Most of the great artists and writers of the nineteenth century are men who feel themselves trapped in their own limitations. They are all stifled by human weakness. And yet at the very time when some men are fighting to get free of this weakness, others are basing their art on the concept of weakness, of human defeat. This is the one clear fact that stands out of our cultural history. One class of men wants freedom; the other builds an ethic of negation. So," Haller said, "what does this indicate? Surely that man is preparing for a new evolutionary leap?" Well . . . perhaps all this sounds commonplace to you. Ten years later, even I thought I had outgrown it, and congratulated myself for becoming a realist. And yet . . . now I believe that I was wrong. Because you see . . .' He hesitated, waving his hand towards the books: 'He feels it too. It is there in his articles. He is also a realist. He writes of hypnotism, of truth drugs, of suicide, as if his only interest is purely scientific. And yet *I* know. I can see what he really feels. . . . Now it seems strange to me that I did not recognize this when he was my pupil. He seemed too nervous and excitable. Perhaps I was too aware of his weakness.' He sat down and scowled at the fire, then suddenly looked at her, as if hoping to catch her unaware. He said, shrugging: 'Now I wonder whether Gustav was right when he accused me of compromise. For it seems to me that there are more ways than one of being a realist.'

She waited to see whether he would go on; then, when he sat, staring past her, said:

'But you still don't explain how a man who believes in freedom can become a murderer.'

'*Was* he a murderer? That is something that I cannot decide. Somehow I find it difficult to accept, in spite of the evidence. . . .'

After another silence, he said:

'But why did he never contact me? I was his teacher. Surely he would want to talk to me about it. . . . Even from the point of view of vanity, he might enjoy showing me that he was not afraid to go further. . . .'

'Into murder, you mean? You wonder why he didn't take you into his confidence about that?'

'No, no. Perhaps. . . . I do not know. . . .'

He stood up.

'What I *must* do now is to spend a few hours alone with Gustav. I must talk to him at length. If they return to this flat in Pelham Place, I shall ring him and ask him if I can go and see him.'

She said, smiling: 'Whatever you do, you'd better eat something. Otherwise, you won't be fit to talk to anyone.'

He laughed, and reached forward to caress her head.

'You are right. I feel hungry now. I shall dress, and then we shall go out to eat.'

He shaved slowly and carefully, enjoying the warm water on his face, and feeling unaccountably happy. He could hear Natasha washing the dishes. As he came back into the sitting-room, knotting his bow tie, the telephone rang. He stood looking at it; Natasha came in, drying her hands on a dish-towel.

'Shall we answer it?'

'It's probably your husband wanting to know when you'll be home.'

'I bet it's not.' She snatched it up, listened for a moment, then said: 'No, I'm afraid he went a quarter of an hour ago. He should be at his home. . . . Yes, Professor Zweig is here. . . .' She handed the phone to Zweig, saying: "Someone from Scotland Yard.'

The voice said: 'Professor Zweig, my name is Chesson. I don't know if Sir Charles Grey mentioned me? Yes? I'm an admirer of yours. But what I was ringing about is this: we've had rather an interesting development, and I think you ought to know about it. We've had Interpol checking on this man Neumann. We haven't got much of value—he doesn't seem to have a police record in France, or Switzerland. But we've got a couple of things. His passport apparently gives an address at Gex, near Geneva. Well he doesn't live there any more, so we might be able to get him on a technicality there —his passport giving an out-of-date address. The other thing is that he has a police record in Germany. Nothing much. He was arrested in Berlin in 1951 for being in unlawful possession of various drugs, including heroin. He got off with a fine of ten thousand marks. Now I think we might have enough there to bring him in for questioning. Do you agree?'

Zweig stared at the telephone as if it was a living being,

wondering what to answer. Chesson's voice said: 'Hello?'
Zweig said: 'I . . . er . . . I cannot really offer an opinion.
I am sure Sir Charles would tell you to do what you think
best. . . .' He wanted to find a reason for delaying Neumann's
arrest, but his mind was a blank. Chesson said:

'All right, Professor, I'll ring him now. But I gather you've
been the chief mover on this case so far, so I didn't want to
do it without telling you. . . .'

'No. Quite.'

'The next thing, of course, is to find out why he was in
England under a false name in 1937 and 1938. But even so,
the case looks a bit brittle, unless we get something more
definite. Of course, there's this Sir Timothy Ferguson—he
might provide evidence against Neumann when he knows the
whole story. But I think the problem is to try to prevent him
from leaving the country and disappearing.'

'Yes, of course. . . .'

'If we bring him in for questioning, we'd probably want
you down at the Yard later today. Is that O.K.?'

'Er, yes. Perhaps you could telephone me?'

'I'll do that, Professor. I don't mind telling you, this is
one of the most slippery cases I've ever dealt with.'

After Chesson had rung off, Natasha said:

'What now?'

'They intend to arrest Gustav at the station—or bring him
in for questioning. They have found out that he was on a
drugs charge in Berlin in 1951. They can probably pretend
that he is an undesirable alien.'

She shrugged. 'Surely it's just as well? It has to come out
in the open sometime.'

'I don't know.' He lifted the telephone. 'I must ring
Charles. . . .' A moment later, he replaced the telephone.
'Engaged. Chesson must be talking to him now.'

'Then let's go and eat.'

'Would you mind if we ate something up here instead? I
no longer feel like a full meal. I could send the porter out
for something.'

'There's no need to do that. I'll go to the delicatessen round
the corner and get something. You stay here.'

When she had gone, Zweig walked up and down the room;
once again he had a feeling of being lost in events that were

moving too fast. After five minutes, he tried Grey's number again; this time, Grey answered.

'Hello, Karl. I've just been talking to Chesson. I think this is probably a good idea, don't you? The alternative is to keep him under observation for another day or so. But I've got a feeling we might be able to hang on to him. I think this business of false identity might be enough to reopen the Maidstone case.'

'Will he be arrested as he gets off the train?'

'I imagine so. Either that, or he'll be followed and arrested later today. Chesson wants to find out whether he has any intention of leaving the country. Gardner tells me he spotted his air return ticket to Munich in his case when you were searching the cottage. There's a Munich flight at seven this evening, and another at eight in the morning. So we may watch and wait.'

'Will you ring me as soon as anything happens?'

'Of course.'

When Natasha returned, holding a paper carrier bag, Zweig was standing by the window, drinking gin and tonic. She said:

'I could do with one of those.'

Zweig poured her one.

'I should not be drinking. I know I have been drinking too much during the past week. But suddenly I feel . . .' He paused, groping for a word, then said suddenly: 'It is all wrong.'

'Drinking?' She looked surprised.

'No.' He laughed, then became serious again. 'Arresting Gustav now.'

'Isn't it just as well, though? If he's not guilty, he'll have a chance to prove it.'

'It is not as simple as that.'

'You believe he's guilty?'

He gestured nervously, as if trying to throw off something that oppressed him.

'I am not sure whether he is guilty or not, and that is not the question. All that I know is . . . that I understand Gustav in a way that no jury is ever likely to.'

She went into the kitchen and unpacked the carrier bag. Zweig sat near the window, drinking his gin and tonic and staring over the rooftops towards Park Lane. When the smell of frying chicken came to him, he realized that he was hungry. He looked at his watch; it was one o'clock. Neumann was now either on his way to Scotland Yard, or being followed by detectives. It was too late to do anything. When the phone rang, he rushed to it, and Natasha came out of the kitchen to listen; but it was only his sister, ringing to ask him to supper. He made an excuse, promised to ring her back and hung up. She smiled sympathetically, and went back to her cooking. He poured himself another gin.

The meal made him feel better. Natasha had cooked the chicken with paprika and a touch of garlic salt; they ate it sitting opposite one another at the table. For Zweig, this made the occasion feel like a celebration; when alone, he usually ate off a tray, sitting in his armchair.

She said: 'Well, I suppose I'd better return to my husband.' She yawned and stretched.

He smiled. 'It might be as well.' He lifted the telephone. 'But first, let me see if Grey has any news.' He dialled, then replaced it. 'His number is engaged.'

He was letting her out of the door when it rang again. He said:

'Ah, I have just tried to ring you.'

Grey said: 'Chesson's been on to me. The idiots have let Neumann give them the slip.'

Natasha raised her eyebrows at the smile on Zweig's face as he asked: 'How?'

'He got a taxi from the station, but they lost it in a traffic jam in Shaftesbury Avenue. When it stopped in Pelham Place, only Ferguson got out. Neumann must have slipped out somewhere around Piccadilly.'

'I see. And what do you propose to do now?'

'We're not sure. Is Natasha there?'

'Yes.'

'Could you ask her if she has any idea where Neumann could go? Does Ferguson have any cottages near London?'

Zweig asked her: 'Has Sir Timothy a cottage anywhere near London?' He did not place his hand over the mouthpiece and Grey could hear her reply: 'Not as far as I know.'

'Do you propose to speak to Ferguson?' Zweig asked.

'Not yet. I don't think it would serve any purpose at this stage. If we get any definite evidence from Interpol, I shall go to see him immediately. But if he's in touch with Neumann, he might warn him off. So, for the moment, we shall ust watch Ferguson. I'll ring you back if there are any fresh developments.'

When he hung up, Natasha said:

'I gather he's escaped?'

'Yes.'

'You're pleased?'

'In a way, yes. And yet . . .'

She sat down on the arm of the chair.

'There's one thing . . . Tim *has* got a cottage. About five miles from Egham.'

He stared at her.

'But why did you say not?'

'Because I thought you'd want me to.'

'But . . .' He changed his mind about whatever he was about to say. Instead, he took her hand, and kissed the palm. She laughed.

'There's only one problem. Joseph knows about it too. If Sir Charles thinks of phoning him, the police'll be there within an hour.'

'Do you think Gustav might have gone there?'

'It's possible, I suppose. There's another thing, too. Tim keeps a car in London—a little Anglia. He has it garaged near Piccadilly Circus.'

'Piccadilly! That is where they think Gustav got out of his taxi.'

'Then we can soon find out. Ring the garage—I've got its number in my little book—and ask them if Sir Timothy's car has been taken out.' She fumbled in her handbag. 'On second thoughts, you'd better let me ring them. They know me.'

Zweig walked up and down the room as she telephoned. The garage kept her waiting. She sat on the arm of the chair, tapping her teeth with the end of a white pencil, smiling at him. Someone had once told Zweig that he looked like a panda when he become agitated, so he forced himself to go into the study and open his Heidegger manuscript which lay on the desk. He heard her say: 'This is Mrs Gardner. Is that Sidney? Oh, Sidney, I wonder if you could tell me whether Sir Timothy Ferguson's little Anglia has been taken out today? It has? Who took it . . . ? I see. . . . And has anyone else rung up to inquire about it? . . . No, it's not important. Thank you, Sidney.'

She came in.

'Yes. It was taken an hour ago by Neumann. He had a letter from Sir Timothy.'

'Do you know where this cottage is?'

'I think so. I've been there once. Do you want to go there?'

He stood there, thinking about it, staring past her.

'I don't know. This is certainly our chance. . . . We could talk to him.'

'There's only one difficulty. If he *is* charged with murder, you might be regarded as an accessory.'

'I know.'

'*Why* do you want to talk to him?'

'Why?' He thought about it, his eyes resting absently on the manuscript. Then he tapped the manuscript with his finger. 'Because of this. Because I shall have no chance to talk to him properly if he is arrested. Because I want him to know that . . . that I understand.'

She was frowning. 'How do you mean . . . because of that? What has your book got to do with it?'

He went past her into the sitting-room. He said slowly:

'If Gustav is a murderer, I shall spend every penny I have on his defence.'

Without moving, she asked: 'Why? Don't you think he'd deserve the death penalty?'

'You can say—if you like—that it is out of friendship to his father.'

'I don't understand you.'

'I will try to explain—but not now. At the moment, there are other things to be done. Will you telephone your husband, and ask him not to mention about the cottage to the police?'

'Is that wise?'

'Do you think he would refuse?'

'No. But . . . if the police find out about this cottage, I can always pretend I'd forgotten about it. But if we ring Joseph now, we're both opening ourselves to accessory charges.'

'Of course . . . it is stupid of me to ask. I am sorry.'

She shrugged, lifting the telephone. He reached out and took her hand.

'No, you are right. It is dangerous.'

She said, smiling: 'I'll risk it.' She was already dialling. He started to speak, then stood back helplessly. She said: 'Hello, Margaret. Is Mr Gardner there? . . . When? I see. Did he leave a message? Thank you.' She replaced the receiver. 'He had a phone call a few minutes ago and went straight out. He didn't say where he was going.'

'Ah . . . then it was probably Grey or the police.'

She said: 'Which means that they're probably on their way to the Egham cottage already.'

He sat down in the armchair, and massaged his eyes with his fingers. He suddenly felt very tired. She said:

'I'm sorry. But there isn't much we can do now.'

'No.'

'Although there's one thing . . . I'd like to see Tim Ferguson before the police get to him.'

She was surprised by the eagerness on his face as he stood up.

'Yes, of course. Perhaps he can tell us something. . . .'

'Do you want to come too?'

'Yes, yes. Let us go now.'

'Very well.'

As they went downstairs, she said:

'You'd better leave a mesage in case Sir Charles or Joseph turn up here.'

'Of course.' He tapped on the porter's door as they crossed the hall. 'I am going out for about an hour. It is possible that someone may call while I am out. If he would like to wait, would you let him into my flat?'

She said, laughing: 'I hope there isn't anything incriminating around?'

'Only my manuscript and the dinner plates.'

Her cream, two-seater Jaguar was parked round the corner. It had a ticket under its windscreen wiper. She glanced at it carelessly and dropped it on the pavement. Zweig climbed in beside her.

'I am afraid that your husband will be thinking of divorce if you stay with me much longer.'

She laughed. 'You don't know Joseph.' The car started with a deep roar. 'I'll tell you a secret. He's hoping to persuade you to write a preface to his new book proving that Atlantis was destroyed by an atomic war.'

As the car turned into Park Lane, he said:

'I may.'

She glanced at him with surprise.

'You'd be mad!'

He said grimly: 'I have done stupider things.'

She parked the car behind the South Kensington underground station.

'There's no sense in advertising who we are. They're probably watching the place.'

But there was no sign of anyone who might have been a detective in Pelham Place. As they went down the path to the house, Zweig observed the familiar stirring of the curtain in the ground-floor window. He smiled towards it, and the startled face of the old lady appeared at the window, dissolving into welcoming grimaces. Natasha went down the basement steps and rang the doorbell. When there was no reply she banged on the door. Zweig went back up the steps and gestured at the window; when the old lady looked out, he called: 'Is Sir Timothy at home?' She nodded and pointed downwards. Natasha rang the bell again, and Zweig rejoined her. Zweig started to say: 'Perhaps he's gone out for a meal,' when they heard fumbling noises on the other side of the door. A moment later it opened slightly and a single bright eye peered at them through the crack. Natasha said: 'Tim, what's the matter?'

'Ah, it's you, Tash.' Ferguson opened the door. Zweig was shocked by the whiteness of his face. He looked as though he had just crawled out of a coffin. Ferguson turned and walked inside, without troubling to ask them in. His walk expressed complete exhaustion. Natasha glanced at Zweig before she went in. She said in a whisper: 'He looks as if he's had another stroke.'

Zweig followed her into a comfortably furnished livingroom; he noticed that the carpet was of the same type as in the cottage at Bury St Edmunds. The room was cold. Ferguson dropped into an armchair and sat there, his head resting on its back, staring up at them. His voice had a perceptible Scottish burr.

'Ah'm afraid ah'm none too good, girl.'

She asked: 'Why is the room so cold?'

He nodded towards the fire. 'Switch it on.' Zweig leaned forward and depressed the switch. The room smelled damp and unlived in.

She asked: 'Can I get you anything?'

'Yes. Could ye reach me a little spot of whisky? There's a flask in my case.'

She said firmly: 'I think you'd better get into bed. You look awful.' Nevertheless, she unlocked his case and took out the whisky flask. When she handed Ferguson a glass with half an inch of the spirit, he raised it slowly and rested it against his chin for a moment before drinking. It made him cough, and whisky ran down his chin. She said:

'I'm going to get you a hot-water bottle and get you into bed. What have you been doing?'

His voice sounded pathetic, like a child's.

'Don't ask me now. I'll tell you later.' He closed his eyes. After a moment, he said: 'Ah'm glad you came, lass.'

The powerful electric fire gradually warmed the room. Zweig sat in the chair, looking at Ferguson's grey face, and refusing to think. Ferguson was breathing wheezily. So far, he had not acknowledged Zweig's presence. Natasha came in from the bedroom.

'I've remade your bed. The sheets were damp. Come and get in.' Zweig observed in her manner a touch of the warmth, almost a tenderness, that she often showed when speaking to him. A stranger might have thought she was Ferguson's daughter.

Zweig helped Natasha get Ferguson to his feet and into the bedroom. As she began to unlace Ferguson's shoes, she whispered: 'Could you go and fill a hot-water bottle? It's beside the kettle.'

When Zweig came in again, the old man was in bed; the pink glow of the bedside light, and the warmth of the electric fire, made the room seem less depressing than when they came in. Natasha handed Zweig a scrap of paper with a telephone number on it.

'Would you telephone that number? It's a doctor. Say it's urgent.'

Ferguson opened his eyes.

'Listen, m'dear, I don't want a doctor. Please.'

'You need one.'

'No. Just bring in my case from the other room. There's some aspirin in there.'

Zweig brought in the case and left it on a chest of drawers. Ferguson was breathing wheezily, his eyes closed. But when Natasha said softly: 'Go and telephone,' he said clearly: 'No, not yet, Tash. Give it another half-hour. Leave me alone for a moment now.'

'How about the aspirin?'

'Not now. Just let me rest.'

She shrugged, and followed Zweig into the sitting-room, saying: 'We're here, if you need anything.'

She closed the door and they sat down. She said: 'I think we should call a doctor.'

'I agree. But he seems not to want one.'

'That's what bothers me. He's usually a terrible hypochondriac. He'd tell us to summon half a dozen doctors once upon a time. . . .'

'What do you think is wrong? Did you say he had suffered a stroke before?'

'Twice. But very mild ones. I've never seen him looking so ill.'

They stared at one another. She said:

'Do you think. . . .'

There was a noise from the bedroom. She hurried to the door and flung it open. Zweig could see Ferguson standing by the chest of drawers, leaning heavily against his case. She said: 'What is it?'

'Nothing.' He reeled backwards and sat on the end of the bed. His hand went to his mouth. She asked:

'What are you taking?'

'Aspirin.'

She went to his case. Zweig saw her hold up a small bottle. 'This isn't an aspirin bottle.'

'There was only one left,' he said.

She stared at him for a moment, shrugged, then said: 'Come on. Back into bed. I'm going to call a doctor.'

'No, please. . . .' He allowed her to help him back into bed and pull the blanket over him. He said: 'Leave it for ten minutes, please.'

'All right, ten minutes.' Her voice now had the hard tone of a professional nurse. She went out of the room without speaking again.

Zweig took the bottle that she held out to him. It was a glass bottle, very small, the type in which saccharins are sometimes sold. But there was no white deposit inside the bottle to indicate what it had contained; it looked as if it had just been washed and polished. The cap was half unscrewed. Zweig removed it and sniffed; the faint smell reminded him of grass.

She said: 'He took something. And I don't believe it was an aspirin.'

A voice from the bedroom called: 'Natasha.' It no longer sounded exhausted. She glanced with surprise at Zweig, then went out. As the bedroom door opened, Zweig could see that Ferguson was sitting up in bed. He sat there, listening to the murmur of their voices. After five minutes, she came in again. She closed the door carefully, then said:

'I don't understand. Come in and see him.'

He followed her; but he could already guess what he would see. Ferguson was now sitting up in bed. Although his face was still colourless, it was no longer devoid of life and energy; he looked now like a man suffering from a headache or a hangover. He smiled at Zweig:

'Ach, my dear man, I'm sorry to put you to all this trouble. We haven't met, but I know about you.'

'You are feeling better?'

'Much better. I had rather a bad turn before you arrived and I could do nothing but sit and catch my breath. . . . Can I offer you a drink?'

'No, thank you. You'd better stay in bed.'

'Yes, sairtainly, I'll do that.'

She was standing by the sideboard, looking in his case. He said:

'What do you want, my dear?'

'To see if you've got any more aspirins!'

'No. I had the last. Do you think I could have another drop of whisky now? Or, come to think of it, a cup of tea'd be very comforting.'

She turned on him suddenly:

'Now, listen to me, Tim. I don't know what you think you're hiding from me. But I'd better tell you, we know quite a lot about your friend Neumann.'

He dropped his eyes, and his head collapsed on the pillow; Zweig recognized the mute appeal for sympathy of the professional invalid.

'I don't know what you mean, lass. He's got nothing to hide, as far as I know.'

She said: 'At the moment, the police are trying to arrest him.'

He looked up, and the look on his face was close to terror.

'Arrest Gustav? But why? They *can't* do that.' He almost

screamed the last words. His eyes turned from Natasha to Zweig. 'Why? Why do they want to arrest him?'

Zweig said gently: 'He came into England in 1937 with a false passport. They have definite evidence of this.'

'But that was so long ago! They can't bring that up now.'

Natasha sat on the bed. Her voice was gentler now.

'Tim, I don't know how much you know about Gustav Neumann, but I can tell you that the police have their reasons for wanting to hold him for a while.'

He sat upright. Zweig was surprised to see that all trace of weakness had vanished from his voice.

'No. They can't do that. Tash, you mustn't allow them to. It's important. . . .'

'Why is it important?'

He reached out and took her hand. His voice was trembling.

'Listen, Tash, you've got a motor-boat at Folkestone, Joe's got a boat. . . . Please listen. Help him to get out of the country. Get him into France.'

'But why? Do you know why they want to hold him?'

Zweig could read Ferguson's uncertainty in the desperate and unhappy expression of his eyes.

'I know what you suspect. Of course I know. But he's *got* to get away, Tash. . . .'

She said: 'Will you answer me just one question?'

'If I can.' His voice wavered.

'Has he been giving you drugs?'

'I . . . I can't answer that.'

'Then there's nothing I can do. The police are looking for him now. They're probably on their way to your Egham cottage.'

He groaned. 'You didn't tell them about that?'

'No. But Joseph may have done. He's with them now.'

'But why? Why do you want to do this to him?'

She said: 'To begin with, because of what he's done to you.'

'He's done nothing to me, except keep me alive.'

'By giving you some drug. How much money have you given him?'

'Not much, yet.'

She said: 'And you won't, either. He'll be in jail.'

'Tasha, my love, don't be so cruel.' He was almost crying. 'You know I've always been fond of you. You wouldn't like to see me die now, would ye?'

She stormed: 'And who'll be responsible if you do? Don't be an old fool. Do you know how many others have died before you?'

Zweig was shocked by her brutality; he was aware of Ferguson's exhaustion, and was afraid that he might have another collapse. He was surprised when Ferguson seemed indifferent to what she said. He only said, in the same pleading tone:

'I know, my dear, but he's got to stay free for the present.'

'Why? What will you do if he gets out of England? Go and join him, I suppose?'

He looked mildly surprised, as if she was being unreasonable.

'But I'd have to go and join him, Tash.'

'Why?'

Ferguson turned to Zweig.

'Can't you make her understand? You were his teacher. Tell her he's not what she thinks.'

Zweig made his voice deliberately soft and reasonable; he wanted to counteract Natasha's anger.

'I agree with you to some extent, Sir Timothy. But you must understand why she feels this way. Could you tell us why you were so ill when we arrived?'

'That was my own fault. It upset me when he went off, and I got into a state. And that brought on the palpitations. He warned me about it.'

She asked: 'And what did you take to improve you so much?'

'I know. I took the emergency tablet he left. But it won't do any harm. Tash, my love, please do something about it.' He reached out again and took her hands. She stood up, sighing.

'All right. I'll see if I can ring Joseph.'

'Yes, would you do that? I'll never forget it. Hurry now. . . .'

Zweig followed her out of the bedroom. When she had closed the door, he asked:

'What are you going to do?'

'There's nothing I can do. I'll go and ring Joseph, but I'm sure he won't be home. But he's in such a state now that I'll have to pretend it's all right. Keep an eye on him.' She unbolted a side door, and went up a flight of stairs. Zweig returned to the bedroom. Ferguson smiled eagerly. 'Is she phoning?'

'Yes. She'll be back in a moment.'

'Good.' He closed his eyes, and for a moment looked peaceful and happy. They sat in silence; the only sound in the room was the tinny vibration that came from the electric fire, and an occasional short-circuit noise like the buzz of a gnat. Then Ferguson said:

'She won't understand, Professor, that's the trouble. He's a fine man, Gustav. You know that. But I can't tell her anything because I've given my word. Try and explain that to her. She gets so stubborn. . . .'

Zweig walked across the bedroom, his feet silent on the heavy carpet; it was impossible to sit still.

'Do you think it a good idea to rejoin him on the Continent?'

'Why not? He's not done me any harm, so far.'

'Are you sure?'

Ferguson opened his eyes.

'Quite sure.'

Zweig said patiently: 'You do see that it looks very bad, don't you? You admit you want to rejoin him. You admit that you'll probably give him money. And he's told you some kind of story about why the police are interested in him.'

'Not some kind of story. He told me the truth.'

'Then why did he come into England on a false passport in 1937?'

'He had to. He'd been in Germany, and the Nazis had a warrant for his arrest.'

'But why should he use his false name in England? There weren't any Nazis here.'

'No. I'm afraid he was a bit of a young fool in those days. I think he enjoyed playing at cloak and dagger.'

They heard voices in the next room. Natasha came in, followed by the young girl Zweig had met upstairs. Natasha said:

'Tim, I'll have to leave you now. This is Sylvia. She's going to stay in the next room and get you anything you want. She'll telephone a doctor if you don't feel well.'

'You're not going?'

'I'll have to.' She paused, then added: 'If I'm going to help you.'

He smiled suddenly. 'God bless you, dear.'

'I'm going back to Joseph now. He'll probably be along to see you later.'

He said eagerly: 'Good, yes, send him to see me. I want to talk to him about . . . about the boat.'

'All right. Try and sleep now. Don't let anything worry you. It's going to be all right.' She beckoned to Zweig. Ferguson said: 'Do you know what's happening? Do . . . they know . . . where he is?' It was evident that the girl's presence constrained him. Natasha said:

'Nothing's happening. No, they don't know about the cottage.'

'Good. And you won't tell them?'

'No.'

'God bless you.' He lay down and closed his eyes. Zweig went out of the bedroom, followed by Natasha.

As they walked back to the car, she said:

'I couldn't get on to Joseph. I tried our flat and Sir Charles Grey's. What do you think?'

Zweig said: 'I'm afraid it all seems rather obvious. Your husband was right about the drugs. I would like to know what he is using. I still have the bottle in my pocket. I shall give it to Grey for analysis.'

'What story do you suppose Neumann told Tim?'

'I don't know. But he claims Gustav swore him to secrecy.' As she let in the clutch, she said:

'It seems to me your Herr Neumann's too clever by half. His cleverness is going to get him into trouble very soon.'

They stopped at the Cromwell Road traffic lights. She said: 'Well, so you still want to go down to this cottage?'

'I don't know. Perhaps we should go back home first.'

'Then come up to our place and have a cup of tea. Joseph will probably ring me there.'

The maid who let them in said: 'No, Mr Gardner hasn't rung back yet. But Sir Charles Grey rang up a few minutes ago to ask if you were home yet. I said I didn't know when you'd be back.'

'Good. I'm feeling rather tired. Could you make us some tea before you go out?'

As he sank into the velvet cushions of the settee, Zweig realized how tired he felt. He leaned his head back and closed his eyes. Natasha came in from her bedroom. She stopped behind him and laid both her hands on his forehead. They felt infinitely soothing. She said:

'You ought to have a sleep. All this rushing around isn't good for you.'

'No. Or for you either.'

'Oh, I'm used to it. Joseph always lives like this.'

He realized that he was taking a sensuous pleasure in the contact of her hands; they were cool, and their touch seemed to restore his vitality. At the same time, he allowed himself to sink towards sleep. The sound of the door opening made her move away, and he came back to reality as if he had been on a long journey. She sat beside him, and he saw that she had changed into a grey woollen dress that showed the soft lines of her figure. The maid wheeled in a trolley with tea and biscuits. He accepted the cup from her without speaking, and they drank the tea in silence. There was no sound in the flat except cutlery noises from the kitchen. A few minutes later the maid said: 'I'll be going now, Mrs Gardner.' When the door closed behind her, Zweig had a sensation of being enclosed in a silence that had the soft quality of the velvet cushions. It came as a shock when she said:

'I wonder what Tim will do when they arrest Neumann?'

He grimaced.

'I'm afraid I had almost forgotten that problem.'

'I know. I'm getting tired of it too.'

He finished drinking his tea. He said:

'All the same, I hope they don't arrest him today.'

'Why?'

'Because I feel I owe him something. . . . It is the same kind of thing that I owe you.'

'What's that?' Her voice had no trace of a desire for flattery.

'A feeling of being alive again.'

She smiled. 'I don't know whether I'm flattered to be included with Neumann.'

He felt too tired to try to explain. When she wheeled the trolley back to the kitchen, he lifted his feet on to the settee, and laid his cheek against a cushion. A few minutes later he was asleep. When she came back in she covered him with a dressing gown, then removed the telephone from its cradle. He slept heavily for two hours.

He found himself in darkness, and for a moment thought that he was in his own bed. Then his hand encountered the cloth of his jacket. He sat up, rubbing his eyes, and his memory returned. He called softly: 'Natasha.' When there was no reply, he reached up and found the light switch of the standard lamp. He looked at his watch and found that it was five-thirty. He went into the bathroom, looked at his face in the mirror, then splashed water on it. He disliked sleeping in his clothes; it made him feel old and dirty. After drying himself and combing his hair, he felt better. He found his way to Natasha's bedroom. The door was slightly open and the light was on. Natasha was asleep under the eiderdown, still fully clothed. He tiptoed over to the bed and took her hand. She stirred, and pulled his hand to her breast with a gesture of a child holding a doll. He said: 'Natasha, wake up.' She opened her eyes, looked at him dreamily, then sat up abruptly.

'Goodness. What time is it?'

'Half past five.'

'Is Joseph not here yet?'

'No. I have just thought. He may be waiting at my flat. You remember, I told the porter to let him in.'

She threw back the eiderdown and stood up.

'We'd better get over there, in any case. Would you ring your flat while I get ready?'

He had some difficulty locating the telephone; she had buried it under a pile of cushions, and it was making a continuous howling noise. When he depressed the rest, the noise stopped, but it became completely silent. He moved the rest up and down for a few minutes, then replaced the receiver. As she came in he said:

'I cannot get a line. Perhaps we had getter go back immediately.'

'All right. I'm ready. Do I look a wreck?'

'Of course not. But you do not have to come with me. I can get a taxi.'

'No need. I'll drive you. If there's no one there, I'll come straight back. Ready?'

●

She stopped the car in front of the flats and said: 'Go in and ask the porter if he's let anyone in. If not, I'll go straight home.'

The porter said: 'Gentleman's been waitin' since five o'clock, sir.' Zweig beckoned to Natasha, and she climbed out of the car. Rain fell steadily. Zweig gave the porter half a crown. He still felt guilty about his sleep, as if the porter could tell from his appearance that he had been sleeping in his clothes. He asked: 'Is it the tall gentleman with the moustache?'

'He's got no moustache, sir.'

Natasha said: 'It must be Joseph.'

Again Zweig felt guilty. If Gardner should ask where they had been, could he reply 'We've both been asleep in your flat?' He thought that the porter glanced curiously at Natasha, with a sly amusement. He turned away irritably, and hurried up the stairs.

The flat seemed empty, Natasha called: 'Joseph.' She said: 'He must be in the bathroom.'

'No, in here.' They both turned sharply. Gustav Neumann was standing in the door of the study, smiling at them, his hands in his trouser pockets.

Natasha was the first to recover.

'Why are you here?'

'Am I intruding? I'm sorry.'

She repeated: 'Why are you here?'

'To begin with, because this is probably the last place in London where the police would look for me.'

She said: 'We could always alter that.'

Neumann ignored her. He said:

'I came to speak to you.'

Zweig cleared his throat. 'Why?'

'I shall be leaving the country tomorrow. I thought we should have a talk first.'

Natasha said: 'You mean you're *hoping* to leave the country tomorrow.'

He continued to speak to Zweig, as if Natasha was not present. 'Why? Is there anything to stop me?'

Zweig said: 'The police want to ask you some questions.'

'About what?'

'About why you came into the country in 1937 with a false passport.'

'I am sure I shall be able to satisfy them.'

'Do you think so?' It was Natasha speaking again. 'They're likely to arrive here at any moment.'

Neumann looked at her with mild surprise.

'Are they? I hope not. I agree that they might cause an inconvenient delay.'

She said: 'You'll also have to explain why Sir Timothy collapsed as soon as you left him today.'

Neumann's casualness vanished; Zweig was glad to see that he looked suddenly startled and worried.

'He did? Are you sure?'

Zweig said: 'We left him this afternoon. He seemed very ill when we arrived.'

'That's bad.' Neumann was staring at the carpet. 'Did he take the tablet I left?'

Natasha said: 'You admit you left a tablet?'

'Oh, yes. But how is he now?'

'He seemed better when we left,' Zweig said.

'Good. This is terribly difficult. . . .'

'What did you want to speak to me about?'

'I'm afraid that may have to wait. This is very awkward.' His eyes travelled from Natasha to Zweig. She asked:

'Am I in the way?'

He said absently: 'No, no.' He looked at his watch. 'I suppose they're watching the air terminal, then?'

'I suppose so.'

'Then I'm afraid I had better leave immediately. That is a pity. I had hoped to have a talk with you. I have been reading your manuscript. I hope you don't mind?' Neumann went back into the study and returned with his overcoat. Natasha said:

'You won't get very far.'

He eyed her thoughtfully.

'That is to be seen.' He buttoned the overcoat, then pulled on a pair of gloves. He looked at Zweig. 'I wonder if you would care to come with me?'

Zweig asked with surprise: 'Where to?'

Natasha interrupted: 'No, he wouldn't.'

Neumann smiled at her. 'My dear Mrs Gardner, I'm afraid you owe me a little rudeness after our lunch the other day. I would be sorry to add to my offence. But I'd really like to hear Professor Zweig's own opinions on the matter.'

She turned to Zweig: 'You can't go with him. I won't let you.'

Zweig put a hand on her shoulder, without taking his eyes off Neumann.

'Where did you want to go?'

'Somewhere where we can talk.'

She said: 'He'd be mad to trust you.'

Zweig said: 'If I come with you, would you bring me back here afterwards?'

'If you want me to.'

Zweig turned to Natasha.

'I'm going with him, my dear. Please don't try to stop me. I also want a chance to talk to him.'

'But you . . .' She hesitated, then turned on Neumann. 'Would you mind going out of the room for a moment while I say something?'

Neumann bowed, his face grave.

'Of course. I shall wait downstairs in the car. It is parked in the mews on the other side of Curzon Street.' He went to the door. 'I hope we shall meet again, madam.' He went out, closing the door quietly. They listened as his footsteps descended the stairs.

She said: 'Please don't go, Karl. You don't know how dangerous he is.'

He took her hand and raised it to his face.

'I must. I want to hear what he has to say. He can't do me any harm. And why should he want to?'

'Because you've given him away to the police! He knows that. He probably hates you.'

'That is possible. But it wouldn't do him any good to kill me.'

'But supposing he doesn't want to kill you! Supposing he gives you some of that drug? He wants to get power over you, the same kind he's got over Tim.'

'He has to make me take it first.' He made her sit down on the arm of the chair, then said: 'Listen. He is now waiting downstairs in the car. For all he knows, I am now on the telephone to the police. He is willing to trust me. And why do you suppose he has come here? He wants to talk to me. Don't you see that I have to trust him? Please don't try to stop me.'

She said: 'And what am I supposed to do while you're away? Sit at home and wonder if you're still alive?'

'I shall be alive.'

'But how shall I know?' She reached out both hands to him. 'I've only just found you. I don't want to lose you so quickly.'

He bent and kissed her white-gloved hands.

'Silly child.'

She stood up suddenly.

'You're not to go. Listen, I'll do anything.' For a moment he was not certain of her meaning. Then she made it unmistakable by taking his hands and placing them on her breasts. She leaned forward so that he could feel her breath against his lips. 'I wouldn't mind giving myself completely ... but I couldn't bear to lose you.'

He drew back; suddenly, he felt only tenderness and pity. He said:

'Please don't worry. But I have to go.'

For a moment, he thought she was going to burst into sobs and cling to him. Instead, he saw a curious calm invade her eyes; she stood back and looked at him; her eyes were sad, but no longer pleading.

'All right. I understand. Go quickly then.' He turned away and opened the door. She said: 'But try to telephone me as soon as you can. I'll be at home.'

'Very well.' He went out and closed the door.

It was still raining, and he was bareheaded. He turned up his collar, and hurried along Clarges Street. The thought of what had just taken place made Neumann seem unimportant. His hands could still feel the shape of her breasts under the thin wool. He said aloud: 'Old fool,' and a passer-by turned and stared after him.

He could see the rear lights of Neumann's car as he crossed

Curzon Street. The engine was idling softly. He opened the passenger door and climbed in. Without looking at him, Neumann let in the clutch and reversed. Neither of them spoke until the car turned into Knightsbridge; then Neumann said:

'I thought you'd come.'

Zweig stared out at the wet road that mirrored the lights. He said:

'She didn't want me to come.'

'Of course.'

Zweig glanced at Neumann's face, but could detect no expression under the tiredness. He said:

'She thinks I am taking a great risk.'

Without taking his eyes off the road, Neumann said:

'Not half as great as I am taking.' He spoke in German, and for some reason it came to Zweig as a shock. He tried to analyse it—whether he was startled by the content of the words, or the language in which they had been spoken. He asked:

'You? Are you taking a risk?'

As the silence lengthened, he thought that Neumann was not going to answer. Then Neumann said:

'If I speak to you frankly this evening, I shall be breaking a rule that I made twenty-five years ago.'

He overtook a lorry, and turned into Cromwell Road. Zweig looked out of the lowered window, hearing the hiss of tyres in the rain, feeling the spots that blew against his face, and thought about what Neumann had just said. It now struck him as strange that this was the first time they had spoken German together since they left Heidelberg. In the hotel in Bury St Edmunds, it had seemed natural enough that they should speak English; both spoke it fluently, without accent. And yet it had emphasized that they had both changed; he thought of Neumann as a different person from the Heidelberg student. Now this no longer seemed true; he wondered it Neumann had done this deliberately.

As they drove over the Chiswick flyover, he asked: 'Where are we going?'

'To a cottage I know.'

'If it belongs to Sir Timothy, I'm afraid it may be watched.'

Neumann looked at him quickly:

'Why?'

'Because Gardner knows about it, and he may have told the police.'

Neumann slowed the car; for a moment, Zweig thought they were about to turn back, then realized they were approaching a red traffic light.

'Are you sure?'

'I am sure that Gardner knows about it. Unfortunately, I have not seen him all day, so I don't know whether he's told the police.'

Neumann started the car as the lights changed. He said:

'It probably makes no difference. If they really want me, they could prevent me from leaving the country.'

'So what will you do if the police are waiting at the cottage?'

Neumann shrugged.

'It would be inconvenient.'

'Why?'

Neumann smiled.

'That I shall explain in due course.'

Neither of them spoke as they drove through Staines. Zweig looked at the policeman on point duty, and at the Saturday evening crowds, and reflected that he felt no strangeness. For the past week he had repeated the question: Could Gustav be a murderer? Now he sat beside Neumann, it no longer seemed important. He had a sense of allowing himself to be carried along, of asking no questions. Instead, he thought: He has become more like his father than ever, and found that his thoughts went back forty years to a rainy evening in a Berlin café. Again the sense of passing time came to him, and made all other ideas unimportant. He looked at Neumann, thinking: He too, and felt something like pity.

The car was turning into the parking space in front of a public house. Neumann caught his look of surprise and said: 'Would you not like a drink?'

'Certainly.'

The saloon bar was empty.

'What will you drink? I shall have a lager.'

'The same for me.'

Zweig took a seat near the fire and watched Neumann ordering the drinks. He thought: He looks absurdly young—

perhaps thirty. His face is unlined. It is obvious that he has not inherited his father's trick of worrying.

Neumann caught his eye as he returned across the room, and smiled.

'They had a German lager.' He placed the glasses on the table. 'I prefer it to Danish.' Zweig raised his glass and said: 'Prosit.' Neumann smiled.

'To the future.'

He drank deeply, then replaced the glass on the table. Zweig was surprised by his smile. He said:

'You look . . . very cheerful.'

He had been about to say: You look happy. Neumann stretched his legs towards the fire and flexed his shoulders. He said:

'I enjoy a good lager.'

Zweig said politely: 'I remember you were fond of it.'

Neumann lifted his glass.

'I stopped drinking it after Georgi Braunschweig died.'

For some reason, the name shocked Zweig; he had not expected to hear it. He asked: 'Why?'

'We used to drink it together. As you know, I was fond of him.'

Neumann's voice contained no self-pity, or even regret; he stated it as a fact that they both knew. There was a silence between them, and Zweig felt no need to fill it by talking. He was waiting. The talk should be in Neumann's hands. When both of them emptied their glasses, the silence still seemed natural.

'Another?'

'I will get them.'

Zweig went to the counter. When he returned, Neumann said:

'I hope the police are not waiting at the cottage. What I have to say to you may take a long time.'

'Then why not stay here?'

'No. It will be crowded in an hour.'

As Zweig was about to drink, he asked:

'Why have you decided to talk to me?'

'For several reasons.' Neumann stared into his glass; there was a fleck of beer foam on his upper lip. 'To begin with, I read some of your Heidegger manuscript.'

'I see.'

Neumann looked at him.

'It has . . . a curious freshness. It reminds me of your early books.'

'Thank you.'

Neumann smiled. It was a one-sided smile that Zweig remembered from his student days; it produced an effect of friendliness and self-mockery.

'I think we have a great deal to say to one another.' He frowned, seemed to hesitate, then said: 'You are an honest man.'

The compliment startled Zweig. His first reaction was to say: 'I hope so,' but he repressed it. Instead, he asked:

'Why did we stop here?' He knew the answer, but he wanted to hear Neumann say it.

'Because I want to tell you something without fear of interruption.' The door opened, and three people came in, talking loudly. Neumann frowned and leaned forward. 'It is this. I said earlier that I was taking a risk in talking to you.' He was staring at the table top as he spoke, and Zweig had to lean forward to catch the words. 'I did not mean a physical risk. But I have spoken to no one about the things I shall tell you. . . .'

Zweig asked: 'Not even Sir Timothy Ferguson?'

Neumann glanced up, and smiled acknowledgement.

'Yes, he knows a little. But not much. You remember how I brought Georgi to see you one evening, and he told you about his most important idea? Do you remember what that idea was?'

Zweig shook his head.

'It was this: that he suspected that every human being who has ever lived has wasted his life completely. Do you remember that?'

'I think so.'

Neumann shrugged. 'I know—it sounds obvious. I often heard him say it, but it never struck me as very important. But after his death, his mother gave me his writings—all his papers—and he had begun to write an essay on the subject. And for the first time I understood what he meant.' Neumann stared at Zweig for the first time, and spoke deliberately. 'He meant that *if* all human life has contained a certain basic error, then the man who realized this would be *completely alone*. He could speak to no one. Other people could only confuse his certainty. Well, when I became convinced that he was right, I also knew that I would have to work alone. . . .'

'But your father . . .?'

'Yes, to some extent, my father. I could speak to him. But only of the superficial aspects.' He paused, then looked again directly at Zweig. 'To you I could no longer speak. You understand why? It was not merely that you were in another country, that you had become a Christian thinker. I had to reject everything you had ever taught me. No doubt I rejected it too violently.' He paused, and took out a packet of small cigars; Zweig accepted one. He wondered if the gesture was intended to be symbolic. 'Even now, I am not certain whether you will understand what I have to say.'

He held out the match, and Zweig lit his cigar. He asked: 'Then why tell me now?'

Neumann shook out the match. 'Because—this reason may strike you as unbelievable—I am a sentimentalist.'

'I believe you,' Zweig said.

Two men and a woman came over to the fire; the woman stretched her hands towards it, then said to Zweig: 'Excuse me.'

Zweig smiled, drawing back his chair. 'Certainly.' Neumann drained his glass and stood up.

'Perhaps we should go now.'

As they climbed into the car, he went on speaking as if they had not been interrupted.

'So it was important that I should get an opportunity to speak to you before I leave the country. And if we are not interrupted . . .' He pulled out on to the road. As they drove along he asked unexpectedly: 'Are you hungry?'

'No. Not now.'

'I have bought food. We can cook it at the cottage.'

Zweig thought of Natasha waiting by a telephone, and wondered if he should suggest phoning her now. Before he could decide, Neumann had slowed and turned to the left, into a minor road.

'We are almost there.'

A few miles further on, Neumann turned off into a narrow lane. Neither of them spoke now. The headlights caught the shapes of trees on either side of the road. Zweig was tempted to say: 'Why not turn back? Stay at a hotel somewhere,' then realized that it would make no difference. If the police were waiting here, they would ultimately find Neumann.

Five minutes later, lights showed in the darkness. Neumann said: 'That is the farm.'

'You have been here before?'

'Once, a few days after we landed.'

'Then why did you not stay here instead of going to Bury St Edmunds?'

'You will see when we get there.' He turned the car off the road. In the farm-house a dog began to bark and a woman's face looked out of a lighted window. The car's headlights showed a narrow, muddy lane, with water flowing along its centre. The tyres skidded, then gripped. A hundred yards farther on, Neumann said: 'I am afraid it will be necessary to open the gate. Would you mind?' Zweig stumbled out in the wet mud and found the rusty wire that kept the gate closed. The sickly smell of pig dung was in the wind. When he climbed back into the car, he saw with regret that the mud had covered his shoes and trouser bottoms.

The car bumped along a winding track with projecting stones; then the headlights showed a whitewashed cottage. Neumann said softly: 'Now we shall see.' He stopped the car, took a key from the glove compartment, and opened the door. Zweig waited until he had opened the back door before he climbed out of the car. Sound of running water came from nearby. When the wind blew, treetops shook rain on him.

He stood in the completely dark, damp-smelling room. Neumann lit a match and fumbled with a gas bracket. As the pale light filled the room, Zweig saw they were in a kitchen. From inside a cupboard in a corner came a scurrying noise. Neumann said: 'Mice.'

Zweig said, smiling: 'But no police.'

'As far as we can see.' He went into the next room and lit another gas lamp. Zweig saw that the fireplace had been piled high with kindling wood and logs. Zweig went to the window and drew the curtains; they were rotten and tore in his hands. Neumann said: 'You see now why we preferred the other cottage.'

He unscrewed a gallon tin and poured paraffin on to the kindling wood. Five minutes later the crackling of the logs made the room more cheerful. While Neumann was outside turning off the car headlights Zweig heard a noise behind him;

as he turned, the firelight caught the red eyes of a rat that disappeared instantly. He swore, and as Neumann came in, said: 'I am more nervous than you are.'

Neumann shrugged. 'It is a place to talk. Would you like another drink? I have some whisky or gin.'

Zweig said: 'A little, perhaps.' He felt no desire to drink, but needed to relax.

'Are you tired?'

'Physically. The past few days have been . . . rather exhausting.'

'I understand.' There was no sarcasm in Neumann's smile. He took a small bottle from his pocket and unscrewed its cap. 'Perhaps you should try one of these.'

'What is it?'

'A discovery of my own.' Neumann shook a small green tablet, about the size of a saccharin, into his hand, and put it into his mouth. 'Try one.'

Zweig accepted the tablet. It tasted bitter, so he swallowed it immediately. Neumann brought two glasses and poured an inch of whisky into each. Zweig swallowed a mouthful, and immediately felt a warm glow in his stomach.

Neumann pulled an armchair nearer to the fire. Its covering was damp and steam rose from the arm that was closest to the flames. Neumann said:

'I was impressed by the opening sentence of your Heidegger book. It seemed to me to go to the heart of the problem. Man's experience of the world is basically an experience of limitation. . . .'

'I noticed something very similar in your article on suicide.'

'Ah, yes . . . I saw it on your desk. But the idea was not my own. Again, it came from Georgi. I could say that it was my starting point.'

Zweig asked, smiling: 'And not your idea of becoming a great criminal?'

'Oh, that. I soon abandoned that.'

'Why?'

'Because I had more exciting things to occupy me. . . . But to return to this problem of limitation . . . what is it?'

The bubble of pleasure that rose up in Zweig had expressed itself as a laugh.

'The effect of this tablet. It's remarkable.'

'How do you feel?'

'Strange. Completely clearheaded. . . .'

It was suddenly amazing to Zweig that he could have found this room depressing. It was true that the walls were flaking and covered with damp spots, and that the ceiling was riddled with woodworm; but these things were not in themselves disagreeable. On the contrary, their suggestion of austerity pleased him. His brain felt like an electric generator working a searchlight; his body and flesh seemed realler than usual, somehow controllable, his own, not a casual extension of himself.

'What is it? What was in the tablet?'

'It would not mean anything to you if I told you. My father did most of the work on it. Unfortunately, he was dead before I perfected his discovery.'

'Is it a drug?'

'Not in the normal sense. You see, a drug affects the body by exciting and stimulating, but also by reducing its efficiency. For example, that whisky is a kind of drug. It gives you a feeling of internal warmth, but it also blankets all your perceptions. It is like wearing a heavy overcoat to keep in the warmth; it also restricts your freedom of movement. Now the stuff you've just tried doesn't repress or stimulate. It simply clears away certain obstacles and allows your energy system to operate without waste or friction.'

'What do you call it?'

'Neuromysin. It's a derivative of neurocaine.'

'What is neurocaine?'

'That is what I shall explain in a moment. First of all, let me explain my basic idea. Do you see now why I attach so much importance to the idea of limitation?'

'I . . . think so.'

'You see? Five minutes ago you accepted your fatigue as a limitation. You were willing to struggle with it, but you assumed that you had to accept it. And this was the idea that Georgi made me think about. You know that he was a serener person than I was. He never lost his temper. Yet in a strange way, he was more of a rebel. Because he made me think about that question: supposing all human life so far has been a misdirection? He used to quote one of the prophets who said: "Take away my life, oh Lord, for I am no better than my fathers." And he said: "That man had real perception. He saw that human life shouldn't be static and futile." He had another favourite quotation: "Life is a preparation for something that never happens." He used to say: "That is what the prophet meant." He used to think that man has some essential faculty that he has never used, whose existence he hardly suspects. . . .'

'You mean telepathy, or something like that?'

'That is what Georgi meant. I am not sure. That is not how the problem came to me. Let me tell you how it first came to me. You remember how we were always having electricity cuts and gas cuts in Heidelberg, with half the workers on strike? Well, one day, my father put on a kettle to make coffee, but the gas was very low, and it took nearly an hour to boil. My father was trying to write an article for a psychological journal at the same time. Suddenly he looked up and said: "My brain is like that kettle—it won't boil." And in a flash, it came to me: that is what is wrong with all human consciousness The pressure is so low that it never boils. We live at half pressure. We are all psychologically undernourished because the pressure of consciousness is so low. My father was right. If his consciousness had been brighter, the article would have been written as fast as his pen could move across the paper.' Neumann was talking fast, smiling as he talked, and he now stood up and walked across the room, away from the fire. 'Ah, it was then that I wished that Georgi was there—so that I could talk to him. Because suddenly it came to me: I had stumbled on the solution to his problem—at least, on the right direction. Because if human life has always been futile, it is because human beings live at half pressure. There are certain moments when the consciousness intensifies—in a sexual orgasm, for example— and we catch a glimpse of the real potentialities of the brain and body. But for the most part, we are like dynamos that turn infinitely slowly because they are fed by a mere trickle of electricity. Now the problem that occurred to me was this: what is the source of the electric current that drives us?' He stopped, leaning back against the old chest of drawers that stood in the corner, looking down at Zweig; it took Zweig a few moments to realize that he was expected to answer. He said slowly:

'The source? Energy . . . will power, I suppose. . . .'

Neumann cut in: 'Quite. And you cannot will without a purpose. It seems a vicious circle. That was how it seemed to me when I first considered the problem. You remember that scandal of the car I stole and drove over the Devil's Shoulder? It was this that provided me with a kind of clue. I admit that I was in an absurd state of mind when I did it. Confused and angry—but angry with nothing in particular, just with life and destiny. Well, I can remember that I wanted some sort of a *sign*, a sign that destiny cared about me. I thought: If I am in this world for a particular purpose, would God intervene if I tried to kill myself? It sounds stupid, yet it seemed obvious and sensible at the time. So I stole the car, and drove it to the Devil's Shoulder, then drove it as fast as I could for the edge of the cliff. And the next thing I knew was that I was lying bruised on the ground, and the car had burst into flame five hundred feet below me. Without an act of conscious will, I had flung myself out of the car within two feet of the edge of the cliff. You see? I *had not willed it*. Something deep inside me—something beyond my everyday consciousness—had flung me out of the car. I cannot explain my feelings as I lay there and watched the flames in the valley, but it was a tremendous triumph. All the doubt seemed to vanish. My dynamo was suddenly working at full power. It seemed that I understood everything. I remember sitting there, repeating: "You fool, you fool." But I was not reproaching myself for stealing and wrecking an expensive car. I was saying: "You fool, why did you ever doubt?" ' Neumann stopped; the excitement left his eyes; he shrugged. 'I am not proud of that episode. It was stupid. And yet it had a certain experimental value. Because I had come to believe that the source of power is completely beyond the reach of human beings—that we have to wait for destiny to grant us a moment of insight. This experience taught me that everything is inside us; all we have to do is pull the switch. But the switch is carefully concealed. . . .'

Zweig spread his hands abruptly, closing them as if grasping at something in the air in front of him; he said helplessly: 'But why did you not speak to me about all this?' He was afraid the answer would be: I tried to; you would not listen. He was relieved when Neumann said:

'Because I was ashamed. At least, a part of me was ashamed. Another part was completely detached. When, the next day, I told my father that I had taken the car, I listened to his reproaches, but I kept thinking: "And why not? I have just performed an experiment that may be of incalculable consequence to the world, as important as any of the experiments of Galileo, Newton, Rutherford." Because I had established, to my own satisfaction, the existence of an *unconscious level of purpose* inside one, a purpose that had good reason for not wanting me to die. It was also at this time that I realized that, in spite of my own inner uncertainty, I seemed able to dominate other people fairly easily. I became interested in the problem of hypnotism, for example. And it was through this that I stumbled on another important recognition: that most people do not like their own identities. Do you remember Gerda Liebknecht? No? The girl who was head of the Catholic Youth Guild and various religious instruction groups? Her personality fascinated me because she seemed so sure of herself and her beliefs. So I deliberately got to know her, and tried to discover the secret of her strength. One evening when she had a headache, I persuaded her to let me hypnotize it away by stroking her forehead. Within a week she had allowed me to persuade her into joining the Communist Party, and had abandoned every belief she held before. And I came to see that her strong personality was a way of disguising her uncertainty. Under hypnosis, she admitted all her fears and doubts. All this, of course, is familiar to you. You have said the same thing in many of your books. Yet its truth was never clear to me until that experience with Gerda. Then I came to realize that men build themselves personalities as they build houses—to protect themselves from the world. But once they have built a house, they are forced to live in it. They become its prisoners. And most people are in such a hurry to hide inside their four walls that they build the house too quickly . . . you understand me? So I was always observing men who seemed at home in the world—confident, at ease—and realizing that most of them hated their homes—I mean the personalities they had built for themselves. My father's friend Gerhardt Seyfert was an example. . . .'

Zweig said: 'Ah. . . .'

'He made his fortune in America, owned a railway line and a newspaper, and hated himself so much that he spent his life having imaginary illnesses. He paid my father alone more than a quarter of a million marks for medical treatment.'

He stopped speaking to observe Zweig, who had stood up suddenly, and was pacing across the room. Zweig said:

'I beg your pardon. Please go on.'

'How do you feel?'

'Quite extraordinary.' Zweig waved his hands. 'Astonishingly clear. Everything you say makes me want to make a hundred comments. I feel as if I could write a book in twenty-four hours.'

Neumann said, smiling: 'Then have some more whiskey.'

'Why?'

'It will deaden the effect.'

'I don't want to deaden it. As you were speaking just then, I was listening carefully, and also thinking about a problem in the last section of my Heidegger book—a problem that has occupied my mind for two years. And quite suddenly I saw its solution—as easily as an athlete vaulting over a gate. Excuse my interrupting like this, but I find this almost terrifying. . . . Do you realize what you're done? You have produced a drug that could alter the course of world history. . . .'

Neumann raised his hand, interrupting gently:

'Pardon me, but you are mistaken. Neuromysin produces this effect on you because you have a highly disciplined mind. Your problem is that you are normally inhibited by the body. You try to think, and the body drags you down. It is like trying to drive a car with the brakes on. Neuromysin releases the brakes. You have spent fifty years disciplining your mind and emotions. Even so, you now show signs of strain and overexcitement. Imagine what would happen if a completely undisciplined person took the drug. His mind would be like a zoo with all the cages open—total chaos. His excitement would burn out the motor of his brain.'

He poured half a glass of whisky, and handed it to Zweig without speaking. Zweig hesitated, then took it and drank half of it in a swallow. The effect came almost immediately; it was like pouring water on a fire. For a moment he felt stifled and choked, and had to sit on the arm of the chair. This passed off in a few seconds. The glow of well-being remained, the sense of control, but a part of his mind felt anaesthetized. Neumann was speaking again, but more softly, as if to soothe Zweig.

'You see my point? The ordinary man has no internal discipline. You spent about twenty years merely learning to think. And that training involved developing a delicate contact between your intuitions and your intellectual mechanisms. And yet how often do you blunder, even now, and discover that you've lost the intuition in the process of turning it into words? Imagine what would happen to an ordinary man after a dose of neuromysin. Take a coal miner and try to teach him higher mathematics, and you'll probably give him a nervous breakdown. It would be like trying to teach an elephant to repair watches. Most of our disciplines aim at restraining the energies. Neuromysin would simply open the floodgates of energy and drive a man insane. It would destroy a neurotic man in a matter of minutes. You see why? You, for example, don't feel hungry now because you are burning only your reserve mental energy. If you were less disciplined, you'd become ravenously hungry because you'd be burning your physical energy too. A man is a series of circuits, like an electronic brain. In the neurotic man, all the circuits are wrongly connected, so that he's continually wasting his energy. Do you begin to understand?'

Zweig said: 'So you were running a risk in allowing me to take the stuff?'

'No. After reading your book on Heidegger, I knew there was no risk.'

'Thank you.'

The fire had died into a dull glow. Zweig threw another log on, sending up sparks; he observed that each spark seemed clearly separated from the next, as if he could count every one individually. His mind had never felt so cold and lucid. He asked:

'Is that what happened to the old men?'

Neumann showed no surprise.

'No.'

'And did they really commit suicide?'

'Yes.'

'But why?'

'That will take some time to explain. However, provided no one interrupts us, we have all evening. Where would you like me to begin?'

'You were telling me about Seyfert when I interrupted you.'

'Ah, yes. Seyfert as I said, suffered from many imaginary diseases. But in the last year of his life, he suffered from a real one—a cancer of the stomach.'

'Are you . . . certain?' Zweig asked the question as an expression of relief rather than because he doubted Neumann's statement.

'Oh, quite. I found out about it accidentally one day when I overheard Seyfert asking my father to kill him.'

'Was he serious?'

'Quite serious. You remember that small closet next to the study, in which my father kept his books on drugs? I was sitting in there reading one day when my father came in with Seyfert. Seyfert had just learned that he had less than six months to live. So he wanted my father to give him some drug that would kill him painlessly. He even offered to leave my father most of his money if he would agree. My father refused.'

'He would.'

'He offered Seyfert drugs to deaden the pain, but said he could not give him anything that would shorten his life by a single day. He tried to convince the old man that there was still hope. Well, that evening I went to Seyfert's home and told him that I could help him. I wanted money. I was tired of being completely reliant on my father. I wanted to be able to conduct some of my own researches. So I told Seyfert that I could keep him free of pain for a few months, with the use of hypnotism and drugs. And I told him that when these methods ceased to be effective, I would give him a drug that would kill him painlessly. I told him my price—a quarter of a million marks.' Neumann paused, his eyes resting on Zweig, as if waiting for a comment. When Zweig said nothing, he went on:

'He agreed, of course. And I immediately began my course of treatment. You know that I had always been fascinated by drugs. In some respects, I knew more about them than my father. I had also taken every opportunity to add to my own private dispensary. This was not difficult, since my father was not a very observant man. So I had no difficulty in giving Seyfert the drugs that would deaden the pain, and in inducing a hypnotic trance in which I suggested to him that he was going to recover.

'After a few weeks of this, I realized something that I had overlooked. When Seyfert died, there would be a post-mortem, and the results would be embarrassing for me. And I realized that he would have to commit suicide in such a way that there could be no doubt about the cause of death. . . . I think you can guess the rest of the story. I explained the problem to him, but he hardly understood. But with the help of post-hypnotic suggestion, I had no difficulty whatever. My only concern was to stick to the letter of my bargain—not to kill him until it was impossible for me to prevent pain. This was not as easy as it might sound, because during the last month he was in a curious stupor so that it was difficult to tell how far he was in pain. But finally, it became apparent that nothing I could do could prevent him from dying in agony. We were in Switzerland at the time, and my supply of drugs was running low. So I suggested to him that he should write a suicide note, then go to a place ten miles away where there was a shepherd's hut on the edge of a ravine. He would then swallow a capsule of cyanide and jump.'

'Why the cyanide?'

'In case his fall left him badly injured but still alive. I must admit that this was my greatest risk. He might have taken the cyanide and been afraid to jump. In that case, there would have been the question of where he obtained the poison . . . not to mention the drugs. However, he jumped. And the fall would have killed him anyway, for his skull was completely crushed. I discovered afterwards that he had left me a great deal more than a quarter of a million marks.'

He stopped, staring at Zweig. After a silence, Zweig said: 'And the others?'

'Ah, there are a great many other things to tell you first. I was sorry about Seyfert's death, but it was inevitable. Still, it gave me an unpleasant sense of having taken part in a crime. Perhaps it was only the affair of the suicide. . . . I remember I was almost sick when I had to identify the body.'

'Did your father know?'

'I told him later—six months later.'

'What did he say?'

'He was horrified, but by that time there was not much that he could do. You see, we were forced to leave Germany, and he lost a great deal of his money. My money, on the other hand, was in Swiss banks. It was mostly my money that equipped our first laboratory near Zurich. We were working together on the drug that eventually became neuromysin. So what could he do?'

'Is that why he killed himself?'

'No. But I shall tell you about that also. We were, as you know, working on the idea of truth drugs. My father was interested in it from the point of view of a brain surgeon—that is, what drugs influence particular parts of the brain. And he discovered, quite accidentally, a drug that influenced the part of the brain concerned with habit patterns. To some extent, it was an obvious step from Pavlov's experiments on the conditioning of motor reflexes. My father was in close contact with Berger and Golla, who were both, as you know, working on the problem of the brain's electrical impulses. My father soon discovered that, using electrical apparatus, and small quantities of certain atropine derivatives, it was possible to completely obliterate some simple habit patterns. To begin with, his idea was to perfect a drug that would destroy the smoking habit and other forms of compulsive behaviour. He believed that this would bring him sufficient money to equip a big laboratory for brain research. Now I was interested in all this for quite different reasons. And when I first learned of my father's idea of a drug to destroy habit patterns, I was so excited that I had to go out for a ten-mile walk before I could control myself. You see why? I was obsessed by this notion of man's limitations. Why does consciousness sometimes blaze into a bonfire that gives us a glimpse of the superman? I see that you have dealt with this problem in your Heidegger book. And you appear to have reached the conclusion I reached—that it is important for human evolution that man's consciousness should be "rationed." Then, in his struggle to achieve intenser consciousness, he creates languages and symbols and all the other apparatus of civilization. Well, it seemed to me that this device of the evolutionary force—limiting human consciousness—has now overshot its usefulness. The sheer complexity of the apparatus we create is beginning to overwhelm us. And yet we cannot break the habit of living in the present, limiting the consciousness. It suddenly seemed to me that my father's discovery would solve my own problem. For I was aware that my own habits prevented me from achieving the vision I wanted. For example, at the time I drove the car over the Devil's Shoulder, I remember telling myself: I have become a different person: I shall never forget this insight. And yet as soon as I was back at home, in the old surroundings, the old habits of thought returned automatically and the vision disappeared. I believed that if I had been able to take a dose of my father's new drug as I stood watching that burning car, the new vision would have remained permanently. The old habits would have been destroyed. And this was why I was happy to use most of my money in equipping our laboratory near Zurich. My father wanted a drug to cure smoking. I wanted a drug to create the superman . . . or rather, to make it easier for the superman to create himself. So from 1933 until 1936, we worked steadily on the problem of our new drug. And then one morning, my father came into my bedroom carrying a glass slide on which there were a few needle-like crystals. It was a crude form of neurocaine, our habit-destroying drug.'

'You mean neuromysin?'

'No. Neuromysin affects the glands as much as the brain. Neurocaine could effect a temporary paralysis of certain habit centres. This was all we knew about it. Neither of us knew what habits would be affected. I suspected, for example, that it might affect habits of thought, ways of seeing ourselves, as well as habits of physical behaviour. A man who had come to think of himself as a weakling and a coward would suddenly realize that he had the power of *choice*—to be a coward or a hero. Habit would lose its grip. You see now why I was so excited? You have written about the human habit of self-delusion, but you have never had a chance to observe what would happen if we lost the habit. I was on the brink of being able to see for myself.

'I wanted to take some of the drug immediately. My father refused. He pointed out that he was older than I, that consequently his life was less valuable. If the drug was harmful, I would remain to carry on his work. So finally I agreed that he should be the first to try it. And the same morning, my father made a solution of neurocaine and injected it intravenously. At first, the results were everything we had expected. After two hours, he felt a tremendous sense of well-being. He suddenly looked twenty years younger. He began to talk of our future work with tremendous clarity and lucidity. I was so excited that I told him everything of my hopes. He agreed with everything I said. I was now anxious to take a dose of neurocaine as soon as possible. He persuaded me to wait for another few days, in case the aftereffects were unpleasant. I can still remember my state of mind during those two days. I was *absolutely sure* that I had stumbled on the answer to the oldest problem of all the philosophers—why man is not a god. I could also see the dangers of the drug—that without his usual habit patterns, a man would need to be absolutely sure of his purpose and direction—he would need to have something with which to replace the habits—new habits of thought and behaviour that would be superior to the old ones. And yet the effect of the drug on my father confirmed our greatest hopes. For two days, his energy was tremendous. He ate and drank enormously, and never stopped talking. He stopped smoking immediately. You remember that he also had a twitch of the left cheek that became more noticeable when he was tired; this also vanished. He told me that the drug produced a strange effect of lightness—yet not of light-headedness. He said he felt like a spirit, as if he could fly or go wherever he liked in a few seconds.

'After the second day, the reaction set in. He became torpid and listless. He also complained that his body felt heavier, and that he found it difficult to walk. I tried giving him stimulants, and these seemed to work. Then, four days after he had taken the drug, he went to his own room and took an overdose of sleeping tablets. I never discovered whether he only wanted to sleep for a long time, or whether he wanted to kill himself.

'For three weeks after his death, I had no time to think about the problem of neurocaine. The place was full of reporters and sympathizers. I gave it out that my father was depressed about the loss of his money and the situation of relatives living under the Nazis. Finally, I was left to myself again, and I decided to take the drug.'

'Why?'

'Because I wanted to know why he killed himself. I reasoned that my father was not a man who lived for great ideas—he was simply a fine brain surgeon. Consequently, he did not possess enough purpose to overcome his bewilderment under the new conditions. I believed that my own will power was stronger than his. In any case, I decided to take only half as much of the drug as he took.

'Its first effect was to fill me with an extraordinary feeling of freedom. I was so excited that I felt I wanted to tell somebody. So I sat down and wrote a letter to you.'

'To me? In 1936? But I never received it.'

'No. I never sent it. Before I posted it, I sent for your latest book from Zurich. It was your book about the hidden meaning of religious symbols. And from it I gathered that you were on the point of declaring yourself a Christian. It seemed to me that you had betrayed the cause of philosophy. You had taught me that man's deepest problem is his lack of freedom. And now, when it seemed to me that I had discovered a new way to restore man's freedom, you were committing yourself to the idea that man has to be redeemed by Christ. I tore up my letter to you.'

'I am sorry. I was never a Christian in the sense you imagine. . . .'

'No. But that is not important. At the time, I didn't care. The first effects of the drug were beyond anything I had imagined. My perceptions became as clear and fresh as those of a child. An adult has made a habit of living, of seeing and hearing, so that his senses become dull. Neurocaine made me feel as if I was living in wonderland, but in a wonderland that no child has ever seen. Because a child is full of all kinds of fears and doubts. His world is strictly limited. My universe was a hundred times as big as a child's, and yet I saw it all with the same freshness of vision. My senses became incredibly keen, and at the same time, my memory began to function with a power and exactitude that I had never known before. I could recall whole days of my childhood in the most minute detail. Every smell brought back some memory. Do you remember Proust's description of the effect of the cake dipped in tea, when he suddenly remembered his childhood? It was like that all the time—for hours and days, not merely for a few seconds.

'Then the reaction began. I now understood what my father meant when he said that his body seemed to become heavier. Things that I had previously done automatically now required an effort of will. For example, it took me several hours to type a short letter. My senses were abnormally sharp, but I was no longer able to ignore things that irritated me; the sound of a woodpecker in the garden drove me half insane until I went out and shot it. I had forgotten—or never realized—how much of living is a habit—including breathing. Neurocaine did not actually affect my breathing—I had not taken enough for that—but it was affecting all my other actions. Every time I did something, I was aware of myself doing it. I was aware that I could choose whether to do it or not.

'I took a heavy dose of sleeping tablets and slept for thirty hours. I hoped that the effect would have worn off by the time I woke up. Instead, it had reached a new stage. When I opened my eyes, I had a strange sensation that everything in the world was real except myself. I felt like a vacuum. And at the same time, it seemed as though I was in the middle of an immense desert—a desert of freedom. For the first time I realized that man needs his habits to save him from too much freedom—that freedom is potentially man's most dangerous enemy. Not in the sense that Hitler or Mussolini meant it—or even Dostoevsky's Grand Inquisitor. I realized what Heidegger meant when he said that man can only know true freedom in the face of death. Because death is the ultimate threat, the ultimate limitation. It makes man aware of his purpose, his desire to live. I realized suddenly: It is not freedom that man needs. He already has more than he can use. *It is a vision of purpose.* Neurocaine had made me aware how little real purpose I possessed. I felt as if I was in a huge factory, all the machinery has been stopped. Imagine a man who works in a factory, and who imagines that he has a wonderful voice. But he can never really know whether his voice is wonderful because he has to sing against the noise of the machinery. Then one day the machinery stops, and he discovers that his voice is actually a toneless wail. This was my position. There seemed to be a great silence behind my thoughts, a silence that asked: What now? It was terrifying, as if I carried all the space between the stars inside me. I remember sitting in an armchair, staring at the wall, and wondering if I would ever want anything again.'

'But surely you still felt the need to eat?'

'Yes, but it went deeper than that. I would find myself asking: What is the purpose of satisfying your hunger? What will you do tomorrow, and next week, and next year? I was aware of myself simply as a tiny naked particle of will power in the middle of a desert. Then I knew why my father could kill himself. The drug destroyed all my instinctive fear of death. I could choose to die or choose to go on living. But I had no *values* to tell me to do either. All my instincts had died.

'I realized that I would have to somehow live through it. I decided to sleep as much as possible. So I kept taking drugs, sleeping for days, then waking up and eating a little. Several weeks went by in this way. Then one day, I realized that the effect was wearing off. I can still remember waking up and no longer feeling the same pitiless glare of consciousness. A fly settled on my face, and my hand was halway to my cheek before I realized that I had done it *automatically*. The world seemed softer. I was taking it for granted again. Within two days, I was back to normal. But I cannot tell you the joy with which I greeted the return of each of my habits.'

He stopped speaking to pour himself whisky. This time he watched Zweig, waiting for him to speak. Zweig felt obscurely revolted, not by Neumann's description of his experiment, but by something more dangerous. The life in him squirmed away from some realization, as from a cold wind. He said:

'What did you do then?'

'I did nothing for a few weeks. I tried to think about what I had learned. I felt a completely different person. You know that Nietzsche talks about the agony of questioning everything, and says: "I do not know if such pain improves us, but I know it deepens us." This was how I felt. All the old nonsense of being a great criminal, for example, had been washed out of me. I felt as if the past month had been fifty years.

'Yet I also knew that I had to have money. I had spent all of Seyfert's inheritance. Yet now I felt it was more important than ever to continue my researches.'

This surprised Zweig: 'Why?'

'Because I felt that I was on the edge of a great secret. I asked: Why do most men live so feebly? Because they are entangled in habits and they possess no purpose. Well, I had snapped my habit patterns and confronted my will to live. I knew that it was only a matter of refining neurocaine. Neurocaine was too absolute. It wiped out all habits like chalk off a blackboard. The problem was to destroy only certain habits, or to weaken their power. Besides, I had come to recognize the importance of purpose in the mechanism of the will. Georgi used to say that the brain secretes will power in the way that the eyes secrete tears, and that we have to learn how to control this gland of will power. For example, a sexual orgasm often releases it; there is a sudden feeling of immense strength. Another remark of Georgi's gave me a clue to my problem. He used to say that the use of will power is more important to physical health than exercise of the body. He

nce said that most men hardly use their will power at all,
nd consequently the will becomes as sick and flabby as the
ody of a man who never takes exercise. On the other hand,
once read somewhere a description of Balzac's tremendous
oy when he thought of the idea of his Human Comedy, and
recognized the feeling, for I had felt exactly the same when
first realized that a lifetime of research might give me the
ecret of human freedom. It was the thought that I would
ave to use my will power with great patience, over a life-
ime. It was a vision of years of steady effort and purpose,
reedom from our usual boredom. I came to realize that no
Irug can solve the problem of freedom. It can only simplify
t at certain points.

'And so I had to continue my researches. But the first prob-
em was money. And in June 1936, an opportunity presented
tself. A former patient of my father approached me, a man
alled Schmoll. . . .'

'Ah. The underwear manufacturer. . . .'

'So you know? You seem to know more than I expected.
Then perhaps you know what happened to Schmoll?'

'I know that he died in a boating accident in Mentone in
August 1936.'

'That is true. This man Schmoll came to me because he was
experiencing suicidal urges since his retirement. He was also
experiencing other urges that horrified him even more—
violent fits of rage in which he tore things into pieces. He was
afraid that one day he would commit a murder. My father had
old him about brain operations that could cure these attacks
—he was studying electrical methods as well as leucotomy.
Schmoll hoped that I would be able to help him. So I told
him a little of our experiments with neurocaine. I must confess that I minimized the dangers. I gave Schmoll a minute
dose of neurocaine one day, and he was astonished and
delighted with its first effects. I told him that I needed a great
deal of money to continue my experiments with the drug. He
was so delighted that he promised me as much as I could
need. Then, when the aftereffects began to set in, I gave him
heavy doses of sleeping tablets, and various other stimulants.
The effects wore off in less than a week, and he felt better.
But I made excuses about giving him another dose—I
wanted to make sure of the money first. In any case, the first
dose had cleared away his violent impulses, which were ob-

viously connected with his sense of frustration on ceasing to work. So for a month he remained as my guest, and made me several large presents of money. Then, when he began to grow restless, I suggested the trip to Mentone. Unfortunately, his fundamentally psychotic nature began to reappear as he became used to me. He grew irritable and suspicious, and on one occasion he called me a common confidence swindler. He apologized afterwards, but I realized that things were coming to a head. He kept pressing me to give him another dose of neurocaine. I tried to persuade him to wait until we could return to Zurich, but this only made him more suspicious. So finally I gave way, and gave him a very mild dose —only half as strong as the first one. This kept him happy for a day, and he declared that I was one of the greatest scientists who had ever lived, and that he would give me his entire fortune for my researches. Then I tried to keep him drugged while the effects wore off. But this time it was not so successful. He got up on the third day, and it was obvious that he was in murderous mood. I seriously considered leaving him there and returning home. It was he who proposed the boat trip one afternoon. We were half a mile out at sea when he suddenly had one of his attacks. His face turned purple. He began to swear at me and accuse me of robbing him. He said that I was a bloodsucker, and that I would cling to him until I had drained him of his money. Then he threw himself on me and we fought. His madness made him a great deal stronger than I, so as soon as I could struggle free I threw myself overboard. He hurled himself after me. That was the last I saw of him. Perhaps his fit ended in unconsciousness—like an epileptic's—and he drowned. I overturned the boat—to explain what had happened—and swam back to shore. Do you know the rest of the story?'

'I think so. I read in a Mentone newspaper about your arrest. That was two years later.'

'Then you read of the man who tried to blackmail me, and went to the police? Luckily, I was able to prove that he had demanded money, and the police released me.'

'And the money?'

'I received some money—not as much as I needed. And his relatives made difficulties.'

They both heard the noise at the same time, a snapping sound like a twig. Zweig turned to the window; Neumann made no movement, but continued to look at the fire. Because of the light in the room, nothing was visible outside. Zweig stood up. At the same time, there was a sound of knocking on the door. Zweig said:

'Shall I answer?'

'Please.'

Before Zweig could reach it, the kitchen door opened, Natasha said:

'I hope we're not interrupting.'

'What are you doing here?'

She came in, followed by Gardner. He said:

'We thought we'd better come and make sure everything was all right.'

'Are you alone?'

'Oh, yes.'

He noticed there was mud on Natasha's shoes; her coat shone with rain.

'Where is your car?'

Gardner said drily: 'We left it at the farm.'

Neumann stood in the doorway. He said politely:

'Please come in. Can we offer you a drink? Or some coffee?'

Gardner said: 'I wouldn't mind a drink. . . .' then stopped suddenly as he caught Natasha's glance. He said: 'Er, no, perhaps not, thanks all the same.'

Zweig said: 'Does Grey know you've come here?'

'No.'

'Do the police know about this place?'

Gardner looked surprised.

'I haven't told them, but they'll probably know by now. They've been trying to get on to Tim's housekeeper all day, so I expect she's told them. . . .' He was glancing from Zweig to Neumann as he spoke; plainly, the situation puzzled him. Zweig said:

'You had better come in. Gustav has been explaining things to me. . . .' Zweig looked at Neumann. 'I am afraid there is no alternative to telling them about it.'

Neumann hesitated, then smiled. 'If you think it necessary. But if the police are on their way here, there may not be time.'

Gardner asked him pointedly: 'Do you want to avoid them?'

Neumann said: 'Yes.'

Zweig said quietly: 'It would be best.'

Gardner shrugged. 'All right, I'll take your word for it. We'd better get out of here then. Here's what I suggest. I know a little pub outside Woking. It won't take us more than half an hour to get there. Let's go there and talk it over.'

Neumann said: 'Very well.'

Natasha asked him: 'Do you know what you're doing?'

Gardner said: 'No. But I'll take Karl's word for it.'

Neumann said: 'Good. Then let us go now.' He went into the sitting-room and turned out the light. Natasha said: 'I have a torch.' As she opened her handbag, Zweig observed the small revolver that lay inside. Neumann turned off the kitchen light. He said:

'We can go down to the farm in this car.'

The drizzle fell steadily. Zweig and Natasha climbed into the back of the Anglia. None of them spoke until they arrived at the farm. The headlights picked out Gardner's car, parked on the other side of the road under trees. Neumann pulled carefully alongside the Rover.

'Perhaps you three should go in the other car. I will follow you.'

Gardner said: 'All right.'

Neumann said: 'You were wise not to park too close to the farm.'

Gardner said gruffly: 'Didn't want to attract attention.'

As soon as the Rover pulled out into the road, Gardner said:

'What's happening?'

Zweig said: 'What he has told me is incredible. But I have no doubt whatever that he is innocent.'

Natasha said: 'But how? Did those old men really commit suicide?'

'He had not finished explaining when you arrived.' As they drove, Zweig told them briefly about Gerhardt Seyfert, and the death of Schmoll. When he had finished, neither of them spoke for a moment. Then Gardner said:

'Frankly, I think he's lying.'

She asked Zweig: 'Do *you* believe him?'

'On the whole, yes. Everything about this affair has puzzled me. But the thing that has puzzled me most is this: how could a man like Gustav Neumann turn into a common criminal? That was to me the unanswerable question. What he has told me explains it. Have you any better explanation?'

Gardner said slowly: 'I don't want to contradict you, Professor, but are you sure you're not being influenced by a desire to see him innocent?'

'You would not think so if you had been with him for the past hour. Everything he has said convinces me that he is telling the truth.'

'And do you think the police will believe him?'

'No. And that is the problem. I intend to do everything I can to help him.'

Natasha said suddenly: 'Joe, how about the *Dragon Fly*? Couldn't you get him to France?'

'Supposing I did? What am I supposed to say to Grey and Chesson? Sorry, but we decided Neumann was innocent, so we helped him to escape. . . . Anyway, what'd be the good? He could be arrested in France or Switzerland just as easily.'

Zweig said: 'No. There is not enough evidence. Here they may try and hold him about the matter of the false passport and the German drug charge. I am certain that he would be safer if he could leave this country.'

'But I don't understand. If you're so sure he's innocent, what's to prevent him from telling the story to the police and proving it?'

'That might take months. They might even bring him to trial, and that would be disastrous. He is anxious to keep his experiments with neurocaine a secret. If it leaked out, he would have every newspaper reporter and every crank in the world interrupting his work. Besides, imagine the forces that would oppose him. All the tobacco companies, to begin with. All the liquor companies. Most of the medical profession, including the psychiatrists. Don't you see that secrecy is of the utmost importance? All that he needs now is money and privacy. And if Sir Timothy intends to supply him with money, then all he needs is to get out of this country.'

'But what about Tim? How do you know he won't die like the others?'

Zweig said with emphasis: 'I am absolutely certain he will not. For a simple reason. After this, Gustav could not afford to have him dying. He *must* keep Ferguson alive.'

Gardner lowered the window, and signalled to turn left,

The car stopped under a tree in the courtyard of a small pub. A moment later, Neumann's Anglia pulled in beside them.

The bar was crowded. Gardner waved to the proprietor. 'Anybody upstairs, Harry?'

'No. Go on up. I'll be there in a moment.'

Gardner led them into a small parlour with a low ceiling. A coal fire burned in the grate.

'Natasha and I used to stay here for weekends when we were first married. This is one of the oldest inns in southern England. Dirty old men used to bring their girl-friends here for little private suppers.' He pulled back a curtain, and revealed a four-poster bed.

Neumann said: 'Charming.' He looked out of the window, into the courtyard. 'A delightful place.' Zweig found himself admiring his coolness. With the possibility of being arrested at any moment, he sounded as polite and interested as a tourist in the museum. 'I noticed, incidentally, that the name of this place is The Goat and Compasses. Isn't that the title of one of your books?'

Gardner looked pleased. 'That's the title of the German translation. The English edition is called *The Day the Moon Exploded*. My German publisher thought it a bit sensational.'

'An interesting book,' Neumann said. Zweig and Natasha, sitting on either side of the fire, were looking at one another; Zweig's face was expressionless; Natasha, her back to Neumann, was smiling faintly.

'When did you read it?' Gardner asked.

'On its first publication. I found the title intriguing.'

'Quite. It's the mediaeval symbol of the devil and God—you know, God encompassing everything. . . .'

'But you know, of course, that your speculations about the psychology of the Wahima have been superseded?'

'What do you mean?' Gardner sounded incredulous.

'My friend Denzil of the Munich Archive spent some time in Ruanda studying their customs. He published some of his results. . . .'

'I know. I read his paper.'

'. . . But some of his most interesting discoveries are still unpublished. For example, he conducted experiments in extrasensory perception with these savages, and established that their telepathic abilities are far beyond those of a European.'

'Are you sure? Are you quite certain?'

'Quite certain. I can introduce you to Denzil. Now if these Wahima are really degenerate members of a tertiary race, how do you account for these psychic powers? Your book claims they were on a lower spiritual plane than our own race.'

Gardner said excitedly: 'No, I didn't. I said that their magic was of an objective kind. They had no idea of the powers of the human psyche. That doesn't mean they didn't possess such powers.'

A waiter came in, saying: 'Can I take your order, gentlemen?'

Gardner said impatiently: 'Yes, yes.' He made an obvious effort to alter the focus of his attention. 'Er, four whiskies. Large ones. And we'd like some sandwiches.'

'What would you like, sir? Ham, chicken, cheese and tomato. . . .'

Gardner interrupted: 'Anything you like. Enough for four. . . .' He turned his back on the waiter. 'Now, look here, if your friend got these results, why didn't he mention them in his paper? After all . . .'

Zweig said: 'Excuse me for interrupting, Joseph, but we have some other problems to discuss.'

'Is it all that important?' When Zweig raised his eyebrows, he said: 'Hmm, yes, I suppose it is.' He said to Neumann: 'We'll have to talk about it later.' He sat down in a chair by the fire, saying to Zweig: 'Sorry, go ahead.'

Neumann said: 'In fact, there is no need to change the subject, because our earlier topic of discussion connects with some of the questions raised in Mr Gardner's books.' He addressed himself to Gardner and Natasha. 'I have been trying to explain to Professor Zweig how an old friend of mine in Heidelberg—he was murdered by the Nazis—started me thinking about the problem of the extension of consciousness. He has told you about my father's search for a drug that would affect habit patterns—smoking, for example? Well, my father always believed that such a drug would also increase human telepathic abilities. He believed that the main obstacle to telepathy is our habit of communicating by speech. And if you consider this for a moment, you will see that it is not implausible. . . .'

'Quite. I agree,' Gardner said.

'A child can easily learn two languages. An adult finds it

more difficult because his own language has become a habit and he takes the path of least resistance. Now my father believed that telepathy is, so to speak, simply another language, another method of communication. Rhine's experiments have proved that most of us possess the power to some small degree. But we never develop it because our speech-language is a habit. My father believed that neurocaine, properly used, could provide us with new methods of investigating telepathy and other forms of mental power—mind over matter, so to speak.'

Gardner stood up. His face had gone pale; Zweig recognized the symptom of intense excitement. But he was surprised when Gardner seized Neumann by the shoulder, and said:

'By God, Gustav, you're on to something really important. If this drug of yours can really affect habit patterns as you say . . .'

Neumann said, smiling: 'Would you like to try some?'

'You've got some here?'

'Not neurocaine. I have a milder version of it called neuromysin. Has Professor Zweig not mentioned it? He has tried some this evening.'

Natasha and Gardner asked at the same time: 'What happened?'

'The results are beginning to wear off now. But it was certainly an astonishing experience.'

Gardner said: 'Let me try it.'

Zweig said: 'Er, Gustav, do you think it's a good idea . . . when we're drinking alcohol?'

Neumann said: 'A small quantity will make no difference.' He took the tube out of his pocket and shook a capsule into his hand. He said to Gardner: 'Professor Zweig may also be concerned because neuromysin is dangerous for excitable people. But your books convince me that your mental discipline will equal the emergency.' He broke the tablet in half, and offered it to Gardner. When he extended the other half to Natasha, she shook her head. Gardner swallowed his half immediately. He sat down again, saying: 'How long will it take to work?'

'Five minutes.'

Zweig said: 'Excuse me, Gustav. It may be wiser to leave here within the next half-hour. So perhaps you could . . .'

'Finish my story? Very well. . . .'

The waiter came in, carrying a tray. Gardner pulled a wallet out of his pocket; as he opened it, it fell from his hand, scattering pound notes on the carpet. Zweig observed that his face had become whiter than ever. When he bent down, his hand grabbed a handful of notes, crushing them. Natasha said: 'Let me, dear.' She took two pound notes and gave them to the waiter, then collected the others up. Neumann handed Gardner his drink, saying: 'Drink this.'

Natasha said: 'I thought alcohol wasn't good with it. . . .'

Neumann said quickly: 'A small quantity increases the effect.' He said to Gardner: 'Please drink it.'

Gardner was staring at his glass; Zweig thought his eyes looked feverish. He said:

'By God, this is astounding stuff. Have you tried it, Natasha? Why not? It's indescribable. It's like getting drunk without getting muzzy. Tremendous clarity. . . .' He took a large swallow of the whisky. 'No wonder it bucked Tim up so much.'

Neumann said: 'Perhaps you could give Tim this tube? Tell him not to take more than one every forty-eight hours—he could get over-excited.'

Natasha asked: 'Is that what happened to the old man at Maidstone—Benskin?'

Neumann was eating a sandwich. He shook his head, and swallowed carefully before answering. 'No. He was suffering from various fevers contracted in the jungle that enfeebled his nervous system. I was treating him with very small quantities of neurocaine. As the professor will tell you, neurocaine has a wonderful initial effect, but its later effects are dangerous—they can cause suicidal tendencies in a man without a sense of purpose. I had to give him strong sedatives to make him sleep through this danger period. Unfortunately, the weakness of his constitution made it very complicated.' He took a swallow from his glass. 'We were very fond of one another—he was one of my father's oldest friends.'

'But how did he die?'

'The neurocaine left him with a profound suicidal impulse. I was not then aware of its effect on a man with traces of malarial fever in his blood. At the same time, he knew that an unexplained suicide might get me into trouble, since I was in this country with a false passport. So he waited until I left the house one evening to summon a doctor—he told me that he needed a fever injection—then went downstairs with a gun and shot himself in front of an open window. He wanted to give the impression that it was an accident—that he had gone down to surprise a burglar and had somehow been shot. There had been a number of recent burglaries in that neighbourhood. . . .'

Gardner stood up suddenly, and laid his hand on Neumann's shoulder.

'You want to get out of this country tonight?'

'Yes, but. . . .'

'No buts. Come on now.'

Natasha said: 'Joseph, do you know what you're doing?'

'I hope so.' Gardner turned to Zweig. 'Do you agree that he should get out of England?'

'Certainly.'

'All right. I agree with you. *We* know he's not a murderer. But the police might be harder to convince, and while he's convincing them, there's no telling what might happen. So I'll take him over to Calais tonight.' He asked Neumann: 'Do you need money?'

'No. I have money in my briefcase.'

'Good. Zweig can take your car back to London. I'll see that Tim joins you in Switzerland as soon as he can travel. I'll probably come with him.'

'I would be only too delighted for your help.'

Gardner turned to Zweig. His voice suddenly had an emotional quality that Zweig had not heard before. His face had now lost its paleness, and was slightly flushed.

'I shall always be grateful to you for involving me in this crazy business, Karl. I've got a feeling that the three of us are on the brink of something that will change human history. I'm going to do everything I can to help Gustav perfect his drug. . . .' He seized Zweig's hand, and Zweig almost cried out at the sudden pressure. 'Good-bye, Karl. See you tomorrow.'

Natasha asked nervously: 'Do you feel all right?'

'I feel splendid. As if someone had switched on a neon light.' He said to Neumann: 'You know, I've often thought that human consciousness is a kind of neon light with a worn motor. You know when you switch on a neon light, and it tries to light up but can't quite make it. . . the light tries to

jump the length of the tube, it starts to glow at both ends, it
flickers for a moment—then it goes out. I used to think a
sexual orgasm's like that—an attempt at real consciousness.
But I can't help imagining that one of these days, the light's
going to leap along the whole tube'—he snapped his fingers—
'and suddenly, just like that, we'll have real consciousness.'
He asked Neumann: 'Do you know what I mean?'

'Perfectly. I could not have found a better image myself.
And you are right to speak of a worn motor. Part of the
problem is purely mechanical. My father used to say that it is
far more difficult to learn to drive a human body than to
learn to drive a motor-car. We all know the basic mechanisms
—how to start the engine and turn the steering wheel—but
there are a million things we do not know. For example, we
don't know how to change gear. Most of us grind through
life in first gear. . . .'

Gardner interrupted: 'Quite. And it's all a question of consciousness . . . the gears. . . .' He suddenly pressed both his
fists against his forehead. Zweig and Natasha looked at him
with concern. He said: 'It's so damned difficult, I feel like a
child . . . trying to learn a foreign language.' He looked at
Neumann and smiled suddenly. 'We've almost got to start
from the beginning.'

Neumann said: 'We can do it.'

'That's right.' Gardner said: 'The three of us. Karl too . . .
because he's working on the same problem. . . .' He smiled
at Natasha, started to say something, then made a helpless
gesture. 'We'd better go. I hope it's not foggy over the Chan-
nel. . . .' Zweig thought he suddenly looked bewildered, like
a sleepwalker who has been wakened suddenly. He said to
Neumann: 'Come on, let's go.'

He went to kiss Natasha. She put her arms round his neck
and said: 'Please be careful. *Very careful*. Don't drive too
fast.'

Neumann bowed to Natasha. 'Madame, we shall meet again
shortly.' He turned to Zweig. 'Join me as soon as possible.
I shall need your help.'

Zweig said: 'Good-bye, Gustav.'

As Neumann moved towards the door, Gardner said
quietly: 'I hope we're doing the right thing.' Neumann heard
the words, and smiled. Zweig said:

'I am sure we are.'

Neumann said: 'Thank you, Karl. I shall not forget.'

Zweig and Natasha stood at the window. The rain was still falling steadily. Gardner and Neumann crossed the yard to the cars; Neumann opened the boot of the Anglia and took out two cases.

She said to Zweig: 'Are you *sure* you're doing the right thing?'

'I am willing to gamble.'

'And what about Sir Charles Grey?'

'I think I can make him understand.'

She said: 'I wish you could make me understand.' They watched the rearlight of the Rover turn the corner, and heard the sound of a car accelerating. She rested her head against his shoulder for a moment, then straightened suddenly and went over to the fire. She said:

'I feel as if this is an awful anti-climax. . . . Somehow, there's something wrong. . . .'

He looked at her with a kind of admiration.

'There is, of course.'

'What?' Her voice was sharp.

'We are frustrating the ends of justice. If Gustav stayed in England, I think that he might have difficulty in proving his innocence.'

'And you think he'll be safe now?'

'Not entirely. It depends on how much evidence the police can accumulate. But he is safer in his own country than here.'

'But why are you so sure he's innocent?'

He said: 'My dear, I am not at all sure.'

'Are you serious?'

He shrugged. 'Gustav explained to me about the death of the old man in Mentone—about the struggle in the boat. All that sounded plausible enough. There was one thing that he forgot to explain—why he was using a false name in Mentone.'

'Was he? Are you sure?'

'The newspaper I discovered in the hotel in Mentone mentioned his name as Gerhardt Seyfert.'

'The first old man? The one who died in Switzerland? But why should he? I mean, why choose that name?'

'Quite. He told me that his absurd ambition to be a great

criminal vanished a long time before. And yet why should he use the name of his previous victim—except out of a kind of bravado?'

She was staring at him incredulously, unable to understand the composure with which he sipped his whisky.

'Do you think he really set out to kill those old men?'

'I am not saying that. But again, why did he come into England under a false name? He allowed us to assume that it was something to do with the problems of escape from Nazi Germany. But he left Germany in 1931. This was six years later. Why use a false passport?'

'Why do you think he did?'

He said quietly: 'My dear, I do not know.'

'Do you realize what you're saying? Do you mean it? You said a moment ago that he was innocent.'

'No. I said that he would have some difficulty in proving his innocence in this country.'

'Then you think him guilty?'

'I think it possible that a court of law might decide that he is guilty.'

She came over to him and looked down into his face. She said: 'Karl, I don't understand you. I'm asking you if *you* think he's guilty?'

'I know what you are asking me. And I tell you: I cannot answer you simply. I believe this: that Gustav has never ceased to be possessed by a vision of his own, and that he has spent his life trying to turn it into a reality. I doubt whether he set out simply to kill these men for money—he is not interested in money. I think that perhaps he hoped to help them. But I think he used them as guinea pigs. . . .'

'You mean he treated human beings as . . . as Pavlov treated dogs? Is that what you mean?'

Zweig stood up; it made him uncomfortable to have her bending over him. He thrust his hands into his trouser pockets as he walked across the room.

'That is a question I cannot answer. All I can tell you is why I want him to escape.'

'Then why?'

'Because I began by suspecting that Gustav had become an ordinary criminal, a killer of old men. . . .'

She interrupted: 'But even then, you wanted him to escape, didn't you?'

'That is not true. But I was afraid that if he had become a mere criminal, then I was partly responsible—perhaps wholly responsible. I was unwilling to condemn him because I was unwilling to condemn myself. Well, I was right about one thing—that my influence has been of enormous importance in his life. But I was wrong in thinking that he could ever be a mere criminal. The true criminal thinks himself a realist. . . .'

'And you're trying to tell me that he can't be a criminal because he's an idealist? But Hitler was an idealist too. How can you accept that kind of reasoning?'

Zweig was deliberately not looking at her; her indignation made him uncomfortable, yet he was certain he was right. He said patiently:

'Please listen to me, Natasha. Sit down a moment and listen.' She sat down on the arm of the chair; he stood still for a moment, now looking down at her. 'There is something you must try to understand. When Alois Neumann and I were students, we shared a common vision—no, not a vision, but a sudden insight. I was the first one to mention it, and he immediately said that he had often felt the same. It was this: there were certain moments when I became quite certain that human beings have always made an absurd mistake in *interpreting* the world. Your senses interpret reality just as a translator translates from one language into another. Well, in this flash of insight, I would understand suddenly that human beings make some subtle mistake when they look at the world. The way we see the world is a lie. That is, it is a complete misconception. I suppose this is what I came to mean by original sin. Now my task as a philosopher has always been to find the source of this error. I was sure that it would only require some tiny adjustment—like turning the knob on the side of a microscope—and everything would suddenly rush into focus. And this focus would come to me in brief flashes when everything would blur again, turn into a labyrinth of shadows. Well, I have devoted my life to trying to discover the principle of this focus. I have always believed that it is the work of the philosopher to undo original sin. When I was younger, I felt this all the time—I was always aware of the stupid imperfection of my vision, as you might be aware of some fault in a radio set, without knowing how to correct it. Since I have grown older, this feeling has disappeared. It takes a great deal of effort to maintain it. Well, it came back again this evening. It has been coming back for days now, ever since I read Gustav's article in the *Monatschrift*. Yet I could not believe Gustav had found an answer, for I know his brain is no better than mine—in many ways, it is worse. Tonight, when Gustav gave me the taste of neuromysin, I knew I had made a mistake. There *is* another way. Gustav has spent his life pursuing it. Instead of using his intellect alone, Gustav has returned to the body. He has recognized in fact what I have only recognized in theory—that part of the problem is purely physical.'

'Are you trying to say that you think all your work has been a mistake?'

'By no means. You remember what Gustav said as he went out: "I need your help." His way can provide the vision, but what good is the vision without purpose? A man needs a lifetime of discipline to make use of such a vision. Why do you suppose the old men committed suicide? Do you think it was a mere physical consequence of the drug? Gustav used a phrase that explained everything. He said that neurocaine gave him a sensation of existing in a desert of freedom. You can observe the same thing when a schoolboy has a long holiday—he loses all sense of purpose after a while. The freedom bores him. He has no use for so much freedom. It makes him aware of his limitations, of his worthlessness. He has to face the paradox that he doesn't want to return to school, yet he doesn't want an everlasting holiday either. His life becomes devalued. Well, Gustav's drug has the same effect, but magnified a thousand times. Do you understand me now? Such a desert needs signposts, and I have spent my life making signposts. Gustav admitted to me that he came close to committing suicide when he tried the drug in 1936. Well, next time he tries it, I shall be with him.'

'Are you really going to try it?'

'There is no alternative. Gustav has certain insights, but, as your husband said, we are all children in this field. . . .'

He stood at the window. The rain had stopped, and the moon showed through moving cloud. She came and stood beside him.

'I don't know what to say . . . I wish I could trust him more. But you saw the way he handled Joseph. When we came in here, I was quite certain that Joseph would never help him to escape. Within ten minutes, Neumann had twisted him round his finger.'

Zweig said, smiling: 'Oh, he is cunning. And a consummate actor. I would like to wager that he has never read your husband's books. He probably asked Ferguson about them.'

'But if he's so cunning, how do you know he's not deceiving you?'

'Because there is one thing that cannot be counterfeited—that passion for order. You know, Natasha, when I was a student I used to go into the university library and look at the works of the philosophers, and think: These men were sick of the meaninglessness of life. They were sick of life slipping away like a confidence trickster and leaving nothing behind. Their works are a protest against the chaos and futility, an attempt to get a grip on life. And yet after more than two thousand years of philosophy, we are not very much wiser. Life is still a confusion. It still escapes us. Yet the true philosophers continue to dream of some simple tool—like a pair of pliers—that will give us a grip on life. This is the passion for order. Gustav has it.'

'And you think he might have solved the problem at last?'

'Perhaps not. But he may have made a completely new kind of start. He has given me hope. I had begun to feel stoical about my life—to accept defeat as inevitable. Do you see now why I had to allow him to escape? His drug may be a new beginning. . . .'

The waiter looked in at the door.

'Is there anything else, sir?'

Zweig said: 'No, thank you. We shall be going now.'

He helped her on with her coat. She opened her handbag and glanced in the hand mirror. Her eyes looked at his reflection as he looked over her shoulder.

'It's funny . . . when Joseph came in tonight, I said: "We've got to get down to the cottage. I think Karl may be in danger." I took my revolver because I was going to kill him if he'd harmed you. . . .' She replaced the mirror, and continued to look away from him.

'But no harm came to me. I knew that before I set out. . . .'

'I don't know.'

'What do you mean?'

She turned to him, and he was startled by the coldness of her face. She said flatly:

'In a sense . . . I think I've lost you all the same.'

He took her gloved hand and kissed it.

'Nonsense, my dear. You're simply tired. Let's get back to London.'

But he knew what she meant. And he also knew that, in the sense she intended, it was true.